Cursed with a poor sense of [...] to read, **Annie Claydon** spe[...] lost in books. A degree in Eng[...] a career in computing didn't lead directly to her perfect job—writing romance for Mills & Boon—but she has no regrets in taking the scenic route. She lives in London: a city where getting lost can be a joy.

Ann McIntosh was born in the tropics, lived in the frozen north for a number of years, and now resides in sunny central Florida with her husband. She's a proud mama to three grown children, loves tea, crafting, animals—except reptiles!—bacon and the ocean. She believes in the power of romance to heal, inspire and provide hope in our complex world.

GREEK ISLAND FLING TO FOREVER

ANNIE CLAYDON

NIGHT SHIFTS WITH THE MIAMI DOC

ANN McINTOSH

MILLS & BOON

First Published in Great Britain 2021
by Mills & Boon, an imprint of HarperCollins*Publishers*
1 London Bridge Street, London, SE1 9GF

Greek Island Fling to Forever © 2021 by Annie Claydon

Night Shifts with the Miami Doc © 2021 by Ann McIntosh

ISBN: 978-0-263-29754-6

MIX
Paper from
responsible sources
FSC **FSC® C007454**
www.fsc.org

Printed and bound in Spain
by CPI, Barcelona

GREEK ISLAND
FLING TO FOREVER

ANNIE CLAYDON

MILLS & BOON

CHAPTER ONE

THE DAY THAT had changed her life had been bright and clear, bathed in sunshine, and every detail was still sharp in Arianna's dreams. She was six years old and had insisted on wearing her new white *broderie anglaise* dress for the journey to the Petrakis family's holiday home on the tiny Greek island of Ilaria.

Her father had frowned when he heard the news that their own launch was out of action, and her mother had smiled as if it was of no consequence and said they'd take the ferry. It had been a new experience for Arianna and her older brother, Xander, waiting with the jostling crowd of other passengers to board, and then finding a place on deck where her mother could sit.

Even her father had loosened up a bit, opening the collar of his shirt and gesturing to their bodyguard to take a family photograph. Then he'd acceded to Xander's excited demands and agreed to take him on a tour of the large, exciting craft. Xander had turned, waving to her as they'd walked away.

Her mother had been wearing a wide-brimmed hat and a red and white fitted sundress, so different from the faded colours she wore now. She'd perched on a slatted wooden bench and started to talk to the other mothers, telling Arianna that she could go and play if she wanted, as long as she stayed close.

The ferry had slowly manoeuvred out of the busy dock, speeding up a little as it entered the blue waters of the Mediterranean. Arianna had wished they could take this route every time, and when Ilaria had begun to loom on the horizon she'd wanted the island to stay away for a while longer, so that they could spend a little more time on the ferry.

Then… Then a juddering, crashing sound. The world tipped suddenly and she fell, grazing her knees on the wooden deck. She heard her mother screaming her name, but she was sliding, falling. Somehow, the water seemed to rear up and grab her, pulling her down.

She couldn't breathe… And then something…someone…was there. Grabbing her flailing arms and holding her tight. Their heads broke the surface, and muffled sounds turned into a chaos of shouting and screaming. She could breathe enough to choke and cry, and when she opened her eyes, blinking against the sting of the salt, she saw an older boy with a shock of blond hair, wet and plastered around his face.

He said something to her, but she didn't understand the words. She understood safety, though, and when he wound her arms around his neck she hung on tight. They bobbed together in the water, and then the boy started to swim, labouring hard while Arianna clung onto his back.

She didn't dare look behind her. Maybe if she had, she would have caught one last glimpse of Xander. But ahead there were small boats, leaving the tiny port of Ilaria and making their way towards them.

Arianna was sobbing now, and the boy stopped swimming. More words that she didn't understand, but which made her feel safe again. The water was pulling them back, towards the sinking ferry, and he began to strike out again, towards the rescue boats. She closed her eyes, reciting the prayer that her mother always said with her before she lay down to sleep.

Then she felt strong hands around her and she was lifted out of the water. One of the boats had reached them, and the boy had pushed her up into the arms of its occupants. A man held her tight as she reached back for the boy, but a wave carried him away. She started to scream and cry as his blond head disappeared amongst the waves and the scattered mass of people in the sea.

And then… The memories lost their clarity. She remembered her mother crying and her father hugging her until she could hardly breathe, when they found her, wrapped in a blanket and sitting amongst a group of survivors in the taverna, which had opened its doors to provide shelter and warm drinks. And she remembered her father, kissing her mother and running back down to the boats that were ferrying people back to the shore.

He'd been gone a long time, but her mother had refused to move, holding Arianna tight as they both shivered in the warm breeze. When he finally *had* returned, he was alone. Her mother had taken one look at his face and screamed in anguish…

Arianna sat bolt upright in her bed, feeling the cold sweat beading her forehead. Returning to Ilaria, to establish a medical practice here, had left little time for anything other than work. Now that the pressure was off during the day her dreams at night had become more frequent and much more vivid. Breathing deeply to steady her racing heart, Arianna told herself it wasn't necessarily a bad thing and that perhaps she needed to get the trauma of that day, twenty-five years ago, out of her system. And it was one more precious chance to see Xander again, along with the blond-haired boy who had carried her to safety and then disappeared amongst the waves.

The boy hadn't drowned. Later, when she was older, she'd traced everyone who had died that day and there was no one matching his description on the list. He'd just disappeared in the melee of survivors. He was out there somewhere, grown up now, and Arianna wondered if he ever thought of her.

It was a bright, warm day. Ben Marsh stepped off the ferry, pulling the map of Ilaria's harbour town from his pocket and looking around to get his bearings.

He'd wondered if he might remember this place when he saw it; he'd thought about it often enough over the years. But he didn't. There was nothing familiar about the ferry terminus, but it was a new building, obviously constructed since he'd last been here, twenty-five years ago. Ben made a beeline for the tourist information booth and a smiling woman welcomed him to the island and marked the position of the health centre on his map for him.

He walked to the main harbour, stopping to scan the small boats moored there. None of them were familiar either, although in truth he'd been too intent on scanning the horizon to look for other survivors to remember much about the craft whose crew had finally pulled him out of the sea. And the people? The frightened little girl who had clung to his back as he'd swum away from the sinking ferry would be beyond recognition now. She could be any one of the young women who passed him in the street, and Ben told himself that searching their faces for any shred of recognition was a waste of time.

But he knew her name. Arianna Petrakis. It had been six months since he'd stumbled on an old newspaper account that had answered the questions he'd wondered about for so long, and since then the name had seemed to resound in his head.

Icy fingers skittered from his neck, down his spine, and he shivered in the sunshine. What if she didn't want to see him? The answer to that was easy; he'd take the next ferry off the island and go. What if she *did* want to see him? How could he explain that the day the ferry had sunk had shaped his life? Could he even begin to say that now he had the strangest feeling that he needed Arianna to rescue him?

Ben shook off the questions, knowing he had no answer to them. Jumping into the water to save Arianna had been the first defining moment of change in his life. The second had been crushingly different. He'd made a solemn vow to love and cherish, and then not been there when his wife had needed him. Emma was gone now, and Ben couldn't turn back the clock and save her.

But he hadn't thought twice when he'd seen the little girl in the white dress sliding across the deck of the ferry and falling into the water. He'd jumped. And now he needed to do that again, to just follow his instincts and jump.

After a steep climb up the hill, away from the harbour, he found the health centre. He shouldn't have worried whether he'd recognise it—the stone wall that bordered the road had a large notice in six different languages, and when he opened the gate he saw a modern building nestled behind a small garden that was a riot of colour and scent. Automatic doors swished open and he found himself in a large reception area, welcoming and cool after the sticky heat. A woman was watering a large plant that stood in one corner and turned to greet him.

Ben's heart jumped. But no, it couldn't be her. Dark

curls could be dyed and straightened into the woman's smart, honey-blonde style, but if he had to guess her age he would have settled at late thirties. Older than Arianna would be. And surely he would recognise Arianna if he came face to face with her?

'*Yassas...*'

The woman's smile indicated that she appreciated him making the effort to greet her in Greek, but it was unnecessary. 'Hello. My name is Corinna. How may I help you?'

'I'm looking for Dr Petrakis.'

'You are sick?' Corinna looked him up and down.

'No... My name's Ben Marsh. Dr Ben Marsh.' Maybe the *Dr* part would convince her that he was here on business of some kind, and she wouldn't enquire any further.

Corinna nodded, shrugging slightly. 'Take a seat, please. Dr Petrakis will be back in five minutes.'

Ben sat down, looking around him. Light and spacey, cool white walls and earth tones for the furniture. Someone had thought through this area carefully, to provide a welcoming and relaxing area, but his heart was pumping hard. He took his phone from his pocket, opening up the app for the British papers and hoping that Corinna would take this as a signal not to engage him in any further conversation.

She finished watering the plants and then returned to her seat, concentrating her attention on the computer screen in front of her. The doors swished open but it was only a courier, bringing a parcel. After fifteen minutes, Corinna spoke again.

'I'm sure she will be here soon. Would you like me to call her?'

'No, please don't. I'm happy to wait until she returns.'

'You would like a drink...?'

The doors swished open again and Ben's heart jumped. When his head snapped instinctively towards the entrance, he saw a young woman and a dark-haired man supporting a blonde-haired girl between them. The man was clearly a passer-by who had stopped to help, calling Corinna by name and speaking in Greek to her, then turning to leave as she began to rap out orders.

'She is having an asthma attack. Sit her down. Dr Marsh, as you are here you must help her. I will call Dr Petrakis…' A flip of her finger towards Ben, and then Corinna picked up the phone.

He wasn't licensed to practise in Greece, but that was a moot point at the moment. The blonde-haired girl was clearly in distress and this was an emergency. Ben hurried over to the girls, guiding them over to the seats.

'Does she have an inhaler?'

'Yes, but she forgot it. It's back at our hotel…' The girl's companion's eyes were wide with panic.

'Okay. That's okay.' It wasn't, but what he needed to do now was to calm both girls. 'What's her name?'

'Helen…'

Ben turned to Helen, taking her gently by the shoulders. 'Helen, I'm Ben and I'm a doctor. Look at me…'

Helen's frightened gaze met his. Ben smiled reassuringly.

'I want you to try to calm down. Try to breathe more slowly for me, yes?'

Helen nodded. The panic and the rush to the health centre hadn't done her a great deal of good, and now that she was sitting down she seemed a little better. Helen turned as her friend started to cry and Ben put one finger on the side of her face, guiding her gaze back onto him.

'Don't worry about anyone else. Just look at me. Try to breathe with me.'

Corinna had finished her call. 'Dr Petrakis will be here in five minutes. She will bring the inhaler from the chemist.'

Ben nodded. 'Thanks. Perhaps you could look after this young lady?' He indicated Helen's friend and Corinna jumped to her feet, guiding the girl away from them and to a spare seat behind her desk.

'What colour is your inhaler, Helen?' Ben smiled again at her. 'Blue?'

A nod.

'Good. Albuterol?' Ben hadn't yet come across anyone with asthma who didn't know exactly what drug they needed, and he hoped this wouldn't be a first.

Another nod. Helen was calming now and her breathing was slower, but she was still having to work too hard to get the oxygen her body needed.

'Okay, that's great.' Ben turned to Corinna, who already had her phone in her hand, the other arm tightly around the other girl's shoulders. 'Will you tell Dr Petrakis…?'

'Albuterol. I heard…' Corinna shot him a stern look, clearly outraged at any implication that she didn't have everything under control, and Ben turned back to Helen again.

'You're doing really well, Helen.' Hopefully the promised five minutes before Arianna Petrakis got here from the pharmacy wouldn't be as long as the five minutes he'd been asked to wait.

'Don't…let me…' Helen was struggling to speak.

Die. Don't let her die. The last few years had shown Ben that he was powerless in the face of life and death, but Helen didn't need to know that.

'I'm not going to let you do anything. Apart from breathe. That's okay with you?'

This time Helen returned his smile, nodding.

'Will you bring her through to surgery?' Corinna had finished relaying the message and put her phone back down on her desk.

'Yes, that would be a good idea.' Anything to keep Helen quiet and away from any hubbub in the main reception area.

Corinna nodded, turning to Helen's friend and telling her firmly not to move. Then she beckoned to Ben.

Helen wasn't ready to walk yet. Ben grinned at her. 'Let's do this the easy way, shall we? Hold onto me.'

He bent, picking Helen up. He could feel her breathing against his chest, as she lay in his arms, and he followed Corinna to a modern, well equipped surgery, putting Helen down on the examination couch and operating the backrest so that she was sitting up.

'Thanks…' Helen seemed to be breathing a little more easily now.

'That's okay. I get extra points on the emergency doctor scale for carrying someone, you know. I'm just glad you aren't too heavy.'

Helen smiled, even though the joke wasn't really so much of a joke. Ben had just done his job, what he needed to do to keep Helen quiet and safe. But somehow, that lost feeling of being able to make a difference had filtered back into the equation. Maybe because of Helen, but more likely because Arianna Petrakis was just five minutes away now, and she'd known him when he *could* make a difference.

Ben saw a light blanket draped across the bottom of the couch and pulled it up over Helen's legs. She was beginning to recover now, although the smallest thing could leave her struggling for breath again. The door to the surgery opened quietly and Ben turned.

Arianna. He'd know her anywhere. Dark curls, cut to frame her face. Liquid brown eyes, and flawless olive skin. There was something about the way she carried herself that reminded him of the bravery of the little girl who had clung so tightly to him, and…there was no getting away from it…she was beautiful. .

'Hi, I'm Dr Petrakis.' Her manner was perfect, assured and relaxed, even though the pink in her cheeks suggested that she might have been running to get here. 'You're Helen?'

Helen nodded, and Arianna put a large paper pharmacy bag onto her desk. 'I've got a selection of inhalers, but Dr Marsh says that the blue one with Albuterol is the one you usually have.'

'Yes, that's right.' Helen seemed much better now, and managed to get three words out without gasping for breath.

'That's good; I have the one you need.' Arianna reached for the bag, taking a box out and reading the Greek lettering on the side, before opening it and taking out the inhaler.

Her English was flawless, and spoken with a slight London accent, the kind you didn't get from just learning the language. The thought that maybe she'd lived in Ben's home town and he'd never known how close she was took Ben's breath away, and then Arianna turned her gaze onto him.

'Thank you, Dr Marsh.' He thought he saw some spark of recognition, but maybe it was just in his imagination. 'I'll examine Helen now. Corinna will make you some coffee, if you still want to wait?'

Yes, of course… He was a tourist who'd just helped out in an emergency, and it was time for him to leave.

'Thanks. I'll wait.' He turned to Helen with a smile. 'You're looking much better now.'

Helen gave him a smile and a thumbs up, and Ben returned the gesture before walking back out into the reception area. He didn't really want coffee, but Corinna insisted on making him some, putting a selection of biscuits on a plate next to his cup. He sipped his drink as he waited, before Arianna appeared again.

'Claire, you can go and see Helen now.' She spoke to Helen's friend, who'd been sitting miserably in the corner, despite all of Corinna's attempts to cheer her up. 'She's much better, but she needs to rest a little. Andreas, our paramedic, has just arrived and he's sitting with her. Be calm and quiet, yes?'

Claire nodded. 'I'm sorry...'

Arianna batted the apology away with a flick of her hand. 'It's frightening to see someone taken ill like that, isn't it? Now that she's here, we can look after her and she'll be fine. What she needs right now is to see you smiling.'

Arianna was being kind. The hurried rush through the streets to the health centre couldn't have done Helen any good; it would have been better to keep her sitting down and get help to come to her. Maybe she'd explain that at some point, but Ben had little doubt that her firm, gentle way would make it sound like a bit of advice for the future rather than a condemnation.

Claire wiped away her tears and tried out a smile, and Arianna gave her an approving nod. Corinna took Claire's hand, leading her towards the surgery, and then Ben's heart started to beat a little faster as Arianna turned to walk across the reception area towards him.

CHAPTER TWO

MAYBE IT WAS the last dregs of her dream. It had been so clear, and Arianna had struggled to break free of it as she'd showered and made breakfast this morning. But when she'd walked into her surgery, the handsome English doctor had made her catch her breath. There was something so familiar about him.

She'd managed to quell the feeling as she examined and treated Helen, but now that Andreas was back from his afternoon visits and would sit with Helen while she recovered it had started to nag at her again. And when she caught sight of Dr Marsh again, sitting in the waiting room, she was even more convinced she knew him. From a day years ago, when a blond-haired, blue-eyed boy had saved her from the sea.

It was impossible. That kind of coincidence just didn't happen, even if it had occupied her daydreams for much of her teens. And her dreams as an adult. Dr Ben Marsh was probably here for…something else. Some*one* else.

He got to his feet as she approached him, all hard lines and male beauty. Maybe that was why he seemed so familiar. He was definitely the kind of man that any woman would *want* to know.

'Dr Petrakis…'

'Arianna, please. Since we've already put you to work.

You're on holiday here?' His casual trousers and shirt didn't indicate that he was here on business.

'I came to Ilaria to see you.'

Okay. Maybe she *did* know him from somewhere. But that still didn't mean Ben Marsh was the man a part of her hoped he was. Although it really shouldn't be necessary to search her memory for someone as strikingly attractive as Ben. Maybe Arianna's resolution to have nothing more to do with any man who looked capable of sweeping her off her feet had worked a little too well.

'I'm sorry… Have we met before?'

'If you're the Arianna Petrakis I think you are, then yes. It was a long time ago, though…'

He was obviously wary, clearly unwilling to spring anything on her, but now Arianna wondered if her instincts had been right.

'You were on the ferry? The one that sank just outside the harbour?' Her heart was pounding in her chest, as if her life depended on his answer.

'Yes. You were there too, wearing a white dress.'

'Broderie anglaise?' The detail seemed suddenly important.

'I think so. It had little embroidered holes—is that what they call it?'

'Yes. You dived in when I fell overboard.'

He smiled suddenly. *'Dived* makes it sound a lot more expert than it actually was. I saw you sliding across the deck and when you fell into the water I jumped in after you.'

'I was drowning…' The memory made her catch her breath. 'You pulled me up.'

'I don't know how I found you. Somehow I did.' He took a step forward, holding out his hand to shake hers. Arianna took it, winding her fingers tightly around his.

Once she did, she couldn't let go. Arianna willed her fingers to loosen around his but they wouldn't respond. She was clinging to him as tightly as she had that day in the water.

Then, she'd been blinded by tears and panic, and the men in the boat had been forced to prise her arms from around his neck. Things were different now. Ben was no longer a skinny youth, and Arianna was old enough to recognise that he now had that indefinable *something* that rendered a man attractive rather than just handsome.

'You still have a tight grip.' He smiled suddenly.

'Uh…sorry.' Still she couldn't let him go.

'Don't be. I needed you to hold on while I swam.'

'Is that what you said to me?' One last detail clicked into place.

'Yes. You didn't understand?'

'No. I didn't speak English then…'

If twenty-five years of longing to see him had taught Arianna anything, it had taught her restraint. She finally released his hand, feeling a chill of regret as she did so.

'We can't talk here. Can I take you for coffee somewhere?'

He shook his head. 'I should come back tomorrow. You have things to do here.'

The thought of him walking away now, of having to wait for a whole day before she could talk to him was impossible.

'It's all right. I start work early and I should be finishing around now anyway. Andreas covers at the clinic in the afternoons and early evenings, so he'll be here with Helen for a few hours and he'll give me a call if he needs me. If she's not well enough to go back to her hotel tonight, we have a three-bed ward here and I can come back and stay the night…'

She was babbling. It would have been enough to say that she had a few hours free and plenty of time for coffee. Maybe throw in a few words about what a pleasure it was to see him after all this time…

'How about this? The last ferry is at nine, and if Helen's well enough then I can go with her and Claire and make sure that they get back to their hotel. In the meantime, I'd like it very much if we could go for coffee.'

'That would be… Do you mind?'

'As long as you're willing to discharge Helen medically, so that I'm just a concerned member of the public travelling with her.' He grinned.

'Of course. I'll go and get my bag.' Arianna flew out of the waiting room, grudging every moment that it took for her to check carefully on Helen and tell Andreas that she'd be down at the harbour if he needed her. It seemed as if she'd been waiting for this meeting all her life, and she didn't want to waste a second of it.

It felt like a dream. Finally Ben had found the girl who'd changed his life, and it felt as if he'd spent every day with her since their first meeting. In some ways he had. He'd got on with his life, but there hadn't been many days when a brief thought of her hadn't flashed through his mind.

Numbly, he followed her out of the health centre and back down the hill towards the harbour. They walked in silence. This was too big a thing for small talk, and Ben wasn't sure where to start with the things that really mattered.

'Is here all right?' She pointed to a small taverna, which looked out over the harbour, with seats outside that were shaded from the late afternoon sun.

'It looks great.' Anywhere would be fine. Ben had the

feeling that Arianna would shine in the darkest of dungeons, and that her dress would still shimmer around her legs in the same way.

She chose a table to one side of the bustle of the main seating area, and sat down. A waiter appeared, greeting Arianna by name, and she asked Ben what he'd like and then ordered in Greek.

'I'm glad you came, Ben. It's good to see you.' Now that they were finally able to talk, she seemed a little unsure of herself.

'I wasn't sure if you would be.' He felt strong suddenly. As if once more he should protect her from whatever she was feeling.

'What makes you say that?'

'I read… What led me to you was a news article. It said that your brother had been on the ferry, and that he drowned.'

'Yes. That's right.' Arianna's frank gaze found his. 'I would have drowned too, if it hadn't been for you.'

Ben shrugged. 'If my coming here is an unwelcome reminder of that day, then…I'd like you to tell me.'

'You think I could ever forget about it?' Arianna raised one eyebrow.

'No. I can't forget and…I had to come…'

She pursed her lips in thought. The waiter reappeared, unloading a tray of drinks and snacks and disappearing just as abruptly. Arianna reached for her coffee, taking a sip.

'I've never forgotten you, and I've always wondered what became of you. And now I know your name at last.' She gave him a smile that made Ben's heart lurch.

'And I've found out that *broderie anglaise* is the correct description for that dress of yours.'

She laughed suddenly. 'So we've both got some answers. I've always wondered about what happened to you after you lifted me into that boat. Tell me what you've been doing all my life.'

It was tempting to tell Arianna that he'd been waiting for *her*. That wasn't entirely true. Ben had done many other things, but wondering about the little girl in the white dress had probably been his most long-term pre-occupation. And, lately, jumping into the water after her had seemed to be one of the few things he'd done exactly right.

Was he about to put all of that at risk? Turn the perfect memory into something vulnerable, which could be destroyed by the present? But when he looked at Arianna he couldn't believe that she would destroy anything.

'Right from the beginning?' He took a gulp of his coffee, feeling the strong taste hit the back of his throat.

'Yes. How did you get back to the shore—did you swim all the way?'

'I was a pretty strong swimmer and I reckoned I could make it. But I was very glad when someone saw me and a boat came to pick me up. It was a bit different from swimming in the pool at home. So was attempting to rescue someone.'

'I'll bet.' Arianna leaned back in her chair. 'Those dummies they use in the pool don't wriggle quite as much as I remember doing.'

'They don't hang on as tight as you did either. You were very brave.'

She smiled suddenly, and Ben wondered if anyone had ever told her that. 'You were the only thing I had to hang onto. I owe you my life.'

Something warm and proud bloomed in Ben's chest. That feeling had changed *his* life and guided him through all of his darkest days. He owed Arianna his life as well, but didn't quite know how to say it.

'Well…' He decided to stick to the bare facts of the matter. 'The boat picked up a few more people and then took us all back to the harbour. I managed to find my parents and my brother and sister, and got a real telling-off from my dad for running off.'

'You didn't tell him that you'd saved someone?'

Ben shook his head. 'No. I felt… It felt so good that… I wanted that feeling all for myself so I kept it a secret.'

'Which is why I could never find any reference to you when I looked back on the news coverage. I knew that you'd survived, though, because you weren't amongst the list of casualties.' Arianna smiled. 'Another mystery solved.'

The thought gave a whole new meaning to his memories. 'You looked for me?'

'Of course I did. You were my superhero, appearing out of nowhere to save me and then disappearing again. Whatever makes you think I wouldn't look?'

He wasn't the hero that Arianna thought he was. He was flawed, capable of the best and the worst, and pretty much everything in between. Maybe this was why he'd decided to come, after all the heart-searching and uncertainty. He wanted to get back in touch with what he *could* do. It was a way of believing in himself again.

He began to tell the rest of his story. How the hotel where they'd been staying had heard that the ferry had sunk, and sent out a boat to bring them back to the mainland. How the holiday had ended and he'd gone back to England. Back to school, and then onto medical school.

'What made you want to be a doctor?' Arianna shot him a quizzical look.

'The same as anyone, I suppose. I wanted to make a difference.'

'Because you already knew that you could?'

'That day on the ferry… I've never forgotten how it felt. When I was younger, I thought my whole life could be like that.' Ben quirked the corners of his mouth down, knowing how naïve that teenage notion was now. He hadn't really meant to discuss this with Arianna.

'It changed you, then. You wanted to feel that way again.'

'Yes, it did. It meant a lot to me.'

It was as close as Ben could get to telling Arianna how much he needed her now. Her gaze was steady on his face and perhaps she understood a little of what he hadn't said, as well as that which he had.

'And after medical school?'

That all seemed easier to say, now. 'I did most of the usual things. Got a job, worked hard. Fell in love and got married. We bought a house and then our son, Jonas, came along, and redefined the meaning of tired.'

'I've heard they do that. Are your wife and son here in Greece? I'd love to meet them.'

'Jonas is here. We're staying at a hotel on the mainland with my sister and her family. My wife, Emma, died in a car accident four years ago, when Jonas was a year old.' The words had lost their sting now. Time was a healer, which had softened the pain of grief. The pain of guilt was a different matter, and Ben never talked about that.

Arianna's hand flew to her mouth. 'Oh. I'm so sorry, Ben.'

'It's…' He shrugged. 'It's not okay, but I live with it. Maybe you feel the same about your brother?'

She thought for a moment. 'I never quite accepted that I was the one who survived.'

That was how Ben felt too, and he had good reason. It had been his fault that Emma was alone in the car with Jonas, and her quick and selfless reactions had meant their son had escaped the crash unharmed. No amount of guilt and regret was going to change that now, and no amount of sharing would either.

Arianna's eyes glistened in the setting sun, and Ben fancied that he saw tears. There was something that Arianna wasn't saying, but he wouldn't press her. There were things he wasn't saying as well.

'Being the one that's left behind is difficult, isn't it?'

She nodded. 'How do you deal with it?'

He didn't. That wasn't for anyone to hear either.

'Let's just say that it took the edge off my belief in being able to change the world. The first year was very hard. The following one was better and then…one evening about six months ago, after I'd put Jonas to bed, I was searching the internet for some ideas on child-friendly holiday destinations. Ilaria came up and it reminded me of you. I couldn't resist searching one more time for information about the passengers on the ferry that day, and found an old newspaper article. I didn't understand it, it was written in Greek, but there was a picture of you and your family. Once I knew your name, I had to find you.'

'And you turned up and saved the day for Helen. As soon as she *could* talk, she told me how kind you'd been to her.'

Ben shook his head. 'I don't believe in turning up and saving the day any more.'

He had, once. But he'd neither turned up nor saved the day for Emma. It had been a salutary lesson.

She leaned forward, taking a matchbook from the holder on the table and lifting the glass shade from the candle that stood next to it. The match flared, and in the candlelight Ben thought he saw hope reflected in her eyes.

'Maybe you should. Ilaria's taught me a few things since I've been here. It might have some things to teach you too.'

Maybe. Ben wouldn't bet on it, but he wouldn't have bet on Arianna having given him a second thought over the years either. Perhaps this was a place where anything was possible.

He searched her face, looking carefully for any clue that she was speaking out of kindness. But even though he'd burst into her life with no warning, reminding her of many things that she'd probably rather forget, he could see no hint of regret. It empowered him to ask, 'Will you tell me what you've been doing with the last twenty-five years?'

CHAPTER THREE

IT WAS THE obvious question. Arianna had asked it of Ben and he'd answered. Now it was her turn, and it felt much more challenging than sitting listening to him.

'You've read the papers. You know who my father is. You probably know all you need to know.'

Who her father was. The death of her brother. The fact that she'd been saved and Xander hadn't. If anyone wanted to sum her up in three short sentences, then they covered pretty much everything.

'Your father is Ioannis Petrakis.' He said the name with an English inflection which made it sound unfamiliar to Arianna. 'That's part of the reason I succeeded in finding you; he's an important man and the newspapers report on what he does. With pictures.'

Arianna turned the corners of her mouth down. The thought that he was only here because of her father's wealth and position left a sour taste in her mouth. Ben was the one thing she'd kept entirely for herself over all these years, and suddenly even that seemed to be slipping away.

'Then you'll know that I was a spoiled rich kid.'

He shrugged. 'I know that your father's a rich man, but...I don't know you well enough to say whether or not you were spoiled. In my experience, when kids are wet through and terrified they're just kids.'

'We were only on the ferry because my father's launch had engine trouble. I loved it; it was so colourful and loud. After Xander died, I didn't get much of a chance to do anything that was colourful or loud. My father wouldn't allow it.'

He nodded slowly. 'It's a temptation, for any parent. My son's beginning to realise that there's a world out there and he wants to start exploring it. When Emma died I just wanted to lock him away and keep him safe.'

If Arianna could have seen Ben's anguished look mirrored on her father's face then maybe she would have understood a little better. But she never had…

'My father…he *did* lock us away. It suffocated my mother, and she sued for divorce when I was fourteen.'

'It's one of the hardest things that anyone can ever face. The death of a child.'

He understood. He'd struggled with his own loss. Her father hadn't seemed to struggle, he'd just ruled his family with a rod of iron, but Arianna felt that she could understand that a little better now.

'There was never really any room for anything else but grief with my parents. I tried to be a good child and not make things worse for them, but I could never really measure up to the son they'd lost.'

Ben shifted in his chair, clearly thinking the matter over. She liked that. He thought about things, tempering his gut reactions with his head and his heart.

'So you decided to measure yourself by what you wanted, instead?'

'Yes. I couldn't make a difference on the day my brother died, but I can make one now. My father threatened to cut me off when I applied to medical school in

Athens but he just reduced my allowance to more than I ever needed.'

'But you've spent time in London.' Arianna shot him a questioning look and he smiled. 'Your accent. No one's second language is *that* good unless they've lived in a place.'

'We came to live in London when I was eleven. My parents' last-ditch attempt to get away from their grief and save their marriage. I went to school in Regent's Park.'

His lips curved suddenly into an incredulous smile that made her shiver. 'You had a straw boater as part of your uniform in the summer? With a blue ribbon?'

'Yes, the blue matched our blazers and dresses…' Arianna had hated the old-fashioned uniform of the high-class school for young ladies that seemed as if it was taken straight out of the nineteen-seventies.

'I was at medical school nearby. Whenever we got a break during the afternoons we'd go and sit in the park.'

They both smiled at the same time, the idea hanging in the air between them. Maybe he'd seen her. Maybe she'd seen him, one of the young men by the lake who'd seemed so free in comparison to her own closeted existence. If fate hadn't managed to engineer a meeting between them, it hadn't been through any lack of effort.

They'd been in the same places, seeing the same things. If Arianna had known that, maybe her teens would have felt a little less lonely. Or maybe not. Somehow it felt as if Ben had always been there. He already felt like an old friend, someone she hadn't been in touch with for a while, but still close enough to pick up a conversation where they'd left it last.

'I came back to London after I graduated from medical school. I applied for a newly qualified doctors exchange programme and worked at a medical centre near Charing Cross.'

He nodded. 'My practice is near there.'

Another chance to pass in the street. To go to the same restaurants and bars. It was tempting to reel off a list of places and wonder if he knew them too, but the fact that they'd breathed the same air seemed enough at the moment, because now they *had* met.

'You must like London then?' He took a sip of his drink.

'London has a lot going for it. But, to be honest, the moving around was partly an attempt to stay one step ahead of my father. It didn't work very well; he's got business interests all over Europe and it doesn't much matter where he's based as long as he's within reach of an airfield. When I went to Athens he decided to buy a house there, and when I came back to London he suddenly felt the need to return and throw a few big parties.'

'Parties?' Humour glinted in his eyes. 'Not the usual kind of parties that newly qualified doctors go to, I imagine.'

Arianna leaned towards him. It felt so natural to confide in Ben, and she wasn't sure whether it was because she owed her life to him or because he seemed to make everyone he came in contact with feel at ease.

'Nice parties. Where I could meet eligible young men who would take me away from a life of doctoring and turn me into a society lady.'

He nodded. 'I'm assuming that they didn't work so well.'

They almost had. Not quite as her father had intended, though...

Lawrence had been the antithesis of her father. He was fearless and unconventional, living for today with no thought of tomorrow. It had been refreshing at first, and he'd swept Arianna off her feet, asking her to marry him before they'd really had a chance to get to know each other. Arianna had said *yes* far too soon.

And then she'd realised. Lawrence's idea of the way they should live was really more a matter of how *he* wanted to live. His plans involved travel and spending her trust fund, and took no account of Arianna's career, because why would she want to work when she didn't have to? Even then she'd known that her work was the only stabilising factor in her life, the only reason she could find for having survived the sinking ferry when Xander hadn't.

That was all in the past now. Arianna had made her decision and her broken heart had mended, leaving her determined not to repeat her mistake. There was no going back, not on any of it.

'No. They didn't work.'

'He throws parties here?' Ben looked over his shoulder, smiling, as if he half expected to see a party heading their way.

'My father doesn't come to Ilaria…'

'Too many memories?' Something soft crept into his tone.

'Yes.' Arianna wondered how it would have been if it had been the other way around, and Xander had lived. If he'd become a doctor and come to Ilaria. Maybe her father would have come then, and maybe Xander's achievements would have meant something to her father.

'But you have your own memories, surely.'

'I love the way of life here, in the islands. I'm needed, and that's what I always wanted to be. But I chose Ilaria in particular because I thought that trying to drive my memories away wasn't the best way of dealing with them.'

'The best way isn't always the easiest.'

Arianna steeled herself against the tenderness she saw in his face. She was quite sure that if she gave into it, it would involve tears, and now wasn't the time for them. Nightmares and tears were for the darker recesses of the night.

'So…how long are you here for? Will I have an opportunity to meet your son?'

'We're here for three weeks, staying in a hotel on the mainland. Jonas is with my sister today; she's here too, with her family. I've told him all about you, though, and he'd like to meet you. I'll bring him with me the next time I come.'

'When can you come next?' Arianna pressed her lips together. Maybe she should have waited for just a few moments and made the question sound a little less a matter of life and death.

'I'm on holiday. I don't have any plans.' His melting gaze hinted at just one plan. 'Apart from coming to find you…'

He was here for *her*. No one had ever just been there for her.

The chemistry that had been flying between them fizzed and bubbled with gratification, like a test tube reaction that threatened to get out of hand and cause an explosion. Arianna's heart began to beat faster, reacting before rational thought could stop it, and she reminded herself again that acknowledging the way that Ben made her feel would be a mistake.

'I worked last weekend, so I have the day off tomorrow. Would you like to bring Jonas over to my house? We can have lunch and he can play on the beach.'

'You have your own beach?' He raised an eyebrow.

'It's…just a small one. He might like it though; it's secluded and safe for him to run around and play.'

'He'd like that. I would too, thank you. If it's not too much trouble…'

'No trouble. You could catch the morning ferry and I'll meet you at the terminus.' There was so much more that she wanted to say to Ben. Arianna wasn't sure what that was yet, but she knew she needed more time with him. A *lot* more time.

He nodded, looking at his watch and pulling a face. 'I guess we should be getting back to the health centre to see if Helen's up to the trip back tonight.'

Where had the hours gone? It didn't seem five minutes since they'd sat down at the table, but the coffee pot that the waiter had brought was empty now, and the sun had sunk low in the sky. But she had tomorrow to look forward to, and it would bring him back again.

They walked back up to the health centre together, and Arianna couldn't resist taking the route that led through the harbour and the older part of town. When Ben took a few moments to appreciate the sunset, she found herself smiling. He clearly liked Ilaria, and that meant rather more to her than it probably should.

Andreas reported back on Helen, saying that she'd been making a good recovery, and when Arianna examined her she found no trace of the painful wheeze that had accompanied her efforts to breathe earlier on. She joined Ben in the empty reception area.

'She's just getting dressed. She should be fine for the journey back. I've made sure she has a spare inhaler and I'll write a discharge note, and give you a copy. What time will you come tomorrow? There's an eleven o'clock ferry.'

There was a long night to get through before she'd see

Ben again, and suddenly she wanted to know exactly how many hours she'd have to wait.

'Eleven sounds great.' He took his phone from his pocket. 'Maybe we should exchange numbers, so I can call you if we're going to be late.'

Good. Why hadn't she thought of that? Something concrete that she could take away with her. Arianna repeated her mobile number to him, hearing her phone ring as he checked he had it right. Now she had *his* number.

'Ben, I'm so glad you came. It means a lot…'

Suddenly, and without knowing quite how she'd got there, she was in his arms. She must have made the first move, Ben was still standing exactly where he had been before, but there was no mistaking his response. This felt so natural, as if time had crushed the getting-to-know-you process into a few short hours and they'd already become firm friends.

His body was strong, and as he returned the hug, she felt tears welling in her eyes. For the first time in more years than she cared to remember, she felt truly safe.

CHAPTER FOUR

'ARE WE THERE YET, DAD?'

There was a glazed glass barrier between them and the sea, but Ben still had a tight grip on his son's hand. An instinct that had survived the years since he'd seen Arianna slip under the metal railings that skirted the deck of the old ferry. That had sharpened since Emma's death.

'Not yet.' He squatted down, holding Jonas protectively against his body, and pointed into the distance. 'That's where we're going…'

Ilaria seemed to shine in the sun ahead of them. He'd texted Arianna to let her know that they were on the ferry, and she'd said she'd meet them at the terminus. Maybe she was already there, shining too.

'How *far* is it?' Jonas was clearly trying to measure the distance that the ferry still had to travel.

'About a mile.' Ben took a wild guess. 'We'll be there soon, but we'll have to wait and take our turn to get off.'

'Okay.' The information seemed enough for the moment, and Jonas pulled away from him, staring at the island ahead of them.

Maybe fifteen minutes before he'd see Arianna again. Ben wondered whether it was possible that Jonas could be as impatient as he was. Their embrace had been echoing through his mind ever since last night.

Now that Arianna was drawing closer with every moment, he should think of it as a hug. A hug which had totally redefined the word and lasted much longer than was strictly necessary. It had said more than broken words ever could.

It had meant something more to Arianna too, he knew. When they'd heard the sound of a door opening and footsteps in the corridor that led out into the reception area, she'd pulled away from him, brushing tears from her eyes.

In that moment he'd felt something flooding back into his heart. The feeling that he wanted to protect her, and the almost painful realisation that maybe there was some way that he could. Ben hadn't allowed himself to feel that about anyone, apart from Jonas, in a very long time and it was almost as if Arianna had stripped the years away and found the man he'd once been. The one he was trying to find his way back to.

Jonas was interested in everything, the people around him, the way the ferry manoeuvred into the dock and the prospect of dry land ahead of him. Ben held his hand firmly, his gaze searching for just one person. When he saw Arianna, wearing a bright yellow sundress, his heart almost leapt into his throat. Dizzily he returned her wave, nudging at Jonas's shoulder to point her out, and the boy waved too, staring at this new person he'd heard all about.

'Hey, Jonas.' She flashed Ben a smile and then turned her attention to his son. 'Welcome to Ilaria. I'm Arianna.'

'Hello.' Jonas was a little more reserved now, watching this new person carefully. How anyone could resist the sudden sunshine of Arianna's smile was a complete mystery to Ben.

'How was the ferry ride? Did you like it?'

Jonas nodded. Arianna looked up at Ben. 'I'm parked

in the harbour. I thought perhaps he'd like to have a look around there?'

'What do you think, Jonas? Shall we go and see the boats?'

Jonas perked up immediately. 'Yes, Dad!'

'Okay. The harbour it is, then.'

She seemed so keen for Jonas to like Ilaria, and for him to like her too. Arianna produced chilled drinks from the straw shopping bag she carried, smiling when Jonas accepted one from her. He'd get over his reticence soon, and then… What was not to like about Ilaria? What wasn't to love about Arianna…?

He amended the thought quickly. The 'L-word' shouldn't intrude into this equation. What wasn't to *like* about Arianna…?

By the time they reached the car, Jonas had been introduced to the men working on their boats in the harbour, and had even been allowed on one. The boy was shining with enthusiasm now, and when Arianna opened the back door of the small SUV he climbed in without a backward look at his father, getting into the child seat and waiting for Ben to strap him in.

It was only ten minutes' drive to the house, which stood in an isolated spot outside the town. When Arianna opened the front door, beckoning them inside, the interior was cool and quiet.

Inside, white-painted walls and irregular exposed stonework were given a modern feel by elegant wooden furniture and pale fabrics. At the back, shutters protected the space from the heat of the midday sun, and when Arianna opened them he saw French windows leading out onto a large patio, edged with flowering plants and shaded by a canopy draped with a vine. Beyond that, a sheltered beach and the blue of the sea.

'You have a lovely home.'

'Thank you. Shall we go outside?'

'Yes!' Jonas answered before Ben could, and Arianna smiled.

'Okay. I'll get some drinks and then you can play on the beach.' She turned to Ben. 'The bathroom's through there if you need it.'

'Thanks. I think Jonas could do with another application of sunscreen.' He pulled the bottle out of the bag he carried, along with Jonas's beach shoes.

The bathroom was white-tiled and shining. Ben stripped off Jonas's T-shirt, applying the sunscreen carefully while the boy wriggled impatiently.

He really shouldn't be noticing that only one toothbrush sat in the glass by the sink. Or imagining what it might look like with two, or three, sitting there. He wasn't looking for a relationship with anyone and, despite the instant attraction that would normally have rendered a love affair between two people practically inevitable, it was unthinkable. Guilt was a heavy burden to carry and it didn't leave much room for anyone other than Jonas in his life.

He found Arianna in the kitchen, adding sliced lemons and mint leaves to a jug of lemonade. She'd taken off her sandals, and Ben tried not to notice the natural grace of her movements, or the way the skirts of her dress moved around her bare legs.

'I'll let you choose a drink for Jonas from the fridge. There's a bottle of ouzo in there as well, if you fancy a dash to flavour the lemonade.'

'Thanks. That sounds good.' This felt like a dream. Ben hadn't allowed himself to have any expectations beyond his initial meeting with Arianna, and he wasn't sure what to say or do. Arianna seemed on edge as well.

She tipped slightly more than a dash into the pitcher,

ice clanking as she mixed its contents thoroughly. Ben took a bottle of orange-flavoured water from the fridge and opened it, and Arianna leaned over, popping a bendy straw into the top of it. She opened a box of sesame and honey snacks and frowned.

'Will Jonas like these?'

'Try him.' When Arianna hesitated, Ben took two of the snacks from the box, giving one to Jonas and popping the other into his own mouth. 'Mmm… They're good…'

As he expected, Jonas followed suit and nodded his agreement. Arianna tipped the whole box into a bowl and added it to the tray that the pitcher stood on, then opened the fridge and took out two covered dishes.

'I'll put these into the oven to warm. I thought something light for now, and I'll cook later…'

'Don't go to any trouble for us, please.'

Arianna laughed suddenly and the tension between them broke, smashing into little pieces on the tiled floor.

'You're on a Greek island. You think you can sit down at *my* table without being fed?'

The warmth was back now, chasing away all the awkwardness. 'I wouldn't presume to do any such thing.'

'Good. Just as well.'

She switched the oven on, opening the kitchen door so that Ben could carry the tray out onto the patio. It was beautiful here, the breeze carrying the scent of flowers along with the tang of the sea. Sand stretched from the back of the house down to the shoreline, with raised ground and rocks on either side forming a small secluded beach. Ben took Jonas's hat from his pocket, putting it onto his son's head.

'Can I make sandcastles, Dad?' Jonas looked up at him pleadingly.

'Okay. As long as you stay where I can see you.'

'He'll be all right. This is a private beach—the land on either side of it goes with the house. I've got some buckets and spades…'

The children's buckets and spades were placed neatly in the corner of the veranda, and it was impossible that they hadn't been put there in preparation for their arrival. Ben watched as Arianna showed Jonas how to dip the buckets into the water butt at the back of the house and wet the sand a little so it would retain its shape. She was so eager to get involved, and all of Jonas's initial shyness had disappeared now and he was hanging on her every word.

He drew a line in the sand, impressing on his son that he mustn't cross it. Jonas was used to the lines that Ben drew; he'd never known anything different, and he was far too interested in his sandcastle to want to bother with the sea.

Hearing how Arianna had reacted to her own father's protectiveness was food for thought, though. It was tempting to believe he might somehow make up for Emma's death by protecting Jonas, but Ben had to admit that his solicitousness for his son was sometimes a little too much of a good thing. If Jonas reacted as Arianna had, it would break his heart.

He could think about that later, though, because right now he had a moat to dig. Jonas stood to one side, issuing instructions and advice, and then decided that if you wanted a job done well it was necessary to do it yourself.

Ben saw Arianna laughing behind her hand as Jonas relieved him of the spade and shooed him away, leaving him to walk back to the shaded patio.

'He's a great little boy. You must be very proud of him.' Arianna was watching Jonas while Ben filled two glasses from the pitcher.

'Yes, I am.' There was no hesitation in his answer. If

her father had reacted in that way just once, then things might have been very different.

'It must be hard. Working and looking after him alone.'

Ben shook his head. 'It would have been harder without him. After Emma died, it was having Jonas to look after that kept me going. And I'm lucky; my sister, Lizzie, has a girl Jonas's age and she'd already made the decision to be a stay-at-home mum. She offered to look after Jonas while I was working.'

'That's a good arrangement. Although I expect he misses his mother.'

'He doesn't really remember Emma. He asks about her sometimes and we talk and look at old photographs together. I think he may start to feel her absence a little more when he's older.' Ben's brow furrowed slightly. 'I guess the two of us will deal with that when we come to it.'

Arianna guessed they would too. Her own loss seemed so long ago in comparison and not nearly as life-changing, but somehow Ben had managed to look forward. Maybe she should take a leaf from his book and shake off her nightmares.

Their conversation drifted, past places they both knew in London, and things they'd both done as doctors. When the timer sounded from the kitchen Arianna jumped to her feet, hurrying inside, and then reappeared with a bowl of warm *tiropita* in one hand and one of *keftedakia* in the other. Ben called Jonas, taking him into the kitchen to wash his hands.

Jonas worked his way through everything that was put in front of him, and then ran back to his castle. Arianna made coffee, and they watched Jonas playing in the sand. When he called his father, Ben slipped off his shoes to walk out onto the beach and Arianna followed him.

'That's amazing. Fantastic work, Jonas. What do you think, Arianna?'

'Best I've ever seen.'

Ben rolled up his trouser legs and knelt down in the sand next to his son, and the boy nestled close. 'That's a great moat. Like the one we saw at Leeds Castle.'

Jonas wrinkled his nose. 'It doesn't have any water, Dad. And I can't go across the line.' He pointed at the line that Ben had drawn in the sand.

'Yeah, good boy. It's okay if you and I go across the line together. Perhaps we'll just flatten the sand a bit first, eh?'

Ben started to tamp down the sand at the bottom of the moat and Jonas followed suit, watching his father carefully. Arianna knelt down on the other side.

'Can I help?' Maybe this was something that Ben and Jonas wanted to do together.

'Hear that? Your castle has its very own princess who doesn't mind getting her hands dirty.' Ben grinned at Jonas. 'I think that'll be a yes please, won't it?'

'Yes! You can do that bit.' Jonas pointed to a segment next to his own. 'Please…'

She could feel Jonas's warm skin against her arm as they worked. His hands pressing on top of hers. The half-remembered feeling of playing with other kids, before she'd lost her childhood and become the little girl who made no noise, and who didn't attract any attention to herself, for fear that the weight of her parents' grief might suddenly break free and crush her.

'Dad…' Jonas frowned. 'You have to do the sides too. *We're* doing the sides.'

'Yep. In a minute. I'll just finish off here…' Ben was packing the sand down at the bottom of the moat first, and Jonas clearly felt that his father wasn't doing things in the right order. Wriggling in between Ben's arms, Jonas started to rectify the problem, tamping the sand at the sides.

Arianna left them, nudging each other good-naturedly out of the way, and went to fetch three large buckets. Ben got to his feet, catching two of the buckets up in his hand, while Jonas followed suit, picking up the two small children's pails. When they got to the line in the sand, he slid one foot over it, grinning cheekily up at his dad, and Ben laughed, picking him up and swinging him over the line, before racing him down to the water's edge. When Jonas reached the sea, he dropped his pails and started to splash water at his father.

'So *that's* the way you want it, eh?' Ben growled, lifting his son up into the air and then threatening to dunk him in the waves.

Jonas shrieked with joy, his arms and legs flailing, and as Ben lowered him he sent a plume of water in his father's direction, hitting him full in the face. Arianna heard herself laugh.

Two blond heads turned in her direction. Jonas flung his arms above his head, beckoning to her to join the game. Ben's smile was less demonstrative, but much more compelling.

Could she cross the line in the sand? The line that had been drawn when her brother died and she'd suddenly been sucked into the emptiness of a family bound by grief. Arianna had thought that the chance to play with other kids was long gone now, but Ben's smile was irresistible…

She walked down to the water's edge and, as soon as she was in range, Jonas sent a splash of water in her direction. She sidestepped out of the way and Ben picked Jonas up, holding him clear of the water.

'Careful, mate. Don't get Arianna's dress all wet.'

Suddenly, she didn't care about that. Arianna gathered her skirts up in one hand, wading into the water and sending a splash in Jonas's direction, then another larger one towards Ben.

'Hey! How come I'm so wet…?'

Because…he looked so much better wet than dry. His T-shirt was sticking to his skin, clearly outlining an impressive pair of shoulders. The temptation to run her fingers across his chest, to see if it felt as good as it looked, was almost too much. His blue eyes were ninety per cent laughter but the other ten per cent were all smouldering heat, which burned right into her soul.

Jonas had decided to even the odds a little, and when his father let him down into the water he filled one of his pails, running over to his father and drenching him.

'Uh…two can play at that game…' Ben filled one of the larger buckets and Jonas ran squealing away to hide behind Arianna.

One look from those mischievous blue eyes that seemed entirely for her, and all about play of a much more adult nature. Then he stepped back, filling the other bucket and walking away up the beach, leaving Arianna to help Jonas dunk his pails into the sea. He gave her one to carry, taking her hand as they walked back to the sandcastle.

Ben carefully emptied the water into the moat, grinning as he passed them on his way back down to the sea. Sudden blinding desire gripped her, and she tried to focus her eyes on his face. But she couldn't resist turning to watch him for just a moment, before Jonas tugged on her hand, impatient to add their water to the moat.

When she looked again towards the water's edge, she saw that Ben had stripped off his T-shirt and was wringing it out in the sea, sunshine glistening on his skin. Its warm fingers seemed to caress him as he moved, and Arianna froze.

'We need more water.' Jonas nudged her and she jumped, pulled back into the moment.

'Yes, we do.' Arianna reached for the last bucket, grabbing her sunglasses at the same time and settling them firmly on her nose. They were a meagre enough defence against the golden lines of Ben's body, but at least it wasn't quite so obvious that she couldn't drag her gaze away from him.

As she walked back down the beach with Jonas, Ben flapped his T-shirt in the breeze and pulled it back over his head. That didn't help as much as it should have done; his image was already burned into her mind. He gave her a cheery smile, dodging out of the way as Jonas splashed more water in his direction, and filling the buckets in the sea.

When the moat was full, and Jonas was busily engaged in building a causeway across it made from stones and shells, Ben came to sit next to her on the steps that ran down from the veranda.

'Would you like a towel?' He smelled of sun, sand and the sea. Like the faraway, much missed summers that she'd spent with her family, here on the island.

'No, I'm fine, thank you. Almost dry now.'

She'd noticed. Had watched as dry patches appeared on his T-shirt, wanting to trace their edges with her finger. They'd spread and begun to join and now she could almost…almost look at him without feeling that her heart was going to stop.

'Your practice here is very different from mine.' He leaned back on his elbows, basking in the sun. 'Different and yet the same.'

'Yes. Some of the problems are unique, but many of

them are the same as the ones I saw when I was working in London. I learned a lot there.'

He nodded. 'My practice would kill for the kind of facilities you have here, at the health centre. But it's a lot easier for me to send people to the hospital for things like blood tests and X-rays.'

'That's true.' Arianna quirked her lips down. 'Although we do have better facilities than some island practices.'

He raised an eyebrow, but didn't ask. Arianna couldn't help answering anyway. There was no holding out against a man who combined beauty and brains.

'When I came here there was no doctor, and no medical centre. If someone was ill they had to go to the mainland. There were funds available to start up a practice, but we would have had to raise a lot more money to afford anything approaching what we have now. Then an… anonymous donor made a very large gift.'

Ben nodded slowly. 'That sounds extremely well timed.' The humour in his eyes left Arianna in no doubt that he'd put two and two together and that four was the correct answer.

'Doesn't it. My father had just about come around to the idea that I was serious about being a doctor, and had been hoping I'd opt for a smart practice in Athens when I came back to Greece. He knew I couldn't turn the donation down.'

'Because it wasn't really for you; it was for your patients.'

'Yes. When I told him I knew it was him, he said that he wanted me to have a nice place to work. Although, if that was all he'd wanted, he could have spent a great deal less.'

'So it was an altruistic move, after all?'

'My father does care about Ilaria. Did you notice that the harbour was a little different when you arrived yesterday?'

He shook his head. 'I noticed that nothing seemed familiar. I was only here for less than a day and it was a long time ago.'

It seemed like yesterday. But it *had* been a long time.

'The ferry that we were on was hit by a larger ferry that had just left the harbour. It had always been a bit of a tight squeeze for the ferries to get in and out of the bay, and my father had a separate ferry terminal built, so that things were much safer for both the ferries and the smaller boats in the harbour. Two men from here drowned as well as my brother, and he made sure that their families would always be provided for. He built the hotel on the other side of the island as well, which has provided employment and allowed people to stay on the island.'

'So he does his good deeds by stealth.' Ben smiled.

'By chequebook. He doesn't turn up in person.'

'Never?'

'No. I didn't expect him to buy a house here and start throwing parties, the way he did in London, but I'd hoped he might finally decide to come back. But he hasn't set foot on the island since the day of the ferry accident. I haven't seen him in two years.'

Ben was watching Jonas playing in the sand, his expression tight and pinched suddenly. Arianna wondered if there was anything that could ever keep him from his son. Maybe if Jonas became an astronaut and flew to Mars…

'Coming here must have been challenging for you.'

'Yes and no. When I first got here, I had to work very hard to oversee the building works for the health centre, and to gain people's confidence. Most of the older people here remember me as a child, and everyone knows what happened, but it took a while to convince them that I could be their doctor.'

He nodded. 'Yeah, *busy* can carry you through a lot of things. It did me, when Emma died, but as soon as I caught my breath I realised I was only postponing the loss I needed to feel.'

Maybe that was what she'd done too. Arianna hadn't told anyone about the nightmares, and after all this time no one had asked. But she couldn't shake the certainty that Ben just knew.

'You had nightmares?' She couldn't look at him for fear that he'd see her own reflecting in her eyes.

'Yes.'

'And they passed?'

'Yes. They did.' His voice seemed to pull her back out of the vortex and offer her a way forward. Maybe if she just clung to him...

Or maybe if she stood on her own two feet and pulled herself together. That was Arianna's preferred coping strategy and it generally worked.

'Good. That's good.' She let out a breath and got to her feet. 'I should make a start on lunch. Is there anything that Jonas doesn't like?'

'He's at the stage where he's beginning to like trying new things.'

'Jonas...' she called over to the boy. 'What's your favourite food?'

'Fingers and chips,' he answered straightaway.

'That's fish fingers and chips.' Ben grinned, beckoning to his son. 'Happy to try something different?'

'Yes.' Jonas's dirty hands found their way onto his father's knees. 'Dad says it's okay if I try something and don't like it because he eats it.'

'But if you have fingers and chips, your dad goes hungry?'

Jonas nodded solemnly and Ben chuckled, pulling a face of exaggerated dismay.

'I'll go and see if I have some fish fingers in my freezer then.'

CHAPTER FIVE

IT HAD SEEMED almost inevitable that they should find something to bring them together again. Sun, sand and sea had done its work yesterday, and Ben had stayed longer at Arianna's than he'd meant to, the two of them talking on the veranda until it was time to hurry down to catch the last ferry.

And today it would be their work. Ben's questions about Arianna's practice had finally led her to laugh, shake her head to catch the sun in her curls and tell him that he could see for himself. A visiting doctor could observe, even if the necessary paperwork to allow him to practice wasn't in place. It had been approximately fourteen hours since Ben had seen her last, and already he'd started to miss her.

She was a mass of inconsistencies. Vulnerable and yet capable, impulsive but measured. Her feet were planted firmly on the ground, yet she was capable of dreaming. Arianna's beauty was the only thing about her that wasn't tempered by an opposite balancing force. His fascination with her was getting to be much the same, never wavering in its intensity.

Maybe that was to be expected. It was as if they'd been fused together that day on the ferry, and then both spent twenty-five years wondering what had become of the other. That twenty-five years hadn't been as straight-forward as either of them might have hoped, but Ben had realised that the one constant thing in his life had been his wish to find Arianna again.

'There!' Jonas had been playing a game with Ben's sister, Lizzie, pointing out every young woman with dark hair who entered the hotel coffee shop and trying to make Lizzie guess whether it was Arianna or not. This time the word was accompanied by a chuckle, and Ben looked up.

Arianna's dress was a mixture of reds and pinks today, and she wore a pair of red deck shoes. She shone, as she always did, and his heart lurched in response. As it always seemed to whenever she was around.

She gave Jonas a wave, and the boy ran to her for a hug. Arianna's awkward delight showed on her face. What kind of fractures had split her own family that she was so unused to the normal ebullience of a child? Ben set the thought aside and smiled up at her.

'You're early. Do you have time to join us for coffee?'

Arianna looked at her watch and sat down in the empty chair next to his. 'Yes, I think I do.'

He left Jonas to introduce her to Lizzie, her husband, James, and their three children, and signalled to the waiter. By the time everyone had decided what they wanted, Arianna and Lizzie had already started chatting.

'It's a shame we didn't get a booking for the hotel on the island.' Lizzie turned the corners of her mouth down. 'Ben wouldn't hear of it, but now it's a bit of a trek backwards and forwards for you both.'

Arianna turned her gaze onto him. 'It would have been a lot more convenient.'

'As things have turned out. I didn't know whether you'd even want to see me, let alone if you'd want me staying on the island for three weeks.'

'Perhaps we could get a swap. I think this hotel's run by the same group as the one on the island,' Lizzie interjected helpfully, blithely unaware that she was sitting with the daughter of the man who owned both hotels. 'What do you reckon?'

James nodded, obviously happy to go with the flow, and suddenly all eyes were on Ben. The idea of moving to the island had occurred to him as well, but he'd far rather have spoken to Arianna about it alone first.

'I'm...um... Perhaps it's better to stay where we are.'

Arianna's face fell. He'd said the wrong thing.

'Or we *could* move.'

'I think it would be better to move, if we can.' Lizzie was committed to the plan already. 'What do you think, Arianna?'

'I know the manager of the hotel on the island. I'd be happy to ask if he can arrange something and you can go from there.'

The idea was agreed, but Ben decided he would find out how Arianna really felt about it later. Because she had already moved on, asking Lizzie where they'd been and what they were planning to do today, and the conversation lasted until their coffee cups were empty.

Ben looked at his watch. 'Should we be going?'

'Oh.' Arianna looked at hers. 'Yes, I think we should...'

She stifled a yawn as they walked out of the hotel and into the bright sunshine, and they walked silently towards the hotel's marina. Suddenly she seemed tired, and Ben remembered that she'd asked him about nightmares. He wondered if the question was a little more personal to her than he'd supposed, and how much she'd slept last night.

She stopped by the neat blue and white boat that she'd pointed out yesterday in the harbour as belonging to the health centre. Something was clearly on her mind.

'If you don't want to stay on Ilaria…' Her lip quivered almost imperceptibly, but Ben had now become used to watching everything about her.

'I just didn't want you to feel crowded.'

Right answer. She smiled again, the lines of fatigue disappearing from her face.

'I don't. It'll be nice to have you and your family there. The hotel has a lovely beach, which isn't as busy as the one here. It's a little more orientated towards relaxing, while this one is better if you want to go sightseeing.'

He reached for her, and suddenly the world around them faded into the background and they were alone on the jetty. His fingers skimming the warm skin of her arm were the only thing that seemed to matter.

She felt it too. Arianna let out the merest hint of a gasp, looking up at him. Locked in the warmth of her eyes, it felt like an embrace. A kiss. The very sweetest one imaginable.

'Lizzie and James can relax, and the kids can play on the beach. What *I'd* really like to do is spend more time with you.'

Her reply was in her eyes. Warm and bright, with the hint of a tear. Someone brushed against her back, and as Ben stretched out his arm instinctively to protect her the moment was shattered.

'I'll…um…give the manager a call, then. I'm sure he can sort out something.'

'You're sure? You've worked hard to make sure that everyone on the island sees you for what you are, and not who your father is. We're not asking for any favours.'

Again, that warmth in her eyes made Ben want to lean in and hold her close. Protect her from all the hurt she seemed to carry with her.

'That's okay. I've never asked the manager for anything before. I imagine he'll be relieved that he has something to report back on to my father.'

Ben raised his eyebrows. 'People report back on you?'

Arianna shrugged. 'I'm sure it's not written into his job description, but my father does always seem to know what I'm up to. It's his way of caring… From a distance.'

She turned suddenly, stepping confidently onto the boat before Ben could extend his hand to steady her. Arianna handed him a life jacket and smilingly refused his help in slipping the mooring lines, before she carefully manoeuvred away from the dock.

'How often do you visit Kantos?' The island was visible on the horizon already, as the boat sped across the blue water.

'I have a surgery there on Mondays and Fridays, and Andreas goes across every Wednesday. And there's a full-time pharmacist on the island as well; he often deals with day-to-day problems. I don't have too many people to see this morning, so maybe we'll have a chance to go up to the Lava Lake afterwards.'

The famous Lava Lake of Kantos was on Ben's list of places to see. Seeing it with Arianna put it firmly at the top of said list.

She steered the boat into the little harbour at Kantos, mooring it. Ben picked up her medical bag and they walked together through the narrow sun-baked streets.

'Here we are…' She unlocked the door of a stone-built house which stood some way back from the road. Inside, the rooms were shaded and cool and a little old-fashioned.

'Waiting room…' Arianna pointed to a large room at the front, decorated with dark wooden furniture and seats arranged in groups. 'My surgery…'

The surgery was at the back of the building. A large mahogany desk and a heavy bookcase gave it an air of gravitas, and when Arianna opened the heavily shaded doors at the back, the light streaming in and her own bright dress added a note of exuberance.

'You're sure you want to sit in on my surgery? You *are* on holiday, and there's a nice taverna in the harbour...'

'If you don't mind. The holiday part is that I'm not responsible for any of your patients.'

'I don't mind at all.' She pulled a heavy leather upholstered chair across the room, positioning it next to hers. Ben grinned at her, pulling the chair back into the corner, and she laughed. 'Okay. Be a fly on the wall.'

It was both the same and different. The differences were immediately obvious. There was no receptionist and when Arianna rang the buzzer to usher a new patient into the surgery, the waiting room just produced the next in line by consensus. She smilingly explained that everyone knew everyone anyway, and that those who couldn't wait were given priority by the others. Jumping the queue was out of the question, and anyone who did that would never hear the last of it.

She knew everyone. Ben couldn't follow the conversations, but she greeted everyone by name without looking at her notes, and when she tilted her head, obviously asking each new person how they were keeping, the long replies seemed to include information of a social nature as well as medical details. Some patients were given stern instructions, accompanied by a look that implied Arianna would be checking up on them afterwards. Others were quietly reassured. In his own practice, and with the best will in the world, Ben couldn't even recognise all of his patients, and only knew their names and some very basic personal details by scanning the computer while they were on their way to his surgery. His approach was necessarily reactive, while Arianna's was more proactive.

One elderly man saw Ben sitting in the corner and insisted on directing his explanations of his medical condition at him instead of Arianna. She waited, arms folded, until he'd finished speaking and gesturing at his left arm, which appeared to Ben to have limited mobility. Something told him that she was well in charge of the situation and that there was no need to intervene, and her murmured words seemed to set things straight. The man turned to her and went through the gestures all over again.

'What did you say to him?' Ben asked while the waiting room was deciding on the next patient.

'I said that you were assisting me today, and that you didn't know everyone's medical history. If he wasn't careful you might try to get him to raise his arm above his head.' She grinned at Ben and suddenly the world seemed to tip a little, as if he were being sucked into the mischief in her dark eyes.

'Ouch. Frozen shoulder?'

'Yes. Do you mind my saying you were my assistant?'

Not in the slightest. Arianna's way of managing her patients was both efficient and charming. He'd be her assistant any day.

'It's a promotion from fly-on-the-wall. I'm extremely happy with it…'

He settled back into his seat as the next patient arrived. For all the differences and personal touches, Arianna's practice was much the same as his. She was thorough and capable, the kind of doctor that everyone aspired to be. But, unlike him, she wasn't one part of a greater machine that provided him with support and backup. She'd achieved all of this by herself.

Ben's Greek extended to 'please' and 'thank you,' and he clearly didn't understand the word *sýzygos*. That was a relief, because it had passed the lips of more than one of her patients this afternoon. Yes, he was undoubtedly good husband material. And no, his name wasn't on her list of prospective husbands because, believe it or not, and most people didn't, she didn't possess such a list.

It was nice having him here, though. He had obviously divined what ailed a number of her patients, just from watching her examinations, but he didn't interrupt with any of his own observations. Compared with her father's constant questions about whether she knew what she was doing with her life, it was a welcome show of respect.

'So.' She turned to him as the last patient closed the door of the surgery behind her. 'What do you think?'

'I think you're making a difference.'

'It's not exactly cutting-edge medicine.' Arianna wondered how he would respond to her father's assertion, that if she was going to work for a living she should choose something a little more high-profile. Or at least some-*where* a little more high-profile, like the city.

Ben winced. 'What do you want me to say? I'm a working GP too, so clearly I think that this makes a difference. What I see here is that if I had the ability to know my patients a little better, then I could make more of the kind of difference you're making here.'

'Okay.' Arianna held her hands up in an expression of willing defeat. 'What I actually wanted you to say was that it doesn't matter where you practice. Now you're telling me that it does and that I'm doing better than you.'

He chuckled. 'Fair enough. It doesn't matter where you

practice, then. You're still doing more for your patients than I can. Are you ready to go now? I'm looking forward to seeing the Lava Lake.'

The conversation was turning into a flirtation, possibly because Ben's smile made everything a flirtation, and possibly because of the warm feeling that his approval gave. Arianna's phone rang and she picked it up from the desk, watching as Ben turned towards the window, staring outside to the large garden at the back, where Mrs Kyriakou and her daughter Athena were bidding their goodbyes to the last of the children they'd been minding while their mothers were visiting the surgery.

The message being relayed to her was the last thing she wanted to hear right now. The Lava Lake, along with Ben, started to recede from her immediate future.

'Ben, I'm sorry but the Lava Lake's going to have to wait. I'll find someone to take you back to Ilaria— something's come up.'

'What's happened?' He was suddenly alert.

'There's been an accident on one of the fishing boats. I have to take the boat out to meet them.'

'Can I help? I'm assuming you have no other medical staff available.'

'Are you sure…?' Arianna swallowed down the objection that Ben was on holiday because she really could use his help. 'I can't wait for Andreas to get here; it'll take him too long.'

'Then let's go.'

Ben carried Arianna's medical bag as they both hurried down to the harbour. A young man was waiting for them at the dock, and Arianna translated what he said for Ben as they all climbed into the boat.

'They're drifting, somewhere over there.' She pointed

towards a clear expanse of sea. 'They had engine problems and a couple of the crew have been hurt, so we'll need to give them a tow as well. Georgios is coming with us, to help.'

At the mention of his name, Georgios held out his hand to Ben and the men nodded a hello. Then he turned to stand with Arianna at the helm, obviously giving her directions. When a fishing boat became visible, Georgios took out his phone, obviously speaking to the people on board and then relaying the gist of the conversation to Arianna.

'Well, they're not sinking, so that's good news.' Arianna was staring ahead of her as she steered towards the boat. 'I think the best thing for us to do is to go across onto the fishing boat and see how badly the men are injured, while Georgios sorts out a towing line.'

'Okay. Just tell me what to do and when to do it.' Ben smiled at her. Arianna was confident and capable, and there was no trace of hesitation in her manner. Clearly she remembered the panic and confusion of the ferry, but it seemed she'd put it behind her and had no fear of the water now.

She manoeuvred the boat alongside the fishing boat, a larger wooden craft with a small cabin towards the back and nets tumbled across the deck at the front, as if they'd been hauled in with haste. One man sat alone, nursing his arm, and the other four were clustered around a prone figure.

He clambered up onto the fishing boat, turning to help Arianna. But she was already beside him, stretching down as Georgios passed her medical bag up to her. Above the clamour of the sea there was no sound other than the moans of the stricken man. Ben's gaze caught Arianna's and she nodded in silent agreement. There was a different note to the cries of a patient in crisis, and it sounded as if someone had been badly hurt.

'If you take a look at the man sitting over there…' She looked around, motioning over to one of the fishermen. 'Dimitris speaks a bit of English. Best we can do, I'm afraid… If you need splints or a sling, there are some in the long chest on the left, in the cabin of my boat.'

'That's great, thanks.' Arianna had given him all he needed, despite the almost unbearable feeling that he should stay with her, be there for her, Ben knew that a division of labour was best for their patients. She'd call him if she needed him. He hoped.

It turned out to be easier just to motion to the man with the injured arm, as Dimitris's attempts at translation weren't all that intelligible. A careful examination showed that the man had a nasty fracture of his forearm, and Ben climbed back onto Arianna's boat and found an emergency splint and a sling. He'd leave pain relief to Arianna; the labels on all the drugs packages were in Greek and although he was pretty sure of what everything was, he couldn't be positive.

Meanwhile, Arianna had called to Georgios and a burns kit was being handed up onto the fishing boat. Not good news. Ben went back to his own patient, carefully inflating the splint around the fracture and positioning the arm in a sling. That should make him more comfortable until they could get him to a hospital, and a thumbs-up and a smile told him that the man was feeling better.

'Anything else?' Ben hoped that Dimitris would be able to translate that correctly, and looked at a small cut on his patient's cheek. The blood was already congealing and there was nothing to suggest any further injury.

'No. *Entáxei*… Okay.' Dimitris glanced over to where

Arianna was kneeling over the other man, rapping out instructions in Greek. 'Go... Go help.'

'All right. You stay here. Watch him...' Words and gestures made Ben's meaning clear and Dimitris nodded, sitting down next to their patient. Finally Ben allowed himself to turn away.

Arianna glanced up at him. 'His leg is badly scalded by steam from the engine. We can't tow the fishing boat back; we'll have to take him on my boat, straight over to the mainland. I've called for an ambulance and they'll meet us back at the hotel marina.'

Ben nodded. 'What do you want me to do?'

'I'm going to get some pain relief for him; will you finish the dressings, please?' Arianna was carefully applying cooling gel dressings to the angry-looking burns that ran from the man's ankle to above his knee.

'Will do.' Ben stripped off his surgical gloves, putting on a new pair from the burns kit. 'While you're about it, the other guy has a fractured arm. I haven't given him anything, and I've no idea whether or not he's taken anything already.'

Arianna nodded. 'Okay, leave it with me. I'll be back in a minute.'

She spoke to her patient, then got to her feet, stepping back down onto the smaller craft that bobbed in the sea next to the fishing boat. Ben finished applying the dressings, keeping a close eye on his face. The man was clearly in a lot of pain and, although the area covered by the burn wasn't enough to make hypovolemic shock likely, he was clearly emotionally traumatised by his injury, and that could well provoke a sudden reaction.

Arianna returned and administered a painkilling injection, then walked over to their other patient to check on how he was doing. Georgios passed a stretcher up to the men on the fishing boat, and then caught a line that was thrown down, pulling the two boats together until they were almost touching.

They worked together silently, Arianna finishing the dressings while Ben assembled the stretcher. When their patient was lifted onto it, he groaned in pain and Ben set about packing a blanket around his shoulders and body.

'Is that…?' He nodded towards the men, who were now lashing the boats together. Ben wasn't quite sure how this was going to work.

'It'll be fine. These men live on the water; they know how to get a stretcher from one boat to another. Just stay back and do as you're told.' She grinned at him suddenly.

'Aye-aye, Captain.' Ben shot her a smile, the warmth of the afternoon tingling through his body.

He stood back and did as he was told. Georgios helped the man with the broken arm into a seat and strapped him in, and Arianna secured the stretcher under the sheltered awning at the front of the boat.

'The blood pressure monitor's in there.' She pointed to one of the chests that lined the cabin. 'Will you keep an eye on him, please?'

Ben nodded. Arianna slid behind the wheel, checking that none of the ropes that secured them to the fishing boat were still in place, and started the engine. They left the stranded fishing boat, the men lined up along the side watching the boat as it headed for the mainland.

The man on the stretcher groaned and retched. The small cabin didn't give him space to turn him on his side without compromising the careful protection around his leg, and Ben sat him up. Arianna's concentration didn't waver as she carefully navigated the waters that were becoming more and more crowded as they neared the mainland. She manoeuvred into the marina, and Ben saw an ambulance waiting for them.

The Greek paramedics who met them were part of one of the best health services in Europe. They were well trained and well equipped, lifting the burns victim out of the boat and into the ambulance quickly. Arianna briefed them on his treatment so far, while Ben helped the other man off the boat and to the back doors of the ambulance.

'*Efcharistó.*' The man held out his uninjured hand to Ben and he took it.

'You're welcome. Take care.' Ben didn't know how to say that in Greek, although he understood the *thank you*. It didn't seem to matter, though, and when one of the ambulance crew came to guide the man into the vehicle, he stopped to shake his hand again.

'Right then.' Arianna jumped down from the ambulance and the back doors closed. 'I suppose we should go and see if the fishing boat still needs a tow.'

There was something brittle about her smile. After her calm efficiency with their patients, the flashed smiles that told him she was happy with the way they'd just fallen into a rhythm of working together, it was slightly odd. When she went to the boat she handed the ignition keys to Georgios, and when the two men made for the cabin, Arianna loitered at the back of the boat, sitting down alone.

He should leave her. Maybe she *did* have qualms about being on the water after all, and they'd just been submerged in her wish to get to an injured man as quickly as possible. She seemed to want to be alone with her thoughts for a moment and Ben stood next to Georgios, his gaze fixed on the stranded fishing boat ahead of them.

But she was always there. Not just as a bright splash of colour on the edge of his vision, but hovering in his thoughts as he helped Georgios secure the towline, and then moved back up to the front of the boat again. Their progress was slower now, and he watched the small harbour of Kantos, which seemed a lot busier than it had been when they'd left, with people gathering on the dock to find out what had happened at sea.

Arianna was all activity again, jumping off the boat before Georgios had a chance to fix the mooring lines, and making a beeline for a group that was standing together at the end of the quay. She spoke to them intently, and Ben saw her reach for the hands of one of the women. These must be the families of the injured men.

Willing hands reached to catch the mooring lines from the fishing boat. The men joined their families, and in the noise of conversation and questions that he could neither understand nor answer he caught sight of Arianna, surrounded by people.

He wanted to make sure she was all right, but he had to wait his turn. Many of the villagers wanted to speak to Arianna and shake her hand, and when he pushed his way through the gathering crowd he could feel people clapping him on the back.

'Let's get out of here...' She flashed him a tight smile when she saw him, and Ben wondered whether that was a suggestion or a plea. He cleared a path for her through people who were milling around them and she followed, silent now and without the smiles that had accompanied her conversations with the families of the men on the fishing boat.

Ben headed for the shaded surgery, knowing that was probably the one place that they could be alone.

CHAPTER SIX

THE NIGHTMARES THAT had been kept at bay for so long had begun to gain focus. As Arianna had begun to relax after the hard work of building her practice they'd become more frequent, and now...

Now they were starting to leak out into her days. Last night they'd been terrifyingly clear and when she'd gone down to the harbour this morning, the sound of the ferry horn had made her jump. The bobbing motion of her own boat had brought tears to her eyes, and then she'd brushed them away, telling herself that she'd see Ben soon.

His presence, and then the urgency of their mission to the stranded boat, had chased her fears away. But as soon as they'd left the injured men on the mainland and she had time to think again, she'd felt suddenly sick, pointless questions echoing in her head. What if...? What if somehow she could go back through time, and the doctor's boat could provide willing hands to pull her brother from the water? Her father had built a new dock for the ferry, to make sure that day could never happen again. She'd come here to make sure that there would be medical help available without having to send to the mainland. None of it seemed enough, because nothing could prevent what had already happened.

Ben walked beside her, back to the surgery, without

saying a word. There was something companionable in the silence, as if he understood everything that she was feeling. Even if that was comforting, Arianna desperately needed *someone* to understand and it felt that Ben, or at least her own fantasy of him, always *had* understood her.

She made it to the building that housed the surgery, proud of the way that her hand was steady when she took the keys from her bag and unlocked the door. Good. Fine. She was doing okay. Her footsteps sounded on the tiled floor and she opened the door into the surgery. Light slanted through the blinds, the same way that it had filtered down through the water when she'd found herself sinking beneath the waves...

'Hey, there.' She felt Ben's arms around her shoulders and squeezed her eyes shut.

'I'm not crying...'

'No. Of course you're not. Never occurred to me that you were.'

Okay, so she *was* crying. And her limbs were shaking too, against the quiet strength of his body.

'I'm fine. Really. Pretend it didn't happen.'

She felt his chest heave in a sigh. 'Pretend *what* didn't happen? The whole of the last twenty-five years?'

That was the glue that held them together. A lifetime that had been spent dealing with the fallout of what had happened that day on the ferry, and Ben's uncanny ability to understand that. His life had been changed by that day as well.

'I'm just... This is crazy.' She pulled away from him, wiping her eyes. 'I'm not going to dwell on the past, Ben. I've never done that.'

He nodded. The smile that hovered at the corners of his mouth had a hint of reproach in it.

'What?' Whatever it was, he might as well just come out and say it.

'You've told me your whole life story, and you've not once been sorry for yourself...'

Arianna frowned at him. 'There's a *but* in there, isn't there.'

'You want to hear this?'

No. Something told her that she really, really didn't want to hear it. But his eyes were mesmerising, and they wouldn't let her go.

'Probably not. Say it anyway.'

'I think you've worked hard and that you're making a difference, but you can't enjoy that because you're still the little girl who's so bound up with her parents' grief that she won't show her own. You're still trying to prove to everyone that you're not the second-best child who survived, but you can't prove it to yourself.'

The emotion swelled inside her.

'How dare you?' Before Arianna knew what she was doing she'd raised her hand, ready to slap him. He didn't even flinch and that somehow made her behaviour even worse. Tears of frustration started to well in her eyes and she brushed them away impatiently.

'I'm sorry, Ben. This isn't all about me, I know that.'

'Do it.' His eyes taunted her. 'It would be the first really honest thing you've done.'

'I don't know what you mean by that.'

'Sure you do. Do it.' He stuck his chin out, pointing at it. 'Right there.'

'No. I'm not going to hit you.'

'Not even if I tell you to grow up. Face your grief and admit that you're *not* second-best, that's just survivor's guilt talking...'

He stepped back as Arianna flung herself at him,

catching her flailing arms. Held her while she cried bitter tears and was still there for her when she wiped her face with shaking fingers. For a long time they were both silent, locked in an embrace. Held together by the day they'd met, when they were both children.

He reached into his pocket, bringing out a handkerchief. Wiping her face gently and carefully was more than just wiping the tears away; it felt as if he were cleaning away the remains of the shell that had kept her imprisoned for so long.

'I didn't think men carried handkerchiefs these days...' She took the scrap of cloth from his fingers, blowing her nose. 'Isn't it a little old-fashioned, having a hanky in your pocket just in case you come across a woman in distress?'

'A hanky comes in very useful when you have a five-year-old. Scraped knees, dirty face, runny nose. It's as well that I haven't been around Jonas too much today, or you wouldn't want to be blowing your nose on it.'

Arianna smiled, putting the handkerchief in her pocket. 'I'll wash it and give it back to you.'

He chuckled. 'Now who's the old-fashioned one?'

Ben took her hand, wrapping his fingers around it. 'I know that my coming here has brought up some very difficult issues for you, Arianna. I'm sorry, and if you'd like me to leave...'

'No.' She laid her finger across his lips.

'You don't have to put a brave face on things, or keep up appearances. If I'm making things worse for you, you don't have to pretend you want me around either.'

She could ask Ben. She really *wanted* to ask him. No one had ever been able to see into her heart the way he seemed to, and it was terrifying and yet liberating.

'I'd like you to stay.'

'Then I'll stay.' His gaze focused on her face and he

tilted her jaw upwards with one finger. 'How much sleep did you get last night?'

'Is that a nice way of saying I have bags under my eyes?'

He grinned. 'I have to look really, really closely to see them. How much?'

'Not a lot.' Arianna turned the corners of her mouth down. The nightmares had been clearer and more disturbing than ever, and in the end she'd wrapped herself in a blanket and sat outside, watching the sun rise.

'What do you say to my cooking for you tonight, then? You can sit on the veranda and watch the sunset.'

'That sounds good. If you're sure, though. You're on holiday, so you should be the one that has the time to sit around watching sunsets.'

His face creased into a pained expression. 'I came here to see you, Arianna. I didn't know what to expect, but if I'd wanted to just laze in the sun then I'd have gone somewhere else.'

'How are you with a barbecue, then?'

He laid his hand on his chest. 'If Jonas were here, he'd tell you. You're looking at the barbecue king.'

Ben shooed Arianna out of her own kitchen and he saw her pick up her phone and take it with her onto the veranda. She sat down, curling her legs up under her, and dialled, speaking in Greek to someone. He heard Lizzie's name mentioned, and guessed that Arianna must be talking about their hotel transfer. Ben turned away from the window and started to unpack the bags of food they'd brought from the village. Chicken for the barbecue, and salad.

The barbecue was housed in its own covered area, to one side of the veranda and outside the kitchen. This was outdoor living at its very best. Shaded places to cook and eat, and the beach and the sunshine to enjoy. Ben could get used to this.

He laid the table on the veranda, and then brought out the dishes of food.

'Very nice. You can come back again.' She smiled at him. Arianna still looked tired, but the light had returned to her dark eyes and she seemed less careworn.

'Thanks. Next time it's pie and chips.'

'Pie and chips is fine. I used to live in London too, remember? Or do you do sausages and mash?'

'Definitely. With homemade onion gravy.'

Arianna grinned and sat down at the table. 'I'm going to need to try that before you go.'

They spent a lazy hour, talking and eating, as the sun went down. Ben had reminded Arianna not to move while he cleared away the plates and made coffee, and he was stacking the dishwasher when his phone rang.

'That was Lizzie,' he called to her from the kitchen door after he hung up. 'She says that the manager of our hotel has arranged for us to move across to the island first thing tomorrow morning.'

'That's good.' Arianna didn't seem much surprised by the news.

'Yeah. I don't suppose you had anything to do with our being upgraded to a suite, did you?' Ben felt slightly uncomfortable about that.

'It was what they had available. There's a similar suite in all of my father's hotels, which is used for family and friends. It's usually empty. And you're *my* friends.' She said it with a touch of defensiveness and Ben relented. A suite would be nice and Arianna had clearly broken her own rule about expecting no special treatment because of who her father was.

'It's great. Thank you.'

The matter was closed. Arianna went into the house, returning with a backgammon set, and he made coffee, taking the two cups out onto the veranda.

It all felt so natural. So unremarkable, and yet so very delicious. Drinking coffee and playing backgammon to the sound of the sea. Watching Arianna's face as she pondered her next move.

He *had* to be here for her. He'd been there on the ferry, and swum with her away from the treacherous undertow that threatened to pull them both down. Now she needed him again. Ben had never had the chance to go back and save Emma, and saving Arianna now seemed all the more important because of that.

But he mustn't get too involved. She needed to find her own way, and Ben's instinct to overprotect the people he loved would only hinder her. It was a fine line, made all the more difficult by the attraction he felt for Arianna. But this was an opportunity he'd never have again.

Before it was time to think about heading down to the harbour to catch the last ferry, Arianna had already begun to yawn. That was exactly what Ben had planned on.

'I should be going. Lizzie wants to leave early tomorrow morning and we'll be on the eight o'clock ferry, so I need to repack everything tonight.'

Arianna got to her feet. 'I'll give you a lift.'

'No, I'll walk.' Arianna opened her mouth to protest and he silenced her with a stern look. 'You think I went to all this trouble just so you could wake yourself up again by driving?'

She thought for a moment, and Ben hoped that she was seeing sense. 'I do feel a bit tired. Would you like to take my car? You can leave it at the harbour and then use it to drive to the hotel in the morning. Then bring it back here.'

'I'm coming back in the morning?' Ben teased her, knowing full well that he couldn't keep away. If Arianna wanted him around, he'd be there for her.

'Are you?' She called his bluff and Ben gave in.

'I'll be back. What time tomorrow?'

He was expecting her to just wave her hand, in the way that many people here seemed to do when time was referred to, but Arianna seemed to want something more precise.

'About ten? Or later if you have things to do.'

Ben wondered if she'd be counting the moments, the way he already was. 'Ten's fine. See you then.'

She dropped her car keys into his hand, and followed him outside. As he drove away he saw her standing in the light from the open front door.

Ben had been careful to curb his expectations when he'd come to Ilaria. He hadn't taken it for granted that they'd be friends, or that she'd even want to see him again. But what he'd found here was beyond anything he could have imagined. They'd just clicked together like two pieces of a jigsaw puzzle.

Being there for her was a challenge, one he wasn't sure he was equal to. But everything depended on getting this right. It was his second chance. The one he'd thought he'd never have to be the man that he wanted to be, and if he let Arianna down now that man would be lost for ever.

Last night, Arianna had watched Ben drive away and then walked, yawning, to her bedroom. She'd gone to sleep, curled up with her memories of him, and then woken again at three in the morning, taunted by her nightmares. Wrapping a quilt around her, she'd gone outside to sit on the veranda. The sun had risen, and she'd had breakfast. And the last thought she'd had was that she must take a shower and get dressed…

Now she was being woken by the brush of fingers against her hand. Nice. She shifted a little on the wide settle, then stretched, and *then* realised that the touch was real and not part of a dream.

'Hey…sorry, I didn't mean to startle you.' Ben pulled back, taking Jonas with him. The boy was staring at her, tilting his head to one side in curiosity.

'Hi, Jonas… Ben…' Arianna rubbed her eyes. 'Sorry, is it ten o' clock already…?'

'Just gone. We paced up and down outside your front door a bit before we decided to come around to the back to see if we could find you.'

Arianna chuckled. 'Don't bother about the pacing. Turning up at my back door and giving me a shake is just fine.' Although Ben's gentle touch had been fine too. A lot better than fine, and Arianna hoped that her half-awake face hadn't betrayed her pleasure.

'Did you sleep last night?'

The opportunity to say that she'd had eight solid hours and that she was feeling entirely rejuvenated and ready to start the day was gone. 'I went to bed straight after you left. Slept through till about three.'

He nodded. 'That's something. You want coffee?'

'Yes. Please.' Arianna remembered that the over-sized T-shirt she was wearing didn't cover her legs, and wrapped the quilt around her body, getting to her feet. 'I'll be back in a moment.'

'Take your time.' Jonas seemed about to follow Arianna indoors, and Ben caught his hand firmly. 'Come and help me, Jonas.'

Clearly coffee-making wasn't as interesting to Jonas as following Arianna into her bedroom, but Jonas reluctantly went with his father. Ben didn't look back, and Arianna decided not to either.

When she arrived back on the veranda she felt a little more awake and rather more embarrassed about being caught napping. Ben said nothing, though, putting two cups of freshly brewed coffee down on the table, along with a jug of iced lemonade and some glasses. Jonas had been sitting on the steps, which led down from the veranda and onto the beach, but when he saw her he jumped up and flung his arms around her waist.

'Are you ill?' He looked up at her and Arianna smiled.

'No, sweetie, I'm not ill. Just a bit tired. Your dad's made me coffee and that'll wake me up.'

Jonas frowned. 'Dad says that *I* have to get a good night's sleep. I'm not allowed coffee.'

Ben flashed her a get-out-of-that-one smile and sat down at the table.

'Dad's right. We'll both make sure we do that, shall we?'

Jonas nodded, seemingly happy with the answer. Arianna sat down opposite Ben, picking up the small coffee cup and draining half of it in one swallow.

'Glad *I'm* allowed coffee.' She leaned forward, murmuring quietly, and Ben chuckled.

'You're not off the hook, though. Sleep's better.'

'Yes, Dad,' Arianna teased him, and he shrugged, pulling a resigned face. 'How's the hotel?'

'It's great. Lizzie loves it and she asked me to thank you for the fruit basket.'

Arianna nodded. 'My pleasure. So what would you like to do today? We have a whole island, and I'll be your tour guide.'

* * *

Ben had been just about to gently put his real purpose here today to Arianna. Maybe casually and a little obliquely, a friendly reminder that a relaxing day might help her deal with her nightmares. Jonas put a spoke in the wheel of his plans.

'Dad says that we're going to look after you.' He frowned, obviously trying to reconcile an inconsistency. 'Even if you aren't ill.'

Her eyebrows shot up. 'Really?'

In for a penny, in for a pound. Now that Jonas had introduced this new approach, he had little choice but to go with it.

'Yes, really. You're tired and your nightmares are beginning to take over. You need to do something Arianna; they won't go away all on their own.'

'Yes!' Jonas chimed in. 'I don't like nightmares. Dad has to grab the monsters and throw them out of the window.' He illustrated his point by acting out the grabbing of a monster and its disposal out of an imaginary window.

'You can do that?' She looked up at Ben, her gaze softening suddenly.

'Yeah. We…um… Sometimes they wriggle a bit and we have to fight them first.'

'Dad rolls around on the carpet, wrestling them. But he always wins.' Jonas threw himself down onto the ground in a life and death struggle with an imaginary monster. 'Monsters don't like it if you fight them; they get scared.'

Arianna was laughing now, but he could see understanding in her eyes. Maybe the monsters that she faced weren't so different from the ones that occasionally inhabited any child's dreams, even if they were much more persistent.

'That would be very nice. So we're going to practise fighting monsters?'

Jonas was nodding his head vigorously, and Ben stepped in before he could invite Arianna to show him her best fighting moves.

'I just thought that a relaxing day might give you a more restful night.' Ben wasn't entirely sure that relaxation was all Arianna needed. Talking about it, voicing the terrors that dogged her seemed to be a more necessary part of the process. Maybe a day spent doing nothing much at all would encourage her to do that.

She slipped out of her seat to bend down in front of Jonas. 'What do you say to making another sandcastle? A bigger one than last time.'

'Yes!' Jonas nodded vigorously and Arianna got to her feet, smiling.

'Looks as if that's today planned out, then.'

Ben had applied all of his ingenuity to the new sandcastle. He'd made a central lake this time and while Arianna and Jonas sculpted a sand cliff that ran up to the level of the veranda, he had constructed an arrangement of beakers and straws, taped together to make a water cascade, which syphoned water over the edge of the veranda in a small waterfall, to fill the lake.

Jonas was so happy with it all. Ben was a great dad, and his own pleasure in playing with his son was obvious. Arianna dimly remembered her own father playing with her and Xander, but then his grief had taken him away from her. Even now, it felt wrong that she should resent that, when her parents had suffered so much at the loss of their son.

Enjoying this didn't feel quite right either. Xander had never had the chance to play again, or to grow up and play with his own children. Arianna got to her feet, brushing sand from her dress and leaving Jonas and Ben to get on with their castle. The wide settle on the veranda was somewhere to sit and watch, without being a part of it all. Here she felt less like a thief, stealing sandcastles from her brother.

When Ben joined her on the veranda they sat together in silence for a while, watching Jonas. Arianna poured two glasses of lemonade from the jug, pushing one towards Ben.

'I was wondering...' She felt so close to him when they talked, but right now she didn't want to think about her own life. Arianna wanted to know more about his.

'Yeah?'

'What did you mean about the day on the ferry changing your life too? I know how it changed mine, but surely what you did couldn't have given you any regrets.'

He took a swig from his glass. 'No regrets. Just an impossible set of aspirations for me to live up to.'

'How so?'

Ben shook his head. 'You don't want to hear about that.'

'Why not? It strikes me that it changed us both, and that maybe we're two sides of a coin. Maybe it only really makes sense if we can see both sides.'

He thought it over carefully, and then nodded. 'It was an odd experience for me. I was so elated, and then there was...nothing. I got to the shore and found my mum and dad—all they were worried about was that I was safe, and I didn't tell them about you because I knew they'd tell me off for jumping in after you. You were my secret.'

'A good one?' Arianna rather liked the idea.

'Yeah, you were a great secret to have. It felt as if I was

a superhero and I could dress up at night and climb out of the window and do things that no one else could do.'

'Did you?'

'I thought a lot about it. I couldn't get a handle on the logistics of how I was going to make my way down from the first-floor window of a suburban semi without breaking my neck, so I decided to leave it awhile until I had my own place. Somewhere to hang my superhero costume where my mum wouldn't find it when she was tidying up.'

'So you went to medical school. Super doc.'

Ben chuckled. 'There was an element of that. I just knew that there was someone in the world who might have drowned without me. It made me feel good that you must be out there somewhere, leading your life the way you were meant to. When I think about it, it was probably quite convenient that I didn't know you. Always best to keep the objects of those kinds of daydreams one-dimensional.'

He wasn't quite making a joke of all this, but he was keeping it light. Somewhere beneath all that there was pain. Arianna nodded, smiling, and waited for Ben to guide her towards that pain. Maybe if they shared their pain then it would make sense to both of them.

'Being a doctor went some way towards injecting a dose of reality. There are things we can't do, but there are also ways that we *can* make a difference. It meant a lot to me that I was able to help people.'

Arianna nodded. 'It means a lot to me too. Surely that hasn't changed for you?'

It had. She could see it from the flash of guilt and regret in his face. He glanced over towards his son, who was busy landscaping his new castle, completely unaware of their conversation.

'When Emma died…things weren't going so well for us. I can't help wondering if her last thought was that I'd let her down.'

Arianna knew full well that guilt had a big part in grief. All the things that could never be changed, never be taken back.

'What do you mean?'

'I wasn't living at home when Emma died. We'd been arguing a lot, and we were both tired. I told her that I loved her, and suggested that we take a couple of weeks out, so we could reconnect with the things that really mattered. I'm not sure she completely understood.'

'I'm so sorry, Ben. Surely you can't think that you let her down, though. From what you say, you were trying to save your marriage.'

'I was. We both were, and I know we would have succeeded, given a bit of time. I just wonder whether she knew how much I loved her and Jonas.' Ben took a deep breath, his face suddenly haggard.

'In my experience—' Arianna puffed out a breath '—not that I have a great deal of experience in making relationships work, but I think you always do know when someone honestly loves you.'

'Maybe. I hope you're right.' He turned his gaze up to meet hers and something in his eyes made Arianna dread whatever he was about to say next.

'When the accident happened, Emma was on her way to do the weekly shop. A lorry swerved to avoid something and skidded out of control. Witnesses said that it was coming towards the passenger side of the car, where Jonas was in the car seat at the back. Emma couldn't avoid it, but she turned the wheel so that it hit her side of the car.'

'Ben, I...' Arianna shook her head. 'That was a very brave and loving thing to do.'

'She was like that. She could be fierce at times, and we used to argue but...I just hope she knew that I would have done anything to be sitting in the driver's seat, so that Emma and Jonas would have been safe on the other side of the car. If there was any way that I could go back...'

'I believe you.' Arianna almost choked on the words. What *she* believed probably meant less than nothing to Ben. But his face softened suddenly, and he nodded.

'Thank you.' Ben reached across the table, covering her hands with his. 'If I'm honest, this is one of the reasons I came here. Those superhero dreams I had when I was a kid were more precious to me than I knew. Since Emma died, I've lost the feeling that I can make a difference to anyone and...I miss it.'

He'd saved *her*. That might not be very important to him, and it might not be so important to her father, who yearned for his lost son. It meant a lot to Arianna, though.

'Thank you for saving me. I know it's not much of a consolation...'

Ben gave her hands a squeeze and then let go of them. 'It's means more to me than you know. But today wasn't supposed to be about making *me* feel better.'

'As I said. Two sides of one coin. It feels as if we both started from the same place.'

He nodded, clearly turning the idea over in his head. 'Maybe you're right...'

'I think that Jonas knows his dad is a superhero, who protects him against monsters. Kids are pretty switched on about that kind of thing and maybe you should listen to him.'

There was no opportunity for Ben to think about it

and decide. Suddenly he was on his feet. 'Jonas, what are you doing? You'll hurt yourself.'

Jonas was upside down in a heap on the sand, and turned himself back up the right way, looking a little shamefaced. 'I want to do somersaults.'

'Not like that, mate.'

'Auntie Lizzie showed Callie how to do one. I want to do them too—show *me*.'

Ben rolled his eyes and then turned back to his son, taking the steps down from the veranda two at a time. 'I can't do a somersault either. And Callie's a bit older than you—that's probably why Auntie Lizzie showed her, don't you think?'

Jonas's face began to crease. 'But, Dad…'

Arianna ventured to the top of the steps. If Ben could come to terms with the past, then so could she. She could do nothing about all the things that Xander had missed out on, but there was one thing she could do for Jonas.

'I can do somersaults…'

Two sets of blue eyes suddenly turned in Arianna's direction. She couldn't resist those eyes, not the father's nor the son's. Ben smiled, heat igniting in his gaze, and then turned to Jonas.

'Perhaps Arianna can show you how to do a somersault?'

Jonas cheered up immediately. 'Yes! Show me!'

CHAPTER SEVEN

BEN HAD WATCHED Arianna on the beach. Her sleeveless T-shirt and shorts accentuated the slim, rounded curves of her figure, and the near-perfect somersaults accentuated its strength. He'd come here with the idea that maybe he could get back in touch with a part of himself that was dying, and which he knew he needed, not just for Jonas but for his patients as well. He'd found a woman who was vulnerable and trying in her own way to deal with the fallout from that day on the ferry, and now it occurred to him that maybe Arianna was right. Maybe they were two sides of a coin, and they could save each other.

Despite all of her protests, he made lunch. Arianna knew what that meant. He was here for her, and he wanted to lift the weight from her shoulders a little so that she could take some time to deal with the grief that had been waiting for her for so long. Her smile and murmured acknowledgement told him that she appreciated the gesture.

They ate, another long, lazy meal. As the sun climbed in the sky and the heat became oppressive, Arianna asked him how Jonas might feel about a siesta.

'I think he could do with one.' Jonas was looking a little heavy-eyed now, after a full morning and a good lunch. 'I was up pretty late last night; I could too.'

She nodded, ushering him and Jonas into a spare bedroom with white walls and a matching white bedspread. It looked cool and calm, and when she opened the windows and door he could hear the relaxing roll of the waves.

Jonas was half asleep already. Ben stripped off his beach shoes and T-shirt and laid him down on the bed, sitting down in the armchair in the corner of the room and watching his son. He'd promised himself that Jonas was all he'd ever want, all he'd ever need and that he'd always be there to protect him. But the lifelong connection with Arianna was stronger than he'd thought, and he wanted to protect her too.

The long net curtains billowed lazily in the breeze, as if cool and calm was something you could see as well as feel. The house was silent, and Ben's eyes began to droop. Maybe Arianna would be getting some much-needed sleep as well.

A sound, carrying through the silence, and his eyes flipped open. Another, which sounded like a strangled sob, and he was on his feet. Arianna's bedroom door was open, to take advantage of the breeze, and he could see her, sitting up straight in her bed, a light cover clutched around her body.

'Arianna…' His voice was a hoarse whisper and she didn't react. Maybe he should go…

And leave her to her dreams? The swirling water, closing over her head? Ben stepped into the room, sitting down on the edge of the bed.

'Arianna.' He spoke again, and this time he heard his own strength, seeping into his tone.

'It's…just a dream…' Her breathing was ragged and her shaking hands moved to cover her face.

'I know.' He moved closer, wrapping his arm around her shoulders. She nestled against him, clinging to him.

'I'm okay. I'm so tired, Ben. I'll go back to sleep now.'

No, she wouldn't. She'd lie here, wide-eyed, as the cool silence provided a backdrop to a terrifying world. In two hours she'd shower and emerge from her bedroom and down another cup of coffee, to banish her sleeping hours and let the day take over again. That wasn't how she could find healing, and Arianna knew that as well as he did.

'Lie down.' He wrapped the bedspread around her and laid her down on the bed. Shifting across, he propped one leg up on the bed, in a sign that he wasn't going anywhere until she was asleep again. 'Is that okay?'

She reached for him, pulling him down next to her. Then she curled her body against his. 'That's better.'

He dared to put his arm around her, and she laid her head on his shoulder. Despite the fact that Jonas was asleep next door and Arianna needed his comfort, it was still electrifying. It had been so long since he'd felt passion, and it made Ben's head swim a little.

He knew he should pull away from her, but he couldn't help it. When he drew her close she snuggled against him. Arousal gave way to a much more potent emotion. Arianna trusted him to quiet her fears, and somewhere inside he felt the stirring of a determination not to let her down.

He lay still, helpless in the face of Arianna's bravery and her determination to keep going, however much she was hurting inside. Unable to defend himself against the feeling that this was exactly where he should be.

'Tell me about your dream.'

'It doesn't matter.'

'Really? You're going to go with that, are you?'

'You're going to fight my monsters? And throw them out of the window?'

'If that's what it takes.'

He felt her heave a sigh. 'It was... Usually I dream about the ferry. About falling off and you coming to get me, and then watching you get pulled away by the tide. This time…I dreamt I was under the water and you didn't come and get me. There was something pulling me down… Trying to drown me.' She was nearing the part that was most disturbing to her.

'What pulled you down?'

'It was Xander. His face was all puffy, as if he'd been in the water for days.' She looked up at him, her face silhouetted against the pillow. 'Why would I dream that, Ben? Xander was my brother, and he wouldn't do anything like that to me. He loved me…'

'You're the one best able to make sense of your own dreams. But maybe it's your own memories of what happened to your brother on that day that are pulling you down.'

'What do you mean?'

'It's just that…you told me that you felt guilty about your brother's death.' Ben ventured the thought as gently as he could.

He felt her whole body stiffen against his, a sure sign that he was getting close to an awful truth that she didn't want to recognise. 'Guilt wouldn't be logical. I was only six years old.'

She felt it, though. He could hear it in her voice. 'Kids have a habit of feeling that the world revolves around them. That they can control things that even adults can't.'

He felt her sigh. Maybe she was in the same world that he was at the moment—two kids in the water, trying to swim to safety. Holding onto each other as tight as they could.

'If you get the dream again, could you tell yourself what you've just told me? That you were six years old, and it wasn't your fault.'

'I don't know. I could try…' She snuggled against him,

slipping her hand into his, and Ben held her close. That same fire, the determination to change her world, was licking around him. He hadn't lost it for good.

'Close your eyes. I'll be here.' That was all she needed to know. He couldn't be here for ever; he had to go home in less than three weeks. Ben hoped that would be enough for both of them.

Arianna had suggested they drive down to the harbour, so that Ben and Jonas could take a look around. She knew everyone and Jonas was made a particular fuss of, being invited to taste slices of succulent fruit and small, sweet baked delicacies in the shops they visited. Ben's presence on Kantos yesterday had already spread to Ilaria and he recognised the Greek word for *doctor* when Arianna introduced him to people. Clearly she wasn't about to tell anyone that they'd met on the ferry, and that was fine by Ben. It had been their secret for so long now that it seemed only right it should remain so a little longer.

They dined at the taverna, their table moving steadily across the floor as people that Arianna knew arrived with their families and friends, and tables were pushed together. By the time the meal had been finished, two hours later, they were sitting with twenty other people, and those who could speak English were vying to translate the jokes that flew across the table for Ben.

When they left, obviously a little early by local standards as there were still children of Jonas's age sitting at the table, Arianna worked her way around the table, saying her goodbyes. Ben was required to do the same, and Jonas followed suit as well. Then they took the coast road, driving around the island to their hotel, bright stars above their heads, the moon reflecting in the dark sea to one side.

'Thank you. We've had a great day.'

Jonas had fallen asleep in the car, and Ben carried him in his arms to the entrance. The foyer was still bustling with activity and even a friendly kiss goodnight seemed too much. It might have started out as something brushed onto her cheek, but the temptation of her lips was far too great.

'Thank *you*, Ben. For everything.' Arianna deposited a kiss on the ends of her fingers and pressed it to Jonas's sleeping brow. It was the perfect way out of the dilemma, and accompanied by a flash of fire in her warm eyes.

'You'll be all right? Tonight…?' Suddenly he couldn't bear to leave her, alone in the darkness, prey to all the terrors that the night brought her.

'I'll be fine.' Arianna said the words a little too quickly, and Ben guessed they were her stock response to any enquiry about her own well-being. 'I sleep on my own every night.'

But tonight… Ben discarded the thought. His role in her life was already a complex mixture of checks and balances. Talking with her and sharing his own feelings, and listening to hers. Being there for her, but not getting so close that his protectiveness became challenging.

'Would you like to go up to the Lava Lake tomorrow?' She seemed determined to leave him on a positive note, and Ben should take a leaf from her book.

'I don't want to impose.' Maybe she had things to do. People to see.

'You're not. I love the Lava Lake and I haven't been up there for ages. This is a great excuse for me to go.'

It didn't take much to convince him. 'In that case, thank you. We'd love it.'

'I'll pick you up at ten? I'll bring lunch.'

'Ten's great. Any time—we'll go to the pool and if you

want to sleep late…' Ben probably shouldn't mention that, since Arianna was clearly skating around the subject.

'Okay. I'll meet you there. Ten o'clock, Greek time. That's any time before noon, English time.'

She turned and walked to her car, waving to him before she got in. As Ben watched her go, the entirely honourable impulse to save her from her nightmares vied with a slightly less honourable yearning to just hold her close while she slept. He turned away, walking into the hotel building and telling himself that both were unacceptable. He hadn't been there for Emma, and he couldn't promise to be there for anyone else now.

Arianna arrived at the pool at ten thirty the following morning, clearly in no rush to get started because she sat down in the chair next to Ben's and when he offered her a drink she accepted it readily, choosing a cocktail of different fruit juices from the bar menu.

'You've brought your bathing suits with you?' she asked, almost as an afterthought, as they walked down to the dock, and Ben nodded. He'd heard that swimming at the Lava Lake was an experience not to be missed.

She had a child-sized life jacket for Jonas, and made sure that it was fitted correctly, before starting the engine of the boat and speeding towards Kantos. She made a circuit of the island, so that Jonas could see it all from the sea, and then slipped into a secluded inlet to moor the boat. Putting on a wide-brimmed sunhat with a blue ribbon that matched her dress, Arianna caught up her straw bag, looping it over her shoulder, before leading them along a gently sloping path.

'How are you doing?' The path had become steep and rocky, and Jonas looked as if he was getting tired. 'You want a lift for this last bit?'

Jonas nodded, and while he was lifting the boy onto his back, Arianna picked up the bag that contained their towels and swimming trunks and they toiled their way up the hill.

'It's worth it when we get there.'

'Yep.' Jonas seemed to be getting both taller and heavier by the hour, these days. And his excited wriggling wasn't helping much either.

'Wait and see…' Arianna seemed to be walking faster instead of slower now and Ben lengthened his stride to keep up with her.

'Woah, Dad!' They got to the brow of the hill and a picture-perfect view revealed itself. The water was the deepest blue he'd ever seen, and the large lake was surrounded by steep slopes, some of them sparkling in the sunshine from the seams of crystalline rock formed by the intense heat of a long-dormant volcano.

'What do you think?' Arianna was looking up at him with shining eyes.

'Spectacular. Far better than I'd expected.'

They slithered down the steep slope to the water's edge, Ben keeping a tight hold on Jonas's hand and reaching for Arianna's when it looked as if she might lose her balance. When she took it, she held on tight.

Jonas ran down to the water's edge, picking up a shiny blue stone. 'Look, Dad. I'm going to take it home.'

Ben shook his head. 'No, we leave everything as we find it. The next person won't be able to see that stone if you take it away with you. You can take some pictures, though, if you want.'

He pulled his phone out of his pocket and gave it to Jonas, who dropped the stone and started taking pictures.

'It doesn't matter,' Arianna murmured, pointing to a glistening blue cliff on the other side of the lake. 'There's plenty left. That's where they've taken little pieces of stone off for the souvenir shops. They're only allowed to take so much, but taking a little has uncovered what's been hidden by shale and vegetation.'

'It's the principle. He's happy taking photographs.'

When Jonas had finished taking photographs of different shaped stones, he decided that he wanted a few selfies. He posed for a while, and then tired of that. Arianna took the phone from his hand, holding it out and taking a shot of the two of them, and then Ben was dragged away from the view to join them. He felt her curls brush his cheek as he leaned in close. Just like a happy family.

He shouldn't think like that. But when he held the phone out to get a shot of the three of them, with the lake as a backdrop, he couldn't help it. He took another shot of Arianna and Jonas, standing at the water's edge, and then managed to capture Arianna in a perfect star jump, her dress flapping around her legs in the breeze. Ben wondered if he'd ever tire of this, but finally Arianna called a halt.

'Shall we rest a while? Then we can go swimming.'

'Sounds good.' Resting generally meant food and a lazy siesta, and this time was no different. Arianna found a grassy spot, shaded by trees that grew almost horizontally out of the sides of the slope, spread out a light quilted groundsheet and proceeded to unpack plastic tubs of food from her bag. Ben took three bottles of water from his bag, and they sat down to eat. Bread to dip into the tubs of tzatziki and hummus, with salads and chicken on paper plates.

When Arianna had collected up the remains of the meal, Jonas curled up beside her, ready to take a siesta now. Ben watched as she lay down beside his son, her arm thrown protectively across Jonas's chest.

This was his for the day, with photographs to remember it by. The pretence of a happy family, just like the one that he'd allowed to slip through his fingers. It might not be his to take, but he could allow himself to enjoy the feeling for a little while.

Ben had been watching over her as she slept. She'd seen him, through heavy-lidded eyes, as she'd dozed, and the knowledge that he was there had chased away her dreams.

He was right. This weekend had been harder than any other, but she was finally facing the feelings she'd been bottling up for years. If Ben hadn't been here she would have retreated into her work again, and pushed them all aside, but now they were bubbling to the surface like a volcano, threatening to explode.

When Jonas began to stir against her, Ben was still leaning on his elbows, still there. Arianna climbed across the rocks, finding a place where she could change into her bathing suit, and then raced down to the water's edge. Ben and Jonas were already there, trying to get each other as wet as possible in as short a time as possible.

The man had everything. Physique, tone, good looks. His blond hair and pale skin were almost golden in the sunshine, and the rivulets of water running down his chest… She just couldn't look. If she looked, then she'd stare.

'It's very quiet here,' Ben remarked as they both bobbed lazily in the water, while Jonas splashed around, doggy-paddling backwards and forwards, never more than an arm's length away from his father.

'Yes. It's not that easy to get to. Although soon there will be more tourists on Kantos. There's a new hotel being built this year; they've already laid the foundations.'

'Yeah? Is that good or bad?'

'It gives me a bit of a problem. It'll mean that I can't cover both islands properly, so I'm going to have to take on another doctor at the health centre.'

'It won't be difficult to find someone, will it. Who's going to turn down the chance to work here?'

Arianna chuckled. It was nice that he thought that this was the kind of place that anyone would want to be. 'A lot of doctors prefer to work in the city. Getting someone to come here for six months or a year isn't too hard, but getting someone who'll stay can be a challenge.'

'I'm sure you'll get the right person. Will the hotel change things here on the island? How do local people feel about it?'

'They're all for it; it brings money here and provides people with jobs. It's going to be away from the village, much like the one on Ilaria. And it'll be low-rise and sympathetic to the local style of construction.'

'Your father's building it?'

'Yes, he is.'

'He seems to have a monopoly on hotels in this area...' Ben broke off, shooting her a querying glance as Arianna quirked the corners of her mouth down. 'Is that a problem?'

'No, what my father's doing in these islands is great; he's developing in a way that supports local communities rather than overwhelming them...' Arianna let out a sigh. 'But I've worked pretty hard to make a place for myself here. I want people to see me for what I am, not what my father can buy.'

'You can't buy your way through seven years of medical training.'

Money obviously didn't impress Ben; he had a different idea about the things that mattered. He valued the same things that she did, and it occurred to Arianna that their ambitions had been forged in the same place and at the same time, in the swirling waters around the sinking ferry.

'Some people think you can. They think that having everything materially means that you have everything you need.'

'Yeah, I suppose so. I was lucky, growing up. We had *enough* in terms of material things and everything we needed. My dad's an academic, and there's a great deal of satisfaction in the job for him, but not a massive amount of money.'

'That sounds nice. Does he teach?' Arianna could imagine Ben's father as a teacher. Ben had that way about him, of listening to what people said and nurturing a conversation.

'Yeah, he's a university professor and he teaches Ancient History. That's what we were doing in Greece; he'd come to meet up with some of his contacts in the museums in Athens. Ilaria was my mum's idea; she wanted to get out of the city and spend some time on the beach.'

'Grandad's going to build me a...what is it?' Jonas had obviously been half listening to their conversation and his ears had pricked up at the mention of his grandfather.

'A trireme.' Ben grinned at his son. 'A model of a trireme, that is, not a full-sized one.'

'No. We don't have room.' Jonas started swimming again, his flailing arms and legs seeming to expend the maximum amount of energy for the minimum amount of progress.

'Try holding onto me if you want to stay in one place, Jonas. Like you do in your swimming class.'

'I can do it, Dad. I don't need to hold on.'

'Yeah, okay. As long as you're managing.' Ben rolled his eyes, and left his son to it. 'Don't let us stop you if you want to go for a swim, Arianna. We'll just stay here and do some pretend swimming.'

'I can do proper swimming.' Jonas's body straightened in the water suddenly and he swam a couple of yards in a very respectable front crawl, before reverting back to doggy-paddle. 'I like this better.'

'Okay. I wouldn't want Arianna to think that I hadn't taught you how to swim properly when you want to.'

'If you like, I can look after Jonas for a little while. You can't come to the Lava Lake without swimming out to the middle and just ducking your head under the water.' Arianna gestured towards the centre of the lake.

'Why, what's there?'

'You have to see for yourself.' She wanted Ben to remember today, and it was difficult to forget swimming in the water above the blue-green crystals that had formed at the deepest point of the bed of the lake.

'You'll be okay here?'

'I won't take my eyes off Jonas for a second.'

Thank you. His lips formed silent words that were only for her, and then Ben spoke to his son. 'Jonas, you'll stay with Arianna, won't you? If she says you're to get out of the water then you get out of the water.'

He waited for Jonas's confirmation that he'd heard and understood and then started to swim towards the middle of the lake. Arianna watched the strong swell of his shoulders, keeping her hand on Jonas's back, ready to grab hold of him if it looked as if he were tiring.

But now that Ben was gone, her fears seemed to swell in her chest. A sudden vision hit her, of Jonas—or was it Xander?—being sucked beneath the surface of the water. She should get a grip, but all she could think about was getting Jonas to the safety of the beach.

'Have you finished swimming now, Jonas?'

The boy was obviously tiring a little but he ignored her, still splashing about.

'Let's get out, shall we?' Arianna tried again.

'Okay.' Jonas swam towards the shore and Arianna heaved a sigh of relief. She felt stupid now, wrapping him in a towel to dry him, and then finding his hat and T-shirt to protect him from the sun. But she did feel a bit more confident.

Ben had reached the middle of the lake and was waving to her. He must be wondering what she was doing, and she waved back. Ben returned her thumbs-up signal, and ducked his head beneath the surface.

Arianna started to count the seconds. She knew exactly what he was seeing right now; she'd swum out and experienced it often enough herself. He was surrounded by iridescent blues, the colours intensifying the deeper he went. Still, she counted. It was tempting to lose yourself down there, and perhaps she should have warned him.

His head broke the surface and he waved again. Arianna cupped her hands around her mouth, shouting across the water, 'Don't stay down too long.'

Stupid. He knew that. He could have stayed and dived again, maybe even for a little longer, but now Ben had turned in the water, and was striking back towards the shore.

He got out of the water, slicking his hair back as he walked towards her. Did he really *have* to do that? Keeping her hands off him was difficult enough…

'You saw it? The bed of the lake?'

'Yes, I did. It's amazing.'

'Don't you want to dive again, and see it a second time?'

He pressed his lips together, puffing out a breath. 'No, once is enough…'

Arianna narrowed her eyes. 'You're the first person I've brought here who's said that.'

He shrugged, bending down to pick up a dry towel and wrapping it around her shoulders. Suddenly he leaned in to give her a hug, and she felt the taut muscle of his arm against her cheek before he drew back again.

'Are you okay?'

Somehow he understood how fearful she'd been. Maybe he'd heard it in the urgency of her tone, when she'd called across the water to him.

'I...wasn't. I am now. I thought I'd be all right on my own with Jonas, but I didn't realise how being in the water with him would make me feel. But you can go back if you want. It would actually make me feel a little better, knowing I haven't spoiled the day.'

He brushed his fingers against her cheek. 'You could never spoil any of my days, Arianna. I'd rather be here if you need me.'

That protective instinct of his again. 'What I really need you to do at the moment is to give me a chance to try again and do it right. We'll be fine, I promise. Jonas has already found something he wants to do.'

Ben looked across to where his son was busy arranging stones into piles, according to their colour. Arianna wondered if he really could bring himself to be a little less vigilant, just this once.

'Fine as in *fine*? Or as in keeping up appearances?'

'Fine as in absolutely fine. And I really want you to go.'

He thought for a moment and then nodded. 'Okay. You'll call me if you want me to come back?'

'I'll call. Don't worry about that.'

Arianna watched as he walked back down to the water's edge, wading in and then diving forward and starting to swim strongly. Maybe if he wasn't so physically perfect, if she didn't crave his touch as much as she needed his comfort, this would all be a little bit easier. But she and Ben were linked now. Linked by their shared past and the way they seemed to understand each other.

She might as well enjoy it. Arianna sat down, pulling her knees up and propping her chin on them. Even at this distance, there *was* a lot to enjoy.

CHAPTER EIGHT

SHE DROPPED BEN and Jonas off at their hotel. It had been a wonderful day, and seeing Ben and Jonas explore the Lava Lake had given a place that she loved an extra lustre.

Arianna had noticed Ben watching her drive away in her rear-view mirror. He'd done that last night as well, and it produced a mixture of emotions. She didn't want him to fuss, he'd been doing enough of that already, and she'd cope the way she always had. But having him there, to help her cope, was a powerful temptation.

One that she had to resist. The smile that lingered on her face as she drove home would be enough to carry her through until tomorrow. It had to be.

It was still early, and she walked out onto the veranda, listening to the calm rhythm of the sea. It lulled her into a half-asleep doze, too drowsy to go to bed, until her eyes snapped open at the sound of the knock on her front door.

Being the only doctor on the island was a twenty-four-hour-a-day job. Arianna didn't mind that, but it always seemed to be the case that people picked the one hour that she most wanted to herself. She stood up, pasting a smile on her face, which promptly slid to the floor when she opened the door and saw Ben.

Is something the matter? He looked as if everything

was right with the world, leaning against one of the pillars that supported the wide porch. His arms were folded and he was smiling in that just-happened-to-be-passing way of his.

He didn't just happen to be anything. He had a child to look after and he'd just walked a couple of miles in the darkness, along the stony path that led directly across the island.

'Where's Jonas?'

'He's in bed. Having a suite makes it easy for Lizzie to keep an eye on him for the night.'

The *whole* night? That sounded challengingly long-term. She supposed the least she could do was to let him in. She stood back from the door, rubbing the sleep out of her eyes.

'I didn't wake you up, did I? All the lights were on.'

What would he have done if they hadn't been? Turned around and walked all the way back? Arianna swallowed the question as it sprang to her lips, not entirely sure that she wanted to hear the answer.

'What's so urgent that it can't wait until the morning, Ben?'

Whatever it was, he seemed determined not to meet her gaze when he said it.

'I…um… I know this weekend has been hard on you, and that my turning up here is one of the things that's caused that. I know that today was difficult in places.'

She couldn't deny what he already knew. 'I have my moments, but they're just moments. I want to just let them go and get on with things.'

This time he could meet her gaze. Perhaps he'd been possessed by the strange spell of the lake, because his eyes seemed even more blue, and more lustrous.

'And you'll let them go tonight? I can't get into your dreams, Arianna, but maybe I can be there to help.'

Who was he trying to kid? Ben had made his way into her dreams a long time ago, and now he played an almost pivotal role in them. He couldn't quite change their course, the darkness always managed to suck her down, but part of the horror of that was that it was carrying her away from Ben's outstretched hands.

'I have to work things out for myself, Ben. You should be with Jonas.'

He heaved a sigh. 'I went back out to the centre of the lake this afternoon because you told me I should. And you were right. I was being over-protective and you and Jonas didn't need me. How about compromising with me now, and admitting that you might sleep a little better with someone around?'

'With *you* around, you mean?' The words *compromising* and *admitting* grated a little.

'This is not an entirely selfless act. I'm here for me just as much as I am for you. I want to be someone who can make a difference again.'

'I'll be up early in the morning. I have to work tomorrow.'

'Then you'll be needing a good night's sleep beforehand.'

She didn't dare thank him or hug him for being here when she really needed him. Just being one step closer to him would only remind her that she should keep her distance and she'd have to step back again and send him away. Arianna walked to the door of the spare room, opening it wide and stopping it from drifting closed again with an irregularly shaped chunk of granite from the sea that served as both a doorstop and a fascinating piece of nature's art. That was an oblique enough hint that they weren't really sleeping separately, and that her bedroom door would be wide open too.

'I should be turning in now.'

'Yeah. Me too.' Ben held her gaze but didn't move, and Arianna realised that it was because she was standing too close to the doorway. She moved aside to let him into the room.

'Just…help yourself to whatever you need. First one up in the morning makes coffee.' Arianna had no doubt that the first one awake would be her. These days, she had so little need of her alarm clock that she might as well throw it into the sea.

'It's a deal.' He turned towards the bed and then changed his mind, as if going anywhere near it when she was in his line of sight was a faux pas. 'I'll see you in the morning. Goodnight.'

'Goodnight, Ben. And…thank you for coming over.' Arianna turned, making for her own bedroom.

Ben had taken a risk, but he'd had to come. He'd spoken to Lizzie, who had told him that if he had things to work out with Arianna then he should go. So he'd kissed Jonas goodnight, waited until he was asleep and left.

He'd faced his own diffidence about whether he was really the one to help Arianna and decided that just because he wasn't in the business of saving anyone any more, it didn't mean he couldn't do something. Then he'd faced Arianna. And now he expected himself to just go to sleep?

He slipped off his shoes, and left his chinos and T-shirt laid out so that he could dive back into them at a moment's notice. Lying down on the bed under a crisp white sheet, he stared in the approximate direction of the ceiling. Nights here were darker than the ones in London, where a little bit of the yellow glow of streetlights had a habit of filtering through into a room.

Ben could hear Arianna moving around, and rejected the temptation to imagine what she was doing. He wasn't here for that, and it was wrong to even give it head room. The house was silent now and he turned over, focusing on a different area of darkness in the room.

Maybe he'd dozed off, but he didn't think he had. He could hear someone moving around, footsteps and the rustle of fabric, but the noises were quiet and measured. Ben stayed still, listening for any indication that Arianna was in distress and not just getting out of bed to fetch a glass of water.

'May I come in?' Arianna's words were almost a whisper, and if he'd been asleep he would have missed them entirely.

'Of course.'

A faint shadow moved across the room and the bed moved as she sat down on it. Ben reached for her hand, but couldn't find it.

'Come here…' He shifted back on the bed, to give her space.

She inched towards him, and Ben reached out again, his fingers connecting with hers this time. And there was no resistance when he guided her hand. Arianna lay down next to him on the bed, and Ben tucked her against the curve of his own body, putting his arm around her.

'That's nice.' She was wrapped in the light quilt that he'd found her under the other morning, but he could still appreciate the scent of her hair, and the feel of her fingers twisting around his.

'Yeah. Much better.'

He felt her relax, her head on the pillow next to his. Ben listened to every breath, the way he'd sat and listened to Jonas's breathing when he was a baby, and sometimes still did. It began to steady and slow, as if she were falling asleep.

She was dreaming. Her fingers clutching at nothing and her legs twitching, as if running fast. Ben pulled Arianna a little closer, careful not to wake her. Maybe she'd feel him there in her dream.

Long moments of agonised waiting. She was quiet and still for a few minutes, and then her body began to move against his again, as if the dream had faded and then returned. And then he felt her jump, a small cry escaping her lips.

'What did you dream, Arianna?' Maybe if she told him now, when she was still half-asleep, she could make a little more sense of it.

'I don't…I don't know.' Her movements were more purposeful now, and she seemed about to pull away from him and sit up.

'Just relax a moment. Tell me about your dream.' Pushing her back into a world that obviously terrified her was a risk. But he couldn't save her from it, and the next best thing was to be with her and try to provide some comfort.

'I'm on the ferry, and then I fall into the water. I'm being dragged down…' Ben could feel her starting to panic, and he found her hand, winding his fingers around hers. 'I'm being dragged down but…I'm telling Xander to let go. I can't help him, and it's not my fault.'

She'd remembered that, at least, and it was reflected in her dream now. 'Can you find me?'

'No…' Her body tensed suddenly. 'No, I couldn't find you, Ben. You weren't there…'

'I'm here, Arianna. Hold on tight.'

Her fingers clutched his almost painfully. And then

she began to relax. Ben suspected that this was usually the point at which she got out of bed and went to sit on the veranda. Sitting up all night had the advantage of clearing your head, but it did nothing for your readiness for work in the morning.

'Go back to sleep. I'm right here, and I've got you. You're safe.'

It had been so long since she'd gone to sleep, wrapped in someone's arms. And Lawrence had never made her feel safe, the way that Ben did. She'd never felt that he could find his way into her dreams and help her fight off the monsters that were waiting for her there.

Arianna hadn't dreamed again that night, and she woke to find herself alone. Lighter, somehow, as if she'd shed some of the weight of guilt that the nightmares always brought with them. She'd thrown off the quilt at some point during the night, and she could still feel the warm thrill of the touch of his skin against hers. Maybe *that* had been a dream, but she didn't think so.

She could hear Ben moving around, and the smell of coffee was tempting her awake. Picking up the quilt from the floor, she wrapped it carefully on top of the sleeveless vest she wore and walked out onto the veranda.

'Coffee! Now!'

Ben's head popped through the open kitchen window. 'Wait! It'll be ready in two minutes. Then we'd better get moving, or Jonas will be wondering where I've got to and you'll be late for work.'

Not a word about the dreams. That was because he'd been there and held her, driving them away. Ben had found two pastries in the bread box and he brought them out with the coffee, sitting down next to her on the long settle so they could both look out at a crisp, clear morning.

'What are you and Jonas up to today?' Arianna took a sip of her coffee.

'We'll probably all go to the beach in the morning. Then we'll take a siesta and I thought I might check out the little museum in the village.'

'Go for three o'clock. It's Andreas's day off today; he's been covering at the health centre this weekend. His father runs the museum and when he has a free day Andreas organises trips down to the harbour, and they teach the kids how to fish. Jonas might enjoy that.'

'That sounds great. I'll take Lizzie's three kids as well, so that she and James can have an afternoon to themselves. My dad's a fisherman and he'd be very impressed if all of his grandchildren come back from holiday knowing how to fish. Do you want to do something this evening?'

Arianna had been hoping that Ben would ask. It would be something to look forward to all day.

'Shall we meet up for dinner at the taverna? About eight?'

'Sounds good. Greek time or English time?' He grinned at her.

'Doctor's time. I'll give you a call if I can't make it.'

That evening Arianna declined the invitations from other diners to join them and they sat alone, under the fairy lights that illuminated the canopy over their heads.

'How was your day?' Ben asked, after Jonas had finished recounting his fishing adventures with his cousins and his new friend Andreas.

'Busy. I was at the hotel this afternoon, but you'd already left to go down to the village.'

'Lizzie said that the manager called her to ask about

the children's MMR vaccinations. Was that anything to do with your visit?'

'Yes. There's a case of measles in the hotel, a little girl from England.' Arianna quirked her lips down. 'The parents gave me a bit of a hard time, actually.'

'How so?'

'Well, they insisted that she couldn't have picked it up in England and that she must have got it here in Greece. They're asking the hotel for compensation.'

'What? How long's she been here?'

'Ten days.' Arianna knew what he was thinking, but the incubation period for measles was between ten and fourteen days. 'She could have picked it up at home, or on the plane, or here. I doubt very much it's here because I haven't had any other cases on the island.'

'Could have been anywhere. What about the other kids at the hotel?'

'I asked the manager to make a list of those who haven't been vaccinated, and I'll be going back tomorrow to see if they have any symptoms. Meanwhile, they've moved the family to one of the separate bungalows in the grounds where they can isolate more comfortably, and deep cleaned their old room.'

Ben nodded. 'That's pretty decent of them. Did you point out to the parents that if they'd had their child vaccinated then she might not have gotten measles in the first place? It's hardly the hotel's fault.'

'That's the thing. I can't really say anything because everyone knows that my father owns the hotel. I can be as even-handed as I like, but that doesn't stop anyone from accusing me of trying to get the hotel off the hook. Andreas is coming with me tomorrow, but he's not exactly impartial either. His wife works as an accountant at the hotel, and he works at the health centre my father built.'

'What about me? No one can accuse me of being partisan.' Ben looked around, as if daring any of the taverna's patrons to do anything of the kind. 'I'd be happy to go along with you. I may not be able to practise, but as a doctor I do know what I'm seeing and I'm happy to tell anyone who asks.'

It would be the ideal solution. Although there was the small matter of last night... 'You're not exactly an impartial witness, though, are you?'

He heaved a sigh. 'We're friends, Arianna. We've spent time together, and that's no one's business but our own. I'm a doctor, and it's perfectly reasonable that I should take an interest in your practice, and be willing to help out in an unofficial capacity if I can.'

It was. Arianna shifted in her seat, feeling a little guilty all the same. 'I suppose... If you don't mind.'

'Of course not. I'll ask Lizzie to keep an eye on Jonas...'

'Dad...' Jonas lost interest in the food on his plate suddenly, and looked up at his father. 'Auntie Lizzie just wants to sit on the beach and read her book.'

'You don't like the beach?'

'I like Arianna's beach. And fishing...' Jonas shot his father an imploring look, and Arianna saw the side of Ben's jaw tighten. For a man as tender-hearted as he was, Jonas's pleading looks had to be difficult to bear. Especially when he was being torn in two directions.

'I've got a better idea.' She nudged his elbow. 'Are you happy for me to organise something with Andreas?' Both Ben and Jonas had spent time out fishing with Andreas this afternoon, and Ben would have had the chance to get to know him and see how good he was with children.

'Yes, of course.' Ben didn't hesitate.

Andreas and Eleni were sitting at a table in the far

corner of the taverna, and when Arianna explained what was needed they agreed immediately. They hadn't started eating yet, and they brought their drinks over to where Ben and Jonas were sitting. Ben fetched a chair for Eleni and Arianna shifted up a bit so that they could sit down.

'Hey, Jonas.' Andreas grinned at the boy and Jonas's eyes lit up immediately when he saw his new friend.

'Andreas has a few hours off work tomorrow. We thought we might go out fishing,' Eleni added.

'Can I come?'

Eleni smiled at Ben. 'We'd like you to come, but you'll have to ask your dad whether it's all right.'

'Dad, *please…*'

Arianna supposed that Ben might have pretended to think about it, but he was already trying not to laugh. 'Of course you can go, Jonas. Thank you both.'

Andreas smirked. 'Thank *you* for getting me out of going to the hotel tomorrow with Arianna. I'd far rather be fishing.'

The five of them ate together, and then Andreas and Eleni bade them goodnight, telling Jonas that he was to be ready at three for their fishing expedition. She strolled to her car with Ben, resisting the temptation to slip her hand into the crook of his arm. The time she had left to ask the question that had been nagging at her all evening was dwindling now.

She wanted the sense of security that only Ben could give her. She knew he wouldn't say no if she asked, but somehow she couldn't quite find the words. Jonas was dozing in the back of the car by the time they reached the hotel, and this was Arianna's last chance. She got out of the driver's seat, catching Ben's gaze.

His eyes always took her breath away. Bright in the

sunlight, and now the deepest shade of blue possible in the darkness. 'Would you…um…?'

'Yes. I would.'

'You don't know what I'm about to ask yet,' Arianna reproved him.

'Whatever it is, it's a yes.' His fingers found the side of her jaw, his touch sending shivers down her spine.

'I could…wait for you. Until you've put Jonas to bed and he's asleep.' Arianna would wait in the car. Sitting in the suite with Lizzie and James seemed awkward, and she didn't want to share what she had with Ben right now.

'Go home. I'll walk across.'

'But…'

He leaned in, brushing a kiss against her cheek. 'Go home. I'll be there.'

Arianna had changed into a pair of sweatpants and a T-shirt, and curled up on the wide settle on the veranda. Listening to the sound of the sea, the waves measuring time as she waited for him. Then she saw him, at the other end of the veranda.

His shadowy figure, walking towards her, made her catch her breath. Ben sat down at the other end of the settle, stretching his legs out in front of him. It felt as if he was coming home to her.

'Jonas is asleep?'

He nodded. 'He's very excited about going fishing *again* tomorrow. But he settled down in the end.'

'And Lizzie? What does she think about you disappearing for a second night?'

She heard his quiet laugh in the darkness. 'Lizzie and I have an understanding. I didn't play the concerned older brother when she was first dating, and she doesn't give me the concerned little sister act now. We have our own lives.'

'And this is dating?'

He thought for a moment. 'Not sure. What do you reckon?'

'I'm not sure either. I'll let you know as soon as I do.'

Whatever it was, it was fine for Arianna to move towards him, snuggling up against him. He put his arm around her shoulders and they sat in silence, the hurricane lamp on the table flickering feebly, a small pool of light in the darkness.

'So do you? Date.' Arianna tried to make the question sound casual.

'Nope. I have enough on my hands with a job and a child.' Ben laughed quietly. 'That's my excuse, and I'm sticking to it.'

He could have found the time. Arianna knew other single parents who managed to hold down a job and a relationship. But Ben just didn't want to. He was manacled, by his own feelings of guilt and the feeling that he could never again be the person he'd wanted to be.

'Do you? Date,' he asked.

'I have enough on my hands, building up a practice. That's *my* excuse.'

'And what's the real story? I've told you mine.'

'I was engaged once. It didn't work out.' Even that had lost its sting. Somehow, when Ben was around everything else really didn't matter so much. 'I met him at one of my father's parties in London.'

'One of the suitors he had lined up for you?'

'Yes.' Arianna could laugh about it now. 'It was a bit like speed dating. Fifteen minutes apiece, and then I got whisked off to the next one.'

Ben chuckled. 'Did they have to form an orderly queue?'

'No, nothing like that. My father's secretary used to be there though; she's always at his parties to oversee things and she's ferociously efficient. I dare say she had a carefully disguised plan, that didn't look like a plan at all.'

'They're the worst. If you're going to have a plan, the least you can do is let everyone else in on it. So how did it feel to have all those guys lined up for your appraisal?'

It had always felt to Arianna that it was the other way round, that she was the one on show. Ben put a different perspective on a lot of things.

'When I met Lawrence the first thing he suggested was that we sneak away somewhere, so that we didn't have to be polite and talk to everyone in the room. I liked that about him immediately. He pinched a bottle of champagne and a couple of glasses and we climbed the railings in the square opposite my father's house. I tore my dress.'

'That sounds *very* romantic.' It was difficult to know whether Ben was teasing her or not. It was just his way—laid-back and without attaching any judgements.

'It seemed so at the time. Lawrence didn't much care about rules; he'd just do whatever seemed right at the time.'

'I can't disagree with that approach to life.'

Arianna dug her fingers into his ribs. 'You're quite different. Lawrence always took the easy way out.'

'Trust me. When Jonas makes his mind up about something, the easy way out seems like a very good option.' Ben chuckled.

'That's different. I've always had nightmares from time to time, and Lawrence just used to tell me to get a grip. He didn't see why I'd want to work as a doctor when I didn't have to. My father didn't much like him, but that was the one thing they *did* see eye to eye about.'

'Because, of course, it's up to them what you do with

your life.' There *was* a judgement there. In the shadows, she could see that Ben's lip had a definite curl to it.

'It became very clear that Lawrence's expectation of marriage was very different to mine. He wanted to live the life that I'd spent all my time trying to get away from. It was one of those tough break-ups where you argue every day for months and finally it's a relief to get away from each other because you're just so exhausted.'

'I'm sorry. It sounds as if he didn't give you what you needed.'

'Lawrence's opinion was that no one could give me what I needed. Too high-maintenance.' Arianna was inclined to agree on that score. She'd never been able to let go of the repercussions that her brother's death had had on her family, even though she'd tried to hide it. Lawrence's observation had hurt, because she knew that it was true.

Ben shook his head. 'That wasn't for him to say. We all need what we need. That's not high-maintenance; it's just a fact of life. High-maintenance is asking for a load of things we don't really need.'

'Maybe…'

He snorted with disgust. 'Come on, Arianna. We're both doctors. Someone comes to see us saying that their leg hurts and we don't tell them to get a grip. We address the problem.'

'Is that what you're doing? Addressing the problem?' Fear lent a sharpness to her tone. She wanted to be more than just a problem that needed addressing to Ben.

He leaned forward slowly, catching her hand in his and raising it to his lips, his eyes dark and tender. A sudden stab of longing penetrated her heart.

'I care about you as a friend. If you want a doctor, you should go and make an appointment with someone else.'

'I don't want anyone else, Ben. I want you, as my friend.' She clung onto his hand desperately. 'I shouldn't have said what I did. I'm sorry…'

'You have nothing to be sorry for, Arianna. We don't need to define our relationship. I wouldn't know how to.'

Maybe that was his way of avoiding the sexual tension that always seemed to hover around them. Maybe it was hers too. Arianna stifled a yawn. All she really cared about at the moment was that Ben was here, with her.

'It's going to be a hot night. Do you want to sleep outside?'

Arianna's version of doing anything was always far more delightful than Ben could have expected. To him, sleeping outside was a bundle of hastily assembled bedding and a tent. But she shooed him off the long settle, pulling at a mechanism underneath it to unfold it into a full-sized bed.

She brought bedding out from the house, spreading pillows and light quilts. And then the finishing touch. A thin muslin drape was suspended from a hook in the canopy above them and arranged around the edge of the bed. It took five minutes to turn the outdoor dining area into a sleeping area with a touch of magic.

She pulled back the drape a little, sitting down on the bed and beckoning to him. 'What do you think?'

'It's wonderful.' They were surrounded by the sounds and smells of the outdoors, caressed by a fresh breeze from the sea to keep them cool. But here, in their own bubble, all that Ben could see was Arianna.

She was still suddenly, staring into his eyes. In the dark depths of hers, he saw an exploding warmth of desire.

So close. So very close to tipping over into sweet

passion. If they did, they could never go back, but Ben couldn't resist. He dropped a kiss onto his own fingers, brushing it against her mouth.

Arianna smiled, raising her hand to her lips and transferring her own kiss to his mouth in return. The feeling was breathtaking, so much from such a small gesture.

'You are so beautiful.' He took her hand, feeling her fingers curl around his. 'But if we do this… I can't stay with you, Arianna.'

She nodded. 'I know. And I want you to stay.'

Could she trust him to stay? He'd made it very clear that he wanted her, and maybe she didn't believe that he could sleep beside her without acting on that. Arianna stood, letting go of his hand.

'I won't be a minute.' She shot him a smile. 'I need to go and get into my pyjamas.'

'Pyjamas? Really?' The idea was oddly entrancing. But then Arianna would be just as entrancing if she chose to wear a suit of armour to bed.

'Don't worry. I'm not worried about having to fend you off in the night. I'm just giving you a minute to get undressed and get into bed, without having to fend *me* off.'

She trusted him. And even though Ben wasn't quite sure that he had the same confidence in himself, he knew that Arianna's trust would stop him from making a move. He watched her go, smiling at the thought.

He took off his clothes, slipping under the covers. Arianna returned in an oversized pair of striped pyjamas, which somehow failed to obscure her lithe frame and the way she moved. And then they were together. Separated by layers of bedclothes, but together in ways that really mattered.

'I'm not sure that anyone could have a nightmare here.' He put his arm around her and she snuggled against him.

'I don't think so either.' She smiled up at him. 'Maybe that's the trick of it. If you dare the nightmares to come, then they don't. It's falling asleep dreading them that lets them in.'

'I don't know. Do you dare them?' Ben wondered if she would. It seemed to him to be a step forward from fearing them.

'Yes. I dare them. They can't get me here.'

He hoped not, with all his heart. Ben held her, listening to the sound of the sea, until she drifted off to sleep.

Arianna had slept soundly until dawn. Ben had carefully disentangled her from his arms, and slipped out of bed to get dressed and make coffee for her. As he brought the mugs out of the kitchen, he saw her stir.

She sat up and stretched. Ben managed to negotiate the muslin curtains without spilling the coffee and she took one of the mugs from him.

'Thank you. This is really nice.'

It was. He sat down on the bed, stretching his legs out in front of him, and Arianna caught up a pillow with her free hand, putting it behind his back. It was like the lazy intimacy that came after a night of passion, only spiced with the sharp tang of unrequited desire. But Ben had told himself that he wasn't going to think about that...

'How did you sleep?'

'Like a baby.' She took a sip of her coffee and Ben chuckled.

'You mean waking up at three-hour intervals, wanting to be fed?'

She wrinkled her nose. 'Like a five-year-old, then. You know, when Jonas just keels over and goes to sleep when he's tired.'

'Funny, I don't recall you kicking me in the night. Or

waking up with your elbow in my ribs.' Ben wouldn't have minded any part of her coming into contact with any part of him. Having her close, knowing that she was safe in his arms, had helped him to sleep and he'd woken in the cool breeze of the morning feeling rested and re-freshed.

'Would you like to take my car this morning? You could bring Jonas down to play on the beach, before you come to meet me at the health centre. He might like to stop off and make a few refinements to his water cas-cade.' She pointed towards the arrangement of beakers and water conduits that still occupied one corner of the veranda.

'Yes, I think he probably would. You're sure you don't need it?' This really ought to feel odd, and yet it was somehow perfectly natural. Drinking coffee together and discussing their day. Working out who was going to take the car...

'No. It's a lovely morning and I think I'll walk down to the health centre. I could do with the exercise.'

CHAPTER NINE

WHEN BEN ARRIVED at the health centre, Andreas and Eleni were waiting for them. Andreas presented Jonas with his very own fishing line, and the three of them left, Jonas chattering excitedly.

'He'll be all right with them.' Arianna seemed keen to reassure him.

'He's fine. He's been looking forward to this all morning.'

Ben ought to feel more guilty about this than he did. He'd always made sure that his holidays and weekends were set aside as time spent with Jonas, but he had to admit that the boy was really enjoying this holiday. He was safe, and loving the attention from both Arianna and the community in the village.

Maybe he was just a little sensitive about it because every moment with Arianna was so precious, and he had to keep reminding himself that he was taking nothing away from his son. He followed Arianna to the car, deciding that perhaps he was overthinking things.

The manager met them in the reception area of the hotel, leading them out past the pool and to a cluster of small guest houses, nestled in the shade of large trees.

'We have another two children that the parents are concerned about. I've isolated them and checked everyone now, and there are only a few of our senior guests who have not been vaccinated.'

'You asked if they had measles when they were children?' Arianna was walking beside him, an intent expression on her face, and Ben guessed she wasn't much looking forward to this next patient consultation.

'They all said they did.'

Arianna nodded. 'In that case they're most likely to be immune. Thanks for doing all that; you seem to have things well under control.'

The manager shot her a rueful smile. 'All except Mr and Mrs Colyer. Mr Colyer is still angry this morning.'

Arianna rolled her eyes. 'Well, *angry* isn't going to solve anything. Let's see if we can come up with something that does.'

The guest houses were the height of understated luxury inside, and Ben began to feel a little less guilty about having been offered a suite here. That was nice, but these were fantastic. But when the manager introduced him to Jem Colyer, he could see straightaway that the hotel's gesture had done nothing to appease him. He shook Ben's hand, ignoring Arianna completely.

'I'm glad to see they've called you in to take a look at Eloise, Dr Marsh. I've been banging my head against a brick wall with these hotel people.'

'I've not exactly been called in, Mr Colyer. I work in London and I'm not licensed to practise here in Greece. I'm here as a matter of courtesy to Dr Petrakis and as an observer only.' He had to make that clear right from the very start.

'Then perhaps you can observe that we're not at all happy about this.' Jem frowned.

'This is lovely, much nicer than the room we had.'

Eloise's mother caught her husband's arm. 'Calm down, will you, Jem.'

'There's nothing to be calm about, Kriss.' Jem glowered at his wife and she let go of his arm. 'I was looking on the internet last night and Greece had an outbreak of measles a couple of years ago. She's caught it here, and the hotel didn't warn us. Don't you think they should refund our money?'

'Dr Petrakis is here to see your daughter, Mr Colyer.' Ben decided to avoid the issue of the hotel's culpability for the time being. 'I think that's the most important thing at the moment.'

'Yes. Of course.' Jem seemed to deflate a little, letting Kriss lead Arianna and Ben out of the main living area, and to their daughter's room.

'I'm sorry about Jem. He gets worked up about things. Especially when it comes to Eloise.'

Arianna was looking at her thoughtfully. She'd not said a word since they'd arrived, and Ben reckoned she must be standing back to look at the interactions between the couple.

'That's all right. Let's take a look at Eloise and see how she's feeling today, shall we?'

She took a pair of gloves from her bag, putting them on. Then she pulled a chair up beside Eloise's bed. The little girl smiled up at Arianna when she recognised her.

'Hello, Eloise. How are you feeling today? You've still got that runny nose, I see.'

Eloise nodded miserably, rubbing her eyes, and Arianna caught her hand, stopping her. 'Your eyes hurt you?'

Another nod.

'Okay, sweetie. I know it's hard but you must try not to touch them. I'll show your mum how to bathe your eyes for you, and then they'll feel much better. And we'll keep the curtains closed, shall we, so it's not so bright in here.'

Kriss hurried to the window, and Arianna smiled up at her. 'Leave them for a couple of minutes, please, until I've examined her.'

'Yes. Yes, of course.'

Arianna carefully checked Eloise's mouth, and Ben saw the characteristic greyish-white spots on the inside of her cheeks. The little girl fretted a bit as Arianna sat her up and removed her pyjama top. The measles rash hadn't appeared yet, but everything else confirmed Arianna's diagnosis.

'Measles. Definitely.' He supposed he should say something. Arianna shot him a smile.

'But she doesn't have a rash…' Kriss frowned.

'No, sometimes the rash doesn't appear straightaway. But Eloise's other symptoms are unmistakable, and by tomorrow she may well be showing signs of a rash. You're giving her the medication I gave you yesterday? Her temperature is a little high.'

Kriss began to blush. 'I gave her the first dose, before she went to sleep last night. Jem said not to give her any this morning. The label on the bottle is in Greek and we can't read it, you see.'

Ben saw Arianna take a breath. Clearly she was holding her own irritation in check. 'This is exactly the same medication that she'd be given in England. Children's paracetamol or ibuprofen will help bring her temperature down, and make her more comfortable, so you're really not doing her any favours by withholding it.'

'Yes. Yes, of course.' Kriss turned to Ben. 'Would you tell Jem that, please?'

Another glance from Arianna. She could easily, in her position as the doctor in attendance, have insisted she tell

Jem that herself. But he'd already seen that Arianna's patients came first for her, and she gave Ben a nod.

'Yes, Mrs Colyer. I'll tell him.' If that didn't work, Ben might just take Jem out and dunk him in the swimming pool.

Arianna watched as Kriss measured out a dose of the syrup and gave it to Eloise, then showed her how to bathe the little girl's eyes with damp cotton wool. There was so much care there, so much genuine warmth, that by the time she'd finished Eloise had begun to talk to her, and professed herself to be feeling much better now.

'You're looking lots better as well. I'll come and see you tomorrow, to check on you.'

It wasn't really necessary; Eloise showed no signs of any complications and measles didn't really require three doctor's visits. But Arianna obviously felt that the family wasn't dealing with this well, and Ben shared her concern.

They'd done all they could for Eloise, but there was still unfinished business. Arianna leaned towards Kriss, asking if there was somewhere private they might talk, and Kriss nodded. She led them through a glass-paned door onto a small veranda, leaving the door open so that she could hear if Eloise needed anything. Ben followed, reluctant to leave Arianna on her own to talk with either Kriss or Jem.

'Is there something bothering your husband?' Clearly she'd seen what Ben had also noticed, and that a case of measles wasn't the most pressing of this family's problems.

'It's… It has nothing to do with this.'

'It seems to be affecting his reactions, now.'

Kriss slumped down into a seat, and Arianna perched

herself on the edge of the seat next to her, so that she could be face to face with her.

'We…lost a pregnancy eighteen months ago. Jem took it very hard.'

'I'm sorry to hear that. It must have been hard for both of you.'

Kris nodded, a tear running down her cheek. 'Yes, it was. We got through it and we were going to try again, but…then last year Jem lost his grandmother. He was very cut up about it; his gran gave him a home and brought him up after his parents died. It was expected, she had cancer, but he never got a chance to say goodbye to her, because of last summer's lockdown restrictions.'

Arianna nodded. 'That must have been very difficult for him.'

She was calm and quiet, giving Kriss a chance to talk. And Kriss seemed to be responding to her.

'He's so angry. He was angry with the doctors, because they wouldn't let him see his gran. Angry with the world. He cares so much about Eloise, and he just wants to wrap her in cotton wool all the time. He tried to get us a flight home last night, but none of the airlines would take us, with her being sick like this. Being isolated again is pushing all of his buttons, and he's worried about what it'll cost to stay on here, and whether he'll be docked pay for any extra time he takes off work.'

Kriss pulled a crumpled paper handkerchief from her sleeve, and started to snuffle into it.

'All right, let's take one thing at a time. See if we can't tick a few things off the list. I think you may well have to stay on for a little while. Eloise shouldn't be in contact with anyone until at least five days after her rash has appeared, and even then I won't be able to sign her off to travel if she's still unwell. But I'll make sure that the hotel doesn't charge you for the extra time you spend here. Kriss looked up at her questioningly and Arianna smiled. 'Being the daughter of the owner here does have its perks.'

'Thank you. I'm sorry about what Jem said about that yesterday.' Kriss looked up at Ben. 'That's why you've brought Dr Marsh with you?'

'He's here to help. That's what I want to do as well. I can write a letter for your husband's employers, saying that I've diagnosed Eloise and instructed that she must stay here and isolate. Maybe you can use it to claim from your holiday insurance, if he loses any money.'

'Yes…thank you, I didn't think of that. I'll have a look at the documents.' Kriss nodded, managing a watery smile. Clearly Arianna's approach was working, and any moment now she'd get around to the most important part of the issue.

'I'm a lot more concerned about your husband's state of mind, though. Has he spoken to anyone about how he feels about the death of his grandmother?'

Right on cue. That was what Ben was most concerned about as well.

Kriss's face fell. 'He won't. He just bottles it all up and rages about everything else. And everyone had a hard time of it last year…'

'Yes, that's true, everyone did. That doesn't mean that he can't ask for help if he's experiencing difficulties. Do you think you could speak to your doctor about this? Either together, with your husband or on your own?'

Kriss shook her head. 'No. Jem doesn't like him and, to be honest with you, I don't feel I get through to him either.'

Ben cleared his throat and Arianna looked up at him,

her slight nod giving him the go-ahead to add his own contribution to the conversation.

'Where do you live, Kriss?' He reckoned he heard a London accent in her speech.

'London. Docklands. Why?'

'My practice isn't too far from there. If you'd like to make an appointment with me, then we could talk over some of the things that might help your husband come to terms with what's happened.'

Kriss hesitated. 'I...don't know. I really don't think I can get him to come.'

'Then you come alone. This is obviously affecting you too.' Ben tore a leaf from his notebook, jotting down his work number and the name of his practice and giving it to Kriss.

'Okay. Yes, I will. Thanks.'

It was the most he could do. Jem Colyer obviously needed help; his anger and grief were spilling over and tainting the rest of his life. Ben could understand that; when Emma had died his own grief had been so overwhelming that sometimes anger had felt like a relief. But he'd known that it wasn't an answer. He hoped that Kriss would take him up on his offer and that he'd see her again.

'Is there anything else that we can do for you, Kriss?' Arianna's tone was gentle.

'No I'm...I'm grateful for what you've done already. I should get back to Jem, before he says something he shouldn't to the manager...' Kriss was gnawing at her lip now, obviously under stress, and she led the way back through Eloise's bedroom and into the main seating area.

Jem had obviously already said something he shouldn't. The manager was standing stiffly by the large windows, clearly looking forward to making his escape, and Jem was slumped in an armchair, seemingly alone with his thoughts. You could have cut the atmosphere with a knife.

Arianna smiled up at Ben, and the warmth in her eyes burned away all of his frustration. He took a deep breath and walked over to Jem.

'Mr Colyer. I know that you're concerned about your daughter and I'd like to set your mind at rest.' He waited for Arianna to sit down and then took the seat opposite Jem's armchair.

'Too right I'm concerned.' Jem smirked at Arianna, as if he imagined that she was about to get her comeuppance, and she smiled back at him pleasantly.

'I'm not licensed to practise medicine in Greece, but I am a doctor—'

'That's all right. I'll take *your* word for it.'

Why? Arianna was a fine doctor, and Jem was being blatantly insulting. Ben swallowed the question down.

'Well, I've observed the examination that Dr Petrakis carried out today, and I concur with her diagnosis of measles.'

'That's pretty obvious; it doesn't need two doctors to tell me that. I'm a bit more worried about the medicine she gave Eloise.' Jem jutted his chin aggressively.

'The standard treatment for measles is paracetamol or ibuprofen, to reduce your daughter's temperature and make her feel more comfortable.' Ben decided to leave out the part about medicines being subject to international standards. 'It's exactly the same preparation as you'd be able to buy from a chemist in England.'

'The picture on the box is the same as the one in our cabinet at home. Eh, Kriss?' Jem looked up at his wife and she pursed her lips, clearly feeling a little impatient with her husband. 'It might have been different, though.'

'Yes, it might. But I can reassure you that it's not.'

Ben resisted the temptation to roll his eyes. 'Dr Petrakis has advised that your daughter be kept in quarantine, as measles is exceptionally infectious, but I believe she intends to exert her influence here and make sure that you're not charged any extra for staying a little longer.'

Jem's lip curled. 'That's another thing. If she's the daughter of the bloke who owns this place she's bound to want to keep us sweet, isn't she?' He turned to Arianna. 'I can tell you now that I'll be putting in a complaint. Like I said, my daughter's picked this up here and we should get compensation.'

Keeping things friendly was one thing. Allowing Arianna to be bullied like this was quite another, and Ben wasn't going to leave her to defend herself. He cleared his throat, and Jem looked back at him.

'I'd encourage you to ask for anything you feel you're entitled to, but I gather you'd been here for ten days when Dr Petrakis saw your daughter yesterday and she was displaying symptoms then. The incubation period for measles is ten to fourteen days, so it's most likely that she contracted it at home.'

Jem thought for a moment. Ben allowed himself to wonder if he was struggling with fourteen minus ten, because it took his mind off the sudden need to protect and defend Arianna.

'Yeah, okay. I see your point, doc. I just want to stand up for my rights, you know?'

Ben nodded. 'I understand that. Are there any other concerns that we can help you with?'

'Nah, I suppose we're good.' Jem stood up, making for the French windows that led out onto the patio. 'I need a bit of fresh air. But I'll be expecting you to come back and see how my Eloise is doing.'

'Dr Petrakis will be coming to see your daughter again

tomorrow. You have her number so you can call if you're worried about anything.'

Jem didn't answer, wrenching open the doors and walking outside.

'Yes. We have your number. Thanks.' Kriss grimaced apologetically. 'He's very stressed…'

'It's okay. I'll see you tomorrow. You take care, eh? And call me if you need me.' Arianna rose, giving Kriss a smile. The manager made for the door with as much speed as he could without breaking into a run, and ushered them out.

The manager wrung Ben warmly by the hand, before giving the room numbers for her other two patients to Arianna and hurrying away. Ben watched his receding figure, as he walked around the swimming pool and back into the hotel.

'Nice guy. Was he like that yesterday?' Ben stopped in the shade of one of the trees, looking out to sea.

'Worse.' Arianna shook her head. 'There's something about him, though. As if all the shouting is really a scream of pain.'

'I just wish that he hadn't felt the need to attack you. That really wasn't fair.'

'He's afraid. He wants to protect his wife and daughter, and he's just lashing out at anyone and anything.'

Arianna was right. She'd borne the brunt of the insults and her ability to look past that and try to help the family was commendable. 'I know. I felt a lot like that when Emma died.'

Arianna leaned towards him. 'I'll bet you didn't go as far as interfering with Jonas's medical treatment, though. Or making the people around you walk on eggshells.'

Ben shook his head. 'No. No, I didn't do that. Jem really needs some help, for his own sake and his family's.'

'Yes, he does. I'll do whatever I can, and maybe Kriss will help him to make the right decision and come and see you, when you get back to England. It was really good of you to offer that.'

Ben smiled down at her. Being treated with such contempt can't have been easy for her, but it was just like Arianna to push her own feelings to one side and concentrate on what other people needed. She did it a little too much for her own good sometimes; he felt sure that ignoring her own feelings was the root cause of the nightmares that plagued her.

'I'll come back tomorrow, when you go to see Eloise.'

She raised an eyebrow. Maybe that had sounded far too protective, but Ben didn't actually care. He *did* feel protective about Arianna, and it was the first time in years that he'd begun to believe he could make a difference.

'You're on holiday, remember.'

'Yeah. Just taking a little holiday from my holiday. A beautiful island bathed in sunshine can begin to grate a little after a while.'

'I wouldn't know. This beautiful island *is* where I work, so I suppose I have the best of both worlds. And I wouldn't have missed your spectacular self-control for the world.'

Ben grimaced. 'It wasn't that obvious, was it?'

'No, it wasn't obvious at all. You were firm with him, but you were really kind as well.'

An idea occurred to Ben. 'Tell you what. Lizzie's taken a liking to one of the cocktails they do here. It doesn't contain any alcohol, so you can drink as many as you like and still drive, but it has umbrellas and cherries…'

'Umbrellas and cherries. Sounds good to me.' Arianna grinned.

'What do you say we go to see how the other two kids are doing, and then go upstairs to my room and order room service. We'll drink the cocktails and you can tell me exactly how annoying this afternoon's been. As loudly as you like.'

She was thinking about it. It was nice to see Arianna acknowledging her frustration instead of bottling it all up.

Suddenly she smiled, reaching up to caress his cheek, and Ben felt a tingle of excitement radiate from her touch. 'Letting off steam over cocktails. You know my guilty pleasures, don't you?'

He could think of a more delicious way of letting off steam. And as to guilty pleasures...

Cocktails were going to have to do.

Arianna had diagnosed one of the other children with measles, and Ben had concurred. The second had a runny nose but none of the other symptoms, and since he'd been vaccinated they'd agreed that it was unlikely he would have been infected. She'd already checked her records, to make sure that all of the children on the island had been inoculated, and it seemed that the outbreak was under control.

They ate at the hotel that evening, with Lizzie and James. Arianna had started to worry what Lizzie might be thinking of her, but her fears were groundless. Lizzie had the same laid-back sense of humour as her brother, and they were laughing together before very long.

Ben walked her out to her car. Arianna had already decided what she wanted to say to him, but he spoke first.

'You're going home alone, aren't you?'

'Yes. I:...It's not that I don't want you there tonight, but I have the foundations to move forward now.'

'And that's something you have to do by yourself.' A flash of regret showed in his eyes.

'Maybe not entirely but...I don't want to define our relationship any more, Ben. You were there for me when I needed you, and I'm really grateful for that. But...' She shrugged, not entirely sure how to explain this to him.

'I get it. We both made very firm limits for ourselves, and I couldn't have stayed with you all night without them. But they feel like restrictions on our friendship now.'

That was exactly how Arianna felt. Being able to hold him at night, but not able to do so for anything other than comfort. Being able to touch him, but not in the way that she wanted. The glimmer in his eyes now was telling her that it wasn't in the way *he* wanted either.

'Let's start again, Ben. I'd rather go back to the beginning and have a friendship with you that can just go wherever it goes. One where we don't feel we're rescuing each other from anything.'

He chuckled. 'Anything apart from each other, you mean.'

They were still there. Her doubts and his, about whether they'd ever be able to be more than just friends. Neither of them were ready for that yet, but at least it was something that was possible now.

Arianna turned to get into her car but he stopped her, laying his fingers gently on her arm.

'Would it be too soon...?'

'No. It wouldn't.' Not a moment too soon. Arianna stood on her toes, planting a kiss on his lips and then drawing back again.

Just a few seconds. That somehow made it even more

intense. When he brushed a kiss against her cheek it felt as if the world was slowly exploding, shockwaves almost bringing her to her knees. There was something to be said for restraint, even if it was hard.

'Goodnight. Sleep well.' His eyes were luminous in the half light.

'You too, Ben. Shall I call you when I get home?'

'Yeah, I'd like that. Just to let me know that you're okay. And if you need me…'

'I know. You're only a call away.' She wasn't going to need him tonight. Because need precluded this delicious wanting, and that was more important to her than anything.

'Quick. Go.' He smiled down at her. 'Before I decide that I'm not done rushing things.'

She got into her car, reversing out of the parking space. Trying to watch Ben and drive at the same time wasn't going to work, and so she dragged her gaze back onto the road in front of her. But when she glanced in her rearview mirror he was still standing there, watching her go.

They'd talked on the phone for an hour before Arianna had gone to sleep. Ben had been there for her when she'd needed him, and now missing him at night had become a matter of quite a different kind of longing. Arianna was determined that if he did end up in her bed again, it wouldn't be out of pity or concern.

'What do you reckon?' She was walking through the reception area of the hotel with Ben, after they'd visited Eloise for the second time together.

'She's not well, but there's nothing to worry about. She should be ready to travel in a little over a week, and Jem and Kriss can take her home.'

'Yes. I think so too.' Arianna looked up at Ben. 'Why are we not happy about that?'

'Because Eloise isn't the one who needs real help.'

'Yes. I don't see what more we can do for Jem, though.' He had seemed calmer and quieter today, and had been positively friendly towards Arianna. But she still had the feeling that nothing had changed with him, and he might explode into another show of anger if he felt his wife and daughter were threatened again.

'Neither do I. Kriss has given me her mobile number and I'll give her a call when I get back to London and see how they're doing.'

'That's nice of you. At least I don't feel as if I'm sending them off into a void.' She sighed. Eloise was very well cared for and there really was nothing more that they could do. 'So what are you up to now?'

'Jonas has discovered the ball pit in the hotel basement. He's completely lost interest in fishing now, and he wants me to build him one when we get home. I'm going to see if I can wrangle him out of there to have some lunch. You?'

'I'm going for a bite to eat, and then picking up some trees. We're going to plant them in the courtyard at the front of the health centre, and the land at the back as well. I've raised the money for it all, and people from the village are coming to help.'

Ben gave her a quizzical look. 'Let me get this right. Your father built and equipped one of the best health centres I've seen anywhere, and you're spending time raising money for a few trees?'

'It does look like a bit of an oversight, doesn't it? But you raise the money, and then go and plant the tree yourself, and it gives you ownership of a place.'

'Ah, yes, that works. I'd suggest it at our next practice meeting if we had any room for trees. Would you like a hand?'

She was hoping he might say that. 'Everyone's welcome. You have to dig if you want lemonade.'

'No problem there; I can dig. I don't suppose you need any more trees, do you?'

Arianna had intended to buy some of the trees herself; it had taken a while to raise the money she had. 'I think we could do with a few extra. Why, would you like to donate one?'

'I think I'd like that very much. I'd better get two, though, because Jonas will want his own. As long as no one minds—this is a project for the village.'

'No one minds.' And Arianna really liked the idea that Ben would be leaving a tree behind, at the health centre. She could tend it and watch it grow, and maybe one day he'd be back, to see it blossom and bear fruit.

'That's great, thanks. Shall we go and have something to eat, then we can leave Jonas here while we pick up the trees and pop back to fetch him?'

She liked the way that planning anything with Ben was so effortless. It was as if she was a part of their small family, and she'd never been a part of a family that had so much fun together.

'Yes, let's do that. Then you can come and decide which square foot of Ilaria you'd like to make your own.'

CHAPTER TEN

ARIANNA HAD TOLD Ben that she hadn't had a nightmare in a week. She didn't jump at the sound of the ferry's horn, and she was happy to spend time on the water. She seemed rested and relaxed, and for now the memories of the day on the ferry had loosened their grip on her. It might not last, but it was progress. She knew there was a way out now and however many setbacks she encountered, she could work her way back again from them.

That brought a whole new set of challenges.

The one where they'd taken Jonas swimming in the hotel's swimming pool and he'd felt the subtle brush of her limbs against his. The one where he'd watched her on the boat, the sea breeze caressing her body. He'd never actually reckoned that a breeze was something to be jealous of before. Oh, and whenever she turned her dark eyes on him and smiled. That was when his whole world tipped into a maelstrom of forbidden possibilities.

He missed their nights together, though. Waking early to find her sleeping beside him had touched Ben deeply. But it had just been a way of being close to her, and yet still keeping himself safe from the conflicting realities of a relationship. Now that their relationship had changed, he hadn't dared go any further than a brief kiss goodnight, and long phone calls before they went to sleep.

Arianna had cooked for Lizzie and James tonight. It had been a good evening, Arianna and Lizzie were becoming great friends and they'd been talking together in the kitchen for a long while, leaving him and James to drink their coffee on the veranda, and keep an eye on the children.

Lizzie had begun to yawn, and declared her interest in an early night. James had called the hotel's taxi service and they'd taken the children with them, telling Ben and Arianna that they didn't want to put an end to the evening for them. Arianna's smile had made it impossible for Ben to leave.

They sat in silence on the veranda, watching the sun go down. 'I'm just wondering if I could ever tire of this. Do you?' Ben asked.

'No, not really. A nice sunset always does it for me. When I was in London and I took the bus to work, I used to always look up from my book when we were crossing London Bridge. The view was always the same, and always different.'

Ben nodded in agreement. 'I always get that feeling when I'm walking past St Paul's. Different skies on different days, but it's always the same.'

'But you only have another week here. You should catch every sunset.'

Every smile and every word that Arianna said too. Each time she surprised him, and whenever he knew what she was about to say or do.

'What do you say…we make the most of the week we have left?' She turned towards him suddenly. This time, Ben knew exactly what she meant.

'I'm not sure that's a good idea, Arianna.' The sudden stiffness in his tone sounded like a rejection, when really all he wanted to do was to gather her up in his arms and make sweet love to her. 'I care too much about you, and…'

'And what?'

'We've only known each other for two weeks.'

Arianna shot him a reproving glance. 'We've known each other for most of our lives, Ben.'

It felt like that to him as well. 'I'm going back home in a week.'

'That's okay. Your place is in London and mine's here. We both respect that.'

Ben was beginning to lose all respect for it. Wondering if he might not fall on his knees and promise to move here, lock, stock and barrel, just to be with Arianna. But that was impossible. He wanted to make promises to Arianna, could even imagine himself doing so, but he still couldn't be sure that he could keep them.

'You know I care about you, Arianna. But—'

'I know. You don't want to hurt me.' She shook her head, smiling. 'Haven't you been listening at all? If you want to protect me, then you should make a start by respecting my decisions.'

She was right, of course. They'd already taken the step of wanting to find out where their friendship would lead, and they'd both known in their hearts that it would be here. He was fresh out of excuses, and he couldn't pretend to himself or Arianna that he didn't want her.

Her bag was hanging over the back of her seat, where she'd left it after rummaging through it to find something for Lizzie. She reached into it, taking something out and concealing it in her hand.

'This isn't a warm night, or a sunset, or a glass of wine with dinner talking, Ben. I've thought about this and it's what I want. I think it's what you want too, but you won't allow yourself to because you *are* going home in a week, and you're too much of a gentleman.' She held up a condom.

He was *not* thinking anything remotely gentlemanly at the moment. 'Have you got just one of those?'

'What do you think? I'm a doctor, and this is a very large bag. I should probably warn you that I'm fully prepared to take advantage of you.'

'Come here…' His head was swimming, with a desire so strong that it almost frightened him.

She got to her feet and walked over to him. Her gaze never leaving his face, she slowly sat down on his knee. Ben reached for her, pulling her close, and kissed her. Hard and strong, feeling her respond hungrily.

'That's what I really like about you, Ben. Underneath, you're not a gentleman at all…'

This was so much better than she'd thought it could be, which sent the feeling firmly into the realms of the unknown. Her whole body was alight with desire and when she pressed the condom into his hand, and he took it, a bright feeling that they could do anything they wanted together consumed her.

'Shall I make the bed up here?' She wanted to make love with him in the cool evening breeze.

'I don't think I can let you go for that long…' His lips curled wickedly. She felt his fingers skimming the fabric of her dress and then his hand on her breast. He kissed her and the effort it took not to scream out loud seemed to concentrate her hunger for him.

'Good thought. My bedroom, then…' Her fingers found the button at the waistband of his trousers, and she heard the soft swish of the zip. A strangled groan escaped his lips.

He threaded his fingers through her hair, letting her

just enjoy his kisses, and the feeling that he was all hers and that she could do whatever she wanted with him. He responded to her every touch, his body hard and his mouth possessive. It almost broke her, right there and then.

'Arianna.' It was his turn now, and he was working slowly and steadily down the buttons at the front of her dress. He lifted her to her feet, slipping the fabric from her shoulders and running his fingers over the lace edges of her panties and bra.

His grin told her that he liked what he saw, very much. And when he reached for her, running his hands along the curve of her waist, she began to tremble.

'Ben… Now…'

He leaned forward, kissing her forehead. 'Soon.'

He was tender, but she knew he could be passionate. And right now Arianna wanted passion. She reached forward, grasping the open front of his shirt. 'Now, Ben. Don't hold back on me now.'

He pulled her close again, and she coiled her arms around his neck. When he lifted her, she wound her legs around his waist and he carried her to her bedroom, a delicious friction zinging between them as he moved.

He laid her down on the bed, and she watched him undress. Beautiful. Pale golden skin, smooth and touched by the sun. The kind of body that a woman could worship, slim hips and long limbs, knitted together by the hard ripple of muscle. And he was looking at her as if she were the most desirable woman in the world.

When he joined her on the bed she goaded him, whispering in his ear to tell him exactly what she wanted from him. Warmth bloomed in his pale eyes and he pulled back for a moment, slipping her panties off. The condom took only a moment and then he leaned in again, kissing her mouth.

Passion fired between them. One hand curled around her leg, pulling it upwards so that he could sink deeper inside. The other slid behind her back, hooking around her shoulder so that there was no escaping the almost unbearable joy of each thrust of his hips. She saw him grit his teeth, making an effort to stay in control as the wild passion in his eyes built. And then she saw nothing, her eyes squeezed shut against the rolling, spreading pleasure as her body surrendered to his.

'Open your eyes. Please…' As the wild pulse of desire began to subside, she felt him nuzzle against her shoulder, whispering in his ear. When she looked up at him, taut muscle and tendon showed that he was near breaking point. Arianna wrapped her legs around him, feeling sharp aftershocks of pleasure pulse through her body as he reached his own climax.

They were both too breathless for words, hearts beating against each other's chest. He kissed her, taking her with him as he rolled over onto his back. She felt him reach around her, unhooking her bra, so that she could slip it off and there was nothing to stop his skin from touching hers. Arianna began to doze, knowing that tonight was very far from over.

Then she felt his hand, smoothing her curls away from her face. 'That was…beyond anything, Arianna.'

'Yes, it was.' He'd demanded a response that she hadn't even known she was capable of. And the knowledge that it had shaken him too, that he couldn't truly put the force of their passion into words either, warmed her. She kissed his cheek, and he smiled lazily.

'Do you want to sleep now?' The light in Ben's eyes told her that he already knew the answer.

'No.'

'You want to play, then?'

Ben's idea of play was scintillating. Hushed voices, talking and laughing together. Watching the strong lines of his body in the soft light from the lamp beside the bedside, as the arms of the ceiling fan revolved slowly. Letting him find out exactly what her body could do, and exploring his. And when finally he tipped her onto her back, and they were joined in the most satisfying way possible, it was just the beginning of a slow, delicious climb back into mindless passion.

'Do you always like to be on top?' she teased him as they lay curled together on the bed. Their own little world, lit by the tender glow of lamplight.

'I'd like to watch you on top of me...' He kissed her tenderly.

'Mm. I'd like that too. Or standing up. Sitting down...'

He chuckled. 'On our sides, so I can touch every part of you. Sixty-nine different things.'

'It's a lot to get through.' Arianna snuggled against him. 'You think a week will be enough?'

'We have time management skills.' He pulled her close, wrapping his arms around her. 'Now's the time for sleep, sweetheart.'

She snuggled against him, falling into a deep, dreamless sleep.

It seemed as if Ben had lived his whole life here. He was getting to know the people in the village and understood a few Greek words now. He knew the best places to shop for food, and when the fishing boats returned with their cargo. And the last four nights had been indescribable. They'd thrown themselves into making the best of what little time they had, and there had been times when Ben had actually thought it was possible to pass out from an overload of pleasure.

He walked up to the health centre to meet Arianna from work. She was sitting in the reception area alone, her face glowing.

'What?' He let go of Jonas's hand, and the boy ran over to Arianna for a hug.

'I…I called my father.'

'You did?'

There was no need to ask whether Arianna's call to her father had gone well. It was written all over her face.

'I called at lunchtime. He was in a meeting but I left a message and he called me straight back, about two minutes later.'

Just what Ben would have done if it had been his child calling him. Jonas ran over to the toy box in the corner, which was his usual port of call when they came here, and Ben sat down to listen to Arianna.

'We talked a bit. A lot, actually, we were on the phone for nearly an hour. He told me all about his plans for the hotel on Kantos.'

'Nothing else?'

She grinned. 'You don't know my father. He always keeps his business interests very close to his chest. Going into details is quite something for him.'

'Okay. Whatever works. Did you tell him all about your work? Your latest brilliant diagnosis?'

'No. I told him about the trees we'd planted. He said he thought it was a really good way of involving everyone.'

Ben had felt it was rather more a labour of love. But Arianna seemed pleased, and that was all that mattered.

'So…you're going to talk again?' That was the main thing. That Arianna's initiative wouldn't be lost, and that she could make her peace with her father.

'Yes, he's going to call me a week on Sunday. He's put it in his diary. Not because he might forget, but to ring-fence that time. For me.'

Ben would be gone by then. But maybe he'd hear all about that conversation as well. It seemed impossible that he and Arianna could just drift away from each other.

'I'm so glad for you. I know it was a difficult step to take…' He broke off as the phone rang. That was one of the downsides of island life. There was only one doctor, and if this was someone needing Arianna's attention, their evening together would have to wait a while.

Arianna picked up the phone, speaking in Greek. As she listened, her face became troubled.

'What's the matter?' he asked as soon as she ended the call.

'Remember that guy, Jem Colyer? The family was going home today and when they were boarding the ferry there was some kind of scuffle. I don't know if anyone's been hurt, but the police are there.'

'You're going down there?' Ben didn't really need to ask.

'Yes. I don't know how long I'll be…' She flashed him a querying look. Arianna didn't need to ask either.

'Is Andreas around?'

'Yes, he can hold the fort here. He can look after Jonas too, if you want to come.'

Andreas appeared, greeting Jonas like an old friend. Ben waved to his son, telling him he'd be back soon, and then followed Arianna down to the ferry terminus.

They were both breathless when they arrived, and Arianna pushed through the people who'd been taken off the ferry, stopping at the police tape to speak to a uniformed officer then turning to Ben to relay the gist of their conversation.

'No one quite knows what caused it all. He was in the bar; apparently someone bumped into Kriss and spilled his drink on her and Eloise. Jem just snapped, and started throwing punches and then grabbed a knife from behind the bar.'

The officer spoke again in Greek and Arianna listened, nodding.

'Someone pulled Kriss away and got her and Eloise out of there, but Jem's still in the bar, threatening anyone that comes near him.'

'He's got nothing to lose now, has he?' Kriss seemed to be the stabilising factor in Jem's life, but now that the police were keeping them apart, he might do anything.

Arianna shook her head. 'No, he hasn't. The police are hoping that Kriss may be able to talk him down a bit, but there's no way they'll let her back in there while he has a knife. There aren't too many good options left, Ben. Someone's going to get hurt.'

'We need to get in there. At least we have some idea of what's driving him.'

Arianna nodded. 'I agree. The police will escort me on, and I'll—'

'*You're* not going to do anything. I'm coming with you.'

She seemed about to argue with him, but then she flashed him a tight smile. 'I don't know why I even bothered to think you might not.'

They were given vests to wear, and a young policewoman checked that they were fitted properly then led them up the gangway and onto the ferry. It looked as if every policeman on the island had congregated on deck, but that still might not be enough to contain Jem without hurting him, particularly if he was in an uncontrollable rage.

He saw Kriss, holding Eloise. They were out of Jem's line of sight from the windows of the bar, sitting with a policewoman. The usual bustle and chatter of the ferry had given way to an almost eerie quiet. Arianna walked straight towards the officer in charge, talking to him briefly before coming back to Ben.

'I told him that we've dealt with Kriss and Jem before. He seems to think that we might have a better chance of getting through to him, he may see us as being on his side a little more than the police.'

Ben nodded. That made sense, but there was one thing he definitely wouldn't allow. 'I'll try to talk to him. I want you to stay back.'

Arianna flushed a little. 'I don't need to tell you that this is *my* practice, do I?'

'No, you don't. And I don't need to tell you that if Jem loses it completely I've got a better chance of fending him off than you do.'

She shook her head. 'I don't like it.'

'No, I know you don't. But if you could think of a reason why it shouldn't be me, you would have told me by now.' He didn't give Arianna the chance to reply, because there was always the possibility that she might get creative and come up with something. 'We should speak with Kriss first.'

She nodded, and Ben walked over to where Kriss was sitting. She was holding it together, no bewildered tears, just a grim look on her face.

'Talk to me, Kriss.' He sat down beside her.

'There's nothing you don't know already. Jem doesn't mean it. I told them that if they backed off and left him alone…'

'They can't, Kriss. He has a knife. The officer told us that it all started when someone spilled a drink.'

'Yes. It was nothing really, but Jem just blew up. I legged it with Eloise, just to get her out of the way of the scrum.'

'Is there anything else we should know, Kriss? Drink or drugs…?'

Kriss shook her head emphatically. 'No.'

'You're sure?' Arianna broke in, a worried look on her face. 'Anything he takes on prescription?'

'No, he hasn't been to the doctor in ages. He says that doctors didn't do his gran much good, which isn't entirely fair. But he likes you, Dr Marsh.'

'Really?' Ben was pretty sure he hadn't done anything to deserve that.

'He respects people who are up-front with him.'

This was only telling Ben what he already knew, that the situation was complex and that there was no one clear answer. He made no apologies for Jem, but right now his aim was to get him out of this situation in one piece. The rights and wrongs of the situation were for someone else to judge.

He questioned Kriss a little more, but she couldn't tell them anything beyond what Ben and Arianna already knew. Jem was volatile, and unpredictable. Ben walked back to the knot of police officers with Arianna.

'This isn't going to be easy.'

'And I was just thinking it would be a walk in the park.' Arianna turned the corners of her mouth down.

There was more preparation; his vest was checked again, and Arianna relayed instructions from the officer in charge of the scene. Jem was pacing up and down inside the bar, obviously becoming more agitated, and Ben had to go now if he was going to have any chance of calming Jem down.

His hand found Arianna's and he gave it a squeeze.

Her whispered, *'Be safe,'* carried him through the line of policemen, and away from her. Knowing that she was watching him allowed Ben to believe that, however hopeless the situation seemed, he could succeed.

He walked to the door of the bar. Jem had stopped pacing and had returned to the bar, reaching behind it to grab a bottle and pour himself a drink. Not a good sign. He had blood on the side of his face, obviously from the fracas over the spilt drink, and he was holding a long chef's knife.

Ben knocked cautiously on the door, keeping his hands in clear sight through the glazing. Jem twitched the knife in his direction, motioning for him to come in, and Ben cautiously opened the door, stepping inside.

CHAPTER ELEVEN

WHOEVER WOULD HAVE thought that your heart could be in your mouth? Or sinking to your boots. Or inhabiting any other part of your body that it wasn't supposed to. Arianna's heart was in the same place that it had been when she was six years old and watched Ben being carried away from her on the tide. With him.

He seemed to be doing everything right, and when she looked up at the officer in charge he was nodding imperceptibly, his eyes fixed on the scene unfolding inside the bar area. Ben appeared relaxed, although the slight twitch of his fingertips showed stress. He was keeping his distance from Jem and moving slowly. Never turning his back, and concentrating all of his attention on him.

He seemed to be encouraging Jem to talk as well. At first, Ben was doing all the talking, with just nods or gestures with the knife coming from Jem. But after a while Jem started to reply to him, although Arianna had no idea what he might be saying. Ben worked his way around to the bar, perching on one of the high stools. Out of Jem's reach, and with his feet still planted firmly on the floor and ready to move, but close enough to feign some sort of connection. Arianna felt sweat trickle down her spine.

'This is taking too long.' The officer looked at his

watch. It had been twenty minutes since Ben had gone into the bar, and Arianna's legs were aching with tension.

'He's still talking...' Arianna wasn't sure whether that was a good thing or not. Jem had already drained the glass at his elbow and had picked up the bottle on the bar to refill it, although Ben had clearly dissuaded him from doing so and he'd put the bottle back down again. Still talking meant that Ben was still in harm's way. Still a target.

Ten minutes more. A small patch of sweat had appeared on the back of Ben's shirt, between his shoulder blades. She loved the scent of him. Fresh sweat, hers and his, mingling with the cool smells of the night. She shouldn't think about that right now, but wasn't it always the possibility of loss that made memories so much more agonisingly clear?

A burst of static made her jump and the officer standing next to her grabbed his radio, quietening the noise and speaking in a whisper to whoever was at the other end. The hostage negotiators would be here soon, and they'd pull Ben out of there. Good for Ben, not so good for Jem, because if Ben couldn't talk him down then Arianna wasn't sure that anyone else could. Right now, she'd take good for Ben. She'd known he would go in there, but she didn't have to like it.

She heard Kriss start to sob. She'd been holding it together up till now, probably for Eloise's sake, but now the policewoman sitting next to them was trying to calm both mother and child. The officer in charge moved swiftly over, bending down in front of them and listening for a moment before guiding Kriss gently to her feet and directing two officers to go with her.

'It's best for her to go,' he responded to Arianna's

questioning look. 'The child shouldn't see her father in this situation.'

A situation that could escalate at any moment. With Ben right in the thick of it. Arianna swallowed down her panic. It seemed that the police now thought that this wasn't going to end peacefully, despite all of Ben's efforts, and it was best if Kriss and Eloise didn't see what was going to happen next.

But the move wasn't without consequences. The gangway onto the ferry was visible from the bar, and Jem had looked up just at the moment that his wife ducked around the officers shielding her, trying to look back. His hand tightened around the handle of the knife and he seemed to be shouting, beating his forehead with the heel of his other hand. Ben moved, getting slowly to his feet, tension showing in his back and thighs. He was still talking, still trying to calm Jem, even though Jem was having none of it, his body coiled with aggression and his face twisted in anger. Arianna willed Ben to just get out of there. Forget about Jem and look out for himself.

Too late. Too late… Batons appeared as the police in attendance stood at the ready and Arianna heard the click of a weapon. Jem must have seen the sudden movement and he jumped to his feet, rushing towards the door.

If he tried to fight his way through, to get to Kriss, the police would deal with Jem. Ben clearly wasn't going to let things get that far, and headed him off. Jem knocked him away but Ben seized him again, and the two men wrestled with each other before a punch to the stomach, followed through by another to the jaw, felled Jem. The knife spun away across the floor, and Ben staggered back to retrieve it.

The police surged forward and Arianna followed, desperate to make sure that Ben was all right. But as she reached the open door of the bar she saw that three po-licemen had Jem on the floor and Ben was kneeling next to him, still talking and obviously trying to calm Jem and inspect him for any injury. She should stay back, and let him finish what he'd started. Hanging onto his neck and kissing him could, and almost certainly would, come later.

The muffled beat of a helicopter was louder now and it was coming in close, hovering just feet above the jetty so that the men inside could jump down from it. The in-cident team had medics with them, who ran ahead to-wards the ferry.

They were taking no chances and Jem was put onto a stretcher and examined before they carried him out of the bar. Ben sat back on his heels, obviously drained by the last hour, his hand moving to his side. It was then that Arianna saw the blood.

'Ben...' She ducked past a couple of the island police, skidding to a halt next to him. He looked up at her, sum-moning a tight smile.

'It's okay. What is it you're supposed to say? Just a scratch.'

'You can let me be the judge of that, Ben.' Arianna loosened the vest, lifting it over his head, and saw a patch of blood on his shirt. The knife must have been deflected by the vest and sliced just below its protective shield.

'Uh... Can't you do that later?' He winced as she un-buttoned his shirt, trying to make a joke of it.

'Be quiet.' Arianna turned to call for a medical kit, but one of the officers had already thought to fetch one, and it was lying on the floor behind her. She examined the wound on his side carefully.

'How's it looking, Doctor?' His tone was still flippant, but Arianna could see pain in his eyes.

'It's superficial.' The wound was bleeding a fair bit, but it wasn't deep. Once the flow of blood was staunched, and Arianna had stitched it, he would be all right.

'I'll dress it, so that we can get you back to the health centre.' She took a wad of gauze from the medical kit, positioning it over the cut. 'Hold that there, will you, while I tape it. Keep the pressure on it.'

He did as he was told, providing the essential third hand that made any dressing easier to apply. The officer in charge of the scene cleared a path as Ben was led to a police car, and got behind the wheel himself, driving them the short way back to the health centre. He shook Ben's hand and Arianna sent him away, assuring him that there was nothing more that they needed.

The health centre was silent, and Arianna locked the main door behind them.

'Where's Jonas?'

Arianna picked up the note on the reception desk. 'Andreas and Eleni have taken him to their house. He's okay; they'll keep him occupied there. I'll get you fixed up and then you can see him, yes?'

'Yeah. Good, thanks.' He went to wrap his arms around her shoulders, and then drew back again. 'I'm sorry. There's a smudge of blood on your dress.'

'That's okay. I keep a change of clothes here and it's not the first time I've had to wash blood out of something.' She hugged him, careful not to touch the dressings on his side. Ben's chest rose and slowly fell, as if now he could finally breathe.

'I've got you, Ben,' she whispered against his chest.

'Yeah, I know. That feels so good, right now.'

She led him through to her surgery and he climbed onto the examination table, rolling stiffly onto one side. Arianna cleaned the wound, anesthetising the area in readiness for the stiches. They had to be perfect. Nothing less would do on his perfect body. She'd leave no scar, even though she wouldn't be there to see the wound knit and the mark fade. Ben lay silently as she worked.

'Done. Would you like to see before I dress it?' Arianna didn't usually offer patients that option, but it would save on a dressing because Ben would be peeling it off as soon as her back was turned.

'Yes, thanks.' He peered into the mirror that she positioned above his side, tilting it a little so that he could see. 'I'm impressed. Very neat.'

He was trying to smile but the lustre had gone from his eyes. Maybe if she waited he'd get around to saying what was on his mind. Arianna picked up his bloodied shirt, holding it up and then throwing it into the bin.

'You can't let Jonas see you in that. Andreas has a couple of scrub tops that he keeps here; he won't mind if you take one.' The V-necked blue cotton top looked enough like the casual shirts that tourists wore that once it was out of the context of the health centre it would hardly draw a second glance.

'Yes, I need to see him.' Ben started to sit up, and Arianna helped him swing his legs down from the couch.

'Of course. Not with blood on your hands, though.' Arianna took a wipe from the box on her desk, picking up his hand and carefully wiping it. However much she cleaned him up, she couldn't restore the light in his eyes, and Jonas would see that. *She* saw it, and it made her heart ache.

'Jem saw Kriss go? Is that why he got so agitated?'

'Yes. He was very on edge when I went in there, but he seemed to be getting calmer. I'd managed to persuade him that there was a way out of the situation for him, and that he didn't need to hurt himself or anyone else. Then he saw Kriss leave with Eloise, and he just flipped. He was shouting about killing anyone who got in his way.'

'So you got in his way.' Arianna tried not to show her disapproval.

'There wasn't much choice. He wouldn't have stopped, and if he'd have got out of the bar there would have been casualties.'

'There was one.'

'It was only superficial, though. You said so yourself.'

She threw the wipe into the bin, collecting a new one to clean his other hand. 'What's going on with you?'

'I just need to see Jonas.'

Of course he did. He hadn't once said that he needed to see her, though, even though Arianna was struggling not to think that way. Of course she came second to his child; she'd never respect a man who thought differently. Being somewhere on the list would be nice, though.

'He needs to see you too. But not with blood all over you and not with that look in your eyes either. What's the matter, Ben?'

He shook his head, as if maybe that might knock his thoughts into some order. 'I've been thinking about what would have happened if I'd been more badly hurt. If I couldn't get back to Jonas…'

Arianna puffed out a breath. Not being there for the people he loved was a dilemma for Ben and probably always would be. 'You are who you are, Ben. Who you are is important for Jonas too.'

It was important to Ben. The man who believed he could no longer make a difference, and who'd made the biggest difference of all to Jem. Without Ben's intervention, the situation would have gone bad very quickly.

'Yeah.' He straightened his back, as if trying to settle

a weight on his shoulders. 'It was easier when I jumped into the water after you. A lot less complicated.'

'Maybe you just thought it was. A lot of things seem less complicated when you're twelve.'

'True. Another fifteen years and perhaps I won't be worrying about Jonas so much.'

'I wouldn't count on it. I've heard reports to the contrary.' Arianna had finished cleaning his other hand, and she threw the wipe into the bin.

'Do you know what's going to happen to Jem?'

'Yes, I heard the police say that they'll be taking him to Athens initially, for a psychiatric evaluation. He'll be in a secure facility, but he'll be well looked after; I know the place. He will be charged, I don't see any alternative, but he'll have a fair hearing.'

Ben shook his head. 'I wouldn't like to be the one to make a decision about that. What Jem did was entirely wrong, but I can still see how it all happened.'

'So can I. But we're doctors and our job isn't to make judgements; it's to do our best for people, regardless of who they are or what they've done.' She smiled at Ben. 'So I think we're off the hook with that, at least.'

He smiled, coiling his fingers around hers. 'What would I do without you to dispense stitches and good advice?'

He should go and see Jonas now. Maybe the gentle walk to Andreas and Eleni's house would finish the job of restoring his spirits. But Ben didn't seem inclined to move just yet and suddenly he reached out, wrapping his arms around her.

'Careful…'

'It's okay. I just need to hold you.' He hugged her tight, and Arianna rested her head against his shoulder.

'When Jem tried to get out of the bar, all I could think

was that you were out there. I had to stop him from getting anywhere near you, Arianna.'

Maybe that was what any woman would want to hear. That a man's only thought was for her, and that he'd risk serious injury to save her. The way he'd jumped into the water after her had fuelled her fascination with Ben all these years.

But things weren't that simple now. He had Jonas to think about, and it was impossible that Ben didn't see the conflict. The things she loved most about him, his honourable nature and his bravery, might just be the things that tore them apart.

Now, in his arms, those thoughts were easy to ignore. She looked up at him, and all the warmth that had been missing from his eyes was there once more. When she kissed him, all of the yearning she felt was in his response.

'You know you'll always be my hero, don't you?'

Ben ached a little, but that was largely across his shoulders, from the tension of trying to talk Jem down. Even after the anaesthetic wore off his side didn't hurt too much, and if he took it easy for a couple of days he'd be as good as new.

He decided to tell Jonas what had happened, carefully leaving out all of the what-ifs and might-have-beens. Arianna had told Jonas that his dad had been very brave, and that the injury was just a scratch. She'd put a very large dressing on it, just to make it look a little more serious than it was.

'Phwoar, Dad!' Jonas had fallen for Arianna's version of the events hook, line and sinker, and was obviously impressed. 'Will you get a medal?'

'No. You only get a medal if you're very, very brave.'

Jonas pulled an indignant face. 'But aren't *you* very, very brave, Dad?'

'No.' The word lost its impact on Jonas, because Arianna chorused a 'Yes' at the same time.

When she heard that Ben's injury didn't preclude him from sitting up or eating, Eleni insisted that they stay for dinner. They ate under a large olive tree in the garden, with Ben propped up on cushions, and Andreas filling his plate from the serving dishes on the table. Arianna took a call, and left for half an hour to visit a feverish child, returning to say that she'd reassured the first-time mother that her little one was fine. Andreas promised to pop in and see her before work tomorrow and the business was concluded with far less fuss and more good humour than the interruption of a dinner with friends at home would have entailed. Along with all its professionalism, the health centre still retained all that was best in the community that surrounded it.

They left early, making their way slowly to Arianna's car. All Ben wanted to do was to sleep, feeling the curve of her body against his, but he should be there for Jonas tonight, to make sure that he answered any questions that the boy had.

'Dad…' It sounded as if the first of Jonas's questions was on the way. 'Can we go to Arianna's house?'

'Why do you want to go there?' Ben took his son's hand, feeling the stitches pull a little.

'So that Arianna can help me look after you.'

'Tonight, you mean?' He could see Arianna smiling out of the corner of his eye.

'Yes. Arianna, you can make sure my dad's all right, can't you?'

'Of course I can. If that's what you want me to do, Jonas.'

'Yes.'

Ben wasn't going to talk about it any more, and he certainly wasn't going to look at Arianna because he'd just start laughing. Or kissing her, and then Jonas might catch onto the fact that her motives for inviting them to stay weren't entirely medical. He reached for the car door and eased himself into his seat.

Arianna had supposed she should sleep in her own bed, leaving Ben and Jonas in the large bed in the spare room. But when it was time to put Jonas to bed, he'd asked her for a story. Ben was tired too, and he'd lain on the bed, listening as Arianna told one of the stories she remembered her father telling her and Xander.

Halfway through, a thought occurred to Jonas. 'What happens if my dad bursts his stitches? Will he bleed all over the carpet?'

'I'm not going to burst my stitches, Jonas.' Ben opened one eye.

'Oh.' Jonas looked slightly disappointed. 'Are you sure?'

'Yes, I'm sure. Arianna's stitches are very special. I'm not going to do any more bleeding, and particularly not all over the carpet.'

'Okay.' Jonas seemed happy with the explanation. He wriggled towards the side of the bed, leaving a space between himself and his father. 'You can lie here, Arianna.'

'Hey! Arianna's got her own bed, you know.' Ben's hand went to his side as he tried not to laugh.

But Jonas shot her a pleading look, and she couldn't resist. Arianna climbed onto the bed, snuggling between Ben and Jonas, and by the time she'd finished the story he was asleep.

She should go, now. But when she moved she felt Ben's hand close around hers. 'Don't. Please.'

He'd been so concerned about Jonas, but he needed a

little comfort too. Carefully she snuggled against him, holding his hand between hers.

Maybe she'd wait until Ben was asleep too, and then leave. But Arianna didn't think so. It felt that this was where she was meant to be, where she would have been if fate hadn't intervened and changed the trajectory of her life. Part of a family that was stronger together than it was apart.

It couldn't happen. But, for this one night, she could pretend it might.

CHAPTER TWELVE

SOME WOUNDS DIDN'T HEAL.

The one on Ben's side was going to be fine. He was a little stiff and sore, but the sudden, unreasoning panic when he'd seen the blood had been an overreaction.

Maybe the result of a greater wound, which had been inflicted when Emma died. Mostly Ben could live with the ache, but at times like these it seemed to be draining the life blood from him. He'd tried to help Jem, because protecting his patients had become second nature to him. But he couldn't even protect the people he loved. Certainly not Emma, and now he'd taken the risk that Jonas might lose the only parent he had left, because instinct had told him that he must prevent Jem from getting anywhere near Arianna.

It was a conundrum. One that could only be solved by letting Arianna go, but that seemed impossible right now. One more wound that might never heal.

The next day was Saturday, and Arianna spent it with him at the hotel, looking after all four of the children while Lizzie and James went out sightseeing together. When there were no demands from the kids to animate her, she too seemed thoughtful and quiet.

'You're staying here tonight?' Arianna asked after

they'd put the children to bed and Lizzie and James had returned to watch them.

'I could…' Perhaps she wanted to spend the night alone, to think about whatever was bugging her. Tonight suddenly seemed an impossibly long time and he drew her close, hugging her.

'Or you could come back to my place?' She turned her gaze up to meet his, and Ben could feel the echoes of the nights they'd spent together shivering through him, driving away all of the doubts and what-ifs.

'I'd really like that…'

As soon as her front door closed behind them, she kissed him. As if she was intent on driving away the silences of the day, submerging them in the chemistry that never failed them when they were alone.

'Come and lie down…' She'd been tending to him all day, making sure he didn't overdo things, but this was clearly quite a different request.

She led him into the bedroom, unbuttoning his shirt and pulling it from his shoulders. Ben let her do it, allowing these moments to blot out the past and the future, everything other than Arianna. She undressed him slowly, carefully, piling pillows so that he could recline on the bed.

'I can be *very* gentle with you.' Her fingers grazed the top button of her dress, the gesture unbearably erotic. Ben grinned.

'I'd prefer it if you left out the *very*. Maybe we could just take a little break to mop up if I start to bleed all over the carpet, eh?'

She smiled, slowly unbuttoning her dress. Stopping for one agonising minute before she let it fall to the floor at her feet.

'You've been wearing that underwear all day, and you never told me?' Ben shot her a reproachful look. Arianna's underwear was a constant fascination to him. Practical but pretty, and *very* sexy.

'I didn't want to give you ideas you couldn't follow through on...' Her wicked smile was the only thing that mattered to Ben right now.

'I can follow through. Don't you worry about that.'

She nodded, her gaze sweeping his body. It must be pretty obvious to her that he had every intention of following through, and then some. Climbing onto the bed, she kissed him lightly on the lips.

'You'll hardly feel a thing...'

He pulled her down, kissing her. Letting her feel how much he wanted her right now.

'Too late, honey. I'm already feeling something...'

Last night had been amazing. As if they'd both been trying to push back the future that they both knew was coming. Ben had driven every other thought from her head, and she knew that he was one hundred per cent there and with her.

But time was trickling through her fingers. England wasn't so very far away—Arianna's father had been known to fly to London for a meeting or a party and be back home within the space of twenty-four hours. That wasn't the issue. The problem was whether she and Ben could reach a place where they felt able to carry on their relationship, and there was so little time before he was due to leave.

She'd thought that maybe one more night, a few hours when passion drove every other thought from their heads, might allow them to gain a little perspective. But she'd woken that morning to find herself alone.

Arianna got out of bed, putting on her light cotton dressing gown. Ben was outside on the veranda, sitting staring out to sea.

'How are you doing?' She nodded towards the dressing on his side, which was visible above the waistband of his jeans.

'Fine. No problem…'

Right. That was the least of her worries settled. Arianna sat down next to him. He didn't move to pull her close, the way he usually did, and suddenly she felt very alone.

'Can we do this, Ben?'

'We *are* doing it, aren't we?'

His words smacked of denial. An attempt to avoid the one thing that neither of them seemed to want to talk about. Only they *had* to talk about it.

'That's not what I mean. You know it.'

He nodded. 'I think the least we can do is part as friends.'

No. That would never work. Arianna took a breath, trying to steady herself. 'Knowing you, Ben…it can't ever be friendship. It's always going to be a matter of wanting you. Loving you, and being loved by you.'

She could see the pain, blooming in his eyes. 'That's something we *can't* do, Arianna.'

Then he must tell her why. Frame the reason into words for her, to give her something to hold onto.

'Why not?'

Ben turned the corners of his mouth down, staring out to sea. 'Emma…'

'You still love her?' If he did, then he should say it.

'That's not it, Arianna. I failed Emma and…I promised myself I'd do everything I could not to fail Jonas. That I'd be there for him, and protect him. The other day—it just reminded me that I can't protect both of you. And Jonas is my child; he needs me…'

Yes. She knew that. Arianna swallowed down the impulse to tell him that she needed him too. 'Do you think I could care for you if you weren't such a good father to Jonas?'

He shook his head resignedly. 'I don't suppose so.'

It was make or break now. All that Arianna could feel was grief, because it seemed impossible that this wouldn't break them apart.

'Has it occurred to you that I don't want you to protect me? I don't need you to look after me; I just want you to love me. Give me a reason why I was the one that was saved and not Xander.' The words came out in a rush of feeling and rather more honestly than Arianna had expected.

He looked at her blankly. Then suddenly his lip curled in an expression of incredulous frustration. 'Surely you don't need me to give you a reason, Arianna. If you're so blind that you can't see how important you are as a person…' He shook his head.

Then she was blind. Before she'd met Ben, her work had been the only thing she could offer to justify her place in the world. She'd begun to see a little of her own worth by looking through his eyes. But now he was going to destroy all of that, by leaving her.

'All I can see, Ben, is that you're ripping us apart.'

He knew what he was doing. Ben had held out one fragile hope that talking about things would stop the inevitable. That was gone now.

'You want to be part of that great experiment, do you? Staying together in the hope that we won't tear each other to shreds?'

She pressed her lips together. Arianna knew just as well as he did that this was exactly what would happen. He was even more determined that he had to leave, now that she'd betrayed how little she thought of herself, because Arianna needed space to grow and thrive, unhampered by his constant need to protect her.

'And you know exactly what's going to happen, do you?' She jutted her chin at him.

'No. I just know that you deserve a lot better than anything I can give you.'

She looked at him, reproachful tears in her eyes. Then suddenly, as if she'd made a decision, she stood up.

'The trouble with you is that you saved me once, and now you think it's your job. And in case you were wondering, yes, I *do* find it infuriating.' She stamped her foot, grimacing as her bare toes hit the wooden boards. 'But you're not going to make me watch you go. I'm going out.'

He knew what she was asking, and it came almost as a relief. 'I'll be gone by the time you get back.'

'I'll leave my car keys…' One last morsel of concern that tugged painfully at his heart. He couldn't accept it; it would weaken his resolve.

'Don't. I'd rather walk back to the hotel.'

She couldn't even look at him now. Arianna turned, storming into the house, and he heard the shower running. Then silence, followed by the sound of the front door slamming shut. It was one of the many things he loved about her, that she never did anything by halves.

Ben stood for a moment, leaning on the rails that bordered the veranda. Willing himself to keep breathing and his heart to keep on beating. If he could get through these moments, stop himself from going after her and promising her anything if she would just stay with him, the next ones would be easier.

Why did doing the right thing hurt so very much?

CHAPTER THIRTEEN

WHEN ARIANNA RETURNED HOME, the house was silent. No mess in the kitchen, no sandy footprints on the veranda. It was as if Ben had never been there. She'd locked herself in her office at the health centre, throwing herself into work, and now, looking around at her empty house, she could feel the tears welling up.

She opened the fridge and surveyed its contents. Wine or ice cream? Neither of them were going to make her feel any better, and she decided on wine now, so that she could keep the ice cream for later.

She knew that Ben was right, and that it was useless. Trying to make this work would only tear them both apart. Their story had started on the day he'd rescued her, and now the fallout from that day had ended it. Arianna poured herself a glass of wine, and even after a large gulp of it she wasn't able to smile at the irony of that, because it was all too cruel.

She topped up her glass and walked out onto the veranda. Every last sign of him was gone, apart from…

Her gaze lit on Jonas's water cascade. Of course, he couldn't take that with him; it was far too complex a contraption, and would have fallen to bits if Ben had tried to move it. They'd had such fun building it.

Tears started to roll down her face and Arianna picked

up her glass, heading out onto the beach. Her life, Ben's life, they'd both better be perfect from now on. Well lived, full of professional success and personal happiness. Because that was about the only thing that would ever compensate her for losing him.

Ben hurried back to his London surgery. Amalie Cutler had an appointment with him this afternoon, and he'd gone down to the hospital himself to get the test results she'd been waiting for. Her consultant was on holiday, and they'd been sitting in his in-tray for the last week. Ben had begged his secretary to give them to him, and she'd relented with a smile. When he'd opened the envelope he'd seen that it was good news.

It was the first time he'd really smiled in weeks. He'd turned the edges of his mouth up for Jonas, even laughed with his son and hugged him, the way he always did. But the staff at the busy London surgery had received short shrift, and more than one apology. He was a little busy, or a little stressed, all codewords for heartbreak. He missed Arianna with every fibre of his being, and as each day passed he only missed her more because it was longer since he'd seen her last.

But finally. This was something to smile about. Ben walked to his surgery, throwing himself into his chair and switching on his computer. Good, Amalie was first in line, so she wouldn't have to wait.

He pressed the intercom and called her name. Amalie was looking well, her blonde hair growing again after the chemo, and she'd obviously been to the hairdresser and had it cut and styled.

'How are you feeling, Amalie?'

'Good. Fine really; it's just…I'm waiting for my results. My consultant's on holiday now and, as you haven't got them back yet, I suppose they'll be another two weeks.' Amalie pursed her lips and Ben noticed the dark rings under her eyes. Waiting had obviously taken its toll.

'I've been up to the hospital and collected them. They were ready; they just hadn't been sent yet. I'm happy to tell you that it's good news.'

Amalie stared at him, her hand flying to her mouth. 'Good news? You're sure, Dr Marsh?'

'Yes, I'm sure. The tests you had at the hospital showed that your cancer is in full remission. We'll still need to see you from time to time, and I'd advise you to continue seeing your cancer nurse for support and to discuss any ongoing issues. But this is an important milestone.'

Ben handed Amalie the envelope he had ready on his desk, and she opened it with shaking hands. She stared at the sheet of paper inside blankly and then looked up at him, tears in her eyes.

'I…I don't really understand what it says.'

'That's fine. Would you like to sit quietly for a moment? Just let it sink in.' Ben suspected that anything he said now would be forgotten in the rush of emotion.

'Yes. Yes, please. I've got to call my husband and tell him. And my mum…'

'I'll get someone to make you a cup of tea, and we'll find you somewhere private for you to make your calls. Then you can come back here, and we'll discuss exactly what the letter says and what your next steps are going to be. Along with whatever it was you came to see me about today.'

'Today…?' Amalie looked at him blankly, and then smiled. 'I've not been sleeping. I've been so worried about my results and I thought I'd have a while to wait still, so I wondered if there was something you could give me, just for a couple of weeks. I don't think I'll need anything now.'

'Okay. We'll leave that then, shall we? Let me know if the sleeplessness continues…'

Amalie had already taken her phone from her bag and was obviously eager to make her calls. She got to her feet, clutching the letter to her chest as if it were the most precious thing in the world. Ben ushered her to the door but she stopped, grabbing his hand to shake it.

'Thank you so much, Dr Marsh. Not just for this but… You've been there for me all the way. You've made such a difference…'

'It's my pleasure.' Ben could hardly get the words out. The warm thrill he was feeling right now was familiar, but he hadn't experienced it since Emma had died. It had taken a trip to Ilaria to find the one person who could show him the way back to finding this feeling of fulfilment. Arianna.

Jonas had taken to the idea of board games, and every evening after tea Ben sat down with him and played draughts. Tonight, the newly established ritual didn't feel quite so painful.

'Are you cheating again, Jonas?'

'No, Dad.' Jonas looked up at him with innocent eyes.

'You're sure about that? How did your counter get from there, to there?'

Jonas studied the board carefully, and then moved his counter back to the proper place. Ben usually allowed Jonas to win, but he tried to stay within the rules while doing so.

'What do you reckon, mate?' Ben took a sip from his glass, and Jonas picked up his juice and did the same.

'What about, Dad?'

That was always the way they started up any conversation that might lead to a decision of importance. And this decision might just be the most important of Ben's life.

'You know what taking a risk means?' Ben took two of the tiny apple cakes that his mother had brought for Jonas yesterday from the plate that lay between them on the table, putting them carefully on the table next to the draughts board. They were just beyond Jonas's reach.

'You can grab one of those easily, right out from under my nose. If you try for two, I might be able to stop you.'

Jonas thought for a moment, weighing the matter up. Then he lunged forward suddenly, grabbing an apple cake in each hand and whipping them out of Ben's reach.

'Gotcha, Dad!'

Ben smiled. There was nothing wrong with Jonas's motor skills and he was constantly having to up his game if he wanted to outwit the boy. Soon enough he'd be applying his full concentration to their board games and Jonas would still beat him.

'So you did. I'll have to be a bit quicker next time, won't I.'

'Yes, you *will*.' Jonas popped one of the cakes into his mouth.

It was an imperfect decision, but the same one that Ben had made when he'd plunged into the water after Arianna. Jonas was willing to take a risk, and set his eye on the greater prize. His actions weren't tempered by the fear of loss, he was a little too young to know what that really meant, but maybe that wasn't an entirely bad thing. Maybe it was the only way out of the dragging unhappiness that had followed Ben back from Ilaria, and wouldn't let him go.

'Your move, Dad.'

'Oh. Yeah, sorry.' Ben studied the board, his mind still

buzzing. Was it really that simple? Later on tonight, when Jonas was in bed, he'd make his decision.

Life on Ilaria wasn't all sunshine and sunsets. The sea around them held harsh realities beneath its sparkling surface. There would always be sickness and strife, disappointment and hardship. Arianna loved the slower pace of life and the beauty of her island home, along with the community who had taken her in and made her *their* doctor, not just the daughter of a man who had the money to make a difference to the island. The sunshine and sunsets weren't bad either.

But now she hardly noticed them. Her body ached when she got up in the morning, even though she'd had a full night's sleep. And the emptiness when she found that Ben wasn't there was worse than any dream.

She'd kept going, though, working hard to dull the pain. And somehow a little of Ben stayed with her. Convincing her that her life had not been saved in exchange for Xander's. His death was and always would be a tragedy, but her place in the world was hers by right.

But she *was* tired. It was late and it had been a busy week, and all she wanted to do now was to eat something and get an early night. Tomorrow was Saturday, and she had the whole weekend in front of her.

She felt her phone buzz in her pocket as she let herself into her house. Dropping her bag on the floor, she sent up a quick prayer that this *wasn't* someone who needed a doctor tonight. She pulled out her phone, looking at the screen. Ben.

Right now, a text summoning her to visit a patient would have been more than welcome, as something to take her mind off the sudden, painful hope. The fear, because she knew that Ben wouldn't get in contact with her unless it was something really urgent. The way that prickles travelled up her spine, just at the sight of his name on the small screen.

She should just delete the text without reading it. Impossible. Perhaps she'd read it and then delete it. Her fingers were trembling so much that the phone slipped through them and clattered onto the floor. Arianna retrieved it quickly, relieved to find that, although the screen had cracked, it was still working.

I want you to know that I love you. Without you I'll always be drowning.

What? Arianna looked for another text that might elaborate on that, maybe give her a clue about what to do next. She knew there wouldn't be one. Ben wouldn't ask her to do anything with this information; he'd just let her know where he stood and wait for her answer.

I love you. He hadn't said that before and neither had Arianna, although it had been on the tip of her tongue. But there had been love in everything they'd done together. Love and trust.

I'll always be drowning. That was Ben all over. The man who saved others, but who brushed the importance of that away without a second thought. He saw only the ways in which she'd saved him.

She could do this. Doing this would be the best thing she'd ever done in her life. The most difficult, terrifying, wonderful thing she'd ever done.

'Wait.' Arianna took a deep breath, admonishing herself out loud. 'Sleep on it. Call him in the morning.'

She got as far as going out to the kitchen and taking a bottle of water from the fridge, before the utter impossibility of the plan hit her. She didn't *need* to think about this. She'd known her answer from the day she'd met Ben.

Taking her phone back out of her pocket, she checked again to make sure that there wasn't another text that she'd missed. Then she dialled.

'Father...'

'Arianna?'

'I need your help...'

She heard her father catch his breath at the other end of the line. It was unusual for him to be lost for an immediate answer to anything, and when he did speak there was an uncharacteristic tremor in his voice.

'Thank you for calling me, Arianna.'

The helicopter swung low over the sea, and landed on a piece of scrubland to one side of the house. The engine cut out and the pilot ran towards her, bending low to avoid the still turning rotor blades. He took her bag, guiding her to one of the doors behind the cockpit.

Her father was sitting inside the helicopter. The shock almost made Arianna stumble backwards and he stretched out his hand, helping her into the empty seat next to him.

Arianna didn't object when he leaned forward to fasten her safety belt. If this was turning into National Surprise Arianna Day, then the world was making a fine job of it so far.

'What are you doing here?'

'In my own helicopter?' Her father shot her an innocent look.

'On Ilaria. You said you wouldn't set foot on Ilaria again.' Arianna frowned at him.

'Technically, I haven't...'

'You're going to rely on technicalities, are you?'

Her father smiled. 'Only you, Arianna. Everyone else allows me to talk them down, but you never did. Even when you were a child.'

Something about the fondness in his face reminded her of the way that Ben looked at Jonas. Warmth curled around her heart.

'I meant it. What I said the other day, about not wanting it to be another two years before we talked.' Saying it face to face seemed to cement Arianna's determination to repair whatever could be salvaged of her relationship with her father. To believe that some part of her relationship with Ben could be salvaged as well.

The lines on her father's face melted into a regretful smile. 'I made many mistakes, Arianna. I told myself that grief had pushed us apart, but it was my job to stop that from happening. I abandoned you and I would give anything for the opportunity to be there for you now.'

Arianna reached forward, taking her father's hand, realising that he was trembling.

'I need to go to England alone. But when I return I'd like to come to Athens, so we can talk. And I'd like you to come back here with me, so I can show you what I've done at the health centre.' Maybe that was a little too much to ask, but if miracles were possible then she might as well think big.

'I would like that. Very much…' The pilot had settled himself into his seat, and the helicopter's rotor blades began to quicken in readiness for take-off. Her father had to shout so that she could hear his final words.

'I'm so proud of you, Arianna.'

Arianna squeezed her father's hand. 'I'm glad you're here. Thank you…'

The helicopter swung out, across the darkening sea. The journey ahead of her, from the private airfield on the mainland to London, seemed very long and lonely. All she could do was hope that Ben would be there for her when she arrived.

CHAPTER FOURTEEN

MAYBE HE SHOULDN'T have sent the text. Ben had been considering the matter all night, before dragging himself wearily out of bed to take Jonas to the day-long play date for a friend's birthday. The other mothers there had taken one look at him and sent him home, telling him to come and pick Jonas up at six. He worked hard all week and he should take a day off.

In truth, a day off was the last thing that Ben wanted, because it gave him even more time to think. Had he worded the text right? Would Arianna understand that he wasn't expecting her to do anything about his great proposition, but that he just wanted to let her know where he stood? If she *did* know where he stood, what would she do about it? And if she rejected him, could he accept that decision, or would he just stubbornly keep loving her?

It was a lot more complex than just grabbing a couple of apple cakes. And the only thing that Ben knew for sure was that he'd never give up hope.

Now wasn't a day for hope, though. Whatever Arianna's reaction, he wouldn't be hearing from her just yet. If she deleted the text then he wouldn't be hearing from her at all, and if she replied she'd probably take a little time to consider what she wanted to say.

The weeds that had started to grow in the garden when

he'd been away in Ilaria, and had continued untouched since then, were threatening to take over. He'd work for a while, until he was truly exhausted, and then take a siesta… No, he'd take a nap. Far fewer memories attached to a power nap than there were to a siesta, even if the two were largely similar.

He worked for an hour and then began to carry piles of weeds through to the front garden, tipping them into the garden waste wheelie bin. A limousine was travelling slowly past the house, and he wondered if someone in the street was getting married. If he'd been in Ilaria, then he'd have known exactly what everyone in the street was doing…

The limousine stopped and then backed up. Ben winced as it drew closer to a small blue run-around that belonged to his neighbour, and wondered whether going out into the road and waving his arms around to help the driver park was going to be necessary. But it seemed that not blocking the road wasn't his first priority, and he got out of the car and opened the back door.

Arianna got out of the car.

Wearing a pair of slim chinos, flat pumps and a striped T-shirt with a wraparound white jacket and standing next to the car, she looked somehow rich. She waved the driver back into his seat and banged impatiently on the front passenger window when he failed to draw away quickly enough, turning to smile and apologise to the driver in the car behind. Then she turned and saw him staring at her.

The car behind her shot forward, almost hitting her, and she jumped out of the way. Ben ran down to where she was standing, in between two parked cars, stopping before he got close enough to touch her.

'Not much of a rescue, if you're going to stand in the

middle of the road.' He knew that he was smiling. Whatever she was here to do, whether it was to sink a dagger into his heart or take him into her arms and save him, he'd accept his fate because it would be at Arianna's hands.

'No. I could have planned that a lot better.' Her eyes were that mix of warmth and fire that made Ben hope against hope that she didn't have any daggers in her handbag.

'Come in.' Ben backed away from her so that she could step onto the pavement and kept his distance, leading her around to the back of the house. Arianna gave him a smile, picking her way around the weeds that were piled up on the path.

She stepped through the patio doors into the sitting room, looking around her. 'I like your house.'

Each one of the books in the bookcase, the toys collected up in a basket by the wide hearth and the chairs, a little faded with wear but still comfortable, took on a new lustre in Ben's eyes. If Arianna liked his house, then he liked it even more.

'I got your text.' She turned on him suddenly. 'So I came straightaway.'

'How…?' She didn't look like someone who'd been up all night, making her way through a busy airport and then spending five hours on a plane. She looked wonderful, like all of his dreams rolled into one.

'I called my father and asked for his help. He came to the island with a helicopter to pick me up, and then put me on his private jet to London.'

That was a story that Ben wanted to hear. Later…

'Do you need to call him to let him know you've arrived?'

She shook her head. 'No, he'll know that by now. The

driver who brought me will be parked up around the corner, reporting back to him.'

Parked around the corner. Ice began to trickle into Ben's veins. Maybe Arianna wasn't planning on staying for more than a few minutes. She had a large leather bag over her shoulder that could contain a change of clothes, but on the other hand, it might be full of things to read on the plane home.

'Arianna. I'm sorry to drop this on you so suddenly. But I love you. Whatever you want to do with that is fine—'

She stepped forward, putting her finger over his lips.

'You made me feel that I'm worth your love, Ben. I want to accept that gift, and love you back.'

She'd changed. Maybe as much as he had. The Arianna who felt that she had no business being saved when her brother hadn't been was accepting his love. Ben almost fell to his knees as hope tugged violently at his heart.

'I meant it when I said I needed you to save me. I can't promise that I won't want to protect you, because I love you, but Jonas doesn't need a superhero and neither do you. I've hung up my cloak, and all I want is for you to love me...'

'I always have.' She smiled. 'So what do you think? You reckon that we *will* break each other, or that we'll be stronger together? I can't let you go a second time, and so you'll be stuck with me. We'll have to face whatever comes, together.'

'That sounds wonderful. You'll be stuck with me too.' He reached forward to touch her, and then realised his hands were covered in grime and his T-shirt had grass stains all over it. Wondering if he could break away for long enough to clean himself up a bit, so that he could feel the softness of her skin beneath his fingertips, was the most delicious of conflicts.

She saw his hesitation and smiled. 'I don't care how dirty you are, Ben. I really need a hug.'

He pulled her close and she melted into his arms. This was for real. It wouldn't break apart as easily as their previous embraces, and they both knew it. Ben kissed her tenderly, feeling the hunger in her kiss and letting it flow through him like a healing salve.

'Where's Jonas?'

'Play date. Back at six.'

'Oh. Good. I mean…not good, but…' Arianna kissed him again.

'I know what you mean. He'll be pleased to see you. Right now I'm *very* pleased to see you.'

She giggled, drawing back so that she could tug his T-shirt over his head. 'I'm very pleased to see you too.' Her fingers moved to the waistband of his jeans and Ben grinned, catching her hand.

'Not so fast.' He took her bag from her shoulder, putting it down on the sofa. 'I hope you've come prepared.'

'I'm prepared for anything, Ben. Everything.'

She ran her fingers across his chest and Ben felt each muscle quiver under her touch. This was a strength he hadn't known he had. He and Arianna, together. He slipped her jacket from her shoulders and then pulled her T-shirt over her head. Her skin was just as delicious as he remembered it.

'*Everything* is going to take a very long time, Arianna.'

'A lifetime?'

He kissed her. Any moment now he was going to carry her upstairs, strip her of her clothes, taking a suitable amount of time to admire the fancy underwear that he reckoned she had on, and then maybe they'd take a shower together, before they made the sweetest love that he could imagine. But for now it was enough just to kiss her, feeling all the warmth of knowing that she loved him just as much as he loved her, and that they'd always be there to save each other.

'I'm not sure that one lifetime is going to be long enough.'

EPILOGUE

Two years later

THE CHRISTENING PARTY for Arianna and Ben's twin baby girls was in full swing. People had spilled out onto the beach, and a good number of them wouldn't be going home until the sun had set and then risen again.

Arianna nudged Ben. 'Are you seeing what I'm seeing?'

She pointed across to where the obligatory photographs were being taken, in the shade and relative quiet of the veranda. The two grandmothers had already posed, laughing and chatting together and insisting on swapping babies for even more photographs. Now her mother was cradling both babies and her father stood beside her, one hand resting on Jonas's shoulder and the other arm around his ex-wife, who was wearing a gorgeous red dress.

'Yeah. Your mother and father are looking pretty cosy these days. You think we need to put them under surveillance?'

Arianna smiled. 'Maybe. Perhaps Jonas can be our inside man and report back to us.'

Jonas would be staying with his beloved Pappous Ioannis and Yia-Yia Alexandra for two weeks at their villa in the mountains, along with Ben's parents. He was looking forward to being the centre of attention of four fond grandparents and it would give Arianna and Ben some time to spend together. After the hustle and bustle of preparing for two new babies, that would be welcome.

It hadn't always been easy, and never straightforward. Where to live, what was best for Jonas and where both Arianna and Ben could work effectively had been their first hurdle. Jonas's love of island life, and the English school on the mainland, where he could learn Greek and transition smoothly onto a Greek high school had been one deciding factor. The fact that there was a lot more left to do on the islands of Ilaria and Kantos, another. And their families got on so well that there was no question of Ben missing his parents or Jonas his grandparents, because they always had at least two invitations to stay for a while from Arianna's extended family. There was talk of them buying a place on Kantos when Ben's father retired, so that he and Arianna's father could spend their summers fishing together. Arianna's mother had confided in Ben that it was about time he slowed down a bit, and loosened his grip on his business empire.

They'd had their challenges. Ben had been required to study hard to get his Greek to a point where he could practise medicine on the islands. Arianna had experienced severe morning sickness at the start of her pregnancy, and as it had progressed the workload of the practice had fallen squarely on Ben's shoulders. Ben had clashed with Arianna's father over his plans for the large house on the island he was planning to build for them, insisting that the proceeds of the sale of his house in London made him perfectly capable of providing for his own family. Arianna had stubbornly refused to live anywhere else but her own house, and they'd come to a compromise that made everyone happy. The L-shaped extension to Arianna's house was in the style of the rest of the house, and nestled amongst lemon and orange trees that Ben had planted. Arianna's father had gifted the shaded open-air swimming pool on the other side of the property for their wedding day.

Ben had taken over responsibility for the new health centre that was being built on Kantos, which would work in the same way as the one on Ilaria, servicing both the hotel and the village. Now, his morning commute was a walk down the beach to the boat moored at the small jetty they'd constructed, so that he could take Jonas to school before he went onto work.

'How did we ever get to be this lucky?' Arianna looked around at the group of friends and family, and the idyllic setting of their home.

'I guess...we didn't rely on luck. Whatever happened, we would have made things work.' Ben put his arm around her shoulders.

'So what do you put it down to, then?'

He thought for a moment. 'A lot of talking. Some arguing.'

'Make-up sex?' She stood on her toes, whispering in his ear.

'Yeah. I'm particularly fond of that. Watch out, I may have to pick a fight with you later.' Ben grinned down at her, then fished his phone out of his pocket, answering the call.

'Don't tell me... *Surely* no one's ill, are they? Isn't pretty much everyone here?'

'Mrs Panagos. Her nephew stopped by to pick her up and she's not feeling so good. He can't find her tablets.'

Arianna rolled her eyes. 'Well, if she went to the

chemist and filled her prescriptions then she'd have them to hand when she needed it, wouldn't she?'

Ben nodded. 'Yeah, I'll have a word with her nephew and see if he can't pick them up for her. I'll be fifteen minutes, tops and I'll bring them back here with me, so we can keep an eye on her.'

'Okay. Good thought. I'll be making good use of my time while you're gone.'

'Interrogating your parents?' Ben knew how much her parents' new-found relationship meant to Arianna.

'Yes. If Jonas helps me out then fifteen minutes should be more than enough to get the full story out of them...'

Ben skirted the house, slipping out through the olive trees that bounded the property. Something made him stop and look back, and he saw Arianna. He wouldn't have thought it possible to love her any more than yesterday, and then today had dawned. Who knew what tomorrow might bring?

* * * * *

NIGHT SHIFTS WITH THE MIAMI DOC

ANN McINTOSH

MILLS & BOON

For my beloved sister, Pia, and all
South Florida medical and hospital support staff.

CHAPTER ONE

SIXTY-EIGHT-YEAR-OLD MRS. MORALES not only looked unwell, she looked terrified, too. According to her chart, she'd collapsed at home, by all indications from an arrhythmia that caused her to faint. After being examined in the ER, she'd been admitted for further tests and monitoring, but although her heart seemed to be the main concern, Dr. Regina Montgomery had her doubts.

"Ask her how long she's been suffering from the swelling in her ankles," Regina requested of the assisting nurse, who, thankfully, spoke Spanish. "And the abnormal itchiness. And ask again if she's been experiencing muscle cramps."

As nurse Amelia Jackson relayed the questions, Regina took another look at the chart, displayed on her tablet. Some of the test results had come back, all focused on heart function, but, like the emergency room doctor before her, she was wondering if heart disease was Mrs. Morales's main problem. They'd asked for a cardiology consult, but it was Regina's responsibility as internist to ensure that if the patient needed additional treatment, it was provided.

"She says the swelling started about eight months ago, but she was itching before that. Only occasional muscle cramps, though," Amelia told Regina.

All classic signs of kidney problems.

"Has she seen a nephrologist?"

That earned her a skeptical look from the nurse, but she dutifully asked the question anyway, and was met with a breathless spate of words in reply.

At the frantic tone in the elderly lady's voice, Regina looked up to see tears streaming down her wrinkled cheeks. Putting down the tablet, she grabbed a couple of tissues from the handy box beside the bed.

"It's okay, don't be upset." Trying to soothe the older woman, she placed a hand on one shaking shoulder and held out the tissues. The last thing they needed was the patient's already elevated blood pressure going higher. She turned to the nurse. "What is she saying?"

"She's scared," Amelia replied. "She's only been in the US for a year, and it sounds as though her medical care has been spotty. I don't think she trusts doctors very much."

Mrs. Morales looked from Regina to Amelia and back again, and Regina was struck by the mute appeal in her eyes. It made her wish she could speak to the older woman directly, explain that she understood.

"I get it," she said quietly, using the tissues, which Mrs. Morales seemed not to have noticed, to mop gently at her patient's cheeks. "My grandparents came to America when they were older, too, and they were the same way—only going to the doctor when the pain got too bad to bear. Tell her not to worry, that we'll take good care of her. Have you been able to contact her son?"

"Yes, but he's in Tampa, so it'll take a while for him to get back to Miami. He's a construction worker, and the group had traveled there together. He's getting on a bus as soon as he can. He also asked his wife to come to the hospital, but she has to arrange for someone to take over her shift before she can leave work."

While Amelia spoke to the patient, gesturing to Regina, Mrs. Morales reached out her hand. Regina hesitated only for an instant before taking it gently and receiving a tremulous smile in return.

While looking at the chart, Regina hadn't put on gloves, and now noticed the texture of Mrs. Morales's skin. The older lady's hand was well-worn, her fingers and palm roughened by work and age. It brought to mind walking hand in hand with Granny through Brooklyn, and with it came the sense of safety and happiness she'd experienced at the time.

How she wished she could give those sensations back to her patient. But all Regina could do was smile and give the trembling fingers a light squeeze. It was tempting to stay where she was, giving comfort, but unfortunately it wasn't possible.

She had too much work to do, and acting as a locum was no excuse to be lackadaisical.

"Please tell her I'll be checking on her test results, and I'll be back in a little while to update her."

Then, with one last squeeze, she let go of the older woman's hand, and left the room to hurry the lab for the rest of the information she needed.

Once Mrs. Morales had been transferred up from Emergency, Regina, as internist on duty, was in charge of her care. It was up to her to ensure the older lady got the appropriate treatment and saw the right specialists. Similar as it was to her usual job of intensivist, there were enough differences to keep her happy, and as she walked toward the main desk, she couldn't help noticing one of the biggest ones.

Any speculative looks she received were because of her newness, not because of her personal life.

She couldn't afford any blemish to her character, because although things had improved, as a woman, and a minority one at that, she had to be that much better than her peers to make it to the top.

And making it to the top—to Chief of Medicine—was her goal.

One unexpected and distressing moment had lowered her reputation, and she'd struggled to continue to act normally afterward.

"Take a vacation," her friend Cher had said. "By the time you get back, the rumor mill at the hospital will have something else to talk about."

But vacations weren't part of her plan. She'd never taken them, unless she needed extra study time or wanted to attend a conference. As far as she was concerned, if it didn't bolster her résumé, it was a bit of a waste.

Then she'd found a site that matched doctors with hospitals in need of locums, and signed up. Accepting a seven-week stint in Miami served two important purposes: taking her far away from San Francisco and the uncomfortable situation she'd found herself in, and showcasing her versatility. She was out of the ICU, where she usually worked, and on the wards, handling a different set of patients and diseases. The variation, and the challenge it presented, appealed to her, too.

"A change is as good as a rest," her mother always said, and after two days in her temporary position, Regina was inclined to agree.

She really felt as though a weight had been lifted off her shoulders.

Getting to the desk, she gave the nurse behind it a slight smile—the kind that showed she appreciated how important all the nurses were but was calculated to keep a professional distance.

"Could you contact the lab and ask them to put a rush on the rest of Mrs. Morales's results, please? Especially the ACR and creatinine level tests."

"Of course, Doctor."

The nurse reached for the phone, and Regina looked down at her tablet, getting prepared to look in on her next patient.

"Please contact me when the results come in," she said, already walking away.

Once she had that information, she could decide whether she needed to bring in a nephrologist or not. Until then, rounds awaited.

Dr. Mateo Herrera shifted to tuck his phone between his chin and shoulder, so he could sign the form nurse Janie Curtis held out to him.

"I don't belong here, Mateo." The sound of tears in his sister's voice wrung his heart. "Everyone is so smart and so put-together, and I'm a mess."

"None of that is true, Serena. You're one of the smartest people I know, and all those people you think have everything together are only pretending, believe me." No eighteen- or nineteen-year-old had it all together, but some were more adept at pretending than others.

"Why'd you make me come all this way to college? I bet you were glad to get me out of the house."

She was working herself up to a full-on anxiety attack, but Mateo knew getting angry would only make it worse.

"Sure I was," he said easily, letting a hint of amusement tinge his voice. "Which was why I was trying so hard to encourage you to go to UM." The University of Miami was only forty minutes away from their house, and Serena could have lived at home if she wanted to. "If I remember correctly, it was someone else who wanted to go all the way to Gainesville."

He heard Serena inhale, and waited to see if his tactic had been effective or she'd go off on him. To his relief, she sighed.

"Yeah. You're right." He could usually count on her common sense to prevail in the end, and today was no different. "But I don't think I'm going to make it here on my own."

Instead of annoying him, her words filled him with deep warmth, since they showed how strong the bond between them was. Yet, he couldn't let his protective instincts win out over the knowledge that Serena needed to spread her wings.

"Okay, listen. You've only been there for a couple of weeks. Give it your best shot, and if you still hate it that much by the time you come home for my birthday, we'll talk about you transferring."

"All right." It was grudging, but at least she sounded as though she'd gotten her frazzled emotions under control. "Oh, hell! I have to be in class in twenty minutes. Gotta go."

"Love you," Mateo said quickly, knowing her habit of hanging up before he was ready. "Call me later, if you want."

"K."

Then she was gone.

Janie gave him a sympathetic look. "Your sister's first time living away from home?"

He smiled and nodded, unsurprised that she knew who it was he was talking to, since most of the people he worked with were aware of his family's story.

"She'll settle in quickly. My daughter cried on the

phone to me every day for three weeks, and then suddenly I couldn't even get her to call me back, she was so busy and happy."

"I hope you're right," Mateo replied.

"You'll see," she said with conviction, then it was back to business. "They've called for a consult on the fourth floor." She slid a slip of paper toward him. "Should I get Dr. Timmins to go?"

Mateo glanced at his watch. He had an hour and a half before the biweekly clinic for patients with chronic kidney diseases started.

"No, I'll go." He picked up the paper and headed for the elevators, but his thoughts were still with Serena.

The child psychologist he'd consulted with eleven years ago, after his parents' deaths, had warned that of his three adopted siblings, Serena would probably have the hardest time coping. She'd been eight at the time, but unlike the other two children who'd been a part of the family for six and seven years, she'd only been adopted by Emilio and Isabella Herrera the year before. There hadn't been time for her to completely accept she was an integral part of the family, and at that age, might even try to blame herself for their deaths.

And the psychologist had been right. Serena needed more reassurance than the other two put together, but the effort had been worth it to see her turn into the beautiful young lady she'd become. Now, if she could just build up the confidence to stay at the University of Florida, he'd be happy.

As he stepped into the elevator, he pushed thoughts of his family responsibilities aside. It was hard to do, since he'd been father figure, caregiver and everything else to his three younger siblings all these years. But they were, for the most part, all grown up now, and he knew he had to start stepping back and letting them live their own lives.

Not that he'd ever stop being there for them, in whatever way they needed. To abdicate that responsibility would be like thumbing his nose at his parents and their wish to give their adopted children a happy, loving family and a good life.

They hadn't lived long enough to see their dreams come true, but Mateo was dedicated to carrying the torch for them, no matter what he had to give up to do so.

On the fourth floor, he went toward the desk to check in, pausing as he heard a voice both strange and familiar.

"Has anyone come down from Nephrology yet?"

"Not yet, Dr. Montgomery."

Montgomery? Regina Montgomery?

Something stirred, hot and low, in Mateo's belly at the name and the memories it and her voice inspired. Drawn forward by excitement and surprise, he took the couple steps necessary to see around the intervening wall to where the woman in question stood.

Wow.

It may have been eleven years since he'd last seen her, but Regina Montgomery was as gorgeous and as sexy as he remembered. Back then, he'd been one of the residents under her supervision and, as such, had to maintain a respectful professional distance. It hadn't stopped him from experiencing hard-to-contain desire each time they'd interacted.

She was tall and statuesque, elegant in a cool, untouchable type of way. Her smiles back then were considered: just enough to show she was amused or engaged, but not enough to draw you in. She'd kept everyone at a firm yet polite distance. With eyes that unusual shade of dark gold, you'd expect them to spark with sunshine, but instead, they gleamed with the hauteur of a lioness.

Everything about her had made him want to ruffle her, get her messy, make her belly-laugh—anything to break that tranquil facade.

But that wasn't all he'd dreamt of doing.

Her smooth, dark bronze skin made his fingers itch to touch. The containment, so essential to her character, had him wild to crack it open and see what lay beneath. Something about her every move, thin smile or brisk order made him want her more.

At the time he'd thought it just a young man's fantasy—lusting after a woman ten years older than him had such a puerile ring to it—but now it seemed he hadn't outgrown the impulse.

In fact, with the way his body stirred and hardened, it seemed the attraction was as strong as it had ever been.

The surprise of seeing her here in Miami sent a seismic shock wave through his system, and he drew a deep breath, pulling himself together before he moved forward.

"Dr. Regina Montgomery." Although he tried to make the words friendly and professional, he heard the hint of roughness in his tone. "Fancy seeing you here."

CHAPTER TWO

HEARING HER NAME in an unfamiliar male voice made Regina stiffen and, for some strange reason, had the hair on her nape stirring. It was difficult not to spin around immediately, but she forced herself to pause and then turn slowly, eyebrows raised.

The sight of the man striding toward her made her breath catch in her throat, even as her brain scrambled to ignore his sheer beauty and come up with his name.

But it was impossible not to take note of every little facet of his appearance. Dark hair cut in a casual, tousled style sat above a wide, intelligent brow. Striking eyes—shaded somewhere between gray and green—held a devilish twinkle. A sensuous mouth was tilted in a slightly lopsided smile, creating slashing dimples in his cheeks and making a frisson of heat skitter along her spine.

Then, like a flash, the name came to her, and forcing a small smile, she held out her hand.

"Dr. Herrera. What a pleasant surprise."

A large, warm hand engulfed hers, sending a shock of awareness up her arm, but she somehow held her smile in place and didn't pull away.

His eyebrows rose, and his smile widened. "I'm surprised you remember me. It's been a long time."

Oh, she remembered him all right. He'd been incredibly gorgeous, intelligent and personable, so much so that women in the hospital had made thinly veiled innuendos about wanting to be on the *night shift* with him. There'd been no mistaking what they'd meant, and realistically, she'd felt as though a shift in his bed wouldn't have been a bad idea. But there was no way she'd risk her reputation and goals by suggesting such a thing, or even intimating it.

Even if he'd expressed an interest, and she'd been willing to indulge, as his supervisor it would have been extremely inappropriate.

But of course, she didn't say any of that.

"I like to think I remember most of the residents I supervise," she lied mildly, loosening her fingers so he let them go. "I take it you're the nephrologist I've been waiting for?"

It seemed very important to move the conversation away from anything even remotely personal, and back to work.

"I am," he replied, that smile still on his face sending another skitter along her spine. "What do we have going on?"

She handed him the tablet, Mrs. Morales's chart already on the screen, and left him to look it over as she spoke to the nurse about another patient. It was, after all, her standard way of dealing with specialists—she provided them with the information they needed, and left them to draw their own conclusions.

Her need to focus anywhere but on Mateo Herrera had nothing to do with his looks, or the warmth swirling just beneath her skin.

Besides, he was probably married, with an equally gorgeous wife—who'd happily given up her own ambitions to become his appendage—popping out beautiful babies at respectable intervals. Somehow that image was enough to tamp down the rush of interest she felt at having those incredible eyes and lovely grin aimed her way.

Interest she had no business feeling, since she was totally and completely off men.

"You're right to be concerned." Regina looked up in time to see Mateo slide a calculator into the pocket of his lab coat as he spoke. "Let's go and look in on Mrs. Morales. I'm going to need to do a full workup on her."

She held up her hand to stop him from walking away.

"Before we go, you need to know that Mrs. Morales doesn't speak much, if any, English. Spanish only."

There went that lopsided smile again. Regina tightened her lips to stop herself from smiling back, but silly heat gathered in her chest, threatening to rise into her face.

"I'm fluent," he replied, waving her ahead of him down the corridor. "There's sometimes a bit of confusion with idioms and localized dialects, but between me and the patient, we can usually work it out."

"Great," she replied, heading off, chastising herself, despite knowing her reactions were normal. No redblooded woman could avoid being affected by this man. She was sure of it.

"That's one of the things I remember best about you—your refusal to make assumptions about anything, even whether a man named Mateo Herrera can speak Spanish or not."

Keeping her gaze firmly trained ahead to avoid looking at him, she replied, "In our line of work assumptions can kill. I'm always checking myself to make sure I'm not taking shortcuts or allowing implicit bias to throw me off track."

"I think I remember hearing you tell one of the residents that exact thing." She could hear the smile in his voice but steadfastly refused to check and see if it was reflected in his eyes. "So, when did you move to Florida?"

The change of subject surprised her, and she replied without thinking. "I haven't. I'm here as a locum for six weeks, filling in for Dr. Nguyen while she's on maternity leave."

"Hmm… Does that mean you've left Charthouse Memorial and become an itinerant doctor?"

He sounded skeptical, and Regina shot him a frowning glance but saw only curiosity in his expression.

"Would that be a bad thing?" She heard the defensiveness in her voice and cursed herself for it. What she chose to do with her life was none of his—or anyone else's—business.

"Not at all. In fact, it sounds interesting and almost idyllic. I just pictured you rising to the top somewhere, and I doubt you'd be able to do that, moving from place to place."

He'd surprised her again, because his assessment of her ambition was spot-on. Somehow hearing that made her relax her usual rigid rules regarding discussing personal matters with colleagues.

"I left Charthouse about six years ago, but I'm still in the Bay Area." Charthouse was the teaching hospital where Mateo had started his residency. She'd been offered a more lucrative position across the Bay, in Oakland, and with the opportunity for advancement, she'd taken it. "I recently decided I needed a change, but not a permanent one, so I took sabbatical leave, and here I am."

"Staving off burnout?"

There was no mistaking his curiosity now, but she'd be hung, drawn and quartered before she discussed with him her reasons for taking time off.

"Something like that," she replied, making her voice brisk and rather quelling.

"I see." They'd reached the door to Mrs. Morales's room, and Mateo took hold of the handle but didn't open it. "Well, I'd like to invite you out to dinner, as a welcome."

Oh, hell no. She hadn't come to Florida to get tangled up in any kind of relationship, even a friendly one. And if she was reading the gleam in Mateo Herrera's eyes correctly, he definitely had a different type of entanglement in mind.

So a crisp but polite "No" was what she intended to say. What came out of her mouth instead was, "With you and your wife?"

His eyebrows rose.

"I'm afraid I don't have one of those. Never got around to it."

A playboy, then. Or a liar, since she couldn't fathom why such a prime specimen of man was still on the shelf.

It would be stupid, though, to lie to her about it, since they were working in the same hospital and it wouldn't take much to check through the grapevine.

Before she could come up with a fitting response, Mateo continued, "What about you? Did you end up marrying that neurosurgeon you were dating?"

That he would remember something so trivial surprised her—and caused her unwanted but unmistakable delight.

"How on earth did you remember that?"

He shrugged, his lips quirking. "I think it was the bunches of red roses he kept filling your office with that made it stick in my mind."

A huff of amusement broke from her lips before she could stop it. "Ah, that was in the waning days of our relationship, when he was trying to convince me that marrying him, and giving up my career to have his babies, was the best thing that could happen to me."

Mateo's eyebrows almost disappeared into his hairline this time. "Did he ask if that was what you wanted?"

"Why would a neurosurgeon want to know what was going on in his girlfriend's brain?" she deadpanned, and was rewarded with Mateo's laughter.

Yet, he was still blocking the door, and it seemed that the sensual gleam in his eyes deepened.

"So you're not married?" he asked, and although neither of them had moved, he seemed closer, and the conversation far too intimate. An electric current ran between them as his eyes darkened, and it took every ounce of control not to lick her lips and to keep her face impassive.

"Never got around to it," she replied, using his own words, but giving them a clipped, almost dismissive edge.

That seemed to get through to him, since he only nodded and opened the door, standing back so she could pass.

As she did, her entire side warmed, as though from his body heat, although she knew full well it was just her heightened physical awareness. There was something about Mateo Herrera that made her decision to avoid men seem far harder than it should.

Oh, she's one cool customer.

Regina sailed past him like a queen, leaving a clean, slightly flowery scent eddying in her wake. Mateo inhaled deeply, savoring it, along with the knowledge that despite her demeanor, the attraction he felt wasn't one-sided.

He wasn't sure how he could be so certain, but he was. Trying to figure out the clues that led him to that conclusion would be an interesting exercise for later, but right now he had a patient to see.

The seduction of Regina Montgomery would have to be delayed—but he was determined it wouldn't be denied. Fate had gifted him with an opportunity he wasn't prepared to pass up.

Since the last of his siblings had moved out of the house they'd all shared, he'd been overtaken by an ebb in energy and a sense of drifting without purpose. Spending time planning out a new, more focused future hadn't stemmed the sense of lassitude hounding him.

Now he suddenly felt rejuvenated. Reinvigorated.

And it was because of the woman who'd preceded him into the room.

She seemed to embody the type of no-strings-attached adventure he needed to get him out of his present funk.

There were four beds and three patients, with Mrs. Morales in the farthest one from the door, on the right. Unlike the other two women, she was awake, and watched as Mateo pulled the curtain around her bed closed.

Then she held out her hand, and Regina took it, as though it were the most natural thing in the world.

That, too, was something he remembered from when she'd been his supervisor—her innate ability to put patients at ease, without seeming to work at it at all. She was neither jocular nor overtly friendly, but something about her calm competence spoke loudly to patients and their families alike. Seeing how she interacted with patients and how they responded to her had stuck with him and given him an ideal to aspire to. While their personalities were very different, he now realized he'd unwittingly adapted his bedside manner to achieve the same result.

Greeting the patient and introducing himself in Spanish earned him a tentative smile, but he saw Regina use her free hand to pat the old woman's, as though to comfort her.

He kept his voice soothing, and coaxed the information he needed from Mrs. Morales in small chunks, hoping to keep her calm. From the chart he knew her blood pressure and heart arrhythmia were problems, and didn't want to exacerbate them by being too pushy.

Besides, she kind of reminded him of his paternal grandmother, so she brought out the gentle side of him.

By the time he'd finished examining Mrs. Morales and gotten her history and symptoms, the elderly lady was smiling and calling him *Papito*. She even reached up and patted his cheek. Glancing at a silent Regina, he saw her fighting back a smile. Or maybe laughter.

He could hardly stop himself from grinning back.

"I've explained to her that, with her symptoms, we need to do further testing on her kidney function, and she's agreed," he said to Regina. "Until I have those results, it's impossible to know whether diminished kidney function is causing her heart problems, although it's a definite possibility."

"That was my concern, too," Regina said, giving Mrs. Morales's hand one more pat before releasing it. "I'm still waiting for Cardiology to send their recommendations, but I'd like a complete picture before I proceed."

The door from the corridor opened as Mateo was making notes, outlining the specific tests he wanted run, and he looked up when one side of the curtain was thrown open, revealing cardiologist Dr. Morgan Welk. Behind him was one of the younger cardiologists, whose expression suggested he'd rather be anywhere else but where he found himself.

Or perhaps it was the company he was being forced to keep that gave him that rather uncomfortable look. It wasn't be any surprise to Mateo, who found Welk to be an irritating bully.

It took every scintilla of professionalism Mateo had to keep his expression neutral and not allow his dislike of the older man to show.

"What are you doing here?" Welk asked, his tone aggressive. "This is a cardiac patient."

Before Mateo could reply, Regina spoke, her voice calm but with an unmistakable thread of steel running through it.

"I called for a nephrology consult on Mrs. Morales."

Welk slowly turned his gaze her way, lifting his chin, looking down his nose at her, despite the fact that he was actually shorter.

"And you are?"

"Dr. Montgomery, internist in charge of Mrs. Morales's care."

"I don't know you." Now he sounded peevish, as though having someone new in the hospital was a personal affront.

"Nor I you," she replied. She even had that cool, distancing smile still firmly affixed on her face, as though neither annoyed nor surprised by the older man's behavior. "Yet, here we are."

Welk's mouth opened and closed a couple of times, as though he could hardly believe what he was hearing.

"Now, young lady—"

"Dr. Montgomery," Regina interjected, her smile not wavering for an instant. "And you are?"

Once more Welk seemed stunned, but then, with something that sounded suspiciously like a curse under his breath, he spun on his heel and headed for the door.

"I won't have my time wasted like this," he said, over

his shoulder. "When you get your act together, let them know upstairs."

"Thank you," Regina replied, making sure he could hear her clearly. "I'll make a note on the file that Cardiology refused to examine the patient or give their input."

That stopped him in his tracks, as it would any doctor in their right mind. Just thinking about what the legal department would have to say should something like that come to light was enough to make even an ass like Welk rethink.

When Welk turned back around, his face was red, and he spoke through clenched teeth.

"That isn't the case. But I don't have time to waste, trying to work around Herrera, while he does…whatever it is he's doing."

"Not a problem," Mateo said, taking a leaf out of Regina's book and giving the older man a thin smile. "I'm finished."

Then he took his leave of Mrs. Morales, telling her he'd see her in a little while, and stepped away from the bed.

"Let me know your thoughts, please, after you reexamine Mrs. Morales." Regina spoke to Welk in the same calm way, but again the hint of steel was clear. "I've been waiting for the cardiology report."

Then, before he could do more than growl, she gave Mrs. Morales a smile and a wave, and was on her way out of the room.

Mateo was only a step behind her when she got to the door, and he held it open for her to go through.

If he'd been attracted to her before, it was nothing in comparison to how he felt now, having seen her so effortlessly and efficiently put Welk in his place. He wanted to see her away from the hospital, finally get a chance to break through that cool shell, to see what lay beneath.

Yet, having seen her handle Welk, he knew he'd have to step lightly, even when everything inside wanted to push, to insist. Even to demand.

But before he could say anything, Regina beat him to it.

"About dinner… I don't think it would be a good idea."

A casual approach seemed the best bet, although he was feeling decidedly eager to get her to himself, even if just for a while. So he gave her a bland smile.

"What's so bad about two old colleagues who haven't seen each other in years having a bite to eat and catching up?"

Her gaze searched his, and her lips tightened just a little at the corners.

Then she shrugged. "When you put it like that…"

Yes!

CHAPTER THREE

BY THE EVENING after her first seven-day shift, Regina felt as though she had a handle on the way the hospital worked. Pouring herself a glass of wine, she stepped out onto the tiny balcony of her executive rental and subsided into a chair.

Taking a deep breath of the warm night air, she let it out again on a sigh. Back in San Francisco, the temperature would be in the fifties—if they were lucky—but here in Miami it was warmer, and dry. She'd laughed to herself, hearing some of her new workmates complain about the January cold. Apparently, anything under eighty-five degrees was an excuse to pull on a sweater, or even a coat.

She was fine with a light cardigan, and was even barefooted, as was her habit at home.

Stretching her tired neck muscles, she tried to relax and let go of the stress that had built up during the week. Although the schedule was lighter here than back in California—seven days on call, then seven off, rather than two weeks on and two off—getting used to a new routine was taxing. As was getting called out three of the seven nights, when a patient needed her urgent attention.

Even building a working rapport with the staff she interacted with the most took its toll, but she felt as though she'd achieved that.

Well, except with Morgan Welk, who seemed bent on trying to undermine her whenever he could. It didn't bother her, since she'd learned, from a very young age, how to deal with people like him. When faced with that kind of opposition, she became more determined, and made sure to ruthlessly cross her *t*'s and dot her *i*'s, so as to never be found lacking.

The only real fly in the ointment, as far as she was concerned, was the upcoming dinner with Mateo Herrera, which was scheduled for the next evening.

Every time she thought about it, an internal battle ensued.

Her sense of self-preservation told her not to go.

But her adventurous side, which she hardly ever let out to play, wanted to see where this all would lead.

Oh, he'd tried to make it sound merely casual and friendly, but Regina hadn't been fooled. The truth was in his eyes, which gleamed darkly whenever he looked at her, and seemed to make all kinds of naughty promises.

Promises she was both eager to take him up on, and a little afraid of, too.

Or maybe she was just overthinking? After all, he was at least ten years her junior. Why on earth would he be interested in an older woman, when he could have his pick of all the younger ones?

So she should go, and they would have a nice dinner, and that would be that.

And if it went any other way, she'd just shut it all down.

That was also something she was very good at—setting boundaries and steadfastly disallowing anyone to cross them.

But each time she'd had to interact with him, she found herself feeling slightly off-kilter.

And excited.

It had taken her all of three days to actually admit that to herself, but her physical reactions whenever he was around couldn't be ignored. Yet, hadn't she decided to cut men, with their ridiculous demands and deceit, out of her life?

That decision had been firm and definitive, brought about by the kind of situation no self-respecting woman ever wanted to be caught in. And even four months later she couldn't shake the shame and anger of being accosted by a strange female in the hospital parking lot and accused of being a home-wrecker.

Regina had been speechless. She really hadn't known Kevin was married. In the ten months they'd been seeing each other, it hadn't even crossed her mind to doubt he was as single as he'd claimed to be. They'd slowly been getting closer to the point where she'd have considered a commitment, which he professed to want from her, but she'd been in no rush. First, she was studying for her master's degree in hospital management, then she'd been putting in a lot of hours to position herself for the next promotion she wanted.

Only afterward, in hindsight, had she realized how easy she'd made it for him to perpetrate his deception.

With her work schedule and complete focus on the upward trajectory of her career, she'd been a prime target. He canceled on her? No problem. She'd just moved on to the next thing on her to-do list, which was always long, and meticulously written down. With her sights set on the long term, she was too busy to worry about a few missed dates.

He'd completely fooled her, and her takeaway from the experience was—no more relationships. No more messy interactions that would detract from her plans or open her up to ridicule. Being the cynosure of all eyes at work because she'd made a stupid mistake had become too much, even for someone who normally paid no attention to what others thought.

Which was why it annoyed her to no end to find Mateo this attractive.

To feel her insides melt and heat and quicken whenever he was around, as she wondered what kind of lover he'd be.

Thank goodness for a well-developed poker face and the ability to keep her feelings to herself. Those attributes had served her well, although occasionally she'd caught him looking at her in a way that suggested he was seeing right through her facade. And what he'd gleaned was as exciting to him as he was to her.

After agreeing to go to dinner with him, Regina had given him her address and phone number, and expected him to call or text sometime over the next few days. Most of the men she'd dated had gone for the hard sell: calling all the time, laying a foundation to get her to sleep with them, treating her like a challenge or competition.

Instead, there'd been radio silence, leaving her to stew about whether Mateo was at all interested in her.

She couldn't remember feeling this way about any other man.

If she were made of less stern stuff, Regina mused to herself as she sipped her wine, she'd be terrified.

There was no way to know which way her dinner with Mateo would go. He'd been completely professional whenever they interacted in the hospital, which was almost daily, as they'd worked together on diagnosing and treating four patients, including Mrs. Morales.

It was a good thing they'd come up with a diagnosis and treatment plan for the elderly lady before her daughter-in-law had arrived. The younger Mrs. Morales was a firecracker, and had made it clear she was there to take charge of her mother-in-law's care going forward.

Regina was glad to see the obvious affection between the two women, and the gentle way the younger woman treated the older. And when Mateo came into the room, her patient waved toward him and called him *Papito*, which made her daughter-in-law laugh.

When Regina had asked Mateo what it meant, he'd looked a little sheepish, and the tips of his ears got adorably red.

"It's just a silly nickname," he'd said, trying to sound dismissive.

"But what does it *mean*?" She wasn't sure why she couldn't let it go, when it was clearly not something he wanted to discuss.

"Um, strictly translated, *Little Daddy*."

She'd bitten the inside of her cheek so as not to laugh at the grudging admission.

When she'd fought for and won back her composure, she'd asked, "Do you get those kinds of nicknames often?"

It had been on the tip of her tongue to actually call him that, but she'd restrained herself at the last minute. It felt too intimate to tease him that way, and the last thing she needed was to get even friendlier with him.

"Occasionally. Now, about her treatment schedule…"

Letting him off the hook was harder than she liked. And she'd subsequently had to stop herself from calling him *Papito* a couple of times thereafter.

There was something about him that brought out her lighter side, and, coupled with her physical attraction toward him, it made him all the more dangerous.

Sighing again, she took another sip of wine and then

lifted her face up to let the night air flow across her overly warm skin. Just thinking about him made her hot and jumpy, and she searched for some justification that didn't involve wanting—quite desperately—to sleep with him.

It was, she decided, just a side effect of all she'd been through, and being in a strange place. A place that seemed to hum with electricity unlike any she was used to. Redolent with a sort of carefree, beach vibe on one hand, and the frenetic energy of a racing, hustling city on the other.

Mateo Herrera was just one more facet of a brief change that had, understandably, given her usually work-focused, driven life a shake-up.

But in the final analysis, nothing that happened here in Miami was going to have a lasting impact on the life she'd mapped out. She wasn't planning on sleeping with Mateo, or on possibly opening herself up to the same kind of gossip and ugliness she'd fled San Francisco to get away from.

If she just reminded herself of that and kept her eye on her long-term goals, it would all work out fine.

Lifting her glass, she silently toasted her own determination, before tipping the last of the wine into her mouth.

Nothing—and definitely no *man*—was going to stand in the way of her achieving her goals.

Not even one as delectable as Mateo.

Mateo pulled into the parking lot of Regina's building on the night of their dinner and drove under the portico. She'd told him she'd meet him in the lobby, but traffic had been lighter than he expected and he was fifteen minutes early.

He wished he'd timed it better, since sitting in the car, waiting, gave him far too much time to think. His nerves were jangling, his pent-up excitement tightening his muscles and making his mouth dry.

It was a while since he'd been on a date, but that wasn't the problem.

What made it nerve-racking was that it was a date with Regina, a woman who made him ravenous each time he looked at her, and brought out in him a fierce, almost feral, desire.

Whenever he saw or thought about her, his brain seemed to freeze, to stumble over itself, even as his body reacted in far more carnal ways.

Waiting for her to appear had anticipation tingling through his body, and made him feel like a teenager again.

It wasn't a comfortable sensation in the slightest.

He couldn't recall feeling like this on past dates. Not that he'd had time to do much dating while raising his siblings.

At first, he'd thought that once they grew up and things settled down, he'd have time to go back to his old life. Of course, he was wrong. As a nominal single parent, things had just gotten more complicated. There was a constant round of school and extracurricular events he had to attend, as well as making sure he was keeping them on track scholastically and emotionally. Even as they became teenagers and wanted to do their own thing, he realized he couldn't release the reins just yet. In fact, to him, that had been the most critical time.

Those early teen years were when so many young lives went off the tracks, and it was his responsibility to make sure they all stayed on the straight and narrow, and were happy.

Now he was free—or as free as he'd ever be—and it seemed he was sorely out of practice when it came to women. The few casual relationships he'd been able to slip in without disrupting his home life apparently hadn't prepared him for this.

But he was probably just being silly, he told himself, as he glanced at his watch. While he was certain of his electric attraction to her, he wasn't 100 percent sure it was reciprocated. And he knew, for a fact, that if Regina Montgomery decided there would be nothing between them, he couldn't change her mind.

She was too determined a woman, and he was too much of a gentleman. Strong-arm tactics weren't in his nature, and he had no intention of adding them to whatever small dating repertoire he still possessed.

They'd probably have dinner, chat about inconsequential things, and that would be that. Not that he wouldn't make his interest known, but no matter how badly he wanted her, he'd make sure to leave the decision on what happened completely up to her.

He'd been watching the lobby, and each time the elevator doors opened his heart skipped a beat. Just as he glanced at his watch again, he saw movement out of the corner of his eye and looked up.

This time his heart not only stuttered but seemed to turn right over, leaving him breathless.

She was absolutely stunning.

Her electric blue long-sleeved top wrapped across her shoulders and under her breasts, hugging every curve and making her waist look tiny. The tantalizing hint of cleavage had him wanting to kiss all the way along it and down, so as to discover the mysteries lying below. A silky skirt in vibrant colors flowed around her legs and clung enticingly to her thighs as she walked. High, strappy sandals completed the sexy ensemble, and her hips swung with each long stride.

It wasn't just her looks that kept him entranced. The way she carried herself—so proudly, regally—made the need inside burn hotter. He was totally enraptured, frozen where he sat, his heart pounding, blood racing through his veins like lava.

Then she paused, looking out through the glass, reaching up to touch her hair, as though to make sure the long waves were still in place. She normally wore her hair up, and Mateo's fingers itched to tunnel through it, rub her scalp until she purred.

He bit back a groan, annoyed at his reaction.

This is ridiculous.

Tearing his gaze away, he reached for the handle of the car door and made himself open it. Wasn't it just a few moments ago he was calling himself a gentleman? Time to get his head on straight and start acting like one, rather than a sex-starved teenager.

As he got out of the car, she saw him, and although her face didn't light up the way he'd have liked, a little smile tipped her lips. And it was a more relaxed, natural one, than the thin, distancing smile she usually gave.

He got to the door to the apartment building just before she did, and when she pressed the lever to unlock it, he held it open for her.

"Hi," she said, sailing past him and leaving a sweet waft of perfume behind. It went straight to his head, like scotch. "I hope you weren't waiting too long."

"Not at all. And I have to say, you look very nice."

Of course, she looked way more than just nice, but he knew better than to be too effusive. He'd seen the way she coolly cut down any comment that even hinted at flattery or kissing up.

His comment still earned him a slanted, sideways

glance over her shoulder, as he reached out to open the passenger door.

"Thank you," she replied, rather wryly, as she slid gracefully into the seat. "I wasn't sure where we were going, so I hope I'm dressed appropriately."

He bent to tuck the end of her skirt properly into the car so it wouldn't get caught in the door, bringing their faces almost level. This close, her beauty stole his breath, but it was her gleaming, lioness eyes that caught and held him.

Was it his imagination, or was there more than just amusement in those molten depths?

"No matter where we go, you're dressed appropriately," he replied.

"So it's the hotdog stand, then?"

Now there was no mistaking her teasing, irrespective of her dry tone. It was there in her gaze and the upward curve of her gorgeous, sensual lips.

He chuckled, wanting to kiss the smile off her mouth, but forcing himself to straighten instead.

"How did you know that's my favorite spot in Miami?" he asked. "I made a reservation for the bench closest to the cart."

"Lovely," came her swift reply. "As long as they serve the dogs with sauerkraut, I'm happy."

"What?" He feigned outrage. "Not on your life. This is chili country, lady."

Light laughter greeted his statement just before he shut her door, and he was still chuckling as he rounded the hood of the car. The silly levity made the evening feel less fraught, although the laughter did nothing to quell his desire for Regina.

If anything, her quirky sense of humor intensified it,

even though nothing in her demeanor led him to think she was interested in him physically.

Either way, he thought, as he opened his own door, the evening should be fun.

And he was content with that.

CHAPTER FOUR

REGINA SETTLED BACK against the soft leather seat and smiled ruefully to herself.

Although she'd dithered back and forth a bit while trying to decide what to wear, in the end she'd dressed for seduction—wearing a blouse that showcased her boobs, and a skirt that tended to outline her legs as she walked. Everything she had on, down to her silky, lacy lingerie, was carefully chosen to scream *Sex!*

Just when she'd decided a little fun and games with the delectable doctor would be okay, she wasn't sure. All she knew was that at some point the realization had struck—this might be the last time she had a chance to totally let loose without fear of the consequences. And she figured she might as well let him know straight up.

And what was Mateo's reaction?

You look very nice.

She had to bite the inside of her cheek not to laugh out loud.

So much for going for the obvious.

Almost even more annoying was how incredible he looked, and her reaction to seeing him get out of the car.

Used to him being in scrubs, which he made look ridiculously yummy, she found that seeing him dressed for the evening gave her an even better appreciation of his good looks and fine body. His white linen shirt made his shoulders and chest seem even wider than usual, and his dark dress pants showed off powerful thighs.

Her heart had trip-hammered, and a surge of heat rushed through her, settling deep in her belly. It wasn't like her to have such a visceral response to a man, and it had taken her aback. Then she'd reminded herself that she'd spent the last week thinking about him and wondering whether there might be something about to happen between them.

Well, since he'd just said she looked *nice*, she could relax and put that thought aside. If he were interested, she was sure he'd be more explicit with his compliments. Most of the men she'd come into contact with were.

Yet, his nonchalance made her tension dissipate, and she decided to simply enjoy the evening. At least it seemed they shared a similar, ridiculous sense of humor, so that would make things easier, although why she felt comfortable sharing that with him was debatable. Only her closest friends were privy to that side of her.

Not wanting to go down that road mentally, she asked, "So where is this hotdog stand we're going to anyway?"

They'd stopped at a red light, and he turned to give her a grin.

"Over on Miami Beach. It has a really nice outdoor seating area with a view of the beach, and hopefully it won't be too cool to sit out there. Sometimes they have a live band, too."

He went on to explain that the restaurant was owned by a famous Miami power couple who'd translated their musical success into a number of lucrative businesses.

"Sometimes she even comes out and sings with the band."

"That would be cool," she said as they got on the highway. "I love her voice."

Just before he could answer, his phone rang, and since it was paired with his car, the name *Serena* flashed on the screen set into the dashboard.

Hmm... Who's that?

"Excuse me," Mateo murmured, before connecting the call. "Hey. What's up?"

"Are you at home?"

The voice sounded young, and the question seemed loaded, so Regina couldn't help watching Mateo out of the corner of her eye, waiting to see how he reacted.

There was no change at all in his demeanor as he responded, "No, I'm not."

"Darn it." Serena's disgruntlement was clear. "I can't find my white, fleece-lined hoodie, and wanted you to look to see if I left it there."

Curiouser and curiouser.

What was the relationship between Mateo and this Serena? Clearly a close one, and the wave of anger and, strangely, betrayal that washed through her made the breath hitch in her suddenly tight chest.

"I know that's not the only warm hoodie you have. We bought a bunch before you left."

"But that's my favorite."

"Unless you've undergone a radical change in habits since leaving home, I suggest you dig through the pile of laundry in your room. It's probably there."

The sound that came though the speaker was clearly a huff, and Regina saw Mateo's eyebrows contract. Then his lips twitched in an abbreviated smile.

"Am I wrong about the pile of clothes?" he asked, letting his amusement bleed over into voice.

After a little silence, Serena sighed. "No."

"Okay, go look there. And if you still can't find it tomorrow, let me know and I'll look in your room."

Another sigh. "Okay."

"Good girl," he said, his gentle tone somehow going straight to Regina's heart. "Talk to you tomorrow. Love yah."

"Wait. Where are you anyway? What are you doing?"

"None of your business," Mateo replied, putting on his indicator, signaling his intention to exit the highway. "Bye."

He disconnected the call just as they were going down the ramp, and Regina could see the still-tender smile on his lips.

"Sisters," he said, ruefully. "Terminally nosy."

Ah, that explained it. Some of it anyway.

"I wouldn't know," she admitted. "I don't have any."

Mateo shot her a glance. "Brothers?"

"Nope. I'm an only child, and now glad of it."

He chuckled, then changed the subject, asking her how her first week at the hospital had gone, leaving her with a bunch of questions she wasn't sure how, or whether, to ask.

Why was his sister calling him about her jacket, rather than their mother?

How old was his sister anyway? Sounded like there was a big age difference.

And did this mean that Mateo—a grown man in his midthirties, at least—still lived at home?

Okay, there were several cultures that expected, even encouraged, their young people to stay in the family home, some even after they married. Was that the case with him, and if so, how did he stand it?

At eighteen Regina had fled her parents' home and never looked back. There was no way she'd have been able to continue living under her father's thumb, being told she'd never amount to anything more than a vessel to carry some man's children. She'd refused to be broken by his outdated and insulting behavior up until the end of high school, but it had gotten harder and harder not to start believing him.

No. The only way to make something out of her life had been to hightail it out of there and succeed in her chosen profession—thereby overcoming her early upbringing.

Even after her father died, it never occurred to Regina to go back home and live with her mom, or have her mother come to San Francisco. She doubted that even crossed her mother's mind, either, since they weren't particularly close.

Clearly, Mateo must have been far luckier in the parent department. But although she tried not to judge, she couldn't help mentally shaking her head. His living at home just seemed so incongruous.

Seemingly, behind that masculine exterior lay a mama's boy!

Yet, even as she had the thought, she knew she didn't actually believe it. No matter his living arrangements, Mateo was definitely his own man.

"How are you finding the schedule? Is it what you're used to?"

His question pulled her out of her contemplations, and she replied, "It's easier, in a way. I'm used to two weeks on call, and two off, and dealing with ICU patients tends to lead to more callouts or nights spent at the hospital. This week I only had to go in a few times for emergencies."

"So what do you plan to do with your time off while you're here?"

"I have some developmental courses I need to get done

before the end of the year, so I'll probably buckle down to those."

He shook his head, those sensual lips coming together in an amused little twist.

"The end of the year, and you're thinking about them now, in January? How about sightseeing, or having some fun somewhere new?"

"It's not a vacation," she said, hearing the defensiveness in her tone. "My time is better served focusing on my professional advancement."

"You say vacation like it's a dirty word."

His amusement had her looking away, out the window. They were driving over a causeway, lights glinting on the water of Biscayne Bay. Somehow the beauty of it brought a sense of melancholy.

"I don't take a lot of them." Unwilling to elaborate, she left it there.

"All the more reason to make good use of the time here," he said easily. "There's so much to do and see within a couple of hours of Miami, it would be a shame to come all this way and not experience some of what's on offer."

Regina shrugged. "I'll see if there's anything that piques my interest."

From her peripheral vision, she saw him slant her a look, but he didn't pursue the conversation any further, instead starting to point out various interesting landmarks as they arrived in the trendy Miami Beach community.

At the restaurant, they were ushered through the sleek, stylish bar and indoor area, and onto the patio. Here, casual elegance was the byword, and the piped music was low enough that the sound of waves crashing on the shore could be heard above it.

"That cold front that came through a few days ago is still affecting the sea," Mateo said as he held out her chair for her. "Listen to those waves."

Regina couldn't help laughing lightly. "Those couple of days when it passed through, you'd have thought it was snowing, the way some of my colleagues were behaving. One came in dressed in a wool coat, scarf and knit cap."

He chuckled with her, laughter lighting his face and making his eyes sparkle.

"We Floridians take our warm weather very seriously, and make a huge stink if it's disrupted. I swear that's one of the reasons my sister has been fussing about wanting to come home. She's at college in Gainesville, and the temperature there was at least ten degrees lower than here."

He'd opened the door to that particular conversation, and Regina couldn't help wanting to walk through.

So after they'd ordered drinks, she asked, "How old is your sister?"

"Serena? She's nineteen. It's her first year at college, and she's having a hard time settling in. She has some social anxiety and self-esteem issues, so I'm trying, as best I can, to help her work through them and be able to stay where she is, rather than transfer back here."

Difficult to know the right questions to ask, so instead, Regina said, "It sounds like you're a very involved brother."

He looked up from perusing the menu, and his brows came together slightly, just for a moment, and then he gave a wry smile.

"I guess you don't know my family story, but I've been guardian for my three youngest siblings for over a decade. They were the reason I gave up my residency in San Francisco and moved back here, after my parents died in a plane crash."

Her heart clenched in sympathy. Despite the time that had passed, she could still hear the sorrow in his voice.

"No," she said softly. "I didn't know. I'm sorry about your parents."

"Thank you, but it's okay. Well, long enough ago that I've gotten used to them being gone, although I definitely miss them every day, especially when one of the youngsters has a problem and I have to figure out the best way to deal with it."

Still trying to figure out the age gap, she asked, "How many children did your parents have?"

"Six. Three biological and, later, when we older ones were teenagers and getting ready to go to college, they adopted Ben, Micah and then Serena." His smile was tender and a little wistful as he continued, "Mom always said that we, as a family, had a lot to offer, but I think they adopted because she just really loved mothering. Lola, Cristóbal and I were all becoming independent, and didn't need that as much anymore, and she missed it."

"So when your parents passed away, you stepped in."

She wasn't surprised by the story, really. It was something she could definitely see him doing.

"It made sense. Lola had just gotten her dream job with a publisher in New York, and Cristóbal was working as a geologist with an oil company, so he was away more than he was home. I could relocate and rearrange my life without too much fuss."

Relocate and rearrange.

The words stood out to her and left her wondering just how much he'd given up to take up the mantle of guardian for his young siblings.

Did he have to rethink his specialty, knowing some were more labor-intensive than others?

What kind of social life had he been able to enjoy, with three kids to look after?

How had he managed, suddenly being thrust into the role of father figure?

Yet, those weren't things she was comfortable asking, so she kept all the questions she had bubbling inside to herself.

Instead, she simply said, "That must have been incredibly difficult for you—dealing with your grief and having to adjust to being de facto parent, too."

He looked back down at his menu, his expression calm, but he also shrugged one shoulder, as though in dismissal.

"It was what needed to be done, and what my parents would have wanted—no, expected—me to do. I have no regrets." Then he glanced up at her and smiled, saying, "So do you see anything that catches your fancy?"

She turned her attention to the menu, but she found herself staring blankly at it, consumed by a rare, tender emotion she had no name for.

This Mateo was a departure from the man she'd thought she was going out with, and she wasn't sure how to handle that revelation.

Instead of the drool-worthy hunk she was considering seducing, now she saw the quietly strong, truly admirable person. A man of stature, who'd shouldered responsibilities others would have run away from.

And as to that question he'd asked, about whether she saw anything she fancied...if she answered honestly, it would be to say, *Yes, you.*

Pulling herself together, she finally got down to picking something to eat, but a swirl of conflicting emotions kept battering her insides, and she wasn't sure what to make of them.

Part of her wished she could just ignore it all and enjoy a lovely dinner in this romantic spot without giving their conversation, and her feelings about it, another thought. But she knew herself well enough to admit that wasn't possible, and the damage had been done.

Mateo Herrera had not only gone up more than a few notches in her estimation but had also increased her attraction to him apace.

CHAPTER FIVE

MATEO LEANED BACK in his chair, replete from the delicious meal. Relaxed in a way he couldn't recall being for a long time.

It felt good to have adult conversation on a Friday night without worrying about getting home. Getting used to this new way of living was taking some time, but having Regina's company made it seem effortless, and well worthwhile.

The sense of loss he'd experienced when Serena left home had taken him by surprise. His older siblings had expressed their opinion that at least now Mateo could have a life of his own, one not predicated on the other kids' needs, and at first he'd agreed. But then reality had set in.

Almost everything, including his work schedule, had revolved around his siblings. With the immediate responsibility gone, he'd been adrift—perhaps even a little depressed.

But he was too young to have empty-nest syndrome, wasn't he? And it wasn't as though Ben, Micah and Serena didn't still need him. Hell, he got calls from one or the other, or all three, almost daily. Although they were all young adults now, he was aware of being the linchpin of the family—the one everyone knew they could count on to be there, no matter what.

Sometimes he thought perhaps he was being egotistical, but the others had said much the same at various times over the last few years.

That they were glad he'd held on to the house their parents had lived in, so they could always come back home.

Or how grateful they felt to have him to talk to, or ask advice of.

Several times a year they all got together for birthdays, Thanksgiving and Christmas, always at the house in Miami, and it was during those times that Mateo felt the warmth of his parents' love most keenly.

His mother and father may be gone, but the family they'd built had survived, and that was the most important thing.

But an evening like this, spent with a beautiful and intelligent woman, made him all too aware of what he'd been missing while holding it all together.

They'd talked about all kinds of interesting topics, and, with some judiciously placed questions, he'd learned quite a bit about her. One of those things was just how ambitious she was, and her complete focus on her job.

"You did a degree in business, and then a master's in hospital management?" he'd asked, in total disbelief. "When did you have the time?"

"Well, I made the time," she'd replied, giving him a small smile. "But remember, I didn't have three kids to take care of, or much of a social life, either."

"Was the sacrifice worth it?"

She'd looked down at her plate for a moment, as though either dismissing or considering his words. Mateo realized which it was, when she met his gaze again.

"It will be, when I become the first black female Director of Medicine at the hospital."

There wasn't a hint of hesitation in what she said, or any doubt that it would, indeed, happen.

The urge had been there to question her confidence, but there was no way to do it without being rude. And it wasn't as though he didn't believe she could do it; he absolutely knew that she could. But there were hurdles ahead of her that he knew were out of her hands, and he couldn't help wondering if she had taken them into consideration.

Then she'd said the most telling thing of all.

"When I set my mind to something, nothing stands in my way. And opposition only makes me more determined."

She'd glanced down again, as though considering whether to say more, and he knew he had to respond. He wanted to understand her better, learn what made her tick.

"It's a good way to be," he admitted. "Not many people have that ability, and they crumble under pressure."

Her nod was curt, and her lips tightened fractionally.

"When they do, they give up their dreams, rather than fighting for them."

"Sounds as if you're speaking from experience."

Those lioness eyes suddenly seemed fiercer than usual, but then they softened with a flash of what he interpreted as sadness.

"My father didn't believe women should be educated, or that his wife should work. My mother wanted to be a lawyer, and she already had been accepted to law school when they met, but he dissuaded her from going back once they'd agreed to marry." She shook her head. "I decided at a very young age not to follow in her footsteps,

and when he tried to browbeat me into looking for a husband right after high school, I left home."

Her words stunned him and made his chest ache.

"How did you manage?"

She shrugged, but he could see the tension in the stiff
set of her shoulders.

"My grandmother took me in, and I worked my ass
off to go to college, and then to medical school. I refused
to doubt I could do it, even though my father said it was
impossible."

Then she smiled and visibly relaxed.

"And after my father passed away, my mother went
to law school after all. She was almost sixty when she
graduated, but now she's an advocate for disadvantaged
kids in Brooklyn."

"That's amazing," he said. "You must be really proud
of her."

"I am."

It had been a sobering discussion. One that made him
even more aware of how lucky he'd been in life. His
father had amassed a fair amount of money in oil ex-
ploration, and his parents had always been totally and
completely supportive of their children's ambitions.

It would have never occurred to either of them not to
be encouraging and uplifting.

And the insight into another facet of Regina's personality added a new layer to the thrum of awareness he constantly felt being in her company, giving it a new depth.

Now, as she paused in the act of eating her dessert and
watched the band setting up on the low, beachside plat-
form, he gazed at her clear-cut profile, trying to discern
what it was that attracted him so.

Yes, she was beautiful, and carried herself with almost regal poise, but that in itself didn't explain his over-

whelming interest. Her razor-sharp intellect certainly contributed, yet also was just a part of the equation.

Then she turned to him and said, in that cool, contained way she had, "It's a shame they're just setting up to play when we're about to leave."

It struck him then, as it had in the past.

He had an overwhelming desire to ruffle her, break through the barriers she placed between them, and see the real woman behind the wall.

Oh, she'd probably say that what he saw was who she was, but now he knew, for a fact, that there were parts of her securely hidden away, and he wanted to see them on full display.

There had been a flash of that other persona in the way she'd taken Mrs. Morales's hand, as though it were second nature.

And another glimpse when she'd spoken about her parents, and the latent pain had so briefly been revealed.

Even the way she'd just spoken, distancing herself from whatever wish she may have to stay and hear the music.

At work she was forthright and fearless, but outside of it there was a subtle subtext of denying her own desires and emotions, as though to indulge them in any way would be a weakness.

"We could have a coffee," he said, catching the waiter's eye. "And at least hear a couple songs."

For an instant he thought she was going to refuse, but as the waiter approached, she said, "I think I'd like that."

As the waiter walked away again to get their drinks, Regina glanced to the left, over his shoulder, and her eyes widened.

"Is that...?"

He followed her gaze, in time to see the owner of the

bar greeting a few people near the door leading to inside the restaurant. The famous singer smiled, exchanging a few words with the customers at each table as she passed.

"It is, indeed," he replied to Regina, unable to hold back his smile when he saw her amazed expression. Even she wasn't immune to being starstruck. "And it looks as though she's making the rounds. You might even get to meet her."

"You wait until I tell my friend Cher about this," she said, regaining her poise, but smiling wider than he'd seen her do before. "We used to belt out her songs in the basement when we were young."

It took a few minutes for the singer to get to their table, and when she did, her gaze tracked from Regina to Mateo, and back again.

"Good evening," she said, in her distinctive, slightly husky voice. "I hope you're having a good time here with us?"

"It's been wonderful." You'd never know from Regina's cool smile and calm voice that she'd just been geeking out over the other woman's presence. "Thank you."

"Will you be singing with the band tonight?" Mateo asked, hoping the answer would be in the affirmative. Hearing some of the songs she used to sing with her friend would make the evening all the more special for Regina, and knowing that made him bold enough to pose the question.

The singer gave him a bright smile.

"I've been thinking about it," she said. "If I do, will you promise to get up and dance?"

"Of course, if my lady agrees," he replied, and gained himself a little wink.

They both looked at Regina, who, after a brief hesitation, shrugged and smiled slightly.

"Why not?"

"Then I will," the Diva said, casting a knowing eye over their table, just as the waiter returned with their coffee. "By the time you've finished those, I should be ready."

When she'd moved on to the next table, Regina lifted her coffee cup but paused with it a few inches from her lips. "Do you even know how to dance to eighties music?"

"Nope," he replied, mirroring her actions and taking a sip of his coffee. "But I'll do my best not to embarrass you."

Her eyebrows rose slightly, and she shook her head. "I won't be the one embarrassed," she replied, with her customary insouciance.

And as Mateo chuckled in agreement, he also thought he was beginning to understand how to deal with Regina Montgomery's wall of reticence.

No pushing, no forcefulness. Make it her decision, always, and see where things led.

Not the easiest of paths for a man used to getting his own way a lot of the time, but one he would stick to, in the hopes of getting what he really wanted.

Regina Montgomery, naked in his bed, crying out with pleasure.

Regina sipped her coffee in silence, her gaze firmly fixed on Mateo's face. Torn between amusement and surprise, she didn't know whether to laugh or frown.

So she did neither.

Instead she tried to figure out his mindset from his expression.

She'd never countenanced being bossed around, and had quite a bit of experience with men who tried to do just that. Most of the time, men tried to push her to do what *they* wanted when she was reluctant. And the approach was either an aggravating macho shove, or a smug *I know what's best for you*.

Nothing got her back up quite like feeling as though she was considered an onlooker in her own life, unable to make the decisions that were best for her. At times like that she beat a hasty retreat, or administered a verbal smackdown guaranteed to let the other person know she wasn't up for it. At all.

Yet, she also wasn't used to being deferred to in quite this way. At no point tonight had she felt him exerting his masculinity, or acting as though to prove who wore the pants. Yet, he was no wimp, either, and their conversations had been spirited and lively, with both of them sticking to their guns when appropriate.

It was an ingrained impulse, this need to question his character and motivations. Unfair, perhaps, but necessary. She knew she wasn't imagining the attraction swirling between them, but past experience told her to be guarded, and watch out for the inevitable domineering traits to surface.

So she'd watch and wait, and enjoy herself in the meantime. The singer they'd just met was best known for a series of fast-paced pop hits of the eighties and nineties, and Regina had no objection to an energetic turn on the dance floor.

It would also be a great way to see Mateo in motion, too.

As she sipped her coffee, she looked forward, if she were honest, with a fair amount of anticipation to see what would come next.

The evening had been enjoyable, even though she'd found herself opening up to Mateo in ways she normally wouldn't. Speaking about her parents was something she rarely did, except with her oldest and closest friends. Yet, talking to him was so easy she'd hardly hesitated. He had a way of looking at her that made her feel see and heard, in the best possible way.

Perhaps even a little bit understood, although that, too, might just be an act.

The band started up, playing an instrumental rendition of a current hit, the upbeat song seemingly setting the stage for their boss's turn at the microphone. As the song was ending, Regina saw the Diva making her way up on stage, and the crowd all clapped and cheered.

Mateo smiled, and when the noise calmed down slightly, he leaned closer and asked, "Are you ready?"

Regina didn't think she was: not for the dance, and not for him, but she nodded anyway and took his hand when he held it out. As he led her away from the table, she was aware of some eyes turning their way, but most people were focused on the woman at the mic, and Regina paid no attention to the others. They didn't concern her.

But what *did* concern her was the fact that when the band started playing again, it wasn't one of the singer's dance hits, but one of her sultry, sexy ballads.

And the way Mateo looked down at her as they stopped at the edge of the dance floor, snagging her gaze and refusing to let it go, the gleam in his eyes making her heart beat an erratic tattoo.

She expected him to pull her close, but instead he simply squeezed her hand, and Regina found it was she who moved toward him and into his waiting arms.

Again he disconcerted her, by keeping a bit of distance between them as he placed his hand on the small of her back and began to move to the music.

Oh, the man could dance!

No rent-a-tile, as her granny used to call it, when she'd

see people locked together on the dance floor, hardly moving. Instead he was master of the smooth, luscious sway and step, his only guidance to her coming from the light movement of his hand on her back, and the gentle motions of the other hand, holding hers.

As they swept across the floor, their bodies brushed occasionally, lighting sparks to flash and sizzle beneath her skin. Regina realized she'd melted into the dance, was letting him set the pace and increase the elaborateness of the steps, and following him with complete trust.

Ceding to his calm, gentle, yet completely masterful control.

How crazy to feel secure and aroused by it all, at the same time.

To feel desire building, just as the singer's voice built with each repetition of the chorus.

To have heat—which had nothing to do with exertion—grow throughout her body, until she was all but aflame.

No longer able to hold his gaze, she let hers fall away, realizing her mistake when it dropped to his mouth.

Those lips, always sensual, were now firm, yet even sexier than before.

They seemed the embodiment of the same control he was now exerting over her body, as he led her through the most erotic dance she'd ever had.

And how she stopped herself from leaning just those couple of inches necessary and kissing him senseless, she would never know.

CHAPTER SIX

As THEY WALKED back to the table, energy still thrummed through Regina, and arousal coursed, thick and hot across her skin. A glance at Mateo seemed to find him amused, unmoved by what had been for her one of the most—if not the most—sensual events of her life.

Mateo pulled out her chair and Regina sank into it, glad to be off her somewhat shaky legs. The Diva started singing one of her Latin-inspired dance hits, and Regina shook her head.

"That's not what I was expecting, when she asked if we'd dance," she said as Mateo helped her push her chair in toward the table. "I think we were set up."

He'd bent closer to hear her over the music, and his breath—warm against her ear—made her have to fight a shiver, when he replied.

"I think we acquitted ourselves well."

"Well, you certainly know how to move."

"It's in the genes. My mother was a dancer," he explained, before straightening and gesturing to the waiter for the bill.

She'd have liked to get more information about that, but the music was too loud, so she waited until after he'd paid and they'd stepped outside the restaurant to wait for his car.

"Did you say your mom was a dancer?"

Mateo smiled one of those tender tilts of his lips that came out whenever he spoke about his family.

"Yes. When she and my father met, she was dancing with a troupe in Buenos Aires, as a way to put herself through university. Once she got her degree, she stopped dancing professionally, but she still knew how to move. She taught all of us kids. Us older ones anyway. She didn't have the opportunity to teach the others."

The regret in his voice wrung her heart. He was clearly so devoted to his family and the legacy his parents left behind that she couldn't help but be touched.

Yet, it distanced her from him, too. Each story about his family seemed to highlight the differences between them. His childhood sounded like the dreams she'd had as a young girl, of a family filled with laughter and loving support—a fantasy to the woman who'd had to scratch and claw and sacrifice to make something of herself. In her mind, there was no point of intersection between them besides both being doctors, and the incredible lust she had for him.

Lust she wasn't even completely sure was reciprocated.

"So did you teach them?" she asked, continuing the conversation.

Mateo laughed, the sound both amused and rueful.

"You were definitely an only child," he replied, still chuckling. "I realized early on that while they'd accept me as an authority figure, none of my youngest siblings had any interest in learning anything like that from me. I offered, but both Ben and Micah looked horrified and declined, and—having learned my lesson—I enrolled Serena in dance class, figuring if she liked it, she could continue going."

Another dream Regina had had as a little girl that never came to fruition, but she pushed the slightly sour thought aside, to ask, "Did she like them?"

The valet pulled up in Mateo's car, and Mateo opened her door for her as he replied succinctly, "Two left feet, in that respect. She's a handy soccer player, though."

Regina found herself laughing as she watched him walk around the front of the car.

As he closed the door and reached for the seat belt, he asked, "Nightcap, before I take you home?"

She hesitated, unsure of how wise it would be to spend more time in his company. Mateo created a rare maelstrom of emotions in her—desire, tenderness and, yes, even longing—that she instinctively knew was dangerous. But Miami was just a waypoint on the path to her ultimate destination. What harm could truly come from enjoying him while she could?

"Sure," she said.

Then, as he put the car in gear, she wondered if the nightcap he offered would be at his house. If it were any other man, she'd think so, but Mateo wasn't like any other man she'd been out with, and constantly surprised her.

And she still couldn't decide whether that was just his usual personality, or she was being played in some way.

Either way, she was determined not to lose her focus because of a pretty face and a winning persona. Not that she was usually susceptible to doing any such thing, but she couldn't be too careful.

The last few months had been stressful, and alleviating that stress by coming to Miami had also left her on slightly shaky ground emotionally. It was the first time in years she'd done something that wasn't directly tied to her long-term goal.

Sure, it would be an interesting addition to her résumé, but it hadn't been in the plan, and she chafed at the thought that this side trip might actually be detrimental to her career. Not that it was in the same category as the initial embarrassment over Kevin's betrayal, but there was always the fear that she'd diminished her worth at the hospital in San Francisco.

All those worries had, she realized, made her question every decision she made, almost obsessively. Even at work, where she was usually at her most confident, she found herself double- and triple-checking actions that were basic or routine.

"So what do you plan to do for the rest of the weekend?" he asked, pulling out of the parking lot and turning the car north.

"Actually, I have a distant cousin who lives in Boca Raton, and I promised to go visit her," she replied.

She'd been dreading going, just because she really didn't know Marilyn very well, and didn't know what to expect when she got there. Now, though, she was glad to have something to do, even if just so Mateo wouldn't feel as though he needed to step in and entertain her.

"I didn't know you had relatives here in Florida."

"This is my grandmother's cousin's family, so, like fourth cousins twice removed or something like that?"

He chuckled. "I've never been able to work out those family connections. Everything is just 'cousin' to me."

They had left most of the nightlife behind and were crossing the barrier island, away from the sea and toward Biscayne Bay.

"Do you have a lot of family here?" She remembered he'd said his parents had met in Argentina, and was curious.

"I have an aunt and some cousins in Texas, but most of the rest of the family is in Argentina. When Mom and

Dad died, my aunt Leona came from Texas and lived with us for about eight years. She'd gone through a divorce the year before, and I think she was happy to get away for a while."

"Did she bring her kids with her?"

Mateo put on his indicator and waited for a car to pass before making a left-hand turn into a dimly lit driveway. On either side were chain-link fences overgrown with flowering vines.

"They were all grown up by then," he replied. "She was older than my father by six years, and married fairly young."

At the end of the driveway was an electronic gate, which opened as the car approached. They drove through into a parking lot with a long, low, brightly illuminated building on the other side. Beyond it, there were glimpses of masts, and the occasional gleam of lights on water.

"Where are we?"

"It's a private marina and yacht club," he replied, slotting the car into a parking space. "It's a nice place to have a drink and see the city from across the bay."

"You have a boat here?"

The more she heard, the farther the distance between their life experiences seemed to grow. Private yacht clubs were still, even at her comfortable stage of life, beyond her reach.

"Actually, the membership belonged to my father, and he'd bought Ben a small sailboat one birthday, after he'd expressed an interest. The boat is still moored here, until Ben is settled and can decide what he wants to do with it, so he only gets to sail it when he comes home for holidays." He gave her a grin, as they both undid their seat belts. "I laugh to myself when I see Ben's dinky little boat up on a rack and compare it to the monster vessels tied up in the water, but, hey, it's still a boat, right?"

"That's true," she agreed, unable to stop herself from smiling with him.

There was just something about his wry amusement that sucked her in every time.

She opened the car door and got out. While his earlier courtesy of opening for her was nice, she didn't want him to think he had to do it every time.

He met her at the front of the vehicle and offered her his arm.

Inside, the restaurant was to the right, and had just one table of patrons, while the bar, which ran the length of the left wall, was occupied by four older men, all huddled together at one end. The bartender smiled when he saw them.

"Dr. Herrera. Good to see you."

"You, too, Keith. How've you been?"

Obviously Mateo spent quite a bit of time here, Regina surmised, as the two men chatted casually for a minute.

"What will you have tonight, ma'am?" Keith addressed Regina, hands poised over the bar, as though just waiting to conjure a drink from thin air.

"A glass of chardonnay, please."

What she'd really have liked was a whiskey on the rocks, but she'd been careful to limit her liquor consumption.

Mateo was enough of an intoxicant as it was.

After Mateo opted for a craft beer, he took her elbow to lead her out through open French doors, across a flagstone-paved patio, and down two stairs to a concrete walkway that curved above the marina itself. The area was beautifully landscaped, and the view across Biscayne Bay was gorgeous.

Regina leaned against the balustrade and took it all in.

The lights of Miami gleaming on the water, and the fabulous yachts rocking gently in the foreground gave the scene an almost dream-like ambience. And she was supremely aware of Mateo beside her, too, the heat of his arm resting on the concrete near hers, the smell of his cologne, his movement as he lifted the bottle to his lips.

She had to stop herself turning to watch him drink.

"How lovely," she said, trying not to fall too far under the spell of moonlight and Mateo, keeping her voice level.

"It's one of my favorite vistas," he replied, his low tone seeming to vibrate between them, causing goose bumps to shiver along her spine. "Whenever I want to think, or just catch my breath, I come here."

"I can see why," she said.

But she was aware of his having turned his back to the view. Now he leaned against the balustrade, and from the corner of her eye she could see him looking at her.

"I was thinking," he said, which was a conversational gambit that rarely boded well. "I have a villa down in the Keys. Why don't you come down with me one weekend? I have clinics on Tuesdays and Thursdays, but I can take Friday and Monday off and make it a four-day weekend. That will fit in with your schedule, right?"

"It would…"

Now she realized what it was about Mateo that confused her and made her hesitate to give him an answer.

Usually by now, she would have a pretty good idea of where things stood on a date—whether the man in question was interested in her, particularly if he wanted her physically. Mateo had been fun, interesting and a perfect gentleman. Once or twice she thought she'd caught a glint of something hot and fierce in his eyes, but it had never lingered long enough for her to be sure.

It made it impossible to know exactly what he was asking her when he offered to take her to the Keys, and because he hadn't made his intentions clear, she wasn't ready with a reply.

She was always ready with a reply, wasn't she? Always on the ball, knowing ahead of time what to say, how and when to say it. Instead, she floundered a little, feeling silly.

Then she pulled herself together. This waffling wasn't her style, at all.

Facing him fully, she said, "It sounds like fun, but I haven't decided whether to sleep with you or not, so I can't judge whether it's a good idea."

His eyebrows rose, and for an instant, his eyes flashed. Then a slight smile tipped the edges of his lips.

"I don't see what the problem is. If you don't decide to be intimate with me, we'll still have a fun weekend."

Taken aback, she instinctively asked, "And if I do decide to?"

His smile widened and his eyelids drooped, giving him a feral, dangerous air.

"Then," he said, his voice low and intense, "we'll have an even better time."

Was it her imagination, or had he moved fractionally closer? Even if he hadn't, her reaction was the same as it would have been if he'd fully invaded her space. Her heartbeat kicked into high gear, and her skin suddenly felt too tight—hot and tingly.

The urge to turn away, to hide, was so strong it was all she could do to hold his gaze, which had once more turned bland, without even a hint of amusement.

"By the way," he asked. "How will you decide?"

"I have no idea," she admitted, taking a sip of her wine and turning back to the view. Trying for insouciance, although she felt anything but indifferent. "I'm sure I'll think of something."

Mateo threw back his head and laughed, the sound of his unfettered amusement taking her already wicked desire for him even higher.

She wished he would just take a hold of her, kiss her senseless the way she wanted him to, but she had already worked it out: he wasn't going to push or demand. Unlike her prior experiences with men, this man was determined to, on at least this level, force her to make the decision on her own.

No coercion.

No coy hints or attempts to get her to agree.

It was, for her, a novel situation.

Not that she was a pushover, just going along if a man crooked his finger. Far from it. If she wasn't interested, she had no problem saying so. But, looking back, she'd also never been the pursuer or the instigator—she was always too busy with her life and plans to expend the energy.

Or maybe just not as interested as she'd thought she'd been at the time. Every intimate relationship she'd had seemed easy at the time. The man chased; Regina decided whether or not she wished to be caught.

Now she was faced with a man who wasn't planning to make it easy for her, and something about that lit a fire in her belly.

Which was both arousing and scary at the same time.

"Well, let me know when you decide, both about the trip and about me," he said, the laughter in his tone still apparent. "Your next weekend off would be good, but I need to let them know by Monday if I'm taking those days off."

"I'll let you know by then," she replied, keeping her

voice firm. Businesslike. But she already knew what she was about to do when she put down her glass on the ledge and turned to him. He was watching her, and she didn't allow herself to hesitate. She stepped close, as she had when they danced, but then closer still.

And kissed him.

Not just a peck, or a light brush of her lips. Regina, having decided on a course of action, never went with half measures. Nope. She went in hot, letting her intentions be known.

But although she instigated it, cupping his face and taking the kiss straight to erotic, Mateo didn't hesitate, either. In a blink he took over, one hand tunneling into the hair at her nape to angle her mouth into the perfect position. The other hand settled, hot and firm, on the small of her back, pulling her flush against his body.

She'd thought of it as an exploratory foray, a way to discover whether her interest in him was worth pursuing. In the past it had always been easy to separate her brain from whatever physical pleasure her body was experiencing. It was, she thought, a part of her nature— detachment was her stock-in-trade, and it had served her well over the years.

Being able to maintain critical thinking at all times was of paramount importance. It was what made her good at protecting herself from distractions, and great at her job.

Yet, in Mateo's arms, with his lips on hers, detachment deserted her before she even realized it was happening.

Sensation after sensation fired through her system, until she was a quaking column of need. His body, hard and hot, against hers. His lips, firm and masterful, not coaxing but demanding response. The sound of their breath, rushing, rushing from lungs laboring to take in enough.

Her head was swimming, and a moan rose in her throat.

That was when she pulled back, and was both relieved and bereft when Mateo let her go immediately.

Forcing herself to turn away, to modulate her breathing, to act as though the ground hadn't rocked beneath her feet, Regina reached for her wineglass. Only as she was lifting it did she realize her hand was shaking.

One more thing to try to get under control.

Putting the glass to her lips, she sipped, but not even the crisp tartness could erase the taste of Mateo from her consciousness.

She scrambled for something to say that would break the unbearable tension tightening her muscles and turning her legs to jelly. A witty remark. An off-the-cuff joke. But her brain was too busy reliving the kiss to spare her the time.

But there was no way she'd reveal to him just how shaken up she was from their brief, explosive embrace. So, gathering every ounce of the containment she was known for, she gave him a cool smile.

"I'll let you know about the trip to the Keys," she said, inordinately proud that she was able to keep her voice level. "By Monday."

"Okay," he replied, before picking up his beer bottle from beside him. Regina hadn't even realized he'd put it down, but the memory of his hands on her told her he must have. "Ready to go?"

He didn't sound as though he cared one way or another. Not just as though he didn't want to kiss her again, but as if the kiss hadn't even happened. And here she was, struggling not to turn back into his arms and do it all over again.

"Sure." Hopefully, she matched his indifference.

And she made certain to pull herself together enough to make light conversation on the way back to her place, although every nerve ending in her body was still vibrating.

She got out of the car as soon as he pulled up outside her building, and he walked with her to the door.

"Thank you for a wonderful evening," he said, causing her to search his expression, which turned out to be unhelpfully neutral.

"Thank you, too." Fishing her keys out of her purse gave her something other than him to concentrate on, and she stiffened when his hand touched her shoulder, and his lips brushed her cheek.

"Good night." His breath was warm against her cheek, and Regina steeled herself not to turn her face and put her lips against his again.

"Good night."

It came out a little breathless, and she stepped away, annoyed, and used her pass card to open the outside door, then walked through without giving him another look.

When she got into the elevator and turned around, he was standing at his open car door, watching her, and even through the glass his gaze caused heat to flare across her chest and back.

CHAPTER SEVEN

MATEO STOOD WAITING for the elevator to go down to the fourth floor the following Thursday, impatiently tapping his toes.

He really shouldn't be this eager to go and see one of his dialysis patients, who'd fallen and been admitted to the hospital, but Rex Knowles was under Regina's care. Mateo hated to admit it, but at this point he was almost desperate for even one glance of the delectable internist.

She'd texted him on Monday, as she said she would, and was as to the point as ever.

I don't think the Keys is going to happen. Thanks for the offer, though.

He'd considered that message for a long time before replying. There were certain responses he was sure would lead to more trouble than they were worth. Asking why was one. Trying to cajole her in some way was another.

He wasn't sure how he was so sure of those things, but he was. So he took his time thinking it through, before sending her a message.

Offer still stands.

And then he'd taken the two days off anyway.

The way he looked at it was, he had at least a week to try to get her to agree to go to his house on Islamorada, and he was going to give it his best shot.

After the kiss they'd shared, he'd be a damn fool not to.

It had almost blown the top of his head off.

He'd never experienced anything like it, and the memory had haunted him every moment of every day since it happened.

The excitement of having her in his arms, the way her soft, curvy body fitted against his and how it trembled kept him awake at night, tossing and turning, as his brain fed him reminders of her scent and taste.

When she'd pulled back, it was all he could do not to drag her close again, to keep kissing her, touching her, searching out the intimate places to make her as wild as he'd felt.

But then she turned away, cool as a cucumber, and he'd thought she'd been unfazed by their encounter, until he'd seen her fingers tremble. Then he'd known she'd felt it, too.

Of course, how she mentally reacted to the desire crackling between them was another thing altogether, and he didn't think her the type to share her personal thoughts and feelings easily. Getting her to open up about what was happening, or not happening, between them wouldn't be simple. She definitely struck him as a woman who could keep her own counsel.

But if he could get her to discuss the situation, maybe they could have some fun together.

The elevator came, and he stepped in, nodding to the occupants but still lost in his thoughts.

Truth was, Mateo wasn't in the market for a relationship. It didn't feel like the right time for him, although his familial responsibilities had diminished markedly. Even if Regina had relocated to Miami full-time, he couldn't see himself getting involved on any kind of deeper level than the purely physical.

He'd put a lot of his ambitions and plans on hold when his parents died, and was only now in a place where he could start contemplating dusting off and reigniting his goals. While he loved his current job, and hadn't come to a firm decision on whether to move on to something else, it was important to him to have enough space and time to think. In his estimation, getting into a relationship would just be a distraction.

But that didn't preclude a fun, sexy romp with Regina. If he could just get her to agree.

Getting off on the fourth floor, he spotted the subject of his ruminations at the nurses' station and, ignoring his body's instinctive excited reaction, walked that way.

She looked up and snared him with those lioness eyes. No smile, just a nod in his direction.

"Ah, Dr. Herrera. Your patient, Rexford Knowles, was brought in after falling at home. I need some further information from you."

Just as he expected, she was as cool as cool could be, as though the kiss they'd shared had been erased from her memory. But although that stung, he had to put it all aside.

"He's due in next Tuesday for dialysis," Mateo noted. "What happened?"

Rex Knowles's polycystic kidney disease was at the point where only dialysis was keeping him alive. His wife of almost forty years was looking after him at home with the help of their grown children, but Mateo knew how hard it must be.

"He hasn't been able to tell us exactly how he fell. His

daughter stopped by to make him lunch and found him. He was awake but confused, and bleeding from a head wound, so she brought him in. When the ER staff pulled his record, they decided to admit him. My main concern now is for his mental state."

She started walking down the corridor, beckoning Mateo to come along.

"The scalp laceration is over the occipital bone, but there's no apparent fracture of the skull," she continued. "But I saw in your notes that he's been suffering some memory issues recently, and would appreciate you evaluating him. Scans haven't revealed any bleeding or swelling in the brain, but I'm worried about concussion. And with his current polypharmacy, we have to be extra careful."

"His wife was the one who mentioned the memory loss, and I had him evaluated for early-onset dementia, which was ruled out. I suspect it's a direct result of his disease, and the corresponding need for frequent dialysis. He's on the transplant list, but so far, we haven't had any luck finding a match. His wife and all four of his children were tested, but discounted."

She made a little sound, just a soft click of her tongue, which he interpreted as sympathy.

"He hasn't had an episode like this before, has he?"

"Not that I'm aware of, and his wife comes to his appointments to make sure he's telling me everything that's going on. We might need to adjust his blood pressure medication, and I'll do some further testing to see if he's suffering any physical impairment."

She paused at one of the doors and faced him squarely.

"I hope you find him a donor, quickly. Is he on the living donor list, too?"

"Yes. And I know, his condition has been deteriorating far too rapidly for my liking."

She glanced down at the tablet in her hand and scrolled back through the record displayed there. "He's checked regularly for hepatic cysts?"

"Of course. And I'd like copies of the brain scans sent to me, directly. It's just about the time when he's due for an aneurysm check, too."

She nodded, a thoughtful frown creasing her forehead, and then, in a blink, it was gone, and she opened the door.

"Come on," she said, rather abruptly.

And she was through the door and in the room before he could even reach for the handle, leaving him with the sense of having been somehow thoroughly dismissed.

There.

She'd had a totally professional and productive conversation with Mateo without letting on that inside she was a mass of conflicting emotions and longings.

The memory of the kiss they'd shared had haunted her, springing into her brain whenever she let her defenses down.

If she'd hoped for an indication of whether she was interested enough to pursue anything more with Mateo, she'd gotten more than she'd bargained for. Every night since then, she'd tossed and turned, her imagination supplying brazen, erotic images of what it would be like to see him naked. Feel his mouth and lips and hands on her. Wrap her legs around him, as he filled her to capacity.

It had taken every iota of her considerable strength of will to put it aside and be a decent guest at her cousin's home, but somehow, she'd done it.

But she knew the true test would be how she reacted to Mateo the next time she saw him.

It had been as bad as she'd feared.

She'd sensed him coming down the corridor even before she saw him, some internal sense recognizing the approach of danger, and her entire body had reacted.

Grown hot and tight, thrumming with erotic energy.

Yet, she'd kept it together, and now, watching as Mateo examined Rexford Knowles, asked him questions and checked the test results a nurse had just brought in, she was quietly pleased with herself.

She could do it—put aside the roaring attraction that gripped her whenever she was in his presence, and get on with her job.

Her life.

So confident was she that later, after they'd discussed the patient's ongoing care and Mateo asked her out to dinner that evening, her heart skipped only one beat, instead of fluttering like a crazy thing.

"I'm on call," she said, as a way to get out of it. "And usually do rounds before I head home."

"You'll still have to eat," he replied, his face serious. "I won't be through with my clinic until about six, and usually don't leave until about seven. We could grab a bite after that. I really want to talk to you about the other night."

That was direct. So to the point that she could only reply, "I'm not sure there's anything to discuss."

But she was annoyed to hear the unusually husky tone in her voice, and knew he'd heard it, too, when his eyelids half closed over his gleaming gaze.

"There's a lot to discuss, Regina." Then he half sighed, half snorted, as though unable to decide whether to be annoyed or amused. "Humor me. It's just a sandwich and a conversation."

And because she didn't want him to think she was afraid, she agreed.

By the time she was satisfied with all she wanted to do before she would leave the hospital, it was almost seven thirty, but when she went down to the doctors' parking lot, he was there, waiting. They agreed on an all-night deli near her apartment, and he followed her in his car to the restaurant.

Ensconced in a corner booth, him with a huge Reuben sandwich and her with a cup of soup and a much smaller toasted cheese, they spent the first little while eating.

Obviously, he was as hungry as she was, and it wasn't until he'd finished half of his meal that he wiped his mouth and said, "I wanted you to know, if you don't already, that I'm very attracted to you."

She put down her spoon and met his gaze across the table. It was on the tip of her tongue to tell him she felt the same way about him, but caution, along with her natural reticence, held her back.

"Okay," she said instead, ignoring the fluttering in her belly and her suddenly galloping heart.

"But I also want you to know, in the interest of full disclosure, that as much as I like you and enjoy your company, I'm not interested in a relationship."

Taken aback, all she could do was raise her eyebrows and say, "Oh?"

He nodded. "Besides the fact that you're only here for a short time, the truth is, I've just started to get my life back since my parents passed away. Along with making the commitment to come back to Miami, there were other plans I had to put on hold back then, too. Now I want to try to work on them, before I'm considered too old to make it happen."

That was something she could totally understand, although it felt weird for the shoe to be on the other foot. She was usually the one telling men she wasn't interested in a relationship.

Now she understood why those men had acted so disappointed. Although God knew she didn't plan on getting seriously involved, either, it felt like being rejected.

But she pushed that thought aside to ask, "What are you planning to do?"

"I want to be a part of a dedicated transplant team. There's a new hospital being built near Plantation, and they're rumored to be aiming at being the place to go for chronically ill patients who need transplants. I've applied for some training courses that I hope will put me on track to be a good candidate."

She could see the anticipation and enthusiasm on his face, and couldn't help grinning.

"Good for you."

He leaned back and nodded, but he was serious once more, and she knew her attempt to sidetrack him from their initial discussion had failed.

"You know by now that I'm not going to try to push you into anything."

"Yes." She made her voice firm, showing with her tone that even if he were so inclined, she was having none of it.

"So, with everything I've said in mind, I'd like to reiterate my invitation to the Keys. No matter what you decide, we'll have a good time."

She took a bite of her sandwich, using the action to put off answering.

He was right. They did have a good time together. Whether or not they decided to take it further, now she knew he wouldn't expect her to get emotionally involved. Best of all, he'd obviously thought it through and was honest about his intentions, or lack of them.

It could be just what she needed: a no-strings, steamy affair, without having to worry about the long-term consequences. They could agree to have fun without expectations, and all without her treating him as though he were a potential life partner.

Weighing and measuring his every move.

Waiting, setting little traps to see what he might do.

Maintaining the tightest grip she could on her own responses and emotions, as though expecting pain at some later, as yet undetermined, date, when their relationship would implode.

None of that was relevant to their situation, and there was no need to be so cagey, when they both knew there would be no long-term relationship to develop and nurture.

And with her track record, wasn't that a great thing?

She could just enjoy herself, without hanging on to all the old habits and norms that had served her so poorly in the past.

Perhaps this was her last chance to experience one of those crazy affairs she'd heard and read about. Not the ones that ended in tears and recriminations, but like those her girlfriends talked about, years after they were over, and both parties had moved on. Where they'd lost their heads for a time, reveling in the hot, steamy sex, and when it was all over, could still sigh and roll their eyes, admitting how good it was, even though it wasn't meant to last.

Regina had never understood why they'd been sucked in, or why the memories still made them fan themselves years later, but she suspected she was about to find out.

Besides, she'd never been to the Keys.

"Can we go to Key West?" she asked, having swallowed. "I want to see Hemingway's house."

"Sure," he replied easily, that sexy little smile touching the corners of his lips. "Whatever you want."

Whatever she wanted?

That made her brain start churning out suggestions, all of which ended with her having orgasms, and she had to yank it back to the present and slam the door shut on that train of thought.

And while she told herself she probably wouldn't end up sleeping with him, she already knew that was a big fat lie.

"All right. I'll go."

The way his eyes lit up, and the slow, sexy smile he gave her told her he knew just as well as she did that their trip wouldn't be a platonic vacation between friends.

As she finished her sandwich, and the conversation turned more general, she realized she didn't mind being quite so transparent.

CHAPTER EIGHT

IF REGINA STILL harbored any doubts about how wealthy Mateo's family was, they were quickly banished when she saw their house on Islamorada Key.

The modern glass-and-concrete house, set on concrete pillars, was gorgeous.

"They build up high here because of the storm surge during hurricanes," Mateo said. "But my father made sure to use high-impact-resistant glass when he built, and I put on a metal roof when the old one needed to be replaced a few years ago."

Regina was too busy gaping at the breathtaking view out over the water to really pay too much attention to what he was saying, though. She walked from where he'd parked beneath the house out onto the flagstone patio bordered by a little strip of grass, overlooking the sea.

There was a concrete seawall and a hoist holding a tarp-covered boat, but what Regina couldn't stop staring at was the confluence of bright blue sky and aqua-shaded water. All the tension of the last week, when she'd worried about whether to give in to her own desires, melted away.

This wasn't a place where stress could easily survive.

"We're on the Gulf side of the island." Mateo had come to stand beside her, and a little shiver trickled up her back at his presence, so close she could smell his cologne. "So the sunsets are gorgeous. We can go out on the boat one afternoon and watch it, if you like, but unfortunately at this time of year it tends to get dark pretty quickly, so it's a little more difficult coming back in through the channel."

"If that's the case, I'll pass," she said. "I'm sure the view from here is amazing."

The house was part of a development, but it was the last one on the dead-end street and sat on a small peninsula, giving it the perfect position for views on three sides.

"Come on upstairs." Mateo touched her elbow, and goose bumps fired along her arm. "We can put away the groceries, and while you settle in, I'll get the boat in the water."

"Sounds like a plan," she said mildly.

She was determined to play it cool, at least for a little while more. There was a part of her, the suspicious part, that was waiting for him to make the move he'd sworn he wouldn't. Waiting for him to try to force a decision on her, or use the attraction between them to coax her into his bed.

But after they'd unpacked the car, all Mateo did was lead the way upstairs and, after opening the door, usher her inside. As she stood, trying to get her bearings, he carried their bags to the start of a hallway and put them down.

"Pick whichever room you like," he said, waving a hand down the corridor.

Without looking at him, she asked, "Which one is yours?"

"The one at the end of the hall. Make yourself at home."

Then he was out the door again, leaving her to her own devices.

The inside of the house was as lovely as the outside. The large L-shaped room she was standing in was an open-plan kitchen, living and dining room in one, and it was decorated in soothing shades of gray and yellow, accented with crisp white. All the fittings and furnishings had the mark of luxury, but at the same time, it had a comfortable, lived-in feel. Big soft couches and chairs created artful seating arrangements, and were positioned to best take in the glorious view visible through floor-to-ceiling windows.

Kicking off her sandals, Regina carried the bags of groceries she'd brought inside over to the kitchen, and started putting them away. When asked what she should bring, Mateo had said he'd take care of everything, and as she opened the fridge, Regina couldn't help smiling, just a little. Clearly, his idea and her idea of what constituted sufficient provisions for the time they'd be there were very different.

Mind you, he had said he usually ate out when he was in the Keys, so maybe bread, antipasto, cold cuts and enough cheese to make fondue for the entire Swiss population would be enough.

Having finished her chore, she strolled over to the windows, and her gaze immediately went to where Mateo was in the process of turning the winch to get the boat into the water.

The sunlight glinted on his hair, and his broad shoulders bunched and flexed beneath his knit shirt. Watching him without his knowledge was a rare treat, and one she definitely had a taste for.

She already knew where she'd be sleeping, and was honest enough with herself to know she'd made that decision a long time ago. What also had to be acknowledged was the fact that she'd wanted him to push for intimacy, and was strangely disquieted by his refusal to do so.

He'd made his desire for her clear, and had been honest about not being interested in a relationship. Nothing about his behavior should cause her this sense of being on the edge of a precipice and being scared she would plummet with just the slightest push.

Mateo got the boat into the water and began to remove the weatherproof cover, and she saw his lips purse, as though he were whistling. Heat bloomed, low in her belly, and excitement spread through her body, as though pushed along her veins with her blood.

Yes, she was going to sleep with him, and suddenly she realized why she'd wanted him to take the decision from her, the way most men she'd been with had done, or at least tried to.

Then, while she would still have sex with him, her liking and respect for him would be diminished, leaving her free to walk away unscathed when she returned to San Francisco.

Instead, she was forced to admit he was a man of integrity and honor, with a devotion to his family that made her heart ache, and made her like him all the more. And when he'd talked about his ambitions, another piece had clicked into place. How could she not admire both his dedication to his family and his renewed decision to pursue the dreams he'd put on hold all those years ago? Most other people would be resting on their laurels, satisfied with where they were.

She could still remain unscathed, though, as long as she reminded herself that they were both in it for the fun. It was all a matter of determination, and Regina was a master at that, wasn't she?

It would mean keeping a firm grip on her signature detachment, and making sure she didn't let him mess with her head.

No problem at all.

Thus fortified, she went and grabbed her bag, taking it straight along to Mateo's room.

Finished with launching and cleaning up the boat, Mateo stood for a moment, just taking in the view and the peaceful scene. The water was shades of brown where the reefs lay just below the surface, to aquamarine in the shallows, to deep aqua farther out into the Gulf of Mexico. There was little chop, the waves running slow and low toward the land, and the tiny islands dotting the water were verdant green.

While he enjoyed city life, these moments spoke to his soul and eased some of the tension tightening his muscles.

Not all of it, though, because he still wasn't sure where things stood with the gorgeous, tight-lipped, sexy woman upstairs, and the uncertainty was gnawing at his insides.

Her caution didn't bother him; he actually understood it all too well.

There was something brewing between them that threatened to be explosive, and it deserved to be carefully considered before any decisions could be made.

But he'd had to draw on every ounce of patience he possessed not to ask Regina what she was thinking, what she had planned.

He wanted her, and the waiting, the anticipation, intensified not just the need, but his desire to break apart her carefully constructed control. To shatter her detachment and bring her into the eye of the erotic storm building inside. He wanted not just her acquiescence, but her complete complicity. He wanted to ravish her senses, give her the utmost in pleasure, leave her weak but still wanting more.

Where that almost savage impulse came from, he didn't know, but he suspected it had everything to do with this waiting game they were playing.

They'd talked easily on the trip down, the conversation flowing from her visit with her relatives to their separate work ambitions, and then to other, more mundane topics. And while he was engaged, he was also terribly distracted, his senses drawn to cataloging her ever move and breath, her scent filling his head.

The memory of her lips on his, the dance of their tongues, was a constant companion, leading his brain to far more intense and arousing imaginings.

He needed to know which way this situation was going to go, so that if he needed to completely put a lid on his desires, it could happen now.

But standing around outside wasn't going to get him any closer to a resolution, so, with one last comprehensive look at the sky to make sure there were no clouds on the horizon, he turned to go back inside.

Upstairs, he found Regina in the kitchen, putting together lunch.

"Wow," he said, taking in the spread she'd laid out. "You've been busy."

She'd rolled sliced meats and cheeses together, made rosettes out of radishes, and had them all arranged on a platter with celery and carrot sticks, olives and fresh mozzarella balls.

"I'm just toasting some slices of bread," she replied. "And then we can eat."

He went to the sink to wash his hands. "You didn't have to go to so much trouble," he said, thinking about the days when he'd slapped a slice of ham between two slices of bread and called it lunch.

She just smiled. "It was no trouble. Besides, my grandfather always said, 'If yuh mek it look nice-nice, people will nyam it up.' He was a short-order cook with the soul of a chef."

"Okay, I give," he said, amazed at hearing her speak with a perfect Jamaican accent for the first time, but not wanting to mention how intriguing it was. "I got the rest of it, but what does 'nyam' mean?"

She chuckled. "Eat, but in this context, more like gobble."

He went around to the other side of the counter and sat on one of the stools so he could see her face while they talked.

"Ah… I have to remember that. Micah had a couple of Jamaican friends when he was in high school, and he used to complain that sometimes they'd be talking and he could hardly understand them."

Regina glanced up, amusement making her eyes glitter. "I only ever spoke patois when I was with my grandparents, since my father didn't like to hear it at home. It was fun to sit around with my cousin and her family the other day and hear everybody. Even I had to ask, every now and again, what they were saying. I'm out of practice."

This was a different Regina, he thought. More relaxed and open, and he couldn't help wondering what had changed.

After they'd eaten and put away the leftovers, he said, "How about a boat ride?"

"Sounds like a great idea," she replied, glancing out the window at the bright sunlight. "It looks perfect out there."

"Although it isn't cold, once we get out on the water, the windchill will kick in. Did you bring a windbreaker?"

"I did," she replied, slanting him a sideways glance. "I'll get it as soon as I wash up these dishes."

"Let me do that." He used his hip to gently bump her away from the sink. "You go and get ready."

He couldn't help watching her as she walked away, the delectable sway of her hips a siren's call it took all his strength not to answer.

She hadn't come back by the time he was finished with the dishes, and as he dried his hands, Mateo debated whether to change into his swim trunks or not. The water was too cold to swim in, in his opinion, but you never could tell what could happen when you were out in the ocean. Should an engine fail, or something fall overboard, it would be better to be in his trunks than in jeans.

Heading to his room, he grabbed his bag on the way, idly wondering which of the other four bedrooms Regina had decided on. Which, of course, led to wondering whether he'd be sharing her bed that night.

God, he hoped so. Being around her was driving him a little crazy.

He was three steps into his room, and in the process of putting down his bag on the low bench at the foot of the bed, before his brain caught up to what his eyes had seen.

There was a bag already there.

A gossamer-thin confection of a nightgown lay across the bedspread, and the sandals Regina had been wearing were placed neatly together just in front of the wardrobe.

Frozen where he stood, Mateo looked toward the door of the en suite bathroom, just as Regina strolled out and stopped, five feet away.

She was wearing a bikini, and had her arms raised as she put her hair up into a knot on the top of her head. Meeting his gaze, she raised one eyebrow but didn't try to speak, since she had a hair clip held between her lips.

Mateo couldn't stop his gaze from falling to devour her exposed body, from full breasts, along her toned, curvy body, wide hips, and down her long, strong legs.

In a distant, foggy sort of way, certain other things registered: the silky sheen of her skin, the glint of a diamond in her belly button, the curl of her toes into the rug she was standing on.

Those toes, and the rapid pulse he could clearly see at the base of her throat, were the only indications that Regina was as affected by the moment as he was.

Holding her hair with one hand, she took the clip out of her mouth with the other.

"I hope you don't mind sharing."

Oh, she was trying to sound amused, but the huskiness of her tone gave her away.

"I certainly don't," he replied, not even trying to disguise the desire in his voice. The blood in his veins flowed hot as lava, and he itched to get his hands on her. "In fact, I definitely prefer it this way."

He hadn't consciously made the decision to move but found himself circling her, watching her watch him as he stepped closer, but she didn't move as he stepped behind her. He couldn't get over how sexy she was, how much he wanted to touch her, although he didn't.

Not yet.

"You're so gorgeous it almost hurts to look at you."

The sound she made was one he couldn't recognize.

"I'm glad you think so," she replied.

She seemed to be fumbling a little with the clip, and he realized it was because her hands were shaking. There was a full-length mirror on the other side of the room, and now he looked at her reflection.

"I want to see all of you."

He heard her indrawn breath, saw the way her breasts

rose and fell. Letting go of the clip caused her hair to come down, and Mateo gently detangled it from the strands before tossing the clip onto the nearby table.

When he looked back up, she was watching in the mirror, too, and for an instant, he couldn't breathe, ensnared by her gaze. No longer golden, it gleamed dark: a night sky of passion.

She reached behind and untied her top. When it dropped to the floor, Mateo thought he might follow it, felled by the beauty of her naked torso.

Slowly she hooked her fingers into the sides of her bottoms and slid them south, bending to push them past her knees.

Then, as she straightened, euphoria rushed to tighten every muscle in Mateo's body, and for a second, as he stepped closer and ran his finger along her spine, he wondered if he were dreaming.

If so, he hoped he never awoke.

CHAPTER NINE

REGINA TREMBLED AS though about to vibrate right out of her skin. The sensation of Mateo's finger down her spine lingered, a line of fire sending waves of heat cascading out over her entire body, tightening her nipples and making her thighs tremble.

He was standing behind her, watching her reflection in the mirror, and the effect of his gaze on her was electric, sharpening her every sense.

The rush of their breathing was like the wind in a storm.

His scent enveloped her, filling her head like an intoxicant.

Her skin was supersensitized, so that even the slightest movement of the air became a caress.

But what held her totally in thrall was the sight of him, looking at her as though she were the most beautiful woman in the world, his gaze intense and hungry.

Ravenous.

She wanted to see him naked, too, wanted to tell him to strip down and to kiss her—touch her, alleviate the need building to an explosive pitch inside. To hurry, before she spontaneously combusted. Yet, she was unable to form the words, mute and rooted in place by his eyes.

When he finally touched her again—a light brush of

his palms along her arms—she shuddered, closing her eyes to savor the sensation.

"Open your eyes, Regina." The harsh timbre of his voice should have shaken her from her arousal, but instead it pulled her deeper. "I need to see your eyes."

She obeyed, and the clash of their gazes made a moan rise in her throat.

Then it was the sight of his hands sliding around to cup her breasts, coupled with the slip of flesh on flesh, that brought her up onto her toes.

It was torture of the most erotic kind, and Regina watched it play out as Mateo skillfully, masterfully took her higher in excruciating increments.

He touched her as though he were learning every inch of her skin through his fingertips. As his thumbs circled her nipples, he set his lips to her neck, and the flick of his tongue echoed across her system, setting off tremors with each pass.

Lower those wicked hands went, and she watched, hardly blinking, as they inched closer to that aching, needy space between her thighs. One touch would send her over the edge. She was sure of it, and craved that contact in a way she'd never desired anything in her life before.

But he withheld that intimacy, caressing her belly, the top of her thighs, her hips and buttocks.

Why didn't she grab his hand and take it to where she wanted it to be? That was what she'd usually do. But somehow with Mateo, as desperately as she wanted culmination, she couldn't bring herself to demand it.

There was something so erotic about his total concentration on her body, and the sight of them together, that all she could do was keep watching.

And feeling.

The slide of hands, and the slip of his mouth across her nape.

The brush of his fingers on her mound, and the scrape of his teeth on her neck.

Tender circles around her tingling nipples.

Just when she thought she couldn't take a moment more, he turned her a quarter turn, stepping around to kiss her, and the passion between them became a flashover.

Where before he'd been slow, each touch filled with intent, now they strained against each other, the wanting driving them to rush.

But although the pace had increased, Mateo never relinquished control. When she tried to undress him, he ignored her efforts, dipping his head to take one straining nipple between his lips.

Regina arched back over the arm he banded around her waist, and it was probably the only thing keeping her upright on her quaking legs. Tunneling her fingers into his hair, she drowned in the moment.

Then his lips were sliding down her body, his hands hard and tight on her ass, keeping her on her feet even as he sank to his knees. When he lifted her leg and put it over his shoulder, Regina was already just a breath away from orgasm.

And the first touch of his tongue was all she needed to achieve it.

She cried out, a sound she'd never heard herself make before in her life, and held his head there, although he'd made no effort to shift away.

She rode out the crashing waves, feeling him still as the final tremors shook her to the core. But before she could catch her breath, he did something wicked-sweet with his mouth, and she was tumbling into another, even harder release.

How had she gotten onto the bed? she wondered, when she finally recovered enough to open her eyes, and found herself lying on the smooth, cool comforter.

Mateo was taking off his clothes, and her body—which had seemed draped in lethargy a second before—tingled back to life at the sight.

Bronze skin stretched over the hard, well-defined muscles of his chest and abdomen, making her want to dig her nails into them and test their strength. A trail of dark hairs led down toward the top of his jeans, and she resolved, there and then, to follow it as soon as possible, with her mouth.

Her breath caught in her throat when he stood up from shucking his pants.

He was, she thought in a distant, stupefied sort of way, ridiculously beautiful.

"You're so sexy," she said, the words falling unbidden from her lips.

Mateo paused, his eyebrows going up as though in surprise, before he replied, "I was just thinking the same thing about you."

She held out her arms, ravenous for him, and when he lowered himself to the bed, there was no need for further conversation.

Their bodies did the talking for them.

And boy, did his have a lot to say.

Hers responded with a series of mind-blowing orgasms. More than should be legal, she thought through the fog of endorphins rampaging in her system. By the time he finally rolled on a condom, she was almost desperate for his possession.

But once again, Mateo surprised her.

He'd been in complete control of her body up until that point, but now he yielded to Regina, pulling her to straddle his hips. Letting her set the pace, and take over.

It was a powerful and somehow empowering moment.

To kneel above him and watch his face tighten with pleasure as she took him deep energized her all over again.

She wanted to make him as crazy as he'd made her, but the moment was too sublime to prolong, and her need was too great. And it didn't take long for her to find release again, but this time she pulled him along with her, and her ecstasy was heightened by his.

Lying beside him, tucked under his arm, Regina yawned, cataloging all the yummy little aches popping up all over her body. Having sex with Mateo had turned out to be better than any cardio workout she'd ever done.

"Tired?"

She shook her head. "No. Although I feel as though I should be, after what we just did."

He chuckled. His arm, which was around her shoulders, tightening just a little. Regina couldn't help wondering if now that they'd slept together, he'd expect them to spend the rest of the trip in bed.

Not that she'd complain. After this first taste, she was more than willing to gorge herself on Mateo's brand of loving. Night shift be damned. The day shift had turned out to be more than satisfactory, and she suspected any shift at all in his bed would be equally mind blowing, if not more so.

But at the same time, it would be nice to see more than just the inside of his house.

As though reading her mind, Mateo said, "I thought we could go to Key West tomorrow. If we leave in the morning, we could stop and get breakfast on the way there, and then explore to your heart's content for the rest of the day."

"Sounds good." Well, that answered her question. "How long does it take to get there?"

"About two hours."

His hand was gently rubbing up and down her arm, and Regina found herself deliciously distracted. Maybe staying all afternoon in his bed wouldn't be such a bad idea.

"Do you want to go out on the boat? There's enough light left for us to go out into the Gulf for a quick run."

His hand was on her shoulder now, just in line to slip down and cup her breast, if he wanted to. She wanted him to, but somehow also didn't want to admit it and appear as though she was getting addicted to him.

"Sounds good," she said, but neither of them moved. Not for a couple of long, drugged beats.

And then he rolled over and kissed her, and she knew it would be a while before they went out on the water.

Mateo went down to the dock while Regina got ready to go for their boat ride. As he checked the gas gauges, he found himself whistling, and abruptly stopped, trying to figure out what it was he was feeling.

Satiated? Sure.

He couldn't tell when last he'd experienced that level of arousal and satisfaction—if he ever had before.

But there was something else making him grin to himself and start whistling once more.

Recognizing it as happiness didn't feel right, so he pushed the sensation to the back of his mind.

When she came down, she was wearing a windbreaker and had put a scarf over her hair. Since he was finished checking the boat, they set off right away.

As he navigated out through the narrow channel, Regina stood beside him, taking in the changing vistas as they moved farther from shore. Normally, he'd have one or more of the kids with him, or be alone, but having her there felt good. Natural.

Once out into the wider channel, he said, "Hold on tight," then opened up the throttle to put the boat up on a plane. As they flew across the water, cutting through the waves, Regina let out a whoop, making Mateo check to see if it was an expression of fear or one of enjoyment.

With her head thrown back, she was holding on to her scarf and laughing, clearly thrilled. He'd never seen her like that before, exhibiting such unfettered emotion, and the sight of it set something free inside him, too. Something hot and wild and possessive.

He had to force himself to turn away, to concentrate on what he was doing and where he was steering the boat.

He passed one of the mangrove islands, and ahead was open water, so he upped the speed a bit more, until the wave heights began to increase, causing the boat to bounce more than he considered comfortable. Throttling back, he brought the boat down to idle, letting it drift and rock.

Turning to face Regina, he found himself the focus of her attention, and even behind her dark glasses, he could tell her eyes were sparkling.

"That was amazing," she said with a wide grin. "I haven't been on a boat in ages. I'd forgotten how much fun it can be."

The flash of jealousy firing through him was insane and ridiculous, but it took all of Mateo's control not to ask her who else she'd been boating with. He wanted to take hold of her and kiss her, and make sure she remembered no other boat ride than the one she was on with him.

But he said and did neither, just smiled at her and said, "We could stay here for a little while, or we can go farther out. It's up to you."

She walked out from beneath the T-top to the rear deck and stood there looking out across the water. She unzipped her windbreaker and shrugged it off, lifting her face to the sun.

"Let's stay here," she said finally. "It's so peaceful."

They were the only vessel in sight, and the tide was pushing them away from the nearest land, so Mateo didn't bother to drop anchor. Stepping to the side, away from the wheel, he leaned back against the console, watching Regina.

She had on a pair of form-fitting terry cloth yoga pants and a loose knit shirt, all of which showed off her luscious figure to perfection. When she bent over to look down into the water, Mateo's body tightened, and his hands itched to cup her gorgeous butt and squeeze.

When she straightened and turned, Mateo tightened his grip on the console, to restrain himself from beckoning her near and begging for more of the closeness he craved so badly.

She froze, and time seemed to waver and stretch as they stared at each other. Then she strode across the deck to him, and she was where he so desperately wanted her to be.

Back in his arms.

She was irresistible, setting off a fire in his blood as soon as those lioness eyes turned on him. The memories of her responses as they made love had him desperate to do it all over again, just so he could see her shatter in his arms.

The exhilaration of their race across the water still thrummed through his veins, and it seemed to have aroused her, too, and she kissed him as though for the first time, leaving no doubt as to her intent.

They'd agreed it was all just for fun—for the physical enjoyment—but when he had her in his arms, it felt bigger. As though there was something growing between them, tying him to her in some fundamental way.

But he didn't hesitate when she walked into his personal space. His arms went around her, pulling her flush against his chest, and he parted his legs so that she stood between them, showing her without words that she wasn't the only one revved up.

Then he kissed her, putting all his need and conflicting emotions into the embrace. She felt so right in his arms, and when she swiveled her hips, he groaned into her mouth.

Her hands roamed his back and then his chest. When she pushed them up under his shirt and slid the pads of her fingers across his straining muscles, desire overtook him.

Placing his hands on her bottom, he lifted her and stepped forward. Instinctively her legs came up to wrap around his waist, and he felt her shudder as her core came into contact with his erection.

Putting her down on the edge of the captain's seat, he broke their kiss to trail his lips down to her throat. Regina arched, giving him full access to her neck. When his teeth scraped along the skin and he followed it with a hot swipe of his tongue, he heard her gasp and felt her tremble.

There.

There was the responsiveness that made him lose his mind and want to make her come over and over again. She was the stuff of every erotic fantasy he'd ever had, and he was willing to lose himself in her arms again, as long as he didn't lose himself in the process.

There was no future between them, he knew, just the

present, and he wanted to gorge himself on her while he had the chance.

She tightened her legs around his waist and arched her back even more, offering her breasts to his lips.

He didn't hesitate.

Pushing her blouse up, he slipped her bikini top aside to suck her already straining nipple between his lips. She moaned, her hips swiveling, and Mateo growled. A sound broke through the fog in his head, and he drew back.

She protested, but he was already smoothing her shirt down, as disappointed as she seemed to be at the interruption.

"Company is coming," he said.

When she became aware of the fast-approaching engine, he saw a wave of color flood her face, but she laughed.

"They're a little late," she said as she took the hand he held out to help her get down off the chair, and then reached under her blouse to adjust her swimsuit. "They missed the show."

Seeing her amusement just made him want her even more, so he didn't answer, just scooped her back into his arms and kissed her until her breath was once more rushing from her lungs.

It was only when the passing boaters cheered that he let her go, and said, "That's it. We're heading home."

She laughed again, and he had to force himself to turn back to the console and get the engines going.

The ride back seemed to take an inordinate amount of time, and by the time they docked, anticipation was like lava in his veins.

All he could hope was that he wouldn't become too addicted to Regina Montgomery, because the craving he had for her was already intense.

CHAPTER TEN

THE WEEKEND SEEMED to fly by, a whirl of sightseeing, boat trips and lovemaking.

Especially lovemaking.

Regina had realized at one point—probably as they sat in a restaurant on Duval Street in Key West, discussing everything and nothing—that she was a little afraid. Not of Mateo—not in the slightest—but of the sensation of being ever so slightly out of control, no matter how hard she tried to reassure herself she could handle whatever came.

But she pushed it all aside, and now, as they drove back into Miami, she was sorry their time together was already coming to an end.

Mateo apparently felt the same way.

"Would you like to stay at my place tonight? I can drop you home before I go to work in the morning."

Oh, she was tempted, but her natural caution reasserted itself, after apparently having taken the weekend off. If it had been firmly in place, surely Regina wouldn't have lost her head quite as completely as she had under Mateo's spell.

"I really have to take care of all the things I usually do on weekends," she said, trying to sound matter-of-fact but hearing the regret in her own voice. "I like to start the week with all my chores done, and of course this week that hasn't happened."

She was getting used to his way of not pressuring her, so it came as no surprise when he replied, "I understand. Maybe later in the week, before you start back up on shift?"

"Maybe." It was the most she was willing to agree to. Right now, she needed a little distance from him so she could think through everything that had happened over the weekend.

It turned out to be a good decision, as she was called in the following morning to cover for the internist on duty, who'd had a personal emergency and had to go out of town.

Regina was glad to be back at work, since she'd tossed and turned all the night before, obsessively going over everything that had happened over the weekend.

No man had ever made her feel the way Mateo had, and not just physically. There was something about the way he looked at her and listened so intently that drilled down into her soul. It was the demeanor of a man completely involved in the moment, not waiting to speak, or thinking about what would happen next.

No, he was totally there, in a way she wasn't used to but knew she could, all too easily, grow accustomed to.

Thank goodness she wasn't contemplating any more long-term relationships in the future, because any man she was involved in would have to put up with being compared with Mateo.

Both in and out of bed.

And she couldn't stop thinking about the "in bed" part, and that was an anomaly for her, since she'd never allowed sex to mess with her head. It was fun, and something she was completely comfortable with, but not an activity she built any part of her life around. Too many men seemed ready to use their sexual prowess as a way to control their partners, and Regina was having none of it.

But if she were inclined to be controlled that way, Mateo would definitely be in the running for puppet master. That man knew his way around a woman's body.

Realizing she was woolgathering again, Regina pulled herself together and started her rounds. Looking over the charts of newly admitted patients, she had a momentary jolt of annoyance when she realized she'd be dealing with Dr. Welk. The pompous cardiologist was truly aggravating.

Then she took a closer look at the young woman's chart and found herself wondering exactly what was going on.

According to Kaitlyn Mignon's medical history, she'd suffered from a variety of nonspecific symptoms for most of her life, but she hadn't been definitively diagnosed with any one illness that could take all of them into consideration.

Stomach complaints. Intermittent fevers. Fatigue and frequent headaches.

What had caused her to be admitted to the hospital was her doctor's suspicion that she'd suffered a series of transient ischemic attacks, which often were a precursor to a stroke. Although the symptoms—in her case an inability to see—had resolved within a few minutes, the doctor had wanted her to undergo further testing, including being on a heart monitor.

Her test results had shown signs of a possible heart valve abnormality, which was why Dr. Welk was on the case. But what caught Regina's eye was another result, which indicated proteinuria.

There was something on the edge of Regina's brain,

nagging at her, but until she could get to a computer station and do some research, the only other thing she could do was call for a nephrology consult.

Somewhere in the confluence of all those symptoms lay an answer, and she was determined to find it.

Having called up Nephrology and being told Dr. Linton would be down in a short time, Regina went on about her rounds, somewhat thankful she wouldn't have to see Mateo just yet.

She couldn't help thinking it would be good to have a little more time before she encountered him, just to make sure she was prepared.

A couple of hours later, Regina was passing the nurses' station on her way to another patient's room, when the nursing supervisor, Lisa Patterson, stopped her.

"Dr. Montgomery, can I have a minute?"

"Sure. What's up?"

The supervisor looked around at the other doctors and nurses in the vicinity, and then said in a low voice, "Can we go somewhere quieter?"

That was never a good sign, but Regina nodded and followed the other woman to the enclosed office space behind the main station.

Lisa closed the door and then said, "There's a situation that came to my attention, and I want you to know about it."

"What is it?"

"Dr. Linton came down from Nephrology, as you asked, but I understand Dr. Welk told him he wasn't needed."

"Oh?"

Despite the mildness of her response and her poker face, she was sure Lisa knew that inside she was livid.

That blasted Welk.

"I wasn't there, but the nurse who was present reported it to me, and I thought you should know."

"Yes, thank you. I appreciate the heads-up."

They exited the room together, Regina's brain racing to figure out how best to handle the situation.

Morgan Welk, she'd come to learn, acted like the lord of the manor because of his long tenure at the hospital, and especially loved to boss around the younger, less confident doctors. Unfortunately, Mark Linton was one of the newest members of the nephrology team, and clearly didn't know how to stand up to a bully like Welk.

Well, Regina was about to show him how.

Back at the nurses' desk, she looked up the extension for Nephrology and put in a call.

"Dr. Linton, please. This is Dr. Montgomery."

"I'm sorry, Dr. Montgomery, but Dr. Linton is in with a patient just now. Can anyone else help you?"

Regina only just stopped herself from grimacing. She'd really wanted to turn the situation into a teaching moment for the young doctor, but she couldn't leave her patient up in the air waiting for him.

"Is there another doctor available?"

"Dr. Herrera is here. Shall I page him for you?"

Her heart fluttered.

"Yes, thank you," she replied, keeping her voice cool, masking her less than professional response. She'd been sure he would be working in the clinic, which was held twice a week for the patients with chronic kidney disease, so she hadn't expected to have to speak with him.

Knowing she was going to have to interact with him here, at the hospital, caused a rush of excitement through her system, and brought to mind all kinds of naughty memories.

And that annoyed her almost as much as Welk's actions.

So her voice was curt when he came on the line and she replied to his greeting.

"Mateo, I have a situation here, and I need someone from your department to attend, stat."

There was a pause, and then he replied, "I can be down in about ten minutes. Will that do?"

"Yes, thank you."

She hung up before he could say anything more, and after she'd given the nurse on duty some instructions regarding the last patient she'd seen, she sat at one of the monitors and began her research.

Mateo wasn't sure what he was in for when he got down to the fourth floor.

Regina's voice had been curt and cold, and he knew something had gone wrong; he just wasn't sure where, or what.

Hopefully, that tone was directed at the problem, rather than him personally.

He should have known that whatever was bothering her would be professionally related. Regina would never allow her personal life to interfere with work.

"Fabry disease?" Mateo said it slowly, turning it over in his head. He looked back at the tablet she'd given him, scrolling up to the section with the patient's history. "Wouldn't it have been diagnosed long before this? According to her chart, she's been exhibiting symptoms for years."

Regina swung her chair around to point at the screen.

"It says that up until the early 2000s many doctors considered females with the genetic anomaly to be strictly carriers. I'm willing to guess not many doctors, even today, are well versed on it, or would even think of it in regard to a female patient."

"That's probably true." Kaitlyn had been diagnosed with irritable bowel syndrome, migraines and a host of other illnesses, but no one had put it together.

Until now.

"I'm going to order the genetic test, if she's amenable, but I need your input for treatment going forward. I also have an issue with Morgan Welk that you should be aware of."

"Oh?" Just hearing that man's name got his back up, and when Regina explained what had happened earlier, he was furious.

"I'll speak to Linton," he said. "And to Welk. If it had come out that you'd called for a consult, and no one had examined the patient, our department would be in a lot of trouble."

"Leave Welk to me," she said with a thin smile. "I'll deal with him myself."

If Mateo hadn't been so angry, he'd feel bad for the cardiologist, but as it was, all he said was, "Go get him, tiger."

Her lioness eyes flashed with grim amusement. "I shall."

Mateo cast a quick glance behind him, and finding the area clear, said quietly, "Come by later?"

Regina shook her head. "No, sorry. I'm on call for the next couple of days, and I never socialize when on duty."

"So you'll be working these shifts, as well as your seven?"

She shrugged. "They haven't worked it all out yet, but they think Dr. Reynolds will be back by Thursday, and if he is, he'll work my weekend shifts and we'll get back on track that way."

"If that's the case, let's do something on the weekend." He didn't want to sound as though he was needy, but he really wanted to see her away from the hospital, and was very aware of her time in Miami marching far too quickly on.

"Sure." She didn't sound terribly enthusiastic, but the look she gave him out of the corner of her eye sent a trickle of heat along his spine. "I'll let you know what's happening."

Then they went to see the patient, who appeared equal parts tired, afraid and angry.

"Okay, *another* doctor?" She eyed Mateo with patent distrust. "I hope at least this one has some manners. That old guy is an asshole."

Mateo bit back a snort of agreement and introduced himself, explaining that her urine analysis indicated there may be some disruption in her kidney function.

"I'd like to do some further tests, if that's okay with you."

Kaitlyn Mignon flushed, and cursed long and hard. Both Regina and Mateo instinctively moved closer to the head of the bed, and Mateo saw Regina reach for the nearby box of tissues.

"My kidneys, now, too? What next? I can't stand it anymore."

"I know," Regina said in that cool, controlled tone that seemed to cut right through to the heart of the matter, but this time all it gained her was a glare and another string of curses.

"You have *no idea*. Every time I turn around, it's something new. Something different, and worse. I can't lead a normal life like everyone else, and there's no answers as to why this is happening."

"We—Dr. Herrera and I—we think you may have a genetic disorder called Fabry disease. That's why we want to do further tests."

Kaitlyn stared at Regina, her mouth agape, and Mateo realized why Regina had grabbed a handful of tissues, when the first tear trickled down the younger woman's cheek.

"You…you think you know what's…wrong with me?" Her hushed tone was such a marked contrast to her previous outbursts it showed how stunned she was by the thought. "Is there a cure?"

"There is no cure, but there are therapies that may help you, if you qualify for them. Otherwise, it's a matter of treating the symptoms and managing the disease in a variety of ways."

Kaitlyn was still staring at Regina, and then she burst into sobs.

It took a while for Kaitlyn to regain her composure, and when she did, her breath was still hitching in her throat as she said, "Just to have some kind of answer to why I've had these symptoms and problems all my life would be a relief."

"It's not a certainty," Mateo said, wanting to manage her expectations. "We'd have to do molecular genetic testing for the mutated GLA gene to be absolutely sure, but your history does seem to point that way."

They were discussing it further with her when Dr. Welk walked into the room. He froze, as though unable to believe his eyes.

Before he could say anything, though, Regina went from cool comforter of the sick to ice-cold avenger.

"Dr. Welk." The frost dripping from her voice seemed to push the temperature in the room down by ten degrees. "May I have a word with you, outside?"

It wasn't really a question, and even Welk seemed compelled to follow her as she strode out the door.

Kaitlyn Mignon watched them go, and although her

eyes were red and swollen, and her nose was pink, Mateo saw the amusement in her expression.

"Wouldn't want to be that guy," she muttered. "Dr. Montgomery looks *pissed*."

"Yep," he agreed. "I wouldn't want to be him, either."

But, oh, how he wanted to be the man who once more melted that ice and had her crying out in ecstasy.

Regina's brand of loving was addictive, and he wanted as much of it as he could get.

CHAPTER ELEVEN

WHAT SHE'D TOLD Mateo was the truth. She never socialized when on call.

Yet by Wednesday morning, she was absolutely contemplating breaking her own rule and inviting Mateo over that evening.

The night before, for the first time that she could remember, she'd felt lonely. Adrift, as though some essential mooring had been slipped over the weekend with Mateo, and she was floating without a destination.

Ridiculous, of course. Her destination was still as fixed as it had ever been—perhaps even more so, since she'd received an email from the hospital in San Francisco, announcing the retirement of the current Chief of Medicine. He'd finally set a date of departure, which was six months hence.

She'd known the retirement was in the works for a while, and that the hospital board had already chosen the Deputy Chief to replace him. It wasn't her time quite yet, but she'd positioned herself to keep moving up in the hierarchy, and was hopeful that all her hard work would pay off with a promotion to the next level.

Then she'd be third from the top, behind whoever was chosen as Deputy Chief of Medicine.

Although it seemed as if her plans and hard work

were paying off, she'd felt no real excitement on seeing the email, and no amount of telling herself she *should* be excited helped.

She'd wanted to call Mateo and tell him about it, so as to get a relatively unbiased view of it all, but that wasn't the kind of relationship they had.

More like, not the kind of relationship she *wanted* to have with him.

There was no future in being his friend, or considering him hers. No use in cultivating the kind of relationship where his opinion and advice were important. That hearkened back to her mother having to take her father's "advice" before doing even the simplest of things, and just thinking about it made Regina's stomach curdle.

She'd thought about calling Cher, just for a chat, but had gotten lost in the memories of the weekend spent with Mateo, and then realized it was too late to phone her friend, who went to bed with the birds.

That had left her with only her muddled thoughts and physical yearnings for company.

It was no good telling herself that she didn't want to want Mateo the way she did, when every nerve ending in her body was set on reminding her of how good he made her feel. So here she was, trying to figure out which was better: another sleepless night of tossing and turning with unfulfilled desire, or setting a precedent she'd probably regret.

She chose the latter, rationalizing that she couldn't go on suffering insomnia and still being her usual effective self at work.

Mateo was the cure for what ailed her.

Besides, it was a carefully considered action, she reassured herself, rather than a spur-of-the-moment loss of control. Wanting to have a physical urge taken care of was natural, and when it could be easily dealt with, and out of the way, there was no need to quibble.

Although tempted to text him, she called instead, from her private phone to his, but had to leave a message.

He called her back thirty minutes later.

"Hi, what's up?" he asked when she answered.

She walked a little way away from the desk, for privacy.

"I was wondering if you—"

"Yes," he said, before she could finish.

Regina couldn't help the gurgle of laughter that bubbled up in her throat.

"You don't know what I was going to ask."

"I don't care. For you, anything."

For some reason that went straight to her heart, and warmth radiated out from that silly organ.

It almost made her change her mind, but she found herself saying, "Come by later?"

"What time?"

She glanced at the desk. It had been a busy day, and she didn't know when it would end.

"Is nine too late?"

"Not at all. See you then."

And she spent the rest of the day with a strange floaty sensation making her want to smile at everyone she met.

Except Dr. Welk, who was intent on treating her as though she was something he'd found on the bottom of his shoe, because of her giving him what-for the day before.

Just thinking about his behavior made her shake her head. He'd been adamant that Kaitlyn Mignon wasn't suffering from Fabry disease, and that they were wasting time and money in testing her for the condition.

"She has a heart valve abnormality and is suffering from TIAs, and that's all there is to it. All this other mucking about is making my treatment of the patient more difficult."

Regina had kept the smile on her face with a great deal of effort.

"Since she's my patient at this time, and I've done exhaustive research into her prior history, it's my professional opinion that Fabry disease accounts for all the diverse symptoms she's experienced over her life."

"Fabry's is only symptomatic in males. Don't you know that?"

"Research has proven otherwise." Disgusted, she'd added, for good measure, "In fact, it's been more than fifteen years since it became common knowledge that females with Fabry's can also be symptomatic, and not just carriers. You really should keep up-to-date on the current research, Dr. Welk."

Apparently, that had been too much for him, and he'd walked away.

Regina was still surprised she hadn't gotten a call from Administration or Human Resources, as she was sure he wasn't going to let it go. Hopefully, the genetic test results would put the entire situation to rest.

And in the meantime, she had tonight to look forward to, and that made the rest of the day seem like an eternity.

She got home just twenty minutes before Mateo was slated to arrive, and dashed into the shower to wash off the workday. When the doorbell rang, she was still wrapped in a towel, with nothing else on, and a wicked impulse had her pushing the buzzer to let him in just the way she was.

His expression, when she opened the apartment door,

made the decision a great one. Just the way his face tightened and his eyes grew dark had her arousal soaring.

He kicked the door closed behind him, just as she gave the towel a tug and it dropped to the floor.

"I've been thinking about this all damn day," he growled, reaching to trace a finger along her throat, and down to her already puckered nipple. "No, that's a lie. I've been thinking about you since the moment I dropped you off on Monday."

Again, that ridiculous warm feeling blossomed in her chest, and she held out her arms.

"Here I am."

They didn't make it farther than the couch.

It seemed he was as ravenous for her as she was for him, and Regina let all the fears about what they were getting into be blown away on the waves of the ecstasy crashing through her body.

They finally made it to her bed about an hour after Mateo had first arrived, and he set about making love to Regina again.

Afterward, as she lay cuddled alongside him, he wondered how, in such a short period of time, he'd become so attached to her.

He hadn't been lying when he said he'd thought about her constantly since they parted. Somehow she'd gotten into his blood, and he was beginning to think he'd never get enough of her.

But it was also clear that she was just in it for the sex, and that wasn't something he could complain about, since he'd been the one to set the rules of engagement.

No relationship, just fun.

Well, it was all fun and games until feelings started

getting involved, and he was pretty sure it was edging past that stage for him already.

He wasn't going to bring any of that up with her, though. Not with the chance that she'd completely shut him out, and their relationship—such as it was—would end sooner than it had to.

"I got an email from my job in San Francisco."

Her sudden words startled him. He thought she'd fallen asleep.

"Oh? What was it about?"

She was quiet for a moment and then said, "The current Chief of Medicine is retiring. I knew he'd been talking about it for a while, but I didn't know when it would happen."

The sensation running through him was a confluence of conflicting emotions, but he pulled his excitement for her to the forefront.

"Do you think you'll be offered his position?"

The sound she made was a cross between a huff of amusement and a snort.

"No, I'm not there yet. I doubt I'm even in the running for the Deputy spot, but it's all getting closer."

He tried to put himself in her shoes, to figure out the parameters under which she was working toward her goal.

"How do they fill those top-tier positions?" he asked. There were varying protocols at different hospitals. "Is it a board decision alone, based on current staff, or by applications?"

"It's usually a board decision, unless there's no one they're willing to promote, but I don't think they have that problem. The current Deputy is slated to be promoted, and I'm almost sure I know who he'll want for his second. All I can hope is that I'm next in line."

Mateo squeezed her shoulders.

"You'll get there. Is there any way to up your chances further?"

She seemed to think about that for a little while, and then sighed.

"I'm pretty sure I've done all I can. No one has faulted my work. I've had no malpractice suits filed against me, or complaints to the board, except for the one doctor who expressed the opinion that I was too sharp with my colleagues." She chuckled. "My defense was that he was too thin-skinned, and the board seemed to agree with me."

"Well, then, unfortunately all you can do is wait."

She rolled over so her hands rested on his chest, and they were face-to-face.

"I don't want to wait. I've worked toward this for so long, and it feels as though it's almost as far away as it was six years ago."

He shook his head, raising his hand to caress her cheek.

"But you know it isn't as far away, and that you've put in the work to get to where you want to, and that's really all you can do."

With a sigh, she nodded. "I know, but I can almost taste it, you know?"

He did know. Fulfilling her goal was of paramount importance to her, and it was eating at her that it was still out of reach.

"Hey, you've come too far to be discouraged. Especially now, when there's some movement in the hierarchy." Then it struck him. "Wait, are you worried that they won't move you up a level when the current Chief leaves?"

Her eyes were shadowed as she replied, "It has occurred to me, although I haven't allowed myself to think about it too much. The reality is, there aren't a lot of women in those higher positions, and only one other African American, who's the Deputy Chief of Surgery, and male. My chances, based on those conditions, aren't that good."

Mateo sought the right words. It wasn't an easy conversation to have, and he wasn't willing to either dismiss her fears, or try to diminish their veracity.

"I think…" he said slowly, trying to gather his thoughts, "I think you're right to consider those circumstances, and wonder if your sex and race might hold you back. We both know the possibility exists. But I also know that no one works harder than you do, or has a better rapport with patients, and you're one of the best diagnosticians I've worked with. I mean, who else would look at a case like Kaitlyn Mignon and put all the clues together that way?"

"I'm sure there are lots of other doctors who would," she replied, but she sounded more relaxed, as though his words were getting through to her.

"Maybe, but I'm telling you, you're special, and really great at what you do. Plus, you've expanded your qualifications beyond what might otherwise be expected, all while carrying a full workload. You've done your part, and if the hospital doesn't appreciate what they have in you, they're idiots."

Leaning forward, she kissed him. It was just a brief, soft touch of her lips to his, but it filled him with warmth and longing.

Not sexual longing, but the kind of longing that made his arms tighten around her and never want to let go.

Then she smiled, her face lighting up, eyes gleaming, and he knew he was falling for her even as he fought against it, knowing it would lead only to heartbreak.

"You're very good for my ego," she said, resting her cheek against his chest.

"I'm not trying to be," he pointed out. "It's all the truth."

Before she could answer, her phone rang.

"Dammit," she muttered, rolling away to answer it. "Regina Montgomery."

Mateo listened to her side of the conversation, and knew, even before she hung up, that she would be heading back to the hospital.

He got up, looking around for his clothes, then remembered they were in the living room.

"Oh," she said, after hanging up. "I meant to tell you, Paul Reynolds will be back on shift on Friday, which means I'm off for the weekend."

"Great. How about a trip over to St. Petersburg? I think you'd like it."

"Sure," she said. She was still naked, hunting in the closet for something, and Mateo cursed the hospital for calling her in. He would have happily spent the night holding her close, instead of going back to his lonely bed. "That sounds good."

"And the weekend after, it's my birthday. I'm having a little party, and I'd really like you to come."

That had her turning around to look at him, and her gaze was extra-searching, as though she was trying to figure out why he'd want her there.

"Will your family be there?"

"Yes," he replied, trying to keep his tone casual. There was no way he wanted her to know just how eager he was to introduce her to his siblings, and see how they interacted.

Although his head was telling him not to get too involved, his heart had other plans.

After what seemed like forever, she nodded.

"I'd like that."

And he felt as though he could once more breathe.

When they were both dressed and ready, they left at the same time, and he kissed her lightly inside the elevator, since her car was parked in the secure underground lot, and his was outside.

"Stay safe," he told her, making her smile.

"Have a good night," she replied as he got out of the elevator and she continued down another floor.

Driving home, Mateo tried to sort through his emotions but couldn't. They were too tangled up and confused. The one thing he was able to decide on was the fact that, with Regina, he was having the time of his life, and he resolved to enjoy it as much as he possibly could, for as long as it lasted.

He'd put off living his life for too long to complain about this new, exciting chapter not being exactly what he would have hoped for.

And he knew all too well that nothing lasted forever.

It made sense to keep reminding himself of that, even while he sought out pleasure in Regina's company.

CHAPTER TWELVE

St. Petersburg was gorgeous, but the weekend flew by, leaving her vaguely melancholy. Her time with Mateo had already begun to wane, like the moon. But unlike that celestial body, their relationship wouldn't rise, full and beautiful, again.

They walked on the windswept beach, visited the Dalí Museum and the Chihuly exhibit, where Regina found herself dazzled by the art glass installations. This was an experience unlike any she'd had before: magical and transformative. The colors and shapes seemed to swirl and dance, leading her into a trancelike state that lasted until well after they'd left.

At lunch, she was still quieter than usual, leading Mateo to ask, "You really loved the glass exhibit, didn't you?"

His smile did something to her insides, adding to the sensation of being someone slightly different than she'd always been.

"I don't have the words to describe how I feel about it," she admitted.

He didn't reply, just offered her his hand across the table. She took it, her gaze locked with his, and it was then she realized why his expression affected her the way it did.

It was the same way he looked when he spoke about his family—his parents and siblings, the life they'd all had together. That tender set of his mouth, the soft crinkling of the skin at the corners of his eyes were indicative of some sweet emotion she knew she had no right to.

Drawing her hand away was instinctive, and far harder than she cared to admit even to herself, but was the right thing to do. They'd agreed to the parameters, and either of them getting attached would negate the whole point of their relationship and cause far more problems than either of them wanted.

On the way back to Miami on Sunday evening, she asked, "What should I bring to the party next Saturday? And how fancy is it going to be?"

"It's casual, and you don't need to bring anything. Lola and Cristóbal are flying in on Thursday, and they're in charge of putting it all together. It'll be maybe twenty people, at the most."

It would be interesting to see him interacting with his brothers and sisters, but at the same time, she had to admit to being a little nervous, and torn about whether she really wanted to go or not.

Theirs wasn't the type of relationship that should be opened up to familial scrutiny, at least as far as she was concerned.

And she was still undecided during the next three days at work, which were hectic, leaving Regina neither the time nor energy to see Mateo in the evenings. One night, as soon as she got home, she got called back to the hospital again.

To make matters worse, she got a call from one of the administrators, who told her that Morgan Welk had filed a grievance against her, citing her "inability to allow specialists to do their jobs unhindered."

"It's not an official complaint," the administrator said cheerfully, as though it was no big deal. "Just an internal matter that will be dealt with on the administrative level."

"Send me a copy of the paperwork so I can file my answer," she said, keeping her cool, although the urge to curse was strong. "I'll only be here for another two weeks, so please do so immediately. I'd like to have the issue cleared up before I go."

"There's no need—"

"There's every need," she interrupted. "I will *not* have an unresolved complaint on my record."

Seeing the cardiologist later, she went out of her way to treat him exactly the same way she always had, despite his smug, condescending manner. Obviously, he thought she should be cowering because of his grievance, but if so, she made it clear she was in no way concerned.

Although, of course, she was. Hers, to this point, was an exemplary record, and she'd be damned if the likes of Welk would spoil that.

The documentation came to her on Wednesday afternoon, and she read it through after she got home.

"He cited the Mignon case," she told Mateo when he came by that evening. She was striving for calm, but inside she was seething. Pacing back and forth in her minuscule living room helped, but only marginally. "Saying I gave the patient a doubtful prognosis while refusing to allow him to properly treat her TIAs or schedule her for heart valve surgery."

"But that case is still open," he pointed out. "We won't know for sure whether it's Fabry's or not until the genetic test results come back."

"Exactly." She jabbed a finger toward him in emphasis. "That's what Welk is counting on—that I'll be back in San Francisco by the time the results are in. And since I won't be here to make sure the complaint is expunged, it'll just remain on my record."

"An internal complaint like that won't hurt you," Mateo said slowly, as though unsure of how she'd respond. "I mean, it's not a malpractice situation, or something the medical board would have to investigate."

She sighed, rolling her head, trying to ease the tension there.

"I know, but it still gets my goat that he'd do something so…so…"

"Underhanded? Ridiculous?"

"Either. Both. Ugh, that man just annoys me beyond reason."

Mateo watched her pace back and forth a couple times more, then said, "Hey, why don't you come to my place and stay the night. I have a heated pool, and we could swim, help you burn off some of that excess energy. I'll drop you off in the morning, when I'm going to work."

It was tempting. In all the time she'd been in Miami, and they'd been sleeping together, she hadn't been to his home, and he hadn't invited her again after she'd turned him down on the way back from the Keys.

She really was curious to see it, and would prefer to do so the first time without all of his siblings there.

"I'd like that," she admitted. "A lot."

"Go on, then," he said. "Grab an overnight bag, and let's go."

The house was very nice, but not as luxurious as she half expected. And although it was silly, she was glad. While she'd gotten over her first hang-ups about Mateo being wealthy, it was nice to find his home to be comfortable and welcoming, rather than grand.

The lived-in atmosphere put her at ease as soon as they walked into the foyer.

"Make yourself at home," Mateo said as he guided her along a corridor toward the family room. Regina paused, looking at the photographs lining the hallway, trying to figure out who was who.

"Those are my parents," he said, pointing to a couple, arms around each other, laughing. "That was their twentieth wedding anniversary."

"You look a lot like your mom," she murmured, ridiculously moved to see his smile on his mother's face. "But it looks like you got your dad's eyes."

"Yeah," he said in that tender tone she'd come to recognize. "Cristóbal has Dad's smile, and Lola is just like Mom."

He pointed to pictures of his brother and then sister as he spoke.

"I can see that."

"And here's Ben, Micah and Serena," he said, indicating a more formal portrait, taken at a graduation. The younger of the men was of Asian descent, while both the elder and Serena were African American.

"Ben's the oldest of the three?" she asked, trying to get them straight in her head.

"Yes, he's twenty-four now, and about to graduate from college with a bachelor-of-science degree. He's going to do his master's in chemical engineering. Micah is twenty-two, and he's very into music production, so he took a year off college and went to LA. It was with the agreement that if he wasn't making a living at the end of the year, he'd go back to school."

"How's he doing?" Regina already knew the answer to her question, just from Mateo's rueful tone, but she asked it anyway.

"Far better than I expected," he admitted. "I think I lost that round, but as long as he's doing well, I can't complain."

She laughed softly. "And what does Serena plan to study?"

"She's leaning toward medical research, which is why she picked University of Florida."

She contemplated the photographs once more. There was an older picture, which must have been taken not long before Mateo's parents died, since the entire family was together, and the three younger children were small. They were all smiling, Serena was in her father's arms, and the love between them all was palpable.

"Beautiful family," she said.

"My dad used to say we were a mini United Nations." Amusement and sadness were mixed together in his tone. "And after they were gone, I worried about being able to raise three kids of different racial backgrounds, and do it justice. Then I figured all I could do was raise them with love and honesty. I think they've turned out pretty well."

"I'm sure your parents would be proud—of them, and of you."

He'd thrown an arm around her shoulders as they talked, and he gave her a squeeze.

"Thanks."

As they continued down the hallway, she said, "I'm in awe of you, you know. I don't think I could do what you did."

"It's the kind of situation where you can't know what you'd do until you're in it," he said. "And it wasn't an easy choice to make." He hesitated for a moment, and then continued, "I'd planned to go into surgery. Renal transplant specialist was my goal. I had to modify that to make sure I was doing right by the kids."

"I'd wondered about that—what you'd given up to be there for them—and I'm sorry." She didn't know why, but the thought of his truncated dreams made her ineffably sad.

He stopped and pulled her around to face him, and when he spoke, his voice was harsh and strong.

"There's nothing to be sorry about, Regina. I'm no martyr. In the final analysis, I didn't have to give up much of anything. My parents left trusts for all their kids, so I wasn't strapped for cash. I was able to get help from my aunt, and could afford a housekeeper, too. We had a roof over our heads, and food enough for any occasion. I don't need sympathy or accolades."

There was no way to explain that his fierce statement only made her prouder, and sadder, so she just smiled and said, "I don't care what you say. You're wonderful, and that's all there is to it."

"I'm not—"

But she didn't want to hear what he thought he was or wasn't. Not when she knew with all certainty exactly who and what he was.

So she pulled his head down and stopped him with a kiss.

When they came back up for air, she said, "So where's this pool? And more importantly, do I *have* to wear a swimsuit?"

"Do you honestly think I'm going to insist that you do?" he asked, nimble fingers already undoing her buttons, stripping her down.

And she laughed, desperately happy to move past a conversation that made her feel so many emotions she didn't want to acknowledge.

She could handle Mateo in a carnal sense, but the tugs on her heartstrings were too much to deal with.

* * *

It had seemed so simple at the beginning. A chance to fulfil a fantasy.

Regina's reentry into his sphere had seemed prescient. Just as he was getting his own life back, she'd appeared, seeming to offer an adventure destined to get him out of his slump.

Well, she'd definitely brought all the excitement into his life that he could possibly need, but along with that, she'd brought a different kind of reawakening.

She made him feel alive, hungry for things he hadn't given much thought to.

Her passions reinvigorated his own; her ambition fired a corresponding desire to do well and do better than he had before.

Not that he wasn't proud of what he'd achieved. Yet, he knew he could go higher, do more.

He wanted more.

The problem was, part of that *more* he now wanted was her.

In his life, in his bed, forever.

And there was no way he could think of to approach a conversation about it that wouldn't have her running away.

She'd shared her parents' story with him, and he knew it had left an indelible mark on her. Even if she hadn't, Mateo had to admit to himself that one of her most attractive traits was her drive to be the best. The ambition that propelled her ever higher in her field.

There was no way he would ever stand in the way of her achieving her goals. Not when she'd worked so hard, and positioned herself so carefully.

Lying beside her in bed, her head on his chest and her even breathing soothing his soul, he dreamed, just for a minute or two, that he could follow her back to San Francisco. Woo her there and show her he was worth taking a chance on.

But that was just another fantasy.

When he'd taken up the mantle of raising his youngest siblings, he'd done so with the knowledge that it was, in a way, a forever job. Just because they'd gone to college, or in Micah's case moved across the country, didn't mean his part in their lives was over.

All of them, even he, needed the stability of their family home: a safe place, no matter what storms life threw at them. It had been over a decade, but they were nowhere near ready to give up what their parents had built and the security it afforded.

Even if all the others were ready to move on, Mateo knew Serena wasn't.

And his responsibility to her was solid and enduring.

It was too late to renege on the trust his family had put in him, and that was all there was to it.

It was hard to swallow, but he'd learned a long time ago some of the bitterest pills were and, in the end, they also were the best medicine. He wouldn't be the man he was today if he hadn't stepped up after his parents' deaths. Raising Ben, Micah and Serena had been tough, but in many ways he knew they'd done more to help him grow than he'd done for them. The trial and error of being a parent, the recognition that sometimes making a decision— even if it wasn't the best one—was better than not making one at all, had helped him become a better doctor.

As had the patience and ability to listen without judgment, which he'd had to learn.

No.

No matter his feelings for Regina, his family had to come first.

But the knowledge that she would soon be gone rattled around in his head, stealing his peace, keeping him awake. So he savored the warm weight of her on his chest, and committed it all to memory.

After all, in a short time, the memories would be all he had.

The next morning, when he was driving her home, he said, "Why don't you come by later for dinner? Lola, Micah and Cristóbal are flying in this afternoon."

But Regina shook her head, and it seemed to him they were once again on the same wavelength when she said, "No. Spend time with your family, Mateo. I'll meet them on Saturday night."

She was right, and her refusal was probably for the best, but it didn't stop it from hurting a lot more than he cared to admit.

CHAPTER THIRTEEN

IT WAS RIDICULOUS to be nervous about a party, but as Regina pulled up outside the Herrera house, her palms were damp, and she had to stop herself from obsessively checking her hair.

She, who would take on any doctor and stare them down until they cried uncle, was apprehensive about meeting Mateo's family.

Telling herself it didn't matter whether they liked her or not, since she wouldn't be around long enough for them to form a proper opinion, didn't make her feel any better. For all her cool containment—which seemed to have gone out the window anyway, where Mateo was concerned—she wanted to make a good impression.

She was only human, and realistically, nobody wanted to be disliked.

Giving her reflection one last, quick look in the mirror behind the sun visor, she forced herself to get out of the car and approach the house.

The front door was open, and when she stepped through, she found the foyer ablaze with lights. Balloons covered the ceiling, and their colorful, curled ribbons hanging down added a festive touch. Beyond the formal living room, the patio doors were open, and people spilled from the inside of the house to out by the pool deck.

As she stood there, gift bag in hand, Serena came in from the hallway leading to the kitchen and, seeing Regina, came to greet her.

"Hi," she said, smiling and holding out her hand. "I'm Serena."

"Regina," she replied, taking the outstretched hand to shake.

"Serena and Regina in the foyer."

The sing-song male voice came from behind her, so Regina looked over her shoulder to see Micah standing there. When she looked back at Serena, the young woman rolled her eyes.

"That's my brother Micah. Just ignore his attempts to turn everything into a rhyme. He can't seem to help himself."

"My rhymes mean money time," he said, giving them a grin. "Let me put that gift on the table for you."

When Regina held it out and thanked him, he took off with the bag, leaving her alone with Serena again.

Still nervous, Regina searched for something to say. "Did you ever find your hoodie?"

Serena's brow wrinkled. "My hoodie?"

"Yes, you called to ask Mateo if you'd left it here…"

"Oh." Serena's confused expression melted away, to be replaced with a speculative one. "You were with Mateo when I called."

"Yes." *Way to keep a low profile, Regina!* "Did you find it?"

"Yeah, I did."

"Was it in the pile of clothes?"

Serena wrinkled her nose, and briefly pushed her lips to the side. "Yeah, it was."

Regina shook her head. "Don't you just hate it when they're right?"

That made the younger girl laugh, and agree. "Yes, I absolutely do." Looping her arm through Regina's, she started for the patio doors. "Come and join everyone outside. What can I get you to drink?"

Outside was bright with strings of lights, and gorgeous floral arrangements in pots were placed at intervals around the pool. The gazebo at the far end of the pool deck was beautifully decorated, too, with the bar and a table with snacks placed there.

The partygoers were clustered in small groups, and as Regina and Serena walked out, it felt as though every gaze turned their way. Serena towed her right over to where Mateo was standing, and his smile had warmth fanning out through her body, although she made certain to keep her smile neutral and polite.

Mateo greeted her with a chaste kiss on the cheek, which she returned.

"Glad you could make it," he said, and to her his voice sounded way too intimate.

"Sorry I'm late," she replied. She'd never let him know, but she'd dithered forever about what to wear, finally settling on a red sundress with a light cardigan.

"You're not," he replied, before turning to introduce her to the rest of his family.

She'd planned to stay in the background but found herself pulled right into the thick of things, not just by Mateo, but by his family, too.

It was evident how close they all were, as they teased and laughed, talking over each other in a way that made their bond easy to see. They'd sung a crazy rendition of "Happy Birthday," which seemed to be a family tradition, while Mateo hung his head as if in shame, although he was laughing. Regina should have felt left out, but instead, she couldn't help laughing, too, at their antics, enjoying the atmosphere.

And although she wandered away periodically to get a drink or some snacks, she kept finding herself gravitating back to Mateo's side.

Or he would come over to hers.

They orbited each other like planets destined to collide, and she didn't think their carefully casual attitude fooled any of his siblings.

They all sought her out at intervals, asking all kinds of questions, obviously trying to figure out exactly what kind of relationship she had with their brother.

She tried to make it clear that she was just in Miami for another couple of weeks, and then she'd be gone again, but that didn't really seem to satisfy them.

"I've been telling him it's time for him to get a life, now that the kids are out of the house," Lola said, giving Regina a straightforward look that put her on guard. "He's probably completely out of practice when it comes to dating."

Regina could tell the younger woman that her brother was in no way lacking in that department, but decided on a noncommittal sound instead.

"He's done so much to keep our family together, but he deserves the chance to get on with his life."

"I'm sure he does." She could picture it: Mateo dating, marrying a beautiful young woman, filling the house he grew up in with children of his own. She wished the future she imagined for him didn't make her feel so terribly sad. To mask it, she smiled at Lola and continued, "Give him time to sort himself out. He's been in one role for so long, it'll take a minute or two for him to decide what to do next."

Lola gave her a long, interrogatory look, then took a sip of her drink.

"I guess you're right. I just worry about him, alone here now. I want him to be happy."

Just then Mateo laughed at something Ben said, and Regina nodded toward him, unable to stop herself from smiling at the deep, happy sound.

"I think he is."

"For now," Lola said darkly, just as her girlfriend, Leticia, came over. When Lola smiled and put her arm around the other woman's shoulders, the resemblance to her brother made the breath hitch in Regina's chest. "Hey, babe. Having a good time?"

Regina was glad to be out of the crosshairs, but the melancholy sensation lingered long after the conversation had ended.

Lola was right. Mateo did deserve to go on with his life, and find happiness. He'd been an exceptional father figure to his youngest siblings, and would be a devoted and loving father to his own children when the time came.

And Regina was forced to admit to herself there was a part of her that wished she could be the one to provide that for him, but it would never be in the cards.

She'd never seriously given consideration to having children, too intent on making her way in the world, and excelling. Pushed by the need to prove herself and rise above the barriers others had tried to put in her way—from her father, to teachers and professors, and even some of her colleagues. There had always been someone telling her she wouldn't make it, and that had just made her work harder, fight more, for what she knew she deserved.

It was far too late now to have regrets for the path she'd taken. Too late to wonder what might have been.

This was reality, and Regina was a determined realist.

When she left to go back to San Francisco, she would leave with dignity, even while admitting to herself that Mateo meant more to her than she could ever have imagined possible.

Trust her to be ridiculous and fall in love at exactly the wrong time, and in exactly the wrong place, with exactly the wrong man. It just went to prove how right she was to have decided to put men—and all the problems they brought—behind her, but she wasn't sure Mateo would be that easy to get over.

If she could have fashioned a man specifically for her, Mateo would have been the result: caring, responsible, loving and supportive. Even the fact that he was incredible in bed didn't rate as highly as those other attributes, although it was a definite plus.

But he wasn't for her, and she would never be able to give him all he deserved. Time to accept the fact, and put the best face on it that she could.

So, as she always did, she hid her thoughts behind a smile and reminded herself that this was a celebration.

And her heartache was nobody's business but her own.

It was great to have everyone back home for his birthday, but Mateo had to force himself to focus on his siblings rather than trail around after Regina like a puppy. Yet, no matter how he tried, he was always aware of where she was, who she was talking to, and what she was doing.

He hadn't even had a chance to tell her how beautiful she looked. The bright red of her dress set off her skin tone to perfection, and the slick of matching lipstick made him want to kiss her more than he wanted to breathe.

It had also been his plan to try to keep his siblings from asking her too many questions, but that hadn't worked out quite the way he'd wanted. He'd seen them all hovering around her at different times, no doubt cross-questioning her, trying to figure out what was going on between him and Regina.

Mateo wished he knew.

Oh, he knew what they'd agreed to, and what the plan still was.

They'd keep enjoying each other until it was time for her to go home, and then that was that.

But somehow, that didn't sit right with him now.

Didn't *feel* right.

Seeing her walk out of the house, arm in arm with a laughing Serena, had made his heart jump and kick into high gear.

And she'd fitted right in with the family, as though she'd always been a part of it.

As if she belonged there.

He was finding it harder and harder to contemplate her departure with any equanimity, but it had to be faced.

Regina had her life planned out, and it didn't include a man with a ready-made family tying him to Miami. A man who, in his midthirties, was just starting to get his life back together, and wasn't sure which way to go. And he would never contemplate burdening her with this change in his feelings.

He just loved her too much.

No one wanted Regina to succeed more than he did, and he'd say and do nothing to stand in her way.

She walked over to the bar, and since she was the only one there, he finally saw a chance to talk to her by herself, where they weren't surrounded by nosy family members with big ears.

As he approached, she glanced up, and he saw a flash of something unreadable in her gaze, but she'd masked it behind a smile before he could figure out exactly what it was.

"Hey," he said, wishing he could put his arms around her, pull her close. "Are you having a good time?"

"I am," she said easily. "Your family is a lot of fun."

"That they are." He moved a little closer, and lowered his voice. "I'm always happy to have everyone home, but would it be terrible to say I wish they'd all leave, so I could have you to myself?"

She laughed lightly, but her lioness eyes darkened just a little.

"That's a horrible thing to say."

"I know." He tried to sound contrite but couldn't quite pull it off. "I'd ask you to stay, but I don't want to give them the wrong idea. I'd never hear the end of it when you leave. They all seem to like you a lot."

She hesitated, and he couldn't resist a spurt of hope. Maybe she'd say she didn't care, and that she'd stay anyway, but that didn't happen.

"I like them all, too," she said and gave him one of those distancing smiles he hadn't seen from her in a long time, before glancing at her watch. "Enjoy your family, Mateo. I'm going to head home before it gets any later."

His heart dropped with disappointment, but he found the wherewithal to smile.

"Drive safely, and call me when you get home, just to let me know you made it okay."

The look she gave him made his heart turn over, and he suddenly didn't care who saw. He had to kiss her.

But he kept it gentle, although it wasn't the chaste touch of lips to cheek he'd given her when she arrived.

For a moment she melted against him, but then she stepped back, to give him a more genuine smile.

"None of that, now," she whispered. "The children will see."

And he laughed with her as they headed back over to the group and she said her good-nights.

He'd planned to walk her to her car alone, but Serena came with them, chattering away to Regina as though they were the best of friends, and the opportunity to give her a proper good-night eluded him.

He couldn't resent his youngest sister, though, and he slung his arm across her shoulders on the way back inside.

"So have you decided whether you want to transfer back down here or not?"

"No, I think I'll stay in Gainesville," she said, putting her arm around his waist and leaning her head against his shoulder. "It's not that bad, and the classes are interesting."

That pleased him, of course. Yet, he couldn't push aside the rush of loneliness her words brought, too.

But he would never let her know how conflicted he felt, so he squeezed her a little tighter and said, "Good girl. You worked so hard to get into that program it would be a shame to walk away from it."

She grinned up at him. "I know you just want me out of the house. So you don't have to pretend you're glad because I'm getting a college degree."

So challenged, he did what he'd always done when she'd teasingly sassed him in the past, and tickled her until she wrestled free and ran.

Later that evening, when all the guests were gone, and it was just the family, plus Lola's and Ben's girlfriends, the subject of Regina came up.

More like it was brought up and jumped on.

"So, what's really going on with you and the Cali doctor, bro?" Micah tried to sound casual, but everyone else stopped talking to hear the reply.

Mateo shrugged, swirling the ice in his whiskey glass. "We're friends."

Clearly, that wasn't sufficient, since Lola got in on the conversation, too.

"I saw how you were looking at her. I think you're more than friends, and you don't want us to know."

"I like her." Serena was wrapped in a blanket on the couch. "She's cool, and easy to talk to. She was giving me some advice on which courses were best to take, and how to balance my time at school."

"She said she's going back to San Francisco in a couple of weeks." This from Ben, who had a speculative expression on his face. "Are you going to try one of those long-distance relationships? Those hardly ever work."

"And isn't she kind of…old for you?"

Micah sounded more intrigued than anything else, but Lola apparently thought his comment a step too far, and said, "Micah, *really*?"

"I mean…"

"That's enough." Lola called on every ounce of her second-oldest position to shut him down, and Mateo held up his hand.

"We're friends," he reiterated, keeping his voice level, not letting his pain bleed through. "That's all."

And although they all gave him a variety of disbelieving looks, they got the hint and changed the subject.

CHAPTER FOURTEEN

On the day after the party, Regina came to a decision.

She would enjoy the time she had with Mateo, without fear and without sadness.

Perhaps she should have been better prepared. She'd never been someone to do anything by halves, and having made up her mind to have a once-in-a-lifetime affair, might have expected to fall in love.

But she couldn't have predicted Mateo's effect on her life and her emotions. She'd felt immune from love, since the men she'd been involved with before hadn't really broken through the shell around her heart. No one had, until Mateo.

Knowing their relationship wasn't meant to last didn't diminish her feelings, or make her too afraid to carry it through to the end. They weren't hurting anyone—except her, and she was strong enough to bear it.

Yes, it would take her a long time to get over him, but surely she could do that, given the right mindset? Didn't she pride herself on her ability to focus on work, to the exclusion of all else? Right now, her focus was on Mateo: the way he made her feel, and her emotional connection to him, but she was sure her drive to succeed would return when she got back home.

Back to the place where the only thing of importance waiting for her was her job.

"No regrets," she reminded herself. "There's nothing to regret."

It had been a perfect interlude, with a man who set her afire in the best possible ways. Even the way he believed in her dreams made her more confident in herself.

He was the only person she'd ever felt secure enough with to show her fears, and be vulnerable with, and that was something she'd treasure, forever.

And seeing him with his family just reinforced her belief that he was where he was meant to be. They still needed him—Serena, in particular. When they'd talked, she'd seen the lack of confidence, the uncertainty in the younger woman's eyes, heard it in her voice. Mateo was his little sister's mooring in a world she'd learned could be unpredictable and filled with pain.

The bond Mateo and all his siblings shared went beyond the normal; it was forged in the loss of their parents and cemented by the care Mateo had taken to keep his family together, whole and strong.

She envied them that sweet, solid connection. Having never known one like it, and having craved it as a child, she would never, ever do anything to damage or destroy it.

And that included telling Mateo how she felt.

He couldn't fool her; she knew she wasn't the only one battling with growing feelings and needs. That look in his eyes, the tender expression when their gazes met, told her far more than he probably wanted. It wasn't hard to distinguish between lust and caring, and Mateo cared for her, just as she did for him.

And that caring would keep them apart as firmly as

if they hated each other, because trying to maintain their relationship would probably make both of them unhappy.

She couldn't bear the thought that eventually he'd regret not being with a younger woman, one who could give him a family of his own. And while they were definitely compatible now, how would their ten-year age difference play out in other ways, later on?

These were things she hadn't had to think about when she had so simply set out to enjoy his company for a while, but now they preyed on her mind.

No, it would be far better for her to go back to focusing on her work and achieving her ambitions, and to keep this time with him as a sweet, lovely memory.

He called her on Sunday evening, after dropping Lola and Leticia at the airport. Serena had left earlier to make the more-than-five-hour drive back to college, and both Micah and Cristóbal had flown out earlier. Although Ben was staying another day, he had gone to visit friends in Vero Beach, and would be overnighting there.

"I'll come to your place," she suggested, when he asked if she wanted to get together. "You must be tired, and you're working tomorrow, aren't you?"

"Yes," he said. Even through the speaker in the car, his voice was a sexy rumble. "But I really want to see you. I'm already on the road, so why don't I just swing by?"

But she refused, and told him she would meet him at his house.

"We can go swimming again," she teased. The last time they'd set out to swim, they'd ended up making out in the pool instead.

He groaned. "Now you're just torturing me."

She laughed, already throwing some clothes into an overnight bag, even while still on the phone. "See you in a little while."

He greeted her as though he hadn't seen her in a month, rather than just a day, sweeping her into his arms and kissing her until her head felt light, and she was floating on a rush of desire.

Making love with him was never predictable, and when he lifted her and put her on the kitchen counter, she didn't know whether to protest or not.

Then she didn't have the mental capacity to do anything more than feel, and ride the waves of the orgasm he so easily created.

Mateo now knew his way around her body better than anyone she'd ever been with, almost as though he'd studied her and discovered exactly the places and actions that drove her wild. There was an added edge to him tonight, though, a fierceness that called to her own pain and determination to wring every last scintilla of pleasure out of their time together. It took their desire to a new level.

She stored up the memories. The way his hands felt, holding and caressing. His scent, so distinctive she'd know him in the largest of crowds. The sensation of his body under her, over her, in her.

The sweet way he whispered loving, joyous words into her ear, telling her how beautiful she was, how amazing she made him feel.

He made her feel beautiful, in a way she hadn't before. Not just physically beautiful, but from the inside out, and for that she'd always love him.

Lying next to him in bed later, she rested her cheek over his heart and listened to the strong, solid beat. How glad she was to have found him, to have loved him, even for this short time. While work had always been the center of her life, now she felt richer, more able to see past her own small box of a life.

She'd always considered love a weakness, something

that reduced you to a diminished state, where you put others ahead of yourself, to your detriment.

Now she realized it was the opposite.

It made you want the loved one to have the very best in life, even if it meant letting them go.

The following morning, she got up at the same time as Mateo, and they had breakfast together. When they went outside to leave, his car wouldn't start.

"I'll drop you off at the hospital," Regina told him. "And if you want me to come back and be here when the tow truck comes, I can do that. I don't really have much planned."

"I'd appreciate it. But I don't want to waste your time doing all that. I can find out when Ben will be back, and get them to come for the car then."

"Don't be ridiculous. It'll be fine."

As she drew up outside the staff entrance at the hospital to drop him off, he jokingly said, "I suppose kissing you goodbye is out of the question?"

She looked at him, noting that tender expression, as she shook her head. "Oh, no, you don't. You have your reputation to think about."

That made him laugh as he reached for the door handle. "Oh, being seen kissing you would definitely up my reputation around here, rather than diminish it."

Then he was gone, leaving her shaking her head, and chuckling, too.

That was another thing she liked about being around him. For so long, she'd taken herself and her life so seriously that she was rarely able to relax and cut loose. With Mateo she could do both.

It turned out there was nothing more seriously wrong with his car than a loose connection, and he called her

around lunchtime to say the garage was sending someone to pick him up.

"I'll have my car back after work. The garage is not
far from your place, so I thought I'd pick up some dinner and come by, if you're up for it?"

Of course, she said, "Yes. I'll see you then."

At a loose end, she called her friend Cher, who worked
from home and often had time during the day for a chat.

"I haven't heard from you in ages. What's going on?
Still enjoying Miami? Although it must be almost time
for you to head home."

"Less than two weeks left," she said.

Cher picked up on her tone, as only a good friend
could.

"You okay? What's wrong?"

She didn't want to get into it; everything was too new
and raw, but this was her oldest and most stalwart friend.

"Remember I told you about the man I went to that
restaurant with?"

"Yes?"

"Well, I've been seeing him."

"Regina Montgomery, what are you telling me? Seeing him, like casually? Or seeing him? Like all of him?"

Despite all her pain, she had to laugh at her friend's
way of expressing herself.

"Oh, I've seen every inch of him, and he is fine..."

The sound Cher made was somewhere between a
whoop and a howl.

"Tell me everything, girlfriend."

It was a relief to let it all pour out, just set it all free,
and ease some of the anxiety and hurt. Cher had always
been a good listener and in Regina's corner, no matter
what, and she was counting on her best friend to bolster

her opinion of why a relationship with Mateo made no sense.

But Cher surprised her.

"I hear what you're saying, Reggie." Cher was the only person with permission to call her that, and she did it infrequently, usually when she was trying to make a difficult point. "But I also get the feeling that you haven't broached any of this with Mateo. How can you know if you're making the right decision without his input?"

"I don't think I could stand to get his opinion." She had to be honest, even though it sounded childish. "I know he cares for me, but…"

"But what?" Cher's voice was soft, but compelling. "You don't want to make the choice, do you? You'd rather be a martyr, letting him go so he can find this mythical younger woman and have babies, rather than ask him what he wants and risk it being you?"

"The fallout could be horrible." She was trying to be smart and reasonable, and it was beginning to annoy her that Cher couldn't see that. "I'm at least ten years older than him. If I'm lucky—and that's a big if—I'll hit menopause in about eight years, if not before, and he'll still be young and vibrant, while I turn into a hag. And what happens if, at some point along that continuum, he does decide he wants kids? How do I deal with that?"

Cher was silent for a few long moments, and then she said, "You know what I find interesting?" It was more of a preamble than a real question, so Regina didn't bother to reply. And as she expected, Cher continued, "You've hardly mentioned your career when talking about the situation."

"I did," Regina objected, thinking back on what she'd said. She had, hadn't she? "And you know that's of paramount importance, even if I haven't emphasized it."

"Hmm…" Cher had the knack of making the simplest sound seem like an interrogation. "Is it really the most important thing right now?"

"Of course." Yet, she almost didn't believe it herself, and her avowal was met with a sigh from her friend.

"I've never known you to be a coward, but you're acting like one now. Maybe you only think you're in love with him, but your feelings don't run as deep as you believe. If that's the case, you're right—it's better not to say anything to him until you figure out what's really important."

"Wow." A little stunned, and rather hurt, she said, "That was harsh."

"Not harsh, girlfriend." Cher said it softly, real sympathy in her voice. "Just truthful, as always. You're looking at his family and career, and your age and career, as impediments. You've made the decision for him about what's important, and what's not. I know you've never thought of love and relationships as vital, but maybe it's time you reevaluated all that."

"I honestly don't know what to do," Regina admitted. When was the last time she'd said that? She was so used to being in control of everything, having a set plan, that even to hear the words coming out of her mouth made her feel a little ill. "But I have a bit more time to decide."

"Put it out into the universe," Cher suggested, as she usually did whenever things were up in the air, or undecided. "And see what comes back to you."

Regina sighed. She really wasn't one for all those New Age types of things, but Cher was, and she'd never hurt her friend by telling her that reason and sober contemplation would trump whatever the ether had to offer.

"Okay, I will," she agreed.

"Let me know what you decide, Reggie. You know I'm here for you, whenever you need me."

They talked for a little more, and after they hung up Regina was as restless as she'd been before they'd talked. Maybe even more so, considering all the crazy thoughts Cher had put into her head.

Seeking something to take her mind off it all, she booted up her computer and started downloading the developmental courses she'd planned on doing while in Miami.

Before she got sidetracked by the sexiest man on the planet, and forgot about her plans and goals.

Funny how emotions messed with even the most level of heads.

Work had always been her solace, the one thing she could count on, without fail, to keep her going, so she went through the first course's lecture slides, and then took the first test.

But only half her mind was on it. The rest was watching the clock, thinking that Mateo should be leaving the hospital soon and coming to her.

It was aggravating and exciting, all at once.

As she rubbed the bridge of her nose, the thought came to her that if the universe had anything to say, it had better get a move on, because time was running out.

In twelve days, she'd be on a flight back to San Francisco, leaving all this behind.

The buzzer for downstairs went just as her email pinged. She got up to let Mateo in and unlock the front door before opening the message from her job in California.

Be careful what you wish for, she thought to herself, dazed and in disbelief after reading the email.

Mateo came through the door, took one look at her face and said, "What's wrong? Are you okay?"

Through lips numb with shock, she said, "I just got offered the position as Deputy Chief of Medicine…"

And her heart ached with pride when he let out a shout, punching his fist into the air in celebration…

…even as that same heart broke, too.

CHAPTER FIFTEEN

WAS IT POSSIBLE to be proud and happy and miserable all at the same time, maybe with a side of angry thrown in?

Maybe not angry, Mateo reasoned to himself. More like resentful, and ashamed of himself for feeling that way.

He'd meant it when he'd snatched the obviously shocked Regina off her couch and swung her around, shouting, "You did it! I knew you would!"

Just as he'd meant it when he'd told her how pleased he was for her.

Yet, once the euphoria died down, reality had set in, and he'd recognized himself for a fool.

Somewhere in the deepest recesses of his heart, he'd hoped she wouldn't get just this kind of offer, because it gave her the ultimate reason to go back to San Francisco.

If they'd passed her over for promotion, maybe she'd get angry and decide to leave that hospital. Perhaps even move.

To Miami.

To him.

Of course, he'd been playing tricks with his own mind, even harboring such thoughts. Regina was well on her way to her goal, and even if the job offer hadn't materialized, she would have still been on track to make it happen.

Mateo knew he was just a diversion on her way to where she wanted to be.

But three days after hearing the news, while on his way to his Thursday clinic, he was still battling with his worst instincts, which told him to bare his heart and let her know how he really felt. That he was in love with her, and couldn't imagine his life, going forward, without her.

Nothing, and everything, had changed in the few short weeks since her reentry into his life.

His obligations to his family remained the same, as did her ambitions, but his love for her and the promise of her new job, which she'd worked so hard for, had turned everything on its head.

He'd had a brief moment of hope when she'd said, "I haven't replied. I need to find out what happened to Evan Logan, the doctor I thought would get the Deputy spot."

"Does it matter?" he'd asked, genuinely curious.

She'd nodded, her gaze unfocused and far away. "Yes, it does. Was it that they wouldn't pay him what he wanted? If so, that's something worth considering. Worse, was he passed over completely? I'd still have to work with him, and if he's going to be resentful, I want to know that, too. If, on the other hand, it was simply that he didn't want the position, that's a different matter."

The way her mind worked truly amazed him.

"How will you find out?"

That made her smile for the first time since he'd spun her around the room. "I have my ways," she said. Then she dropped her voice to an overly dramatic whisper. "There are spies everywhere."

There was nothing to do, he realized, but to accept that next week she'd be gone.

He should take a leaf out of her book and concentrate on work, to the exclusion of everything else.

He'd seen only three clinic patients, when one of the senior nurses came to find him.

"There's an urgent telephone call for you, Dr. Herrera. It's from the renal support network."

His heart skipped a beat, but he kept his cool. The support network, while it usually was the conduit through which they found organ donors for their patients, also provided other services. It wasn't unusual to field calls from them, but hearing the name never failed to give Mateo hope that one of his patients was about to be a lucky kidney recipient.

"Dr. Herrera," he said, picking up the call.

"Dr. Herrera, I'm calling to let you know we've found a match for one of your patients, Rexford Knowles."

For the second time in three days, he had the urge to punch the air in excitement, but this time he restrained himself.

"Is it a live donor?"

"No, Doctor."

"Local?"

"No, the kidney is being flown in from Texas. We have two possible recipients, but Mr. Knowles is first on the list. Please advise us as soon as possible if he's fit for surgery, and where the operation will take place."

The hospital didn't have a dedicated transplant team, so they either had to bring a surgeon in, or have the operation done elsewhere.

"I'll get right back to you on that. What's the ETA on the kidney?"

"The donor is on life support, and will remain so until early tomorrow morning, so you should have the organ by early afternoon tomorrow. I'll keep you updated."

"Thank you."

Then it was a flurry of activity.

Finding a surgeon was easier than he'd thought, since Tim Janowitz, who he'd been a resident with, had recently moved to Florida and was free the following day.

"I'd prefer to do the operation there," Tim said. "You'll be able to keep an eye on your patient afterward, rather than have someone he and his family aren't familiar with, post-op."

That was a relief, since Mateo had worried about the same thing.

Then, while one of the nurses made arrangements for the operating room and surgical staff, Mateo had to call Rex Knowles and his wife.

Pat Knowles tried to maintain her usual brisk, no-nonsense persona, but he could hear the fear and excitement in her voice as she said, "I'll get a bag packed and bring him around."

"I'll let them know downstair, to take him straight to a room, and I'll come by to examine him. Also Dr. Janowitz, the surgeon, will be by later to check his fitness to have the surgery."

He heard her deep breath and a whoosh of an exhale before she replied, "We'll be there in about an hour. Hopefully, the traffic isn't too bad."

And hopefully, Rex was well enough for the surgery.

And hopefully, the kidney was viable and got to them in perfect condition.

There were so many variables, but this might be Rex's last chance of survival. The decline in his health and his mental acuity had been marked over the last few months.

Turning to the nurse at the desk, Mateo said, "Could you contact whoever is on call today, and ask them to come in as soon as they can to take over the clinic for me?

Also, advise Admissions that patient Rexford Knowles will be coming in for preoperative tests, and he'll be staying overnight."

"Of course, Doctor."

Once Rex got to the hospital, Mateo would be with him, doing full panels and screening, so as to have the results on hand when Tim Janowitz came in.

With patients waiting, he had to get his head back into clinic mode, but it was difficult. It was an unfortunate fact that they didn't have as many patients receiving kidneys as there were ones who desperately needed them, so transplants were dishearteningly rare.

He sent up a little prayer that all the variables came together, and then stepped into an empty office to call Regina and let her know what was happening.

When Mateo called her on the ward phone, rather than her personal one, she knew it was work-related, but that didn't stop her silly heart from turning over when she heard his voice.

Aware of being surrounded by people, including the odious Dr. Welk, who'd been called up for a consult, she made sure to keep her tone neutral.

"Yes, Dr. Herrera?"

"They've found a donor for Rex Knowles, and the kidney should be here tomorrow afternoon. He's coming in for pre-op testing, and I've already advised Admissions to send him right up."

All pretense of impartiality fled, and she said, "That's really great news."

"Let me know when he arrives, and I'm writing up the order for the tests I want run, so if you could get that started, I'd appreciate it. I only hope it works out well. So many things can go wrong."

The strain in his voice was real, and she wanted to reassure him, but from the corner of her eye, she could see Welk, not even pretending he wasn't eavesdropping. Yet, really, who gave a fig?

"We'll all have our fingers crossed for a favorable outcome."

When she hung up, she turned to find Welk standing there, a smarmy little smirk on his face.

"Taking personal phone calls on the hospital line is frowned upon here."

The drip of ice along her spine was a surprise, but she pushed her instinctive defensiveness aside, so as to give him a narrow-eyed stare.

"Excuse me?"

He waved toward the phone. "You shouldn't tie up the line with personal calls from men friends. Those are for hospital business only."

The urge to smack his smug face was real and visceral, but it wasn't the first time, and it wouldn't be the last, she'd have to deal with someone like him. So she hid her rage behind a thin smile, before turning to the nurse who was standing there, mouth agape.

"Ona, we're having a renal transplant patient of Dr. Herrera's, Rexford Knowles, being admitted in a short time. When he gets here, please let Dr. Herrera know, and get the panels started."

Then she turned to Morgan Welk, that dismissive smile still on her face. "Dr. Welk, I believe there's a patient waiting for you in Room 436?"

She walked away then, before she could say or do something that would make her lose her cool completely.

He caught up to her, almost running alongside her to keep up.

"I saw you the other morning, dropping Herrera off."

The way he said it, his tone, speared through her. It made all the beauty of her experience in Miami seem tawdry and wrong, and she felt her anger start to peak.

Stopping abruptly, she turned to face him, holding on to her temper by a thread.

"And?"

"And? You're a disgrace, running after that young man. You should be ashamed of yourself."

She loomed over him, glad of her superior height, and she knew her voice was shaking, but she didn't care. Her words were cold and precise. Measured.

"What is shameful is that you would spend more time speculating about things that are none of your business than you would looking after your patients. What's also shameful is that you bully and bluster your way around this hospital, rather than putting your mind to doing your job."

He sneered but stepped back, and before he could say anything, Regina continued.

"Luckily for me, I don't have to put up with you much longer, but I suggest you remember in the future that not everyone is frightened by your disgraceful attitude, and one day you may bite off more than you can chew."

Then she turned on her heel and walked away, and Welk had enough sense not to try to follow her again.

Ducking into a staff bathroom, she locked the door and took several deep breaths, trying to dissipate the rage.

She wasn't ashamed, not in the slightest. It wasn't as though she was going to hang on to Mateo, or pretend she was right for him, but Welk's words clung to her like cobwebs, making her feel as though she needed a shower.

Was the entire hospital talking about it—about her and Mateo?

Like they had about her and Kevin?

Knowing Welk, he was probably spreading his poison far and wide, but it wouldn't hurt her, because she'd soon be gone.

Okay, that was a lie. It did hurt, and she had to admit it was because he'd brought up the age difference, and it, with all its implications, bothered her terribly. Not because there was anything wrong with a woman being ten years older than the man she dated. Hell, it could be a thirty-year gap, and still be all right. Men had been dating and marrying much younger women for centuries, and hardly anyone batted an eye.

And if Mateo had been married before and already had kids, she'd feel different.

But he hadn't. And he didn't.

So she couldn't be sanguine about any of it.

Mateo deserved the chance to be a father to his own children, not just his siblings.

Damn Morgan Welk and his nasty insinuations. He'd made her lose her temper, and it would probably earn her another one of his complaints.

They still hadn't got Kaitlyn Mignon's genetic test results back, and that was another annoyance to add on top of all the others.

Telling herself she had the offer of the Deputy Chief of Medicine job back in California should have made her feel better, but it had somehow refused to fully sink in. Intellectually, she knew it was hers for the taking, but whenever she thought about it, it didn't seem...real.

Maybe because she hadn't immediately jumped at the chance, the way she was sure she would have just five weeks ago. Instead, she'd been turning it all over in her mind, and had told the board she would speak with them when she returned home.

According to her sources, Evan Logan simply hadn't

wanted the job. He was older, having gone to medical school after serving in the army, and had mentioned to more than one person that his main concerns at this stage were his grandchildren. If he took the job, he'd be spending even less time with his family, at a time when he wanted to spend more.

It was a sound decision, and cleared the way for Regina's advancement.

If she could just talk herself into being happy about it all, rather than wishy-washy.

Thinking about it allowed her temper to cool, and Regina shook her head. She washed her hands, her mind back under control.

This trip to Miami had stirred up nothing but trouble, and she should be glad it was almost over.

Of course, she was anything but.

Pulling open the bathroom door, she marched to Room 436, determined to hang over Welk's shoulder while he examined the patient.

She knew how much he hated that, and right now, she hated him just as much.

As petty as it may be, it was retribution time.

CHAPTER SIXTEEN

MATEO SPENT THE rest of the day assembling the transplant team, acting as transplant coordinator, supervising everything going on. He made sure all the instruments and equipment the surgeon would need were available. Then there were the surgical transplant nurses, dietician and social worker to be booked, provisional, of course, on whether the transplant actually took place.

There couldn't be anything overlooked or forgotten, not in such a specialized operation, and the aftercare of the patient was almost as important as the surgery itself. Rexford Knowles would have to learn a new way to live, to ensure the success of the transplant.

Luckily, Mateo had the ability and know-how to get things moving, but this was the first time he'd actually coordinated a transplant himself, so his tension built with each passing hour.

When Tim Janowitz arrived in the late afternoon, Mateo felt he had everything under control.

They shook hands, and the surgeon grinned at Mateo.

"Don't you age?" he asked in mock anger. "You look exactly the same as when I last saw you eight years ago, at that conference in Las Vegas."

Mateo laughed. "You don't look much different, either."

Tim pointed to his head and replied, "Except I don't

have much left on top. How on earth can you still have all your hair?"

"Genetics."

"Yeah, that's the only thing that really works, isn't it?"

They went up to the surgical floor so Tim could approve the room they'd been assigned and look over the preparations Mateo had made. Then they went down to meet Rex and his wife.

When they got to the room, Regina was there, along with a nurse. Tim paused, then said, "I'm getting a flashback. It's like homecoming in here today."

"Good grief," Regina gave him a smile and held out her hand. "How are you, Dr. Janowitz? I haven't seen you since you finished your surgical residency at Charthouse."

"I'm well, thank you. I didn't realize you worked here."

Mateo shook his head, déjà vu rushing at him. Regina and he had had a similar conversation when she'd just arrived, but suddenly it struck him, harder than ever, that she would soon be gone, forever.

The conversation swirled around him as Tim introduced himself to Rex and Pat Knowles, and then set about explaining the procedure for the following day. Regina slipped out of the room, after telling the patient she'd be back later.

"I'm sure Dr. Herrera has warned you that there's no guarantee that the kidney will be viable," Tim said, and Rex nodded. "Unfortunately, I can't make that determination until it gets here and I examine it, but I'm going to act as though the surgery is going forward, so as to make sure you're fully informed about what to expect."

Then he went through the procedure and the aftereffects. "You're going to be kept here in the hospital for a few days after surgery so we can keep an eye on you and make sure there are no complications. Until the new kidney starts producing urine, you might need to continue dialysis."

Pat Knowles looked concerned to hear that, but Mateo gave her a little smile, trying to be reassuring.

"Dr. Herrera has lined up all the specialists you'll need, including a couple of transplant nurses, who'll be here to look after you before you go home."

Mateo had gone through most of this with them before, but in his estimation, there was no harm in hearing it again. It was a major surgery, with potentially life-threatening effects. It was better for them to hear it twice and absorb it, than once and not remember.

On leaving the room, Tim said, "Regina Montgomery, eh? Remember how all us residents thought she was hot?" He glanced down the corridor, as though looking for her. "She's still damned gorgeous, isn't she?"

Mateo bit his tongue, not allowing the heated words building there to come out, knowing he was being ridiculous.

Tim sighed and grinned. "But now I'm a happily married man, with two-point-five kids. All I can do is look, nowadays."

"Two-point-five?" That was a safe subject. "Your wife is expecting?"

"Yep. Another little boy due in about four months. That'll make two boys and a girl."

"Congratulations."

"Thanks." They started walking to the elevator. "What about you? You have any kids yet?"

"No." He'd done his time, raising the youngsters, and didn't relish the thought of going through it all again. But he didn't elaborate. While he'd known Tim for more than a decade, they weren't close friends.

Thankfully, Tim didn't pursue it, instead saying, "I want to tell you, I like the way you put this whole transplant together. I know this isn't something you do here very often."

Mateo shrugged. "It's a special interest of mine, and I knew this particular patient was high on the transplant list. I've been preparing for a while, networking to make sure I had the contacts, in case the surgeon wanted to do the operation here—like you did."

"It makes for a better recovery, in my experience, if the patient is familiar with his or her surroundings. He's comfortable with you as his nephrologist, and I trust you to keep an eye on him, once my stint with him is over."

"I've been treating him for about eighteen months, so, yes, we're pretty comfortable with each other, and maybe even more important, his wife is comfortable with me, too. She's the one who works hard to keep him on track."

Tim chuckled, "Well, everything looks to be in order, and the patient seems to be in good hands. Let's just hope the kidney is in acceptable condition when it arrives. Do you know the circumstances of the donor?"

"From the records that the support network sent over, it was an industrial accident that caused a traumatic brain injury. The donor is on life support until his parents arrive tomorrow morning."

The corners of Tim's mouth turned down, and he nodded soberly. "Well, thank goodness he'd signed up to be a donor. There are far too few people who do." His elevator came, and they shook hands before he stepped in. "I'll see you in the morning."

Mateo's phone chimed, and he took it out to see there was a message from Regina, saying she'd gone to get something to eat, but would be leaving to go home at about six.

Without a pause, he messaged back.

See you at seven.

If ever he was in need of her company, tonight was the night.

With the surgery set for the following day, he was on edge, but there was nothing else he could do to improve Rex's odds, so he'd rather spend the evening losing himself in Regina.

Regina walked through the door into her apartment and dropped her bag on the console table in the hallway, before going to the couch and flopping down on it.

What a day.

The residual effect of her run-in with Welk was still a bad taste in her mouth and had left her with the urge to punch something. Or someone. Preferably Welk himself.

Thank goodness she only had a short time more to deal with him.

Luckily, the rest of the afternoon had been mostly uneventful, and she'd had a chance to check in on Rexford Knowles before she left. He'd looked apprehensive, but still optimistic about the operation the following day.

"I know they said it wouldn't be a surety until they got the kidney here and took a look at it," he said. "But I'm staying positive and believing it's going to happen."

"Good for you." Regina discreetly checked his temperature and BP, and was relieved when they were both within normal parameters. The last thing they needed was for him to show signs of an infection. "Try to get some sleep tonight, although I know being here in the hospital makes that difficult."

"I'm used to it," he replied with a little shrug. His wife nodded, patting his hand.

"Well, hopefully, after tomorrow you can get unused to it again."

That made them both smile, as she intended.

She really hoped the transplant would go ahead the following day, and be successful. Rex Knowles had been living on borrowed time.

And, she thought, how strange was it that the surgeon who would be operating was another of the Charthouse alumni? She'd seen the name on the chart but hadn't recognized it. Thinking back to how she'd easily remembered Mateo, after not seeing him for over ten years, she shook her head.

That alone should have been a red flag.

Glancing at her watch, she realized it was too late to think about showering before he got there. She'd left the hospital a little later than she'd planned, and he was invariably punctual.

Her mind circled back to Welk, and what he'd said.

Should she tell Mateo?

She chewed on her lip, considering it, then decided it wouldn't be a good idea. The two men already disliked each other, and this would just make Mateo despise the older man. When she was off in California and out of the situation, Mateo would be left to deal with the cardiologist here in Miami. There was no need to make a bad situation worse over her hurt feelings.

She'd just got up to get a drink of water when the buzzer went off, and she crossed instead to the door to let Mateo in. With just one glance, she could see the stress rolling off him in waves, and she walked right into his arms to hold him tight.

He buried his face in her hair and sighed.

"What a day."

"No doubt," she said, rubbing his back. "Have you eaten?"

"I had something at the hospital, late in the afternoon. I'm not hungry."

"I know what you need," she said. The idea had popped into her head, and seemed a great one. "A bubble bath."

He leaned back to look at her, eyebrows up in his hairline.

"A what?"

She grinned at his bewildered expression. "A bubble bath. Nice and hot."

He wrinkled his nose. "But won't I smell like a flower garden?"

"You can shower after, with some manly soap, and we'll never speak of the flowery scent again."

That had him chuckling as she led him through to the bathroom and set the bath. One thing she'd enjoyed immensely about the apartment was the deep, long bathtub, and they put it to good use.

They started out facing each other, legs entwined, and Mateo talked about the preparations for the surgery the following day, as though obsessively trying to make sure he hadn't forgotten anything.

To divert him, she said, "How crazy is it that another of my Charthouse residents is doing the operation? You're all coming out of the woodwork."

He smiled, resting his head back against the wall, his eyes half-closed. "I was surprised when I saw his name on the surgeons' list. The last I heard he was in Illinois."

"Do you know what brought him here?"

"No clue. Maybe he got tired of the winters, although I think he was originally from Maine or some other northern state." He sat up a little straighter and said, "You know what I don't like about this bubble bath?"

"What?"

"The bubbles." He waved his hand through the froth. "They hide your body."

She laughed and carefully shifted around, so as not to cause a tsunami onto the bathroom floor. Settling back against his chest, with his legs on either side of her hips, she asked, "Is this better?"

"Mmm-hmm," came his reply, as he stroked along her arms. "Much better. Your skin is so soft I can't stop touching you."

There was a note in his voice that made her glad she couldn't see his expression, which she knew would be tender. Loving.

Having her back to him made it easy to joke.

"Yours will be, too, with all the flowery moisturizer in the bubbles."

He chuckled, as she meant him to, but his hands shifted to her breasts, and suddenly she wasn't laughing anymore.

No fear. No regrets.

Those words drifted through her mind as she sank into the delicious sensations Mateo created with those talented hands and fingers.

But soon they were in danger of trying something silly, like making love in the slippery bathtub, so they quickly showered off the bubbles and retired to the bed.

There was an urgency to the way Mateo touched her, and she forced him to slow down, wanting to savor each moment, each kiss, every caress. She wanted the chance to love him, so he'd always remember her and the nights they'd shared.

It was made more magical by the bitter knowledge

that there would only be a few more nights like this, and she stretched out their pleasure, taking control in a way she rarely did.

And when he groaned her name, it was one of the sweetest sounds she'd ever heard.

Afterward, she curled up against his side, in the position she'd learned was her favorite. When they slept together, they'd end up spooning, but before they fell asleep, she lay listening to his heartbeat, content and replete.

"There's something I want to tell you."

His voice was soft, and something about the timbre of it made her pulse go haywire. It was on the tip of her tongue to tell him she didn't want to know—that whatever it was, was best left unsaid—but before either of them could say anything more, his phone rang.

Mateo cursed, and she rolled out of his way, relief at the interruption making her feel a little weak as she turned on the bedside lamp.

"Yes, Mateo Herrera here."

His face tightened as he listened to whatever was being said on the other end of the line, and fear suddenly gripped her.

Was there something wrong with Rex Knowles? With the donor?

Or was it something to do with one of his siblings?

"Yes, I'll be there as soon as possible. Let me know when you get in touch with Dr. Janowitz."

He was out of bed, heading for the bathroom, as he said over his shoulder, "The donor's family got there early and said their goodbyes. The kidney should be here in about four hours."

As she heard the shower start up, Regina sat on the edge of her bed, clutching the sheet in both hands. She didn't know where the fear had come from, when he'd said he had something to tell her, but it had rendered her ice-cold, terror-struck.

And she knew why.

She didn't want him to tell her how he felt. What would happen if she were too weak to resist admitting how much she loved him, too?

Call it cowardly, but she couldn't face that. Not now, with all her resolutions to walk away made shaky by the force and beauty of his lovemaking.

"Saved by the transplant," she whispered to herself, knowing she had time to get herself together before such a moment may arise again.

Hoping she had the strength to stick to her plan to leave, and not falter.

CHAPTER SEVENTEEN

THE TEXT CAME at two in the morning, and Regina was half-asleep, having tossed and turned, unable to fully surrender consciousness, worried about what was going on.

"Thank goodness," she muttered, reading the message that the kidney was viable and the surgery was underway.

Get some sleep.

His order made her shake her head, both because he knew her so well, and because he wouldn't follow his own advice. No doubt he'd stay at the hospital until he knew the outcome of the operation, even though he wasn't actually in the OR.

But somehow, probably from a mixture of relief and exhaustion, Regina actually did fall asleep, so deeply that when her alarm went off, it was startling.

She rushed through her morning routine, getting to work early and going straight to the surgical ICU unit to check in on Rex Knowles. Tim Janowitz was there, examining the still-sedated patient, and she waited outside the room for him to finish and come out.

"Morning," he said, looking surprisingly chipper for a man who'd been up most of the night. "The patient's doing really well. I think we'll have him out of bed for a little while later."

"Good to hear," Regina replied, knowing that it boded well that Tim wanted Rex ambulatory so soon. Although that wasn't unusual, if there were any complications during the surgery, getting patients out of bed would be postponed. "I take it everything went well?"

"Very well. The kidney was in really good condition, and there were no surprises during the operation itself. Now we just have to wait and see how it functions, and hope his body doesn't reject it."

He started walking toward the doctors' lounge on the ICU floor, and Regina walked with him. It was on the tip of her tongue to ask where Mateo was, but she restrained herself.

"Pat Knowles has gone home?" she asked instead.

"Yes. I sent her home, telling her we were going to keep her husband under for a while, and she should get some rest." At the door of the lounge, he added, "Do you have a few minutes? I want to ask you something."

"Sure. I came in a little early, so I have time." He held open the door for her, and she stepped through, saying, "What can I do for you?"

The lounge was empty, and Tim made a beeline for the coffee machine. "Coffee?"

"No, I'm good." She held up her travel mug. "I have some."

Once Tim had his filled cup, he waved her to a seat and sat at the table across from her. He looked serious, and Regina's curiosity was piqued.

"So, what's up?"

"I wanted to ask you about Mateo."

Her heart skipped a beat and her stomach dropped, but she kept her expression as neutral as she could, even as her brain whirred. Was Tim asking in a professional capacity, or a personal one? Had Welk's nasty comments and speculation reached even a surgeon who didn't work at the hospital but had been brought in for one operation?

There was only one way to find out.

"What about him?"

"This is confidential, okay?" Tim waited until she nodded, before continuing. "I moved down here because I was offered a job at a new hospital being built north of Miami. It's still under construction, but they offered me a salary, office space and the ability to pretty much freelance until they're ready for me, because otherwise I'd have extended my contract in Illinois, and not moved."

"Okay," she said, her pulse kicking into high gear. Was this the same hospital Mateo had mentioned? The one in Plantation? Something stopped her from asking. It was better if Tim was allowed to tell the story in his own way, but she wished he would get to the point.

"One of my jobs is to assemble my own team, for when the hospital opens, and I think Mateo would be a great candidate."

Yes!

Regina took a sip of her coffee to hide the elation she was sure had sparked in her eyes. This was what Mateo had hoped for but hadn't been sure was achievable, and she was so proud and happy for him that she felt fit to burst.

"I want your opinion of him, since you've been working with him, and I trust your judgment."

The elation drained away, leaving her feeling cold and trapped.

"Are you asking for an official recommendation?" she asked carefully. "Because there are a couple of issues I have with giving one." When his eyebrows rose, she lifted a hand and added quickly, "Not reservations about Mateo's capability, but realistically, I've only worked with him for the last five weeks. That's not a long enough time to fully assess someone professionally, especially when they're in a different department."

Tim nodded. "Understood, and no, I don't need anything in writing, just your observations."

"One last thing," she said, determined to be completely honest. "Mateo is…my friend. So I may be a little biased."

To her surprise, Tim just shrugged.

"Doctors recommend their friends for positions all the time, so I don't see the big deal."

He obviously hadn't picked up on her hesitation, and had taken "friend" at face value. She probably shouldn't be surprised at that, or hurt, but she was.

It seemed just one more indication of how mismatched they were, if people were either disgusted or disbelieving that they could be in a relationship.

Yet, she had to put that all aside, if it would help Mateo.

Assuming her business persona, the one that had seen her through all of the hardest parts of her life, she said, "From my observations he's a dedicated nephrologist, willing to work with other doctors to get to the root of a patient's disease. He's not territorial, but will fight for his patients, and isn't intimidated when people try to bulldoze him. I think his bedside manner is exemplary, too, and his patients seem to trust him."

Tim nodded, holding her gaze. "He put together that transplant like a pro, and I know it's not something he does every day. I've had less well-organized surgeries at established transplant hospitals."

She didn't have a useful response for that, so she just nodded, taking another sip of her coffee.

But the wheels were turning in her head, and her brain ping-ponged between excitement at the opportunity seeming on offer for Mateo, and dread if their affair became public and it came out she'd vouched for him.

"When will you speak to him about this?" she finally asked. It would give her a better idea of how to handle the information.

"Sooner, rather than later." Tim rolled his shoulders, the events of the night probably catching up with him. "The hospital will be operational in about six months, and I need to get my staff in place. I'll also need to figure out if he has a contract in place here, and whether he can get out of it." He sighed. "I can't wait to relinquish the hiring responsibility to the administration, when we're up and running. I don't like this part of the job, at all. I'd rather be in the OR, hands-on, helping people."

She smiled and pushed back from the table, ready to take her leave.

"Well, good luck with your new endeavor," she said, shaking the hand he offered. "And remember my caveats when giving you my answers to your question."

Tim smiled and walked her to the door. "I remember you from back in my Charthouse days. You were tough but fair, always scrupulous in how you handled things. You word carries some weight with me."

Regina nodded, giving him as much of a smile as she could manage.

Scrupulous? She didn't feel that way, at all. In fact, despite her joy for Mateo, she felt completely unscrupulous.

Not that she hadn't told the truth about his abilities, from her perspective, but she was in love with him, so how unbiased was she, really?

As they exited the doctors' lounge, she saw Morgan Welk further along the corridor, and the way his eyes narrowed. He started toward them as she took her leave of Tim but walked right past her, without even acknowledging her presence.

"Dr. Janowitz," she heard him call. "A moment, please."

What did Welk want with Tim?

Regina had to stop herself from looking back, not wanting to seem concerned, even as her heart rate went up a notch and her stomach clenched.

She'd taken the coward's way out by not being completely truthful to Tim, and now there was the added worry about what Welk was up to.

She had to figure out how to handle the situation.

If she somehow messed up this opportunity for Mateo, she'd never forgive herself. He'd been so supportive of her goals and ambitions. If she owed him anything, it was reciprocity in that respect.

What would be best?

Going back and telling Tim the truth of their relationship?

Maybe reiterating that her recommendation was strictly unofficial?

Something else completely?

This new wrinkle in their relationship threw her into crisis mode.

She couldn't be sure what Mateo had been about to say the night before, but if he had been about to make some kind of romantic declaration, she was even more glad he'd been forestalled.

There were more important things than their feelings at stake. His family. His future.

Regina wouldn't let anything destroy or damage what he'd built.

She was still desperately running through her options when she got to the fourth floor, and had to force herself to fully concentrate on getting ready for rounds.

Losing herself in work usually centered her thoughts, but it took all her energy to keep her focus. On a break, she saw there was a text from Mateo, saying he'd gone home for a nap but was now back in the hospital, and asking what she wanted to do that night.

It was Friday night, which meant he didn't have to work the following day, while she was still on call.

She already knew what she had to do when she replied to his text, telling him she'd come by his place later, after she got everything squared away at work.

Putting her phone back into her pocket, she realized her hands were shaking, and she left the cafeteria to go to the ladies' room and try to pull herself together.

She'd hoped to keep seeing him until she left, but it was getting too hard to manage her emotions. Now it was easy to put aside all other feelings and concentrate on the fact that his dream of working for a dedicated transplant unit was within his reach.

She'd make sure nothing stood in his way.

Especially not her.

Mateo yawned, almost nodding off in his chair as he waited for Regina to arrive. The short nap he'd had earlier hadn't really revived him, just given him enough energy to get through the rest of his shift and make it home.

He was grateful that Regina was coming to him this evening, rather than the other way around. She'd messaged to say she'd be a little late, but that was okay. He didn't mind waiting.

Regina was worth waiting for.

And tonight he'd tell her how he felt, and ask her to keep seeing him, even after her time in Miami was over.

He'd thought it through. At least he'd tried to. But he'd be the first to admit his emotions, his love for her, tended to muddle his thinking. Yet, he was sure they could work something out. It wasn't optimal, but maybe they could do the long-distance thing for a couple of years, until Serena got fully on her feet.

Then he'd be willing to move wherever she wanted, just so they could be together.

It was funny that he would feel that way, considering it meant, once more, giving up what he wanted for the sake of love. Yet, he didn't resent the thought. His parents' lives and deaths had taught him the most important things in life weren't actually things, but people.

Regina was as important to him as any of his siblings, even though he knew he couldn't let go of the family reins just yet.

That sense of having been entrusted with his parents' wishes hadn't diminished. Not even after eleven years. That responsibility had to be fully taken care of before he could move on, and he thought Regina would understand that and, hopefully, be patient.

What they had was too special to throw away.

But when he opened the door to her, he found her almost unrecognizable, and the sense of being thrown back in time by her distancing smile kept him silent, stilling the urge to take her in his arms.

And if nothing else, this Regina Montgomery was completely efficient.

As efficient at breaking his heart as she had been putting her patients at ease, or Morgan Welk in his place.

She turned and looked at him, her lioness eyes clouded, but direct.

"I've decided it's best that we don't see each other socially, for the rest of my time here."

Each word was a blow, but he wanted to understand, so he could, just as efficiently, plead his case.

"Why?"

It looked as though she were about to shrug, and he was glad when she didn't. Any sign of nonchalance would have set him off.

"It's time to put this behind us and start looking ahead," she said cryptically. "I have a lot to do, professionally, before I go back, and I don't need the distraction."

Was that what he'd been? A distraction? Nothing more?

He wanted to ask her, but his pride wouldn't let the question pass his throat.

Hell, he could hardly breathe, much less articulate.

She shifted, one hand coming up slightly from where it hung at her side, and then falling back.

"I've had a great time with you. You know that. And I hope you had fun, too. But I have to start concentrating on my future, and these last few days that I'm here are valuable. I don't want to waste them."

So he'd been both a distraction and, apparently, a waste of her time.

He felt the first spark of anger but tamped it down. If he allowed his rage to overcome him, he didn't know what he might say.

"Okay." His voice was rough, rusty, passing with painful difficulty through his tight throat. "If that's what you want."

For a moment, a brief hopeful moment, he thought she might change her mind. It was there in her eyes, in the glimpse he got behind the mask she'd donned to speak to him.

Then it was gone, and she nodded.

"It is."

At least it seemed she knew better than to thank him, or try to initiate some tender parting moment. Instead, she just walked away and let herself out, leaving him there, feeling as though he'd been hit by a truck.

How long he stood there, staring at the door, he didn't know. The sound of her vehicle had faded, and the murmur of the television was the backdrop to his numbness.

Not even the anger, which had so briefly stirred inside, came back to sustain him.

He was…empty.

Shell-shocked and dead inside, because the only woman who'd ever touched his heart and soul had just tossed him away like he was a used tissue she no longer needed.

And he didn't even have the wherewithal to wonder exactly why.

CHAPTER EIGHTEEN

YOU CAN DO THIS, REGINA. Make it through the next seven days, before you go home.

But she wasn't absolutely sure she could.

She hurt, even physically, whenever she thought about Mateo. She hoped he was all right. That the shock and hurt she'd seen in his eyes on Friday night had morphed to anger or indifference. Either of those would be preferable to seeing him in pain.

Or having him look at her with contempt.

She had enough of that for herself, without him horning in on the act.

Thinking she'd be safe from seeing him over the weekend, she remembered too late that he'd undoubtedly be in to check on Rex Knowles, and she went to ICU on Saturday morning.

When she got there, Rex was sitting up. The improvement in his appearance was marked, and wonderful to see.

"It's working already," he told her with a wide grin. "The kidney is actually working, so they've taken me off dialysis. Dr. Janowitz is transferring me out of ICU today, although he wants me to stay in the hospital another night or two."

"That's wonderful," she told him, even though her

stomach twisted. If he was transferred back down to the fourth floor, there would be no avoiding Mateo. All she could do was hope Rex would be sent to one of the other floors instead.

That was when it dawned on her that, as his nephrologist, of course Mateo would want to check on his progress personally, and before she got a chance to scuttle back to the fourth floor, Mateo walked in.

Her heart turned over, and it took every ounce of strength to greet him with cool professionalism.

He replied in kind, his expression frozen, his gaze blank. Then they both looked away, and Regina said goodbye to Rex before beating a hasty retreat. She'd held it all together this far, but she wasn't sure how strong her composure actually would be under prolonged exposure to the man she loved.

And she definitely wasn't strong enough to survive an interrogation, should he put her to one. Hell, just a simple question might break her.

Which was why she'd avoided calling Cher, the one person she could count on to tell it like it was. Her friend had already pointed out facts Regina didn't want to think about right now. Instead, she preferred to concentrate on the good she was doing for Mateo, rather than anything else.

Nothing could convince her that she hadn't done the right thing. He'd been through too much, given up too much, to have anything more taken away from him. Mateo deserved the world on a string, and everything in it as his own.

He deserved a woman who could give him everything he could ever need, or want, and that was not her.

And if she kept reminding herself of that fact, she might feel a bit better.

Hopefully, Rex would be sent to one of the other floors, but she wasn't so lucky, and later that afternoon, he was indeed transferred back under her care.

There was no way to avoid seeing Mateo again, later that afternoon.

"Regina."

Oh, the ice in Mateo's voice, as he nodded his head in her direction. Unlike earlier, now his gaze was angry. When it snagged hers, her blood froze, but Regina refused to let the pain show.

"Mateo. Here to check on Rex Knowles?"

"Yes. He's doing exceptionally well."

"So I see from his charts."

"I'll leave instructions for his care, for overnight, but I'll be back periodically over the weekend to keep an eye on him."

That sounded almost like a threat, despite his banal, curt tone, and it was more agonizing than she'd expected, and that was saying a lot.

She'd been expecting to hurt, but not this much. Surely it would be less painful to have him just plunge a knife straight into her chest.

"Excuse me," she murmured, affixing a habitual smile to her lips. "I have a patient I have to deal with."

And she forced her trembling legs to propel her away before she lost all control and started to cry.

She avoided him as best she could over the rest of the weekend, feeling like the coward Cher had accused her of being, and the strain of it had her dragging by Monday morning.

Not even seeing Kaitlyn Mignon's genetic test results, and finding out the Fabry disease diagnosis was correct, lifted Regina's spirits, although she was glad for the younger woman's sake.

"Please forward these results to the patient's primary care physician," she instructed the nurse at the desk, remembering to smile, although for the last few days her face had felt stiff. As though it didn't actually belong to her.

Glad of something to distract her, she made the decision to call Kaitlyn herself and alleviate some of the stress the other woman clearly exhibited regarding her ailments. Waiting for the report to get to her physician, and then hoping they'd quickly pass on the news, seemed cruel when she could just handle it herself.

And she was glad she had, when Kaitlyn, clearly in tears, wouldn't stop thanking her.

"I know you said there's no cure, and maybe I don't qualify for the treatment, but just knowing, after all this time, is such a relief. I don't know how to thank you for that, Dr. Montgomery."

"Just take care of yourself," she said, not wanting or needing the thanks. "And there are both support groups and organizations with information that will be helpful to you. The best thing to do will be to learn as much as you can about the disease, and then you can advocate for yourself, or at least know who to turn to, so they can help if you hit a roadblock."

After hanging up, she took another look at the report, and realized she didn't even care enough to forward it to the administrator who'd handled Welk's complaint. That could die a natural death, as far as she was concerned. It meant less than nothing.

All she wanted to do was make it through today and the two days after that without losing her mind, and then she could go home and lick her wounds in private.

Then the administrator called and asked if she could

stay another day, as the doctor she was acting for couldn't come in until Friday.

"Her baby is ill, and her husband couldn't get Thursday off to take care of him."

Regina's flight wasn't until Friday, and although she really wanted to say no, it would have been churlish, so she agreed.

Now, if she could just minimize her contact with Mateo, she'd be okay.

Right?

Mateo tried to remind himself that no one had died. That the end of his relationship with Regina was no comparison to when his father's Cessna had gone down in the Everglades, and he, along with his siblings, had been orphaned.

But the sensations he was experiencing seemed to belie that assertion.

The cycles of numbness, anger and bone-deep pain were familiar, even after all these years. The force of will it took to keep going, and put one foot in front of the other, was the same.

Each time he saw her, the anguish was amplified, until he could hardly stand it. When he heard through the grapevine that she'd been asked to stay on another day, he was torn between anger and gratitude. His head wanted her gone—sooner rather than later—but even now his heart wanted her to stay. Forever.

Because it was clear, even in the midst of his pain, that his feelings toward Regina hadn't changed, and if nothing else, he deserved to understand why she'd rejected him the way she had.

Surely the connection he felt when they were together wasn't completely one-sided?

Even if she reiterated her disinterest in continuing their love affair, she owed him more of an explanation than she'd given.

He knew he had to talk to her, but he wasn't ready. His emotions were too raw, his anger too sharp. Trying to have the conversation he knew they had to have would have to wait until he achieved some modicum of control.

Maybe, he thought in the middle of Tuesday night, when he was trying to work it all out, she needed an opportunity to work through her own feelings. Perhaps, although it would hurt more than he wanted to contemplate, he should let her go back to San Francisco. Give her some time back on her home turf before following her, and making a declaration she couldn't ignore.

So on Wednesday he put in for a week off the following month, and booked a ticket to San Francisco.

Rex Knowles was one of the few bright spots in the days following Regina's bombshell. The transplant recipient was so happy to be alive and feeling better that no amount of warnings about the antirejection drugs and what he needed to do to stay healthy would bring him down.

"Dr. Janowitz is supposed to come to give me one last checkup," he said on Wednesday afternoon. "And then it's up to you to send me home."

"What, are you tired of us already?" Mateo couldn't help teasing, happy to see the other man smiling, the unnatural pallor he'd developed over the course of his disease starting to dissipate.

"Well, of you, sure." Rex's grin was cheeky. "But I really don't mind that Dr. Montgomery. She's easy on the eyes."

Keeping the smile on his face after hearing her name was almost impossible, but somehow, he managed it.

"I said the same thing." Tim's voice, coming from behind him, startled Mateo, and he turned to see the surgeon already at the foot of the bed. "Much better-looking than this mug."

Mateo didn't answer, and was thankful when the conversation moved to the surgical site and postoperative care.

Tim and he left the room at the same time, and although he didn't feel like having a conversation, Mateo forced himself to walk with the other man.

"I actually need to talk to you. Do you have some time?"

"Sure."

"Walk with me down to my car."

Under different circumstances, Mateo would be intrigued, but nothing mattered right now, except perhaps politeness.

Tim didn't start talking until they were outside the hospital and heading toward the car park.

"I want to know if you'd be interested in coming to work with me, at the new transplant hospital in Plantation."

They were passing a bench, and Tim sat down, then looked up at Mateo expectantly.

It was what he'd wanted, the next best dream to his original one of doing the surgery himself, but he felt no enthusiasm. No spurt of adrenaline brought on by surprise and delight.

Yet, that was no reason to dismiss it out of hand.

Just like the pain of his parents' passing had eventually faded to bearable, if he couldn't win Regina back, her loss would, too.

"I would be," he said, sitting beside Tim. "Tell me more."

As Tim outlined what he was involved in, and the role

he envisioned Mateo taking, a small spark of interest was kindled deep inside. By the time Tim finished, and they had talked about his status at his present job, and whether he would be able to leave it without difficulty, Mateo realized the fog he'd been battling was lifting.

Just slightly, but enough to give him back some hope for the future.

"I'm actually very surprised Regina didn't mention it to you," Tim said, capturing Mateo's complete attention. "Even though I asked her not to, I didn't think she'd keep that promise."

"You spoke to her about this?"

"I asked her opinion of you, as a doctor, and if she thought you'd be a good fit for what I was looking for. She gave you a solid recommendation, but she did warn me that you were her friend. I got the impression she was telling me she wasn't unbiased, without coming right out and saying it."

"We were more than friends." The words popped out of his mouth, propelled out by a brain churning to work all this new information out, mold it into something that made sense.

"Duh," Tim said, sounding like he was doing an impression of a twelve-year-old girl. "Wait, were?"

"Yeah, she broke it off, last Friday."

"Huh. That was the day I spoke to her." Tim got up and stretched. "And in case you were wondering, even knowing the two of you were an item, I still trusted Regina to be honest with me. I saw your capability for myself, too, but I still valued her opinion. She was always a straight shooter. I'll be in touch."

Mateo stayed where he was after Tim walked away, turning all he'd heard over in his head, trying to fit the pieces together.

He'd been about to tell her he loved her, ask her to wait for him. He'd been willing to give up his life in Florida for her.

Had she realized that?

And knowing he was about to achieve his dream of being on a dedicated transplant team, decided that was more important than their relationship?

Or did she really not feel anything for him, the way she'd implied?

There was really only one way to find out, and one person who could tell him the truth.

And he was no longer willing to wait to find out what that was.

CHAPTER NINETEEN

REGINA HAD DAWDLED at the hospital for so long that by the time she'd decided she needed to go home and get some sleep, it was almost eight o'clock, and exhaustion tugged at her every muscle.

Thankfully, she hadn't seen Mateo that afternoon, although she wasn't actually sure whether she was thankful or not. She'd seemed to spend an awful amount of time looking for a glimpse of him, as though compelled by forces beyond her control.

It was long past the time he normally left the hospital, barring emergencies, so as she dragged herself down to her car, the last person she expected to see was him.

He was leaning on the wall in front of her vehicle, and her first muddled thought was to wonder how he'd known where she'd parked. After all, there were three staff parking levels.

There was an urge to turn and walk away, but she wasn't one to run, so she kept going toward him, even though she got the sense that she was walking into some indefinable danger.

"I need to talk to you." His voice was hard, but she couldn't tell whether with anger or hurt. "We can do it here, but it might get loud, and I don't know if you want an audience like that."

She narrowed her eyes, unsure of whether he really meant that, but she wasn't willing to take the chance. Not with him behaving so uncharacteristically.

"I'd prefer not to air my dirty laundry in public," she told him, tipping up her chin to let him know she was in no way intimidated. "But I'm still on shift, and I need some rest. Can't this wait?"

"Your place or mine, then," he said, as though he hadn't heard her question. "Your choice."

She sighed, trying to appear nonchalant, when her pulse was all over the place. "Just come to my place. It's closer."

"I'll drive." It wasn't a request, or a question, and when he waved her toward where his car sat, three spaces away from hers, she decided discretion was the better part of valor, and preceded him there.

The short trip to the apartment was undertaken in silence, and Regina didn't try to break it. She was using the time to muster her defenses, staring out the window so she wouldn't stare at him instead, but just being in such close proximity was delicious torture.

Still silent, they went into the building. There was a group of young people in the lobby, already waiting for the elevator, and they all got in together.

One of the young women eyed Mateo in the mirrored door and flipped her hair, as though trying to entice him into talking. Regina didn't know how he didn't notice, but when she shifted her gaze to Mateo, it was to find his fixed not on the other woman, but on her.

It was impossible to look away. His eyes were fierce and wild, and the heat that rolled through her abdomen and flared out into her veins was a visceral reminder of the passion between them.

The got out on her floor, and she fumbled with her keys, her trembling fingers refusing to cooperate. Mateo took them from her, and the brush of his fingers sent a jolt of electricity up her arm.

Once inside, she dropped her bag on the console table and turned on the lights.

"I spoke to Tim Janowitz this afternoon."

She wanted to face him, to pretend this meeting meant nothing to her, but she couldn't. So she walked over to the sliding glass door overlooking the city lights, and watched his reflection instead.

"About?"

"About a job on a dedicated transplant team. He said you knew about it."

"He asked me not to say anything, so I didn't."

Mateo paced closer, and she saw him stab his fingers through his hair, as though in frustration.

"Did that have some bearing on you breaking up with me?"

She wasn't a good liar. Had never cultivated the art, since she despised people who glibly told untruths without batting an eye.

"Some," she admitted, leaving it there.

"Did you do it because you knew I loved you, and would have passed up the opportunity to be with you, if you asked me to?"

She closed her eyes for an instant, wishing they didn't have to do this, or that it didn't tear her up to have to tell him the truth. But they had gotten to this point, and maybe only the truth, all of it, would do.

"Tell me, Regina. If you don't love me, don't want me, then just tell me."

His hand tore through his hair again, and her heart broke at the angry, pain-filled gesture. Finding courage from somewhere deep within, she turned and faced him, finally.

"This…thing between us was beautiful and glorious, but it's not meant to last. I can't be all that you need or deserve."

His eyes narrowed, and he stepped closer.

"What kind of answer is that, Regina? It was a simple damn request. Tell me you don't love me, and don't want me, and this conversation will be over, and you can fly back to California to the job you've always wanted."

She almost laughed then, at him thinking she was throwing him over for a job, but her chest was too tight with agony to spare the breath.

"I'm too old for you." It came out as a whisper, each word cutting her throat at it passed. "You deserve someone who can make a home for you, give you kids, not a driven loner who's never been able to sustain a relationship, not even with her own family."

"No. No, no, no, Regina. You don't get to come into my life, make me love you, make me need you almost as much as I need air, and tell me BS like that. I don't need to hear whatever cockamamie excuses you've come up with in your head to make this seem right."

He was so close now she could feel the heat pouring off him, and it took everything she had not to reach for him, to seek the solace she so desperately wanted in his arms.

"Tell me you don't love me."

"I broke up with you because I knew we couldn't last—"

"Tell me you don't love me."

"And I didn't want Tim to use my recommendation and then find out we were sleeping together—"

"He's not a fool. He knew we were sleeping together. Tell me—"

"And I didn't want to disappoint you, later on—"

"Do you think I care about any of this—about a job, or your age, mythical kids I don't even want or anything else—more than I love you?" His voice was low, vibrating with so much anger he might as well have shouted.

"Your family needs you, and you need them."

He shook his head. "Nothing can come between me and my family, but that has nothing to do with you and me, and whether you love me."

He reached out, as if he couldn't help himself, and traced his finger down her cheek. Then he drew his hand back, and the fierce light in his eyes almost took her to her knees.

"You know what to do to get rid of me, Regina. Just say four little words: I don't love you."

"I can't."

The admission was dragged from her throat, and had hardly emerged before she was locked in his embrace, and he was kissing her, as though never to stop.

When his lips left hers, it was to trace a path to her ear, and he whispered, "Nothing else matters, Regina. Believe me. Only love. Everything else is just window dressing."

"I'm afraid." If there was going to be truth, then it needed to be complete, so he could understand. "Afraid that I won't be enough for you. That I won't know how to balance a life with you, and still be true to myself. And afraid I'll hurt you, or your family, because I don't really know how to be a part of a unit as close as yours."

He leaned away so he could see her face.

"Do you love me?"

There was no avoiding it and, truth be told, she didn't want to avoid it anymore.

"I love you so much it hurts."

His eyes gleamed, and he had that tender set to his mouth that had first told her how he felt about her.

"Then we'll make it work, however we have to. Didn't you tell me, a while back, that there's nothing you set your mind to that you can't achieve."

"That's true."

"Then just set your mind to loving me, and we'll take care of the details later."

"I can definitely do that," she said, cupping his face. And setting her mouth against his, she whispered, "Easily."

EPILOGUE

"ARE YOU SURE?" Mateo sounded stunned.

He leaned across the table, as though getting closer and searching her expression would give him some information he was missing.

Regina smiled and reached for his hand. Twining her fingers around his, she gave them a squeeze.

"Perfectly," she replied, her smile widening as she watched him try to process what she'd just said.

Outside the restaurant's windows, lights gleamed on the dark waters of San Francisco Bay, and the trees undulated in the cool, salty breeze. They were at a secluded table for two, at her favorite high-end eatery. Mateo had flown in the day before, and she'd hugged her news to herself, wanting the setting to be perfect before she revealed it.

Although, with the way they'd made love, ravenous for each other after almost a month apart, nowhere could be as perfect as being in his arms, hearing him declare, over and over, his love for her.

"Which hospital?" He didn't so much ask as fire the question at her—a true sign of his discombobulation.

Only once had he ever been that forceful when talking to her, and it was the night he'd gotten her to admit to loving him.

When she answered his question, his eyes widened.

"That's a premier hospital. One of the best in the state, if not *the* best."

She chuckled. "You sound surprised. Didn't think they'd want me?"

"Darling, any hospital that gets you is lucky," he replied, still sounding a little dazed. "But it's a step back, isn't it? I don't want that for you."

How could she have ever thought that a job, of any kind, could be more important than the love of a man as true, noble and supportive as Mateo?

"It really isn't," she reassured him. "Think of it this way—in the normal course of things, the position they've offered me is exactly what I was expecting to get here, and—" she held up her hand to stop him from butting in "—*and*, it's at a more prestigious facility. I'll be second in line for Chief of Medicine, and they already know that's what I'm interested in, in the long run."

He chewed on the side of his lip, looking so adorable doing so she wished she could kiss that spot, soothe the sting of his teeth. Then, as he pulled back his hand and she noticed the distant, faraway expression in his eyes, a little trickle of cold water ran down her spine.

Mateo had told her that once Serena was out of school, he'd be willing to move to be with her, and the enormity of his proposed sacrifice had driven straight through her heart.

Give up his home in Florida, and with it his post as linchpin for his family? And also give up, after only a few years, his dream job?

For her?

It didn't seem right, even as she recognized it as proof positive of his love.

"We can travel back and forth," he'd said. "As often as

we can. Or meet somewhere in the middle, if that works better. I could buy a place in Texas, so we'd always have somewhere to go that's halfway for each of us."

When she'd thought about it, that didn't sit right with her.

Oh, she had no doubt they'd both make the effort, but with his new position and its attendant unpredictability, and the duties she'd take up as Deputy Chief, they probably wouldn't see that much of each other.

And she'd learned, perhaps far later in life than most, how important it was to be happy personally, as well as fulfilled professionally. There was no way she was waiting four years to be with Mateo on a permanent basis.

Regina had never been a halfway kind of woman. She was all or nothing.

Now, watching him wrestle with what she was saying, she wondered if she'd somehow got it all wrong. If he didn't see this as the perfect solution.

She was willing to make the sacrifice instead, and take a job in Miami to be with him, but his reaction made her doubt herself, and him.

"I thought you'd be happy," she said slowly. "That you'd see it as a good thing."

His gaze snapped to hers, and before she realized what he was going to do, he was on his feet, and tugging her up, too, into his arms.

It was only then that she realized he was trembling; his hard, warm body was shaking with some undefinable emotion. And his eyes were anguished as he gazed deep into hers.

"Darling," his voice was hoarse, choked, little more than a whisper. "My darling love. I would love nothing more than to wake up every morning for the rest of my life, and see you beside me. To go to bed and know you're there. Reach for you. Make love to you. But I never, ever, want to hold you back. It would kill me if you ever looked at me with disdain and accused me of getting in the way of your dreams."

Her heart soared then, as she lifted her hand to press the palm to his cheek.

"Mateo, I love you more than I ever thought I could love, and there's nothing that's going to keep me from your side. Not my job, or yours. Not even your family. This is my new dream. To be yours, and have you as mine, forever. Is this a dream we can share, and be happy with?"

He kissed her, uncaring of the appreciative audience around them, and she grew hot, melting into his body, as he ravished her mouth.

"You have just made me the happiest man in the world," he said. "And there's nothing more that I could ask for."

"She said yes," the woman at a nearby table stage-whispered to her companion. "Isn't it romantic?"

Regina felt an unaccustomed wave of heat rising into her face, and turned toward the window, so no one would see her blush. Somehow that comment made her self-conscious and unsure.

Mateo dipped his mouth close to her ear and whispered, "I change my mind. There is one more thing that I would ask for. Will you marry me, Regina? I have this ridiculous urge to tie you to me in every possible way known to man, so you don't stride off into the sunset without me."

A bubble of laughter rose into her throat, but it got caught on the wave of love swelling in her chest.

"I will. I'm yours, my love," she replied. Then a mischievous urge arose in her as she thought back to when they first met. "And I will be, for every shift hereafter."

* * * * *

MILLS & BOON

Coming next month

CONSEQUENCES OF THEIR NEW YORK NIGHT
Tina Beckett

Nicola's mind was wandering, and her thoughts slid in and out of places that were best left for another time. The hospital was huge and the names of people she'd been introduced to were starting to squish together inside the confines of her skull.

And as the space grew even tighter, something had to give. So squeezing between the cracks came the memory of a night five weeks ago. And the tall stranger she'd fallen into bed with.

She swallowed. She still couldn't believe she'd done that. What had she been thinking?

She hadn't been. And that had been the idea. She hadn't wanted to think, to talk…to remember. She'd just wanted to feel. And, God, had she ever. She'd…

"Kaleb, could you come over here for a moment?" Harvey Smith's voice shocked her back to reality, making her blink. "I want you to meet the newest member of our team: Nicola Bradley. Her specialty is internal medicine with an emphasis on diagnostics. She'll be helping us crack the tough cases."

As the hospital administrator continued to speak, she turned to greet the newcomer, and a wave of shock knocked her flat, setting off all kinds of sirens and alarms.

"Nicola, meet Kaleb Sabat. He's New York City Memorial's chief of reconstructive surgery."

She somehow met the man's cool blue eyes without flinching. How was this even possible? Was this some sort of cosmic joke? If so, the punch line was lost on her.

The man she'd shared a crazy, impulsive night of sex with was NYC Memorial's chief of reconstructive surgery? Oh, God. What should she do? What *could* she do?

Quit? Run down the hallway until she found the nearest exit? No. Nicola was no chicken. At least she hoped not.

She was going to pretend it never happened, that's what she'd do. And hope that he did the same. Or maybe he didn't even remember her.

Please, God...

"Nice to meet you, Dr. Sabat," she murmured, placing the slightest emphasis on his title.

The man's head tilted sideways for a second, his eyebrows coming together as a host of changes came over his face, the last of which was sardonic amusement.

Oh, no. He remembered. *Remembered!*

They'd both had a little too much to drink that night five weeks ago, and she'd hoped...

If she'd had any idea he'd worked at the hospital she was transferring to, she would have moved off that barstool quicker than anyone believed possible. But she'd been grieving and needed to forget.

Kaleb had given her a few hours of respite...and more.

Continue reading
CONSEQUENCES OF THEIR NEW YORK NIGHT
Tina Beckett

Available next month
www.millsandboon.co.uk

COMING SOON!

We really hope you enjoyed reading this book. If you're looking for more romance, be sure to head to the shops when new books are available on

Thursday 18th March

To see which titles are coming soon, please visit

millsandboon.co.uk/nextmonth

WE'RE LOOKING FOR NEW AUTHORS FOR THE MILLS & BOON MEDICAL SERIES!

Whether you're a published author or an aspiring one, our editors would love to read your story.

You can submit the synopsis and first three chapters of your novel online, and find out more about the series, at **harlequin.submittable.com/submit**

We read all submissions and you do not need to have an agent to submit.

IF YOU'RE INTERESTED, WHY NOT HAVE A GO?

Submit your story at:
harlequin.submittable.com/submit

MILLS & BOON

LET'S TALK

Romance

For exclusive extracts, competitions
and special offers, find us online:

- facebook.com/millsandboon
- @MillsandBoon
- @MillsandBoonUK

Get in touch on 01413 063232

For all the latest titles coming soon, visit
millsandboon.co.uk/nextmonth